THE GATES OF ZION

Books by Brock and Bodie Thoene

THE ZION COVENANT

Vienna Prelude
Prague Counterpoint
Munich Signature
Jerusalem Interlude
Danzig Passage
Warsaw Requiem

THE ZION CHRONICLES

The Gates of Zion
A Daughter of Zion
The Return to Zion
A Light in Zion
The Key to Zion

THE SHILOH LEGACY

In My Father's House
A Thousand Shall Fall
Say to This Mountain

SAGA OF THE SIERRAS

The Man From Shadow Ridge
Riders of the Silver Rim
Gold Rush Prodigal
Sequoia Scout
Cannons of the Comstock
The Year of the Grizzly
Shooting Star

NON-FICTION

Writer to Writer

BODIE THOENE

THE GATES OF ZION

BETHANY HOUSE PUBLISHERS
MINNEAPOLIS, MINNESOTA 55438

The Gates of Zion
Copyright © 1986
Bodie Thoene

With the exception of recognized historical figures, the
characters in this novel are fictional and any resemblance
to actual persons, living or dead, is purely coincidental.

Cover illustration by Dan Thornberg,
Bethany House Publishers staff artist.

Published by Bethany House Publishers
A Ministry of Bethany Fellowship International
11300 Hampshire Avenue South
Minneapolis, Minnesota 55438

Printed in the United States of America by
Bethany Press International, Minneapolis, Minnesota 55438

Library of Congress Cataloging-in-Publication Data

Thoene, Bodie, 1951–
    The gates of Zion.

    (The Zion chronicles ; bk. 1)
     1. Palestine—History—Partition, 1947—Fiction.
I. Title. II. Series: Thoene, Bodie, 1951–   . Zion
chronicles ; bk. 1.
PS3570.H46G3   1986   813'.54   86–18870
ISBN 0–87123–870–5 (pbk.)
ISBN 0–7642–2107–8 (mass market)

THIS STORY IS FOR MAMA,
BETTIE RACHEL TURNER,
WHO ALSO HAPPENS TO BE
MY BEST FRIEND.

because she believed the promises
first among us all.

"The Lord loveth the gates of Zion . . ." Psalm 87:2

BODIE THOENE (Tay-nee) began her writing career as a teen journalist for her local newspaper. Eventually her byline appeared in prestigous periodicals such as *U.S. News and World Report, The American West*, and *The Saturday Evening Post*. After leaving an established career as a writer and researcher for John Wayne, she began work on her first historical fiction series, THE ZION CHRONICLES. From the beginning her husband, BROCK, has been deeply involved in the development of each book. His degrees in history and education have added a vital dimension to the accuracy, authenticity, and plot structure of the Zion books. The Thoenes' unusual but very effective writing collaboration has also produced three other major historical fiction series with Bethany House Publishers.

Contents

Prologue

Pale smoke from the oil lamp curled to the ceiling and hung suspended in the corners of the small stone room. Simon Bar Gideon blinked hard, and wearily rubbed his tunic sleeve across his aching eyes. Leaning back against the wall, he gazed at the unconscious form of his seventeen-year-old brother, so still on the pallet beside him.

"Reuben," he whispered sadly, reaching out to touch a finger to the blood-soaked bandages that covered the frail young man's head. "So young—so young."

The physician of the brotherhood only a short time before had predicted that the boy would not live through the night. Clucking his tongue in sad despair, he left Simon alone in his sorrowful vigil.

Simon leaned close to Reuben's head and gently smoothed back a lock of dark brown hair from beneath the bandage.

"What of Mother?" he whispered quietly. She and his three sisters were still in Jerusalem, surrounded by the brutal Roman legions of Vespasian and Titus. "Can you not give me even one word of hope, Reuben?" he pleaded. "Did you come so far over the wilderness to the city without a word ever crossing their fate?" He wiped a trickle of blood from Reuben's temple, then stared at the dark red stain. Had the blood of those he loved already been spilled in the streets of Jerusalem by some Roman sword?

"Speak, little brother. Only one word. Do they live still?" He lay his lips next to Reuben's ear, his question answered by the shallow breath of the beardless young man whose wounds spoke more dramatically than words. "Your blood is mine," Simon said quietly. The tears stung his eyes. He took Reuben's limp hands in his own and began to recite the Shema: "Hear, O Israel, the Lord our God is one Lord . . ." His voice was joined by another, steadily chanting from the doorway behind him. As

9

they recited the ancient invocation in unison, Reuben's breathing became even more labored until at last the rattle of death filled his throat.

Simon bowed his head and pressed Reuben's hands against his cheek. "When he was a baby, these hands reached out to me," he said, his voice ragged with pain. "He took his first step into my arms."

"I am sorry, Simon," said the voice, his tone filling the simple words with deep compassion.

"They must all be dead, all of them now," Simon mourned. "And I deserted them. Instead of fighting, I turned away to this— a life of peace, of studying the Word of God. I would have done better to have died with the Zealots!" Bitter pain raged through his voice, and he clenched his fists.

"Jerusalem has fallen. You have a greater purpose for your life than to die of plague or famine behind those gates," his companion comforted. "You are not finished yet."

"What is the use?" Simon threw the words at him. "Who will know or care what we do here?"

"Jerusalem has fallen," the voice said again. "What good would it have done to have numbered yourself among the starving and the dead? Even the wife of the high priest was driven to wander through the alleyways of the city in search of scraps. Those who stole out beyond the city gates after dark for roots were crucified by the hundreds each night. Every tree has been hewn down, all made into the crosses which line the roads into the city. And when they have served their evil purpose, they fuel the bonfires that burn the dead bodies of our people. Such a death is not noble, Simon. It is only death."

"How do you know these things?" Simon asked, his eyes still fastened on Reuben's blood-streaked face.

"Only an hour ago two Zealots stumbled into the compound. They escaped death once, but it will find them soon enough, I think. They say legions are coming here."

Simon sighed, nodded, then crossed Reuben's hands on his chest. "Then I have urgent work to complete." He drew a deep breath and straightened his shoulders. "Is everything lost then? Everyone dead?"

"They say Titus began his assault on the North Wall. By day he crashed battering rams against the fortifications. By night the Zealots struggled to repair the breaches, resting only after collapsing with exhaustion—or when death came. Two weeks ago the outer wall fell, then the second wall. And last week the third wall crumbled. When the legions swept through the streets of the city, the survivors retreated to the temple and continued to resist. For six days the battering rams echoed in the courtyards of the Holy Citadel, then it, too, was taken. The soldiers butchered—killed everyone they found alive. Some escaped. A few—like your brother, like the two men. But as they escaped, the smoke of the temple blackened the sky behind them." He paused, then said gently, "I am sorry, Simon. Your family is dead. We will say Kaddish for them."

"And when the Romans come here, who will say Kaddish when the last Jew is dead?"

"Perhaps God," he answered slowly.

"Then we must preserve the words of His promises." Simon wiped his eyes and stood. "And when the words are sealed, then we, too, may die in peace."

"Yes, Simon. We have another way to fight against those who say there is no God in Zion. Though we all descend to the grave and Israel be empty, God still lives."

Simon turned toward the speaker in the doorway, a kindly, gray-bearded old man. "Then I will return to my pen and fight my enemies with peace in my heart."

Simon walked slowly across the dark, deserted courtyard to the now-empty writing room. He unlatched the door and opened it, looking around the long stonework area as though he were seeing it for the first time. Two dozen scrolls lay neatly wrapped in linen on the wooden table at the far end of the room. Tomorrow they would receive a final coat of pitch before being sealed in the clay jars and hidden in the caves on the barren hillsides around Qumran. Only this scroll, the book of the prophet Isaiah, remained unfinished. Wiping his hands on his robe, he crossed to his writing table and sat down, lovingly touching the new leather stretched out before him. How long, he wondered, before the eyes of man would read the words he so carefully copied from the worn and faded master scroll? In the dim light of the oil lamp, he strained to read the next line of the column: "How beautiful upon the mountains are the feet of him that bringeth good tidings . . ."

His own voice echoed hollowly against the stone walls of the room. An ache filled his heart as he remembered Reuben stumbling into the community only two days before. His feet had not been beautiful. Without sandals, they were bloody, lacerated to the bone.

". . . that publisheth peace; that bringeth good tidings of good, that publisheth salvation; that saith unto Zion, Thy God reigneth!"

The triumphant declaration seemed to mock him. *There will be no salvation, no news of peace,* thought Simon as he carefully dipped his pen in the inkwell and copied the words of the promise he had just read. Only the Romans reign in Zion now. The promise of Isaiah would have to wait for another age, another lifetime. *Or would it ever come?* he wondered fleetingly.

In a matter of days the legions would come here to the community and kill, burn, and destroy in the names of Titus and Vespasian. Only the sacred writings would be safe. The Word of God would sleep quietly in a cave until another time to come— who knew how long?—and men would hear the promises and see their fulfillment.

Slowly, Simon reached out a trembling finger and reverently traced the words of the prophet. He did not fear his own death. But he did fear the fire that would inevitably follow the slaughter. *The scrolls must be preserved! Help us, Yaweh!* His silent cry reached out to the God of Abraham.

He drew a breath as the faces of his family crowded his memory. Surely the God of Israel would not forget His promise; surely He would remember Jerusalem!

Simon brushed away the tears with the back of his hand and once again pushed his pen into the ink. Every letter, every jot must be perfect. Nothing can be changed or deleted. *The temple has been burned,* he mourned. *Were any of the Holy Scrolls saved, or do I, Simon bar Giora, hold the last of the word that promised a nation would live again where now there are only ashes?*

The thought of the legion filled his mind. Only a few days' march from where he now sat, someone was sharpening the sword that would end his life. *Quick! I must do this carefully but quickly,* he resolved as he dipped his pen. He and his compatriots would steal the final victory from the Roman holocaust. *Together,* thought Simon, *we will be Guardians of the Promise even as we die in silence.*

PART 1

The Celebration
November 29, 1947

*"I know that God promised all of
Palestine to the children of Israel. I do
not know what borders He set. I believe
they are wider than the ones proposed. If
God will keep His promise in His own
time, our business as poor humans who
live in a difficult age is to save as much
as we can of the remnants of Israel. . . ."*

David Ben-Gurion, 1947

1 The Discovery

"Antikas! Antikas!" the old Bedouin shepherd shouted as El-lie Warne entered the mahogany-paneled study of her uncle's home. After six months in Jerusalem she understood the word well enough. For an unsuspecting tourist lost in the maze of the Old City souks, it usually meant that a piece of the true cross or the actual crown of thorns was being offered for sale to the highest bidder.

"Antikas!" The old man smiled a broad toothless smile and whacked his young companion on the shoulder in hopes of making him a little more enthusiastic.

Ellie rubbed a hand wearily across her forehead and resisted the urge to turn around and go straight back to bed. *What*, she wondered, *had old Miriam been thinking of when she let these two con-artists into a room filled with actual archaeological antiquities?* Not to mention the fact that she had roused Ellie out of bed with the worst case of flu *ever*, just so she could look at what was most likely phoney junk. For three days Ellie had stayed home from her work at the dig. Sick and weary, she wanted only to rest, to sleep. Her uncle Howard Moniger, after all, was the archaeologist; she merely photographed the finds.

Not a half-bad job, she thought, *if a girl likes taking pictures of 2,000-year-old jar handles.* It beat waitressing in Long Beach while all the prime photojournalism jobs were snapped up by GI's returning home from Europe and the Pacific. Even with a B.A. in photojournalism from UCLA, she was lucky to have a job, she knew that. Good old Uncle Howard had really come through on this one. Her pay with the American School of Oriental Research was miniscule but steady. Nothing in her education, however, had equipped her for this.

"Antikas! Antikas!" the old Arab repeated, gesturing wildly toward the battered leather pouch he carried slung over his bony shoulder.

"All right! Just wait a minute!" She motioned impatiently for them to sit, then muttered, "Stay right there; I'm going to strangle a sweet little old lady; then we'll take a look at the treasures you've brought." She turned and glanced toward the open door into the hall. "Miriam!" she shouted. "Come in here—immediately!" Ellie turned back to look at her two unusual visitors. Rigidly seated in straight-backed leather chairs, they stared wide-eyed at the walls of books and the displays of artifacts that filled the room. *They look like artifacts themselves*, Ellie thought, *on display among the potsherds and Bronze-age tools in Uncle Howard's glass cases.*

As the Bedouins investigated the room, Ellie looked them over. *Wonderful photographic studies they'd make*, she thought. Both were dressed in the traditional sandals and long robes, and were crowned with the keffiyah, the head covering of nomadic tribes in Palestine. One looked to be about eighteen or nineteen years old. His scruffy beard framed a thin face, with a nose hanging between his eyes like a large beak. The older had a curly gray beard and high cheekbones; he reminded Ellie of a roosting buzzard blinking in the sun.

"Miriam!" she shouted again, and Uncle Howard's old housekeeper finally appeared in the doorway. "I think I'm going to need you—" she gestured vaguely in the direction of the two shepherds, still sitting erect, still waiting, watching.

When Ellie turned back to them, they apparently had changed tactics for their sale. The older of the two sprang to his feet and whacked his young companion sharply across the head. Ellie, at 5'5", towered over the old man. The younger, tall and stoop-shouldered, rose to his feet a bit more slowly.

"Salaam." Both men spoke in unison and bowed majestically to Ellie.

"Salaam," Ellie returned. The three of them stood for an awkward moment until Ellie broke the silence. "Please sit down," she said. "The professor is not here, but he will return in the next few days . . ." Her voice trailed off as the two continued to stand, smiling at her.

"Antikas—" the elder began again.

"Miriam—" Ellie pleaded, looking toward the door where the old woman stood.

But before Miriam could translate, the old Arab man suddenly dashed between Ellie and the door. He pushed the battered leather pouch toward her. "Antikas!" he insisted. Then he raised his palm toward her solemnly, like an Indian chief, and motioned for her to stop.

"All right," Ellie groaned. "Let's see what you've got. The silver chalice? The very nails from . . ." Before she could finish, the wizened brown hand pulled from the pouch an object that looked like a miniature mummy. It was about ten inches in height and several inches thick, and seemed to be wrapped in shreds of linen. Her sarcasm diminished, replaced by cautious curiosity. The old man smiled a toothless smile and reverently held the object out to her.

"Antikas," he repeated quietly and sincerely. "You see, real antikas."

Suddenly ashamed of her flippancy, Ellie stared at the object for a long moment before she put her hands out tentatively, looking at the old man to see if he meant for her to take it. He nodded at her and smiled again.

"Yes, you look. Truly." He put it carefully into her hands and backed away.

Even Ellie's untrained eye could see that she held a scroll. It was surprisingly heavy. Tan in color, the edges seemed to be crumbling; indeed, it had the appearance of something very old. In the field of archaeology, however, the term "old" was quite relative. She had been around long enough to know that something a mere two hundred years old was of little value.

"Very old," the man encouraged.

Ellie looked up at him and smiled. There was no way to tell if what she held had existed for a hundred years or a thousand.

"I'm sorry," she said. "I just don't know enough about it. The professor is gone and won't be back for several days . . ."

"Open," insisted the old Arab, snatching it away from her. As he grabbed it, fragments from the edge broke off and fell to the floor. "Look, antikas." He laid it down on the broad surface of the desk and unrolled it without ceremony. "There," he said beaming. "Very old."

The inside of the scroll was covered with columns of neatly ruled writing in what appeared to be Hebrew. Pieces of the scroll were stitched together and Ellie guessed that the material was leather. She looked carefully at it and tried to remember what Uncle Howard's colleague had told her about the Hebrew scrolls that were stored in genizahs after they were worn out. This might be just such a scroll, its value insignificant. But still,

17

there was something about the shape of these letters. They were different than anything she remembered Moshe showing her before.

"Yes, very nice," she nodded to the Arab.

He turned to his young companion and beamed triumphantly.

"Two hundred English pound," he announced. "Cash."

"Listen," Ellie tried to explain. "I can't. I mean, I don't know anything about this sort of thing. My uncle, the professor . . ."

"Two hundred English pound," he said again.

"Where did this come from? Where did you find it?"

"Cash," he replied, holding out his upturned palm.

Ellie looked first at the gnarled hand outstretched before her, then at the eyes, filled with the delight of greed. "What we have here is a communication breakdown, my good man. You are looking at the Betty Boop of the archaeology world. No. No. A thousand times no." She blew her nose and motioned impatiently to Miriam, still standing in the doorway. "Explain this to him, Miriam." There was no talking to a man whose entire English vocabulary consisted of "antikas, very old," and "cash."

Miriam pried herself away from the doorway as the old Arab rattled off a stream of words, jabbing at the air with one hand while he held the other still outstretched for the money. Miriam rattled back at him in response, and Ellie noticed an instant change in his demeanor.

"Bah!" he spat, lowering his itching palm. He glared at Ellie as if she were an interloper in the world of high finance, then began to gather up the scroll like an angry executive stuffing disappointing quarterly statements into his briefcase.

"Miriam!" Ellie shouted. "Don't let him do that!—Don't do that," she told him, hurrying over to the desk.

"Bah!" he spat again, not even looking at the upstart.

Miriam began talking rapidly, mowing down his obstinance with a barrage of Arabic until, midsentence, he pulled the scroll out of the leather pouch once again, sniffed indignantly, and gazed steadily at Ellie as Miriam finished speaking.

"Hmmm," he said, rubbing his chin thoughtfully. "Hmmm." Then his toothless smile reappeared. He whacked his young companion on the shoulder and the two of them once again took their seats.

"There," said Miriam to Ellie. "You see, one simply must

know how to talk to these desert peasants."

"What did you tell him?" Ellie asked, awed.

"I tell him that you are the most utmost authority on ancient scrolls and that you will not pay him until you can see them all."

"Authority!" repeated Ellie miserably. "All? You mean there are more of these things?"

"He did not tell you?"

"Why, no."

Miriam gave the ancient shepherd a good tongue-lashing, which he followed by a tirade of his own while Ellie groped her way to Uncle Howard's massive leather desk chair and sank down into it.

"Well," Miriam sniffed, "this lying dog says he tells you there are more. He says he tells you how his son finds them in jars in a cave when he goes to find a lost goat."

"He might have," shrugged Ellie. "I couldn't understand a word."

Miriam's eyes narrowed and she shook her head. "Ha!" she barked at the shepherd. "Speak the King's English, please."

The old man looked at the young shepherd beside him who had been gazing intently at a case of ancient tools. Then the old man slapped him on the arm. "King's English, please," he snorted, then mumbled a few Arabic curses.

The young man cleared his throat nervously and rubbed a dirty hand across his lips as if to loosen up a frozen tongue. Then he drew a deep breath and began. "My pardon, ma'am." He nodded to Ellie. A decided trace of British accent in a deep and pleasant voice tempted Ellie to look over her shoulder for the ventriloquist who might be throwing such educated tones into the mouth of this sack of bones and dirt.

"My father is quite an ignorant man," he explained. "He told me he must handle this enterprise himself, and I must learn." A smile cracked his lips as he looked out of the corner of his eye at his brooding father beside him. "He means no harm."

"Obviously, since you speak so well, you must also understand that I am not the authority the housekeeper makes me out to be."

Miriam turned to leave. "I'll bring tea," she announced in an injured tone.

"Thank you, Miriam," Ellie called after her. "And, Miriam—" The old woman paused. "Thank you."

19

The young shepherd's eyes followed the old woman. "She did well. My father would be gone to the antique dealers in Bethlehem if he knew."

"Tell me how you came by this." Ellie leaned her aching head back on the leather chair.

"My youngest brother, Mohamed the Wolf, found a cave filled with jars and some scrolls such as this. Many were in pieces, and there were many broken jars and fragments. He had lost a goat, you see, and tossed a stone into a cave to see if it had wandered in. He heard the sound of breaking pottery and fetched me. We found this and six others whole."

"Where is this cave?"

"There are many caves in the desert," he replied with an evasive smile. "This is one of many by the Dead Sea. I know where it lies, but this is not the time to say."

"I see." Ellie understood his meaning. Until he was paid, he would say nothing. The old man, thought Ellie, would have done well to take lessons from his son. "You know I cannot promise you anything until the professor sees this."

"Then perhaps we should go to Bethlehem to the dealers," he replied with a sigh.

"No. Let me keep it until you bring the others."

"Alas, no. I fear that we will be gone many days to the desert. Two weeks until we return to Jerusalem. We leave in the morning." He began to stand.

"No, wait." Ellie motioned him to sit down. "I am the photographer for the archaeological team. If I weren't ill, I would be with the professor now."

"May Allah grant you health, blessed be His name." The shepherd bowed his head.

"Well, He hasn't, and I'm here," she said under her breath. "So, would you let me keep the scroll overnight? I can photograph it and show it to the professor when he returns. If he likes what he sees, then perhaps you can let your father complete the transaction?"

The young man cleared his throat thoughtfully. "Excuse me, please," he said to Ellie, then addressed the old man, who was staring suspiciously at her. For a period of several minutes they argued back and forth in Arabic, debating the wisdom of leaving such a valuable item in the hands of this red-haired, unveiled, infidel woman who could not even speak the language of the country she now resided in. In the end, Ellie pulled a five-pound note out of her pocket, and the discussion swung decidedly in her favor.

"Tell him this will be a deposit. Good faith, you know." Ellie said as the old man eyed the bill. "He can have the scroll back in the morning, but I want the money back too."

"No, a thousand times," replied the young shepherd, shaking his head firmly. "He keeps the money, and we take the scroll in the morning."

"But you promise to return two weeks from today with the rest of the scrolls?" asked Ellie. "And the five pounds is off the purchase price if the professor decides to take them." Her eyes narrowed shrewdly as she tried out her bargaining ability.

The young man repeated the offer to his father who immediately was lost in deep thought. After a moment of coy consideration—*more show than substance*, Ellie thought, amused—he snatched the bill from her hand, rejoicing in a torrent of happy Aramaic. Just as Miriam entered with the tray of steaming tea, he embraced his son energetically and strode out of the study and through the front door, triumphantly waving the five-pound note. *Scroll rental*, thought Ellie. *Something new in Palestine.*

"Tomorrow morning, then." The young Arab bowed and took his leave.

"Yes, if I'm still breathing," moaned Ellie, laying her head on the desk.

"May our gracious Lord will it so," said Miriam matter-of-factly as she set the tray on the desk. "Will you have tea in bed?" she inquired.

Ellie raised her head and peered at the old woman. "No, Miriam. Tea in the photo lab."

———

As Ellie prepared the scroll for photographing, moving about the lab to gather up materials, she mused over her earlier confrontation with Miriam. The eighty-year-old housekeeper fancied herself in charge, determined to make a respectable young woman out of the professor's flighty, unconventional niece. Eccentric, dominant, yet solicitous of Ellie's welfare, Miriam had taken upon herself the responsibility of the red-haired photographer.

"I told them you were not well," Miriam had said when she

21

woke Ellie to meet the Bedouin shepherds, "but it is very important they speak with you. Utmost urgently. For if they go they may not come again for some time. Drink your tea and I will help you get dressed." Miriam had shuffled over to the closet and begun sifting through Ellie's clothes. "So many beautiful dresses that you have, yet never wear," Miriam chided.

"You want me to wear an angora sweater to the dig?" Ellie sniffed defensively.

"Should we not share our abundance? If you do not wear these things, there are so many Jewish refugees at the docks. Poor women . . ."

"I'm not planning on rooting around Palestine forever. When I'm done here I'm going to Europe. Paris and London. Civilization, you know." She blew her nose and sat up. Catching a glimpse of her reflection in the mirror, she groaned and sank back to her pillow. "Look at me, Miriam. I'm death warmed over. I can't see anybody. . ."

"No matter how you look. This is only Jerusalem. The men who wish to see you, only Bedouin shepherds. They are very ignorant. All day they look at goats. They will think you are beautiful." There was an amused twinkle in the old woman's eyes as she selected a pair of khaki trousers and a shirt to match. "It is more important you look like an archaeologist right now I think." She laid the clothes on Ellie's bed.

"You're getting me up to see Bedouin shepherds? Out of bed?"

Miriam placed a cool hand on Ellie's forehead. "The professor shall be much relieved that you have no more fever."

"Great."

"If you like I shall bring the Bedouins here to your bedside?" Miriam suggested mildly.

Ellie sat up and swung her legs out from the covers. "This better be something, Miriam. It better be." She had been helpless under Miriam's firm gaze.

Ellie chuckled as she remembered the bluff, her hands moving expertly to load the film and set the light meter.

As Miriam came in with the tea, Ellie was spreading out the scroll across the large table in the center of the laboratory.

"Jesus looks out for you, my Ellie," Miriam said, "but you got to help yourself as well. Come, have tea. And here—" she offered Ellie a box of tissues.

What I wouldn't give right now, Ellie thought, *for American Kleenex!* The toilet paper was bad enough, but the stuff these people blew their noses on was a hybrid of cornhusks and sandpaper—guaranteed to scrape away the germs, skin and all.

"Thanks," Ellie grunted, her tone not at all evidencing any thankfulness. But she sniffed appreciatively at the scent of the tea and sat down heavily, cup in hand, to examine the scroll.

Miriam lightly touched the back of her hand to Ellie's forehead. With that, the old woman shuffled out the door and closed it behind her.

Where in the world, Ellie wondered, *did Uncle Howard ever find Miriam?* This Arab woman could hold her own with the best of her nation's bargainers, yet her sharp tongue was tempered by her instinct to mother anyone who needed her care; she was a woman who, to Ellie's amazement, believed in God and spoke of Him as if He were real. Most of the Jews in Jerusalem had given up the hope of Messiah; those who still held on to their hope expected a military zealot. But Miriam, this ancient Arab, believed in Yeshua, and took Him as her Allah.

Wiping her hands on her khaki slacks, Ellie gently touched the fragile scroll. Ellie believed little of religion for herself; indeed, she had rarely thought deeply enough to come to the right questions.

She sighed and looked up at the wall, where hung a random scattering of photographs she had taken during the last few months in Palestine. She studied the faces of those she had met in the crooked streets of Jerusalem. They weren't bad as photographs go. Professor Tierney back at UCLA might have packaged them up and sent them off to *National Geographic*, or at least had them mounted for display in some Graduate Middle Eastern History class. All things considered, Palestine was a photojournalist's heaven. An armed Arab dressed in flowing robes and a tarboosh was better than a picture of a sorority girl at the prom any day of the week. And the cobbled alleyways of the Old City were in every way superior to Westwood Boulevard for photographic interest. For some time now, Ellie had quietly nursed the suspicion that anyone with an ounce of ability could take fantastic photographs in this place. Moshe disagreed. Praising her talent, he told anyone who would listen that she was the Rembrandt of the world of film; that no one had ever captured Jerusalem as she had.

"Something you capture in the faces," he would say, his voice trailing off. "There is something . . ."

Ellie was flattered, of course, but she had the feeling Moshe knew about as much concerning photography as she knew about Babylonian cuneiform writing. Still, as she gazed back at the silent eyes looking down at her, there was enough life and soul in those faces that she longed to speak to these she had seen only through the camera's eye.

What was it they all had in common? An Arab merchant framed in the doorway of his shop, a veiled Bedouin woman with a water jug steadied on her head, an Orthodox Jew standing by the Wailing Wall, a small Jewish boy, one of the refugees, standing proudly with his first orange in hand—somehow they were all the same picture. They spoke of the same—the same *something* . . . What had made her snap the shutter? She stared at their eyes, and then she knew. These people all belonged somewhere. Not like her. Not like David. They were all like Moshe; all somehow in focus.

Moshe! The thought of him brought a smile to Ellie's lips as she remembered not only his praise of her work, but the lovely richness he had brought to her life. Moshe Sachar was an archaeological linguist at Hebrew University in Jerusalem. Tall and slender, with rough-hewn features and a deep tan from the sun of his native land, this Jew was a striking contrast to Ellie's fair skin sprinkled finely with freckles, copper-colored hair and green eyes. He was at home among both the souks and the cabbis of the Old City. Arab merchants called out to him and he answered in their native tongue while Ellie stood by bewildered and impressed by the haggling. As often as not, the bargaining centered around her. Rarely did a stroll go by without Moshe being offered twenty camels in trade for the red-headed woman who wore no veil. A deal no sane man would refuse, in the opinion of the male Arab population.

"You're never even tempted?" Ellie teased.

"What? For twenty camels? You're worth at least fifty, and a couple of goats besides," he said, dodging her playful blow.

At age thirty-two, Moshe was unmarried and absolutely devoted to his profession. He was, in fact, the most in-focus man that Ellie had ever known. They had met the same week Ellie arrived in Jerusalem, when Uncle Howard had invited him to dinner to discuss the discovery of jar handles inscribed with the name of the ancient town of Gibeon.

Ellie had heard such excitement in a man's voice only when her brothers discussed the Rose Bowl or laid odds on whether the war would end before they could enlist. For three hours Ellie sat quietly while Uncle Howard and Moshe mulled over the possibility that they had indeed found the ancient site where the men of David and the men of Saul had done battle. Ellie was about to yawn politely and excuse herself when Moshe looked up at her with the deepest brown eyes she had ever seen and said, "I must apologize. For me to babble about ancient battles is sacrilege in the presence of such a beautiful woman. I am afraid I do not provide much of interest to normal conversations."

Ellie had gazed back into the deep pools that looked at her so searchingly and felt herself melt. "Oh, no, Mr. Sachar," she fibbed. "I find it all extremely interesting. Please tell me more about it." A sweet smile and fluttering eyelashes were all it took. The next few months had been filled with heavenly discussions about Babylonian cuneiform writing and the benefits of leather scrolls over copper ones. She found herself actually becoming interested in the subject as well as her teacher.

She truly liked Moshe; maybe their friendship was moving on toward something deeper. Most importantly, when she was near him she never thought about David, never daydreamed of the way he used to hold her or what he had meant in her life.

Ellie's eyes regained their focus on the cryptic writings before her. *What*, she wondered, *would Moshe think of these scrolls? Most likely*, she thought, *I've just paid five pounds for the Brooklyn Bridge*.

2   The Contraband

The sharp prow of the ancient fishing boat rose and fell in cadence with the rhythmic thud of the gasping diesel engine. Moshe Sachar gripped the slippery rail and braced himself against the swells of the Mediterranean. Like a living figurehead, he searched the midnight darkness, whipped by the wind and biting salt spray. They were, he knew, only a few miles from their destination, and still there was no sign of the inevitable British gunboats. Perhaps they would make it through the blockade and unload their precious smuggled cargo on the shores of Palestine. Perhaps they would be spared the bullhorns and the searchlights and the gun-toting sailors who pushed their way below deck to remove their treasures.

Moshe could picture in his mind the human contraband, huddled together below as they quietly endured the misery of seasickness and unbelievably cramped conditions—eighty-four human souls jammed into a space designed to carry a dozen fishermen. But these people were survivors—*the survivors* of Auschwitz, Ravensbruck, and Birkenau—places where millions of men, women, and children had died simply because they were Jews. They faced starvation, forced labor, brutality and torture—because they were Jews. Ultimately they succumbed to the gas chambers, the ovens, and the anonymity of mass graves—because they were Jews.

Moshe remembered many of the faces of the eighty-four he had helped transfer in midocean only the day before. The deck of that rusting hulk of a freighter was jammed with nearly eight hundred refugees waiting for small boats to carry them through the British blockade. Faded, silent, gaunt and frail, even the very young somehow seemed old and fragile as they gazed down at Moshe and the rickety fishing boat. Then, welcoming rainfall after a drought, the cries of hope had risen from those who lined the freighter's rail, cheering the eighty-four being lowered to this deck.

"Hey, Aram," joked one as his friend took Moshe's hand and stepped aboard, "did you ever learn to swim?"

"La Chaim!" cried others. "To life!"

"*This year in Jerusalem!*" called an old man tearfully, remembering the promise of his fathers. There were no good-byes. There had already been too many good-byes for one lifetime. In the names of those who had died without hope, the survivors would touch the soil of their ancient homeland and find new life and lasting hope—because they were Jews. That is, if they could make it past the British warships patrolling these waters in search of "illegal" immigrants.

Moshe's keen eyes scanned the blackness of the night in

search of a patrol boat. In the distance, the lights of Tel Aviv sparkled—so very close, but oh so far. Tonight every radio in Palestine was tuned to the news in faraway America where the United Nations met at this very moment to decide on the partition of Palestine into two states: one Jewish, one Arab. Perhaps the British Navy had taken the night off to listen to the vote which would decide the issue of Great Britain's presence in the Middle East once and for all. Moshe pictured the English officers lounging in their mess halls, sipping whiskey and commenting on each nation's vote. If Partition passed the U.N., the British would withdraw and these secret trips would end. No more "illegal" immigration of Jews. They could come openly, permits in hand, to their own homeland. They could live in freedom and decide their own fate. And Moshe Sachar, secret member of the Haganah, blockade runner by night, archaeologist and scholar by day, could be simply Moshe Sachar, archaeologist, once again. He wiped salt spray out of his eyes, prayed for the outcome of the vote, and half-envied those who warmed themselves by their fires, listened to their radios, and shared coffee as the world made an end to "The Jewish Problem."

He thought of Ellie then, beautiful and unconcerned. What a refuge she was to him; she never suspected the double life he led. And if indeed she had known, she simply would have asked to come along and photograph the adventure for the fun of it. With Ellie there were no politics or issues, only people and her camera. Ships of state might collide and sink, but for Ellie all that mattered was that people survived it in the end and that she had enough film to photograph the event. *She's a true journalist at heart*, thought Moshe. Beyond his deep feeling for her, ⸻ the British authorities and known as "The Kangaroo" for his expertise in smuggling. He was never seen with anyone even remotely suspected of being a member of the Haganah, the Jewish underground organization. Ellie and her camera were his only contacts with other members of the organization. Photographs of hieroglyphics and cuneiform symbols provided the codes of his movements to those who needed them. A series of Hebrew scriptures photographed from scrolls communicated plans and intentions. Ellie took the pictures, and an Arab runner delivered them to other "members" of the archaeological community, all very neat and safe. She never suspected a thing, and if she had, Moshe was not so sure it would have mattered to her. So, not only was her assistance convenient, she was one of the most delightful women he had ever known.

Sometimes he thought he might actually be in love with her. He hoped there would be time later to explore the possibility a little deeper. Right now, however, there was too much else at stake—the future of a Jewish homeland. He could not afford to look or love too deeply. Love gave a man too much reason to stay alive. It turned courage away from its ability to stare at death without blinking. It made a man hesitate when risk loomed over his head. So Moshe would wait before he let Ellie have too much room in his heart. Already she had made life dangerously precious to him.

The lights of the coast grew more distinct, and still there was no sign of pursuit by the authorities. Moshe pulled the collar of his blue wool coat up close around his ears and yanked his cap down. The little boat slapped against a particularly large swell, and he stumbled backward into someone else, a woman, nearly knocking her to the deck. He made a grab for the rail and managed to keep her from falling. It was one of the refugees. How long had she been standing there watching him think?

He held her by the arm as he found his footing. "Forgive me," he said, finding a secure handhold for her on the railing. "You should be below with the others."

"Rough sea tonight," she replied, avoiding his comment and moving away from his grip.

Moshe could just make out her features by the starlight. Her voice was young and her skin very white against the dark frame of her hair. She was wrapped in a large bulky shawl, but from their collision he knew how light—almost fragile—she was.

"Is the sea always this rough?" she asked seriously, looking up at him with bright, luminous eyes.

Did he detect apprehension in her voice? "Sometimes it is much worse than this. Nothing to worry about."

She peered over the rail into the black churning water. "I cannot swim," she said quietly.

"So swimming is not part of your tour package," he smiled.

She looked at him for a moment without acknowledging his attempt at humor, then turned and stood quietly watching the shoreline.

"That is it, isn't it? Palestine?" she asked.

"Yes," he answered. "Palestine-England. Under the control of His Majesty's forces."

"So close," she said sadly. "Will they come for us?"

"Possibly," Moshe answered. "If they catch wind . . ."

"I cannot swim," she said again. "I will not be taken."

"You should go below with the others," he insisted, becoming anxious about what she might do if a gunboat appeared on the horizon.

"Please," she begged, gripping the rail with a firm resolve. "I cannot. It is so close, so crowded down there. Just give me a moment to breathe free air."

Moshe backed away from her a step and stood in silence, wondering what agonies this young woman must have passed through to come to this moment. "Our landing site is only a few miles to the north," he said quietly. "Your home, your new home, is a kibbutz not far—"

"I am going to Jerusalem," she interrupted. "I have family there. I am not the only one left. I have family, not like the rest of them!" She spat out the last words, and in the tone of her voice somehow cut herself away from the other eighty-three human beings who hoped for the Promised Land.

"I see," said Moshe also a bit doubtfully, not comprehending the anger in her voice. "You are lucky, then."

"Lucky," she repeated flatly. "I had forgotten there was such a word." Then she turned and, staggering against the roll of the ship, disappeared down the hatch. Moshe scanned the horizon once again, then followed the young woman down the stairs.

Young and old they sat, crammed together on the floor of the hold. A small child cried and an old woman tried to comfort him, but the rest were silent. A dim lantern swung from the center beam, casting evil shadows on their gaunt faces. Every eye turned hopefully toward Moshe as he appeared on the ladder—all except the eyes of the young woman he had met on the deck moments before. She held herself apart from the others, braced in a corner. Her long, dark hair swung with the shadows, damp wisps clinging around her face. *She is*, Moshe thought fleetingly, *very beautiful*. Her nose was straight and aquiline above soft, full lips, remarkable in such a thin face. She gazed at the floor, steadfastly refusing to look at the man who had called her "lucky." She was, indeed, not like the others. Distractedly, she rubbed her fingers over the inevitable tattoo of her identification numbers on her forearm. *As if*, thought Moshe, *she hopes to rub them off*. A wave of compassion swept over him. He knew she suffered still.

A ragged vagabond of a man followed Moshe's gaze to the young woman then asked, "Have you news for us, sir?" bringing Moshe back to reality.

"We are—" Moshe began, swallowing the lump in his throat. "We are very near to our destination." He smiled at the light that transformed the weary faces before and the murmurs of joy which rippled through the group. Only the beautiful young woman remained unresponsive.

"How soon?" was the first question. "What of the British?" "When will we land?"

"Maybe an hour," answered Moshe. "We have been traveling under radio silence. So far it does not seem that the British have got wind of us. Be hopeful. We are almost home." Moshe glanced one more time at the young woman's downcast face, and turned on his heel to resume his topside vigil.

A welcome blast of wind hit Moshe full in the face as he came out of the stale hold. He adjusted his collar and lowered his head, then staggered forward around coils of rope and fishing nets. When the leaky vessel was not carrying illegal passengers, it doubled as a sardine boat. *Appropriate*, mused Moshe, *the way they jam everyone into this tin can*. Its captain, a surly Rumanian Jew named Ehud Schiff, actually made a legitimate living as a fisherman. For his illegitimate activities his only reward was the satisfaction that the cargo he delivered to Palestine passed right under the noses of nearly the entire British fleet. Moshe knew that Ehud ran the blockade as much to spite the English as from a sense of patriotism or compassion. Grizzled and hairy, smelling like yesterday's catch, Ehud Schiff was the elite of the blockade runners. He and his wretched little boat had tallied a neat total of twelve hundred refugees in the last four months alone. Considering that the British legally allowed only fifteen hundred Jews into the country each month, his was an impressive accomplishment. And he was only one of many who risked the loss of their boats and imprisonment if they were caught. Bits and pieces of other small craft often floated in the water near Tel Aviv and Haifa after attempting the same feat. Moshe looked up toward Ehud at the helm and smiled. Many were the times he could remember coming in after a particularly difficult run, and as they passed the wreckage of a less fortunate vessel, Ehud would murmur to the old ship, "Close your eyes, my darling. Take no notice, my love." Then he would run his gnarled, weather-cracked hands over the ship's wheel as if he were caressing the face of his beloved. Perhaps the most amusing detail about Ehud and his sardine boat was her name: *Ave Maria*. To name a Jewish sardine boat "Hail Mary" seemed odd, to say the least.

"I bought the boat in Italy," Ehud would growl when questioned. "Mary was Jewish and she carried a Jewish child. Is this not a proper name for my angel?"

No one argued. A rabbi or two might have looked askance, but the British Navy had never once detained the *Ave Maria* when her hold was "with child." And those to whom she gave life in the land of Palestine blessed her barnacle-encrusted hulk.

Moshe again braced himself in the prow of the ship and gazed toward Tel Aviv. He could see the outlines of battleships resting at anchor. He strained his eyes for details, then lifted the binoculars that dangled around his neck. There, in the reflection of the city lights, he saw something that made his heart catch and then beat a hard counterpoint to his boat's chugging engine. From between two anchored British ships, the running lights of a third ship moved out in a direct course toward the *Ave Maria*.

One glance told him all. Moshe turned on his heels and bounded up the ladder to where Ehud stood at the helm.

"I spotted her too," growled Ehud as Moshe sprang to his side. "A gunboat."

"Yes," said Moshe feeling the tingle of sweat between his shoulder blades. "She's moving top speed out of the harbor."

"Got someone in her gunsights."

"We're directly on her course. No use trying to make a run for it," said Moshe. "I make it we've got five minutes at most before she intercepts us."

Ehud stroked the smooth wood of the wheel. "Ah, my darling," he said sadly to the ship, "you are beautiful, but you are too slow, eh?"

"So if we can't outrun them, we'll have to outtalk them. They won't board with seas like this."

"But they can force us back out into the harbor. Or blow us out of the water."

Moshe started back down the steps. "Turn around, Ehud," he instructed. "Out to sea."

Moshe groped his way back down the hatch as the *Ave Maria* swung wildly around. The swinging lantern in the hold illuminated the fear on the faces of the men and women. They needed no explanation. It was plain enough from the vessel's change of direction and Moshe's face that something had gone wrong. Moshe's gaze briefly touched that of the young woman. Her eyes were filled with resignation and accusation. Why had he given them hope? She quickly looked away.

"Are any of you men fishermen?" Moshe demanded. "We need a crew topside at once."

Three thin remnants of what had once been strapping young seamen, stood and picked their way to Moshe's side.

None of the three looked the part of Mediterranean fishermen. From their worn street shoes to their long black coats and baggy vests hanging on shrunken frames, the men told the story of European Jews sneaking in the back door of Palestine. They would be spotted at once if the *Ave Maria* were stopped.

Moshe scanned the group for caps and coats that might pass the inspection of a British Naval officer.

Several of the refugees wore caps that resembled those of Greek fishermen. Close enough. Moshe snatched them from the heads of their startled owners, then tore through the compartments beneath their seats in search of slickers and boots. He found one oil-soaked cable knit sweater and a torn wool coat. He took off his own coat and handed it to one of the three who was most nearly his size.

"Put this stuff on," he instructed them. "And keep your shoes out of sight. It wouldn't take a detective to see that you are not shod for the deck of a sardine trawler. Stand behind the nets or something, eh?"

The motley crew followed him up the steps and took their stations—one in the wheelhouse with Ehud, the other two mending nets that littered the decks. Moshe stood near the hatch, nursing a cold cup of coffee: the picture, he hoped, of nonchalance. It was his hope that the *Ave Maria* would be thought to be just leaving the harbor rather than returning from a long voyage.

As the small craft bobbed through the swells, the British gunboat dashed through them like a terrier after a rat.

The ominous drone of the gunboat's engines rose and fell with the winds and seemed to growl the warning: *Run, run, run.* But there was no running. There was only the thin shred of hope that by some miracle the gunboat would pass by them without seeing. "God of Abraham," Moshe prayed, "remember us."

If that miracle did not happen, the next would be if the British let them pass as sardine fishermen heading out for the morning's catch. "Remember how these, your children, have suffered."

Moshe thought of the cages that lined the decks of the British deportation boats; cages for apprehended immigrants on their way to the detention camps of Cyprus. More barbed wire; more imprisonment for children, some of whom had never drawn a free breath. "We don't dare go over our monthly quota of Jews," a British colonel had explained to him over a beer at the King David Hotel. "Why don't they just go back to where they came from? Stop stirrin' up the Arabs."

In the eight years he had spent smuggling Jews out of Nazi-dominated Europe, Moshe never had come closer to giving himself away. With steely eyes and a fixed grin, Moshe had answered, "Back to the ovens of Auschwitz, eh?" The colonel had laughed uneasily, then sniffed self-consciously under Moshe's glare.

"You know what I mean. Man, you're a native here. Surely you see immigration means nothin' but trouble. We'll have another holocaust on our hands, and this time it'll be the Arabs doin' the dirty business, won't it now?"

Yes, thought Moshe, *under the passive eyes of the British Mandatory Government in Palestine, the Arabs could do what they wished. Not only were Jews prohibited entry into the country,* but the Sabra, the native Jewish Palestinians, were forbidden to carry anything even vaguely resembling a weapon. A Jew could be stopped and searched at will by British soldiers and arrested for having a pair of scissors on his person. An Arab, on the other hand, could openly sell a rifle in the marketplace.

The British predict a bloody massacre of Jews by the Arab world if the Partition Resolution passes tonight, Moshe thought. *Arabs vowed to drive the Jews into the sea. Perhaps it would happen as they prophesied, but never again would Jews die like sheep without a fight.* "Never again," Moshe murmured, watching the running lights of the gunboat charge through the sea like the red eyes of a bull.

Run, run, run, chanted the gunboat.

"Never again!" answered Moshe. "We will not run again." He felt the hot charge of anger rush through his body. Like David against Goliath, if the little state of Israel was indeed born to-night, it would stand and fight. And the *Ave Maria* would also fight and die rather than give up her children to the detention camps of Cyprus. There had been enough useless suffering.

"God of Abraham," prayed Moshe, "remember us." The gun-boat was less than a quarter of a mile off stern, and still it had not veered from its straight course toward the rescue vessel. Searchlights now clicked to life and split the dark night with their shafts. Moshe was reminded of the lights that had searched the skies of London for Nazi bombers during the Blitz. Now, with the same earnest determination, the lights searched for the vic-tims of Nazi tyranny. In a flash of disbelief, Moshe said, "To them we're all the same. All the enemy."

Moshe glanced up toward the wheelhouse where Ehud held the little ship steady. Just a few moments more and they would be discovered. The *Ave Maria* chugged bravely ahead. The lights reached out and felt the sea a mere four hundred yards behind them.

"God of Abraham—God of Zion," Moshe whispered. Then he was hit from behind with the force of someone bursting through the hatch and onto the deck. He stumbled forward, spilling his coffee and falling over a rope coil.

"I will not be taken!" cried a desperate voice. "I cannot! Let me die!" It was the young woman. She clambered over Moshe's prostrate form and ran to the railing.

"Stop!" shouted Moshe, fighting to regain his footing. "Don't jump!"

But the young woman didn't even pause as she threw herself over the side of the boat.

"Oh, God!" Moshe cried; then, without thought, he too was over the rail and in the water. Cold blackness engulfed him, in-stantly filling his boots and pulling him downward. He knew he could not be more than a few feet from the young woman. Struggling to the surface, he gasped for air, then awkwardly treading water, fought the heaviness of his boots and clothing as he searched for her. Her body would struggle to survive, he knew, even though her mind longed for death. Three yards from him he heard her choke as she battled the seas that sought to claim her. He plunged beneath the surface and pulled off his boots, then with one more breath he swam through the foaming wake of the *Ave Maria* to her side. She flailed wildly against the pull of death, striking Moshe hard across the cheek. He went under and grabbed her around the waist. Then he burst up for air, pulling her into a hammerlock as he kicked his powerful legs to stay afloat.

"Stop fighting, you idiot!" he shouted. "You'll kill us both!" She lay still in his arms. Had she slipped into unconsciousness?

"Let me die," she moaned, coughing and spitting out sea water. "Oh, let me!"

"Shut up, or I'm liable to." His left arm circled under her chin and kept her head above water while his right arm worked to keep them afloat. She struggled briefly as a wave slapped her across the face, filling her mouth with brine.

"Relax!" he shouted angrily. What in heaven's name had he done? Jumping into the sea after a lunatic two full miles from shore?

The *Ave Maria* chugged farther away to his left, the fishing boat's engine stuttering as she dipped down behind another wave. To his right, the gunboat loomed. Moshe didn't relish the idea of ending his life beneath a British gunboat as chopped fish food.

"God of Abraham!" he shouted against death's whirlpool. There was no time to swim away from the path of the gunboat. No time unless he left the young woman to die alone. "God!" he called again.

"Let me die!" screamed the woman. "Please! Save yourself!"

"Shut up!" he demanded, treading water as death approached.

"Swim away," she pleaded. "This was my choice, not yours." Her dark wet hair floated around him like seaweed and clung to his face. He did not want to die. Not like this. "Hear, O Israel . . ." He began to recite the Shema, the death prayer of the Jews. "The Lord our God is one . . ."

"Save yourself!" she cried again.

"The Lord our God . . ." He struggled to swim but his burden weighed him down. He held tight to the young woman as the bow of the gunboat loomed only a hundred yards from where

35

they waited in its path. So this was what it meant to die.

"Hear, O Israel . . ." Moshe shouted louder. "Say it with me," he demanded. "Say it!"

"Hear, O Israel, the Lord our God is one God," they gasped together.

Then, as they gazed in disbelief, the gunboat began a slow turn away from them, away from the path of the *Ave Maria*. Shafts of light skated across the swells like water spiders, passing within a few feet of where Moshe and the young woman bobbed helplessly. If they were trapped in the light, they would be dragged from the water to the relative safety of a British prison.

The lights moved nearer, sweeping inches from them.

"Let me go," the young woman struggled feebly. "I cannot be taken."

In an instant, Moshe knew that for this woman at least, death would be more merciful than the detention cages.

"Be still!" he shouted as the drumming engines covered his voice. "When I say *now*, hold your breath." She nodded desperately, eyeing a bright circle sliding directly toward them.

"NOW!" shouted Moshe, filling his lungs and pulling her under. The spot passed over them, illuminating the water in an eerie green wash, then sweeping back again over the place where the young woman's hair fanned out on the water's surface. "It's nothin', sir," Moshe imagined a sailor saying. "Nothin' but a bit o'kelp."

The gunboat slid by, a mere fifty yards from where they surfaced, filling their lungs with precious air. The dim outlines of sailors moved across her deck, little suspecting that they were passing only seconds from a catch. The strong wake of the gunboat swept toward them, pushing them hard through the three-foot swells toward shore.

"Ride with it!" Moshe yelled, holding tight to his charge. "Kick your feet! Kick them, I say, and we both might live!"

The gunboat continued her wide sweep, shutting down the searchlights one by one as Moshe watched. He began a slow crawl toward the lights of the harbor.

What was it that had made the British ship turn away when she was so close to her quarry? Moshe glanced back at the gunboat's retreating hulk as she cut a broad semicircle back to Tel Aviv. She had simply not known what lay a few yards beyond her probing lights. Moshe thought of the *Ave Maria*. With the gunboat safely away, Ehud might try to look for the two of them. The "crew" had no doubt witnessed her dramatic leap into the sea. "God, don't let him turn back to search. Tell him it is hopeless," prayed Moshe.

The weight of the young woman's skirt pulled him down and wrapped itself around his rapidly tiring legs. He stopped his slow crawl toward shore to tread water, as she lay back against him in misery.

"You'll have to take your skirt off," he instructed. "I cannot fight the sea and that, too." He felt her stiffen in a protest of fear.

"I'll drown," she choked.

"Oh, so now she wants to live!" he mocked. "Take your skirt off or we both drown."

As Moshe supported her, she awkwardly unbuttoned the heavy wool skirt and kicked it away. Choking on salt water, she struggled to pull her arms free. Her lightweight slip floated about her body, and she immediately felt more buoyant.

Finally she relaxed in Moshe's grip, exhausted. "I can't go any farther," she moaned.

"You fancy burial at sea, eh?" he said sarcastically. "Kick your legs, woman. I'm going to let go for a moment."

"No!" she cried, clutching at his arms.

"I have to take my trousers off. My sweater." He shoved her hard away from him, confident that she would still be thrashing when he took hold again. His head slipped beneath the surface as he pulled his sweater over his head and kicked off his heavy trousers. Careful not to let go of them, he pulled them to the surface. In one strong stroke he swam to her side and grabbed her by her hair, pulling her to him. "Relax," he demanded, "or I let you go again." She coughed and sobbed in protest, but he felt her slender body go limp.

Moshe swung his heavy trousers through the water in front of her. "Your hands are free," he instructed. "Knot the legs at the cuff."

With some effort, the young woman worked on the trousers, obeying commands now even though she could not understand them.

"Finished," she said.

Stopping to tread water once again, Moshe took the trousers from her and opened them at the waist trapping air bubbles solidly inside the water-saturated fabric. He wrapped the trouser legs beneath her arms, holding the waist beneath the water so the air would not escape. "There. A life preserver." Moshe tucked his arm around her. "Now kick," he demanded, "or I'll turn you over to the British myself."

3   Yacov

Nine-year-old Yacov Lebowitz opened his eyes and stared into the darkness of the basement room. The kerosene stove had long since stopped sputtering and popping with warmth, and the room had reverted once again to the cold, damp chill of Jerusalem's early winter. He shuddered and pulled the ragged woolen blanket tighter around himself.

He reached his hand down to the floor beside his iron cot and felt for the warm, shaggy dog sleeping beside him. "Psst, Shaul!" He snapped his fingers and was greeted by a soft whine as the dog shook himself to his feet and licked Yacov's hand expectantly. "Come on," Yacov whispered. "Up." The huge animal jumped onto the cot, causing the rusty springs to groan and sag. He lay squarely across his young master, grateful to be off the cold stone floor.

Grandfather had forbidden Yacov to sleep with the dog, and during the summer months he had obeyed, since the old man's bed was only an arm's length away. But tonight his bones ached with the steadily dropping temperature in the tiny one-room apartment they shared.

He hoped Grandfather would not wake up and throw Shaul out on the street as he had threatened. Yacov listened to the even cadence of the old man's breathing. It had not changed. The dog nuzzled close, and Yacov was thankful for the living, furry blanket that shielded him from both the chill of the night and the loneliness of his existence.

"Jackal!" Grandfather had called the filthy puppy Yacov had found cowering among the discarded crates and garbage near the Dung Gate. "Hiding among the baggage like King Shaul, eh?" And so the name stuck.

He had been lost, Yacov guessed, by some careless shepherd who brought his sheep to the Old City markets for sale. Half-starved and afraid, but mostly alone, the puppy had shivered when Yacov had gathered him up to go begging scraps at Solomon's Kosher butcher shop in the New City. "So," Grandfather had said, "this jackal is eating better than we are? Tell him, Yacov, he must eat his soup bones, we will not share our soup!"

That had been two years ago. Shaul brought home the bones from Solomon's; Grandfather made soup, and they all ate well. "So we're not starving anyway," Grandfather would say.

Shaul had grown into a strange-looking mix of every stray dog in the city. He had a sharp, wolf-like muzzle that could look vicious when he showed his teeth. But his light-brown eyes were kind, almost human when he gazed at Yacov. His coat was a mosaic of gray and black and tan, the length and texture of a collie's over massive shoulders and narrow hips. Shaul had no tail. Occasionally he would cower and slink, but that was only when Grandfather growled at him, "You son of seven fathers! I'll sell you for Arab stew meat!"

For Yacov, the dog became the brothers and sister he had lost, the sweet comfort of a mother and father vanished in the smoke of the Auschwitz crematoriums.

Yacov stroked the dog's broad head and tried again to remember the face of his mother. "Such a beautiful girl she was," Grandfather had said in a tender moment as he showed Yacov a faded photograph of a young Orthodox girl. She had married one of Grandfather's Yeshiva school students, a bright boy from a good Jewish family in Warsaw, who had come to Jerusalem to study. She had returned to Poland with him.

Grandfather showed him her letters, carefully penned in Yiddish. She was a scholar herself, unusual for a young woman. Her letters spoke of happy times, a good life in Poland, and the birth of a daughter and three sons, of whom Yacov was the youngest. Together he and Grandfather had gazed for a long time at the picture of his mother, father, sister, and brothers, with the baby Yacov sitting properly on his mother's lap.

Yacov had studied the face of his father: dark, serious eyes, full beard, high cheekbones and a large, straight nose. *Handsome*, Yacov thought, *but not at all like the face I see in the mirror each day.* His oldest brother, however, nine years old then as

Yacov was now, seemed a reflection of himself; curly light-brown hair, small and fine-boned. Grandfather often said that the boys' clear, gray-blue eyes were just like their mother's. And the older sister was more beautiful still. Even in the photograph, though there was no color, Yacov had seen the resemblance and longed to reach out and touch the faces that were so much like his. Tonight he wondered again why he alone among those six precious human beings had escaped.

After the Nazis had come to Poland, the happy letters had stopped. Six months later, Yacov was smuggled into Palestine under the noses of the British, then into Jerusalem, into the basement room, and into Grandfather's impoverished life. Yacov remembered nothing of the days before Grandfather. But sometimes at night, with Shaul smuggled onto his cot and breathing against his cheek, Yacov thought that he could *feel* what he had forgotten. Once again the pretty young woman in the picture held him on her lap and sang to him. He must have never been cold then, or lonely.

Grandfather was a rabbi and an Old City Yeshiva school-teacher who delighted in the law of Moses and whose daily hope was the coming of the Messiah to restore Israel. He resented these new Jews who had invaded Palestine with programs and politics of Zionism, demanding a Jewish homeland without a Messiah.

Years of endless study and prayer had stooped his frail shoulders and streaked his once-black beard with gray. For him, the needs of this life were minimal, the needs of a small boy incomprehensible. He survived, as many others of his vocation, on the charity and donations of others—threadbare coats, cabbage soup, and the Torah. It was not enough. Never enough. So Yacov survived by becoming a thief.

Selective about whom he robbed, he targeted mainly the British soldiers who roamed through the marketplace souks of the Old City looking for souveniers to take home. Yacov picked their pockets without conscience and quickly passed the booty to Shaul who faithfully trotted home as Yacov escaped over the rooftops.

He knew the most obscure routes of escape from the grasp of some angry British sergeant in hot pursuit. The rooftops were second nature to him—a hiding place and a playground.

In quiet moments he feared the disapproval of Grandfather

more than the wrath of God or the British. But he had decided long ago that he could not wait for the Messiah to come and bring His blessings to the bare cupboards of their basement room. He knew the commandments, but hoped that somehow God would understand the ache of hunger that sometimes gnawed at him and kept him from sleep. Besides, he reasoned, were the British themselves not thieves? Had they not stolen the land of Palestine from her people?

But now his most immediate worry was that of losing his quarry. There was talk, so much talk he didn't understand. Many people in the Old City thought perhaps the British soldiers would be leaving Palestine and the streets of Jerusalem forever. Tonight, he knew, someplace far away in America, men who had never even seen Palestine were voting about something called Partition.

Grandfather and the other rabbis raged against it and against the young Zionist Jews who supported it. The baths and coffee-houses of the Old City had become centers of hot and angry debates. Should Palestine become two states, one Arab and one Jewish? Shouldn't we put our faith in the restoration of Israel when Messiah comes?

Yacov understood little of the issues. But if the soldiers left, whose pockets could he pick? Arabs? Many of his playmates were from the Arab Quarter, friends and neighbors who came to light the lamps for him and Grandfather on Shabbat. He could expect no mercy from God if he stole from his neighbors. That much Grandfather had taught him. But the British—they were the enemy. And like David who took Goljath's sword, he was determined to take whatever he could win in his battle against the British "Philistines" who roamed the streets of his city. Whatever this Partition was, whatever his motive, Yacov stood by the rabbis' stand: "May the English thieves stay until Messiah comes," he whispered softly to Shaul.

The boy softly rubbed Shaul's ear as he turned these things over in his mind. Sleep began to settle on him as he grew warmer beneath the dog's weight. Scenes of tall British officers in kilts and tunics bulging with money drifted into his mind. The souks were crowded with Arabs and Jews and soldiers. A strong wind began to blow through the streets, tearing at robes and tunics until the English soldiers' pockets burst open and the streets became littered with British pound notes. Yacov scrambled to retrieve the money as a captain shouted, "Mind the little Jew beggar; they're all thieves, you know!" Yacov filled his pockets and stuffed his yarmulke full, then scampered across the rooftops as the captain chased after him, blowing a horn and shouting, "Stop, Jew!"

Then through his dream he heard a sound that made him sit straight up in bed, sending Shaul tumbling to the floor. Seconds ticked past until beyond the darkness of the room, the sound of a solitary Shofar cracked the stillness of the night.

Shaul whined impatiently. "Shhh," Yacov warned, listening closely. Had it only been a part of the dream, he wondered?

He knew the sound he had heard—the ram's horn, the ancient call to freedom for the Jewish people. Why was it being blown this night? Had Messiah come?

Wrapping the blanket tightly around his shoulders, he climbed out of bed and stumbled to the shuttered window. Too small to reach the latch, he felt in the darkness for the one wooden chair they owned. He carried it carefully to the window and climbed up, unlatching the shutters and peering out into the darkened streets of the Old City.

Then, clearly, he heard the sound of the Shofar as it filled the Old City with its mournful echo. The solitary blast of the horn was joined by another, then another until the streets reverberated with the sound. A knot of warm excitement grew in the pit of his stomach and chills caused him to pull the blanket tighter around him.

For a moment he was unaware of Grandfather standing behind him. The old man put a gnarled hand on the boy's shoulder, and neither of them spoke for a long moment.

"What does it mean, Grandfather?" Yacov asked quietly.

"The ending of things as we know them, I fear," the old man answered. "But tonight they will celebrate because they do not understand."

The old man turned away and carefully lit the oil lamp on the table. "So get your trousers on," he instructed. "This is a night for every Jew to have his trousers on."

Yacov barely noticed the cold fabric of his trousers as he pulled them on. Grandfather sat down and scrawled out a short note to the chief rabbi and mayor of the Old City. He folded the paper and sealed it carefully with the wax drippings of a candle before handing it to Yacov.

"You think you can deliver this to the mayor tonight without getting yourself into trouble, eh?"

Yacov looked at the note in Grandfather's hand and nodded slowly. Never before had Grandfather sent him out after dark. *Surely this night is as important as the first Passover*, thought Yacov.

"For the mayor's hand alone." The old man looked wearily into Yacov's eyes. Yacov looked down, trying to conceal his happiness at being part of some unfathomable adventure. But there was no joy in Grandfather's ancient, lined face, and somehow Yacov felt ashamed of the excitement that must surely shine through his eyes.

Grandfather took the boy's face in his hands knowingly. "So you think this old man is blind? Hmmm?" he asked. "Maybe soon, but not yet can you hide feelings from me. It is the stirring of battle you feel now, boy. But you must think what that will mean."

Yacov met his gaze and tried to understand the old man's words.

"We here in the Old City try to live in peace with our neighbors, Christian or Muslim Arab, eh?" said Grandfather solemnly. "We try to live in the ways of peace. We wait for Messiah, Yacov. Until He establishes Israel we cannot be a nation, there can only be more killing. This Partition is a nasty business for everyone. Christians will die, Muslims and Jews as well. It is a nasty business, Yacov. Those who celebrate tonight do not know they dance on the edge of their own graves. Remember that, will you?"

Yacov swallowed hard and nodded. "Yes, Grandfather."

Grandfather mussed his hair and half smiled through his thick gray beard. "So go. What are you waiting for? The Messiah?" He stood and walked Yacov to the heavy wooden door. Then he began to double over with coughing. Yacov wondered if he really should leave him alone, even to deliver such an important message. Yacov put his hand on the old man's back and patted him gently between his bony shoulder blades. "So go already," Grandfather wheezed.

Yacov pulled on his coat and Shaul sprang to his feet, expectantly wagging his entire hind end. Grandfather glared at the dog disapprovingly. "Jackal!" he exclaimed. Shaul cowered and lay back down. "So you're going to lie here? Go with the boy," he shook his fist and kicked at him and Shaul scrambled clear. "And see that he gets home, or tomorrow it's an Arab stew pot for you!"

Yacov unbolted the heavy wooden door and Shaul gratefully followed him onto the steps that led up to the street. *Always Grandfather threatens*, thought Yacov. *Always he kicks and misses and growls about Arab stew, and always he sends my big dog out on my heels.* Briefly Yacov wondered if it was all some sort of game the old man played. One thing was certain: Grandfather knew that as long as the dog was able, he would protect Yacov.

In the dark streets of the Old City, Shaul's shaggy presence was a comfort to the young messenger. Soon, the old man knew, it would not be safe for a Jew in the Old City streets at any time of day.

Yacov bounded up the steps two at a time. He paused for one incredulous moment as lights began to wink on throughout the Old City. An eerie glow seeped through the shuttered windows and fell in uneven puddles on the cobblestones.

He stood and listened. In the distance, in the direction of the New City, came another sound. Like waves against a sea wall, the blaring of automobile horns crashed against the hand-hewn stones of the Old City Wall.

"They are celebrating," Yacov said to Shaul as they set out. "The Zionists are celebrating. That's the difference between them and us. On this side of the wall we still blow the Shofar, eh?"

4 Partition Night

The blare of automobile horns penetrated the thick walls of Ellie's darkroom. She paused to listen, squinting in the dim red light. "Something's up," she said aloud, startled at the sound of her own voice. Then she rinsed the final prints of the old Arab's scroll and hung them to dry with the others.

The fumes from developing chemicals had seeped through

her stuffy sinuses until, after six hours' work, she felt better than she had in days. With a sigh, she washed her hands and dried them on the tail of the nightgown which had long since inched out the back of her trousers. Then she switched on the light and plopped down on a three-legged stool to admire her efforts. Row after row of dripping, eight-by-ten photographs hung around the little room like laundry on a clothes line. *Chances are very good*, thought Ellie, *that I have just spent six hours working on a 1925 copy of the Jewish code for kosher butcher shops, or something equally ridiculous*. Moshe and Uncle Howard would probably laugh her out of the house. "Oh, well," she said to the pictures, "I might be an archaeological nitwit, but after I'm dead they'll say I had stamina."

She sneezed then, like a roaring lion, rattling the prints hanging nearest her. She reached for the now-empty box of tissue. Staring at the overflowing trash can, she considered using photographic paper on her nose before reaching for the tail of her nightgown. "What I need right now," she muttered miserably, wiping her nose on the soft cloth, "is a shower and a good hot cup of Irish coffee." *The shower was easy enough to arrange*, she thought, opening the darkroom door and taking one last look at the photographs before she switched off the light. The Irish coffee would be a little more difficult, however.

Uncle Howard was a teetotaller, the son of a hellfire and brimstone preacher who would sooner die than take a sip of anything alcoholic, even for medicinal purposes.

"The smaller the drink, the clearer the head," he would say sternly, refusing a drink even at a cocktail party. Ellie had yet to figure out why anyone needed a clear head to celebrate, but many times she had seen Uncle Howard's stout, serene figure wandering from group to group with a half-consumed bottle of warm Coca-Cola in his hand. Early in the evening she might overhear him discussing various aspects of Baal worship with people obviously less clearheaded than himself; but as the night wore on, he changed his topic of conversation considerably more often than his soft drink. Spotting some half-loaded British colonel expounding on the problems of Jewish immigration in Palestine, he inevitably moved to the fringe of the officer's audience. "It's only a matter of time, you know," Uncle Howard would interrupt with a benevolent smile on his face, "before the Jews have their own nation. Right here in Palestine.

We'll be asking *them* for passes to get in, eh, Colonel?"

Nothing gave him quite as much pleasure as watching a British officer choke on his whiskey soda. When all eyes turned to Uncle Howard, he would add, "Read it and weep, Colonel. It's written in the Good Book. You might as well pack your bags." Then before anyone could say another word, he would smile, sip his Coke, pat the choking colonel on the back and saunter off. Clearheaded, that was Uncle Howard. So there would be nothing to make her coffee Irish in *his* house.

Ellie glanced at her watch. It was after midnight. Even the bar at the King David Hotel would be closed up tight. After three days in bed, Ellie felt wide awake and cursed her luck to be in a city that rolled up its sidewalks after a nine o'clock curfew. She listened to the crescendo of automobile horns, wondering what had happened to cause such a clamor in the streets. It was some political demonstration, no doubt. Probably Jewish terrorists or Arab terrorists had blown up another building.

She tiptoed down the dark hall toward the bathroom, startled as she passed the kitchen and heard the sound of the radio. She pushed gingerly at the swinging door and peered in. There, at the small table, sat Miriam and her gray-headed 50-year-old son Ishmael, listening gravely to an Arab newscaster speaking in undeniably angry tones. *Must be the Jews that blew something up this time*, thought Ellie, quietly stepping into the kitchen. She stood for a moment until Miriam glanced up, dark circles beneath her eyes, her ancient face a mask of weariness. Ishmael looked up too, concern etched deep into the lines around his eyes. Ellie blinked back at them, offering a half smile.

"I know I look terrible, but it's nothing to get upset about," she quipped. Miriam and Ishmael solemnly stared back at her. "Excuse me," she mumbled, turning to go. "I was just looking for the locker room. Quick shower . . ."

"Sit," commanded Miriam. "Always making jokes; well, nobody is laughing tonight." The old woman pushed back her chair and went to the stove. "Sit!" she said again, narrowing her eyes. "I'll fix tea."

"Well, actually, I was in the mood for an Irish coffee, you know—with a little whipped cream on top," said Ellie, pulling up a chair. "What's going on? Why are you still up?"

Without a word, Ishmael reached across the table to the radio and adjusted the dial, searching for the BBC of Palestine, the English-speaking broadcast of the Middle East. Miriam opened a canister on the counter to prepare coffee. *No Irish*, Ellie mused, resigning herself to temperance, *just coffee*.

"Listen to the radio," ordered the old woman. "Maybe you learn something." Then she grumbled in Arabic while Ishmael fiddled with the tuning of the old radio.

"Do not worry about Mother. Pay no mind," Ishmael whispered. "She always talk like that when her feet hurt," he said confidentially.

Ishmael continued to work the knob, passing over announcers that chattered in jubilant Yiddish and others in angry Arabic until finally the voice of the BBC slid in clearly.

". . . The vote passed with a narrow two-thirds majority, thirty-three nations voting for Partition and thirteen voting against. Among those abstaining were Great Britain and . . ."

"Oh," Ellie exclaimed in relief. "I thought somebody blew something up!"

"Not yet," said Miriam sadly. "That will happen tomorrow."

"I forgot this was the day of the vote." Ellie leaned closer to the radio.

"What can one do with such a girl?" Miriam threw her hands up in the air.

Ellie ignored her. "The British are leaving, then." She looked at Ishmael with her eyebrows raised.

He nodded slowly. "There will be a war here very soon. The Mufti has returned to Jerusalem. I hear it but this morning. He stirs the Muslim Arabs to passion. What will become of us then, the Christian Arabs? Who can say!"

"Only our Lord knows," Miriam said as she filled the cups. Jesus, be our defender," she murmured.

"So who is this Mufti anyway?" Ellie asked.

"You see, Ishmael, she does not even know of the Mufti." Miriam shook her head in disbelief at Ellie's ignorance.

"A man of great power over the people," said Ishmael. "In 1929 and again in 1936, for many months he stirs the people to riot against the Jews, when before they are friends and neighbors. He proclaims a Jihad—a holy war—against all who are not Muslim."

"You too?" Ellie frowned and leaned forward. "The Christian Arabs too?"

47

"It was this wicked man who has been responsible for the deaths of my younger brother and my father," Ishmael explained.

Ellie glanced quickly at Miriam who simply sighed and shook her head at the memory. "I . . . I'm sorry," Ellie said quietly. "I didn't know."

"It was in 1920," said the old woman. "And your kind uncle, the professor, he took this old woman in when I had no place to go."

"For a Jewish child," Ishmael continued, settling back in his chair, "the Mufti is the one they have nightmares about when the lamps are put out and they are afraid in the night."

"The bogeyman?" Ellie queried.

"Yes. The same. Of course, he is only mortal. This is a fact he knows well. He does not go anywhere without six tall, black Sudanese bodyguards."

"Sudanese?" Ellie asked.

"As a young man he worked for British intelligence in Sudan. He believed that Britain would become the liberator of his people. Then in 1917 the British signed a paper that planned an independent Jewish homeland in Palestine."

"The Balfour Declaration." Miriam stirred the coffee. "How the young Zionists celebrated in Jerusalem! And we Christians all came to believe that soon the Lord Jesus would return to this earth!" She smiled.

"Each Sunday after church services we would all picnic on the Mount of Olives and say one to another, 'Perhaps this will be the day of His return.' " Ishmael, too, smiled at the memory.

"We were a large and happy family then," added the old woman. "But this Haj Amin, the Mufti—he began to hate the British. He quit his job and returned to Jerusalem. All day in the souks of the Muslim Quarter he talked about the evil British and the evil Jews and the evil Christians who believe that this is written in the Word and must be fulfilled that Jews return."

"Not all Christians believe this, Mother," Ishmael interrupted. "Some don't agree with that and some are only Christians in name. For political reasons."

"Like Democrats and Republicans in the States?" Ellie questioned.

Ishmael nodded. "Yes. Political. But many of us here in Palestine believe in the Christ. He is the Messiah. When there is once again a nation of Israel, He must return, and perhaps soon." He rubbed his forehead as if trying to remember something. "But this fellow Haj Amin Husseini, he hates all who stand by the promises for Israel. When I am yet a young man, this fellow stirs the Arabs of the Muslim Quarter to riot during the Holy Easter season. They fall upon the Jews and Christian Arabs at Jaffa Gate. They swarm from the quarter and fall upon us. My father is killed before my eyes. My brother is knifed, and so am I." Ishmael pulled back his shirt collar, revealing a jagged scar six inches long from his throat to his chest. "My brother does not recover. I am near to death for many weeks."

Miriam stood with her head bowed and her back to Ishmael and Ellie. Her voice muffled, she said, "The British did nothing to punish this man. Instead, they hoped to win him over, and they appointed him to the third highest Muslim post. They created him Grand Mufti of Jerusalem. And no Muslim official secures office without swearing absolute loyalty to him. He despised the intelligent and built his power on the ignorant."

"And there are many who followed him. It was he who frightened the British to halt Jewish immigration with the White Paper of 1939," Ishmael added.

"How could one man do all this?" Ellie asked.

"He declared a Jihad—a holy war against all Jews," he explained. "So the English think they will save a lot of trouble in Palestine by keeping Jews out. After all, England was fighting the Nazis. Perhaps they thought the Arabs would kill all the Jews anyway if they came to Palestine. So this white paper stopped the Jews from escaping and Hitler killed them all the same."

"The Mufti fell from favor with the British and fled to the side of Adolf Hitler. There he remained throughout the war. Two madmen, supping on their hatred of God's chosen. So Hitler is dead, but the Mufti returns to Jerusalem in this hour to stir the Muslims to passion once again," said Miriam.

"What does he look like?" Ellie asked, wondering if the unspeakable evil of such a man could ever be caught on film.

"He has a red beard . . ." Ishmael began.

"Red?"

Ishmael nodded. "And bright blue eyes. He is always courteous, they say. Most elegant and with much dignity. He condemns a man to death with a wave of his hand."

"And he has six black bodyguards?" Ellie smiled. "He'd be hard to miss."

"But it is better if you miss him all the same," said Miriam sternly. "You must not hope to find this man and take a photograph."

"You read my mind."

"The darkness of his hatred cannot be seen," Miriam warned. "But it can be felt. Every Jew who dies by his violence is but another victim of what this Hitler believed in. He is in Jerusalem. Soon we will all feel his presence."

"There are Jews also whose hatred is just as dark," Ishmael added solemnly. "They think that violence is the only response to violence, and so they, too, have the blood of the innocent on their hands."

"It is their senseless acts that turn the hearts of the world against a Jewish state, I think." Miriam shook her head sadly.

"Well, considering what has happened to them, can you blame them if they don't turn the other cheek?" asked Ellie.

"There is no blame," Ishmael shrugged. "But even the leaders of the Jews, good men like Ben-Gurion and Weitzman, they know that when Jews become terrorists and murder innocents as the Mufti does, it undermines the Jewish dream of homeland. And the world looks at those they murdered and says, 'See, those Jews are killing the innocent, also. How are they different from the Nazis, eh?' "

"Not long before you come to Palestine, the English executed two Jewish terrorists who were guilty of murder." Miriam poured another cup of coffee for Ellie. "So then other Jewish terrorists kidnap two British soldiers and hang them. They died only because they were English. This old woman wonders how it shall all end."

"Shhh." Ishmael raised his index finger for silence.

The announcer droned on with a thick British accent. "Palestine will be divided into two states, one Arab and one Jewish. On the recommendation of the commission, Jerusalem has been declared an international city and will in fact be governed by the United Nations . . ."

"There, you see," Ellie chirped. "Jerusalem belongs to everybody: Christian, Jew, Arab. You'll all be okay."

Miriam looked up at her with an unfathomable glance, causing Ellie's smile to quickly fade.

"I tell you, Miss Ellie," broke in Ishmael kindly. "The Mufti will not rest until the Jews are driven into the sea, until Jerusalem is capital of the United Arab Nation of Palestine. No Jews. You see?"

Ellie nodded her head. "War?"

"Yes," mourned Miriam, "and those of our faith shall be trapped in the middle."

"All the horns," Ellie nodded her head toward the sound of the automobile horns.

"The Jews celebrate. At least some of them. But the old rabbis will not rejoice tonight. They know that too many will die," said Ishmael.

Miriam rose and set the coffeepot on the back of the stove. "Our lives will change most certainly. Perhaps this is the time our Lord the Christ spoke of, but I think right now would be a good time to take a holiday to America if I were not so old and if the bones of my family for a thousand years were not planted so near Jerusalem."

"Representatives of the Arab nations," droned the announcer, "have vowed to drive the Jews into the sea the day after the last British soldier leaves the soil of the Holy Land. Zionists have countered with the . . ."

"Surely the United Nations—" Ellie began, gulping back her words as the radio continued.

"The British government has vowed to remain neutral in all disputes between Jews and Arabs, but will continue to enforce the laws of the mandate until British evacuation."

"You see, Miss Ellie," explained Ishmael. "The laws of the mandate declare that Jews may not have weapons. The Arab nations have many weapons, and may buy more, for they are recognized nations. The Jews must wait until the mandate ends before they may buy, and then it will be too late. There will be no one to protect them. Unless God makes a miracle, they will be wiped out in only days, you will see."

"They have wanted a state of their own," said Miriam, sitting down heavily at the table. "I fear they have purchased only a cemetery for those who shall die. Here is a night to mourn, I fear. The night of Partition."

"Well, it will certainly give Uncle Howard something to talk about at social events," Ellie smiled, trying to lighten the mood.

"What can you do with such a mind as this?" Miriam peti-

51

tioned the Almighty with hands raised. "Miss Ellie, you care about nothing but that camera," she chided. "Always making jokes, and no one is laughing. Only dying."

Ellie resisted the impulse to say it wasn't so bad to die laughing, and instead took a sip of her coffee and stood up. "Well, thanks for the coffee. Now for that shower." She waved and walked to the door, then turned and smiled sweetly at Miriam. "Hope your feet feel better soon," she said, quickly closing the door behind her on a stream of exasperated Arabic.

As she passed Uncle Howard's darkened study, the telephone began to ring. Ellie glanced at her watch. Nearly one a.m. *That means only one thing—a long-distance call*, thought Ellie. And at this hour it had to be *really* long distance, perhaps her mother in the States. "Mother never can remember the time difference," she murmured as she picked up the phone.

"Hello," she said loudly, expecting the dim reply of a long-distance operator. Instead, she was greeted by the excited voice of Darla Makewith, a student at the American School of Oriental Research who rarely surfaced from her books for anything.

"Is that you, Ellie? What are you yelling about?"

"I thought you were—" she began, only to be cut short by Darla's frantic babbling over raucous laughter in the background.

"Can you believe what's happening? I mean, the place is going crazy. Everyone is so excited! Hey, I thought you were sick or something. You want to go out with us for a while? People are dancing in the streets, like V-day!"

"Give me half an hour. I've got to shower first. Then come by." Ellie chuckled, amused at the unusual phenomenon of Darla speaking more than two sentences at once. This must be some street party to blast Miss Makewith out of her books.

Ellie hung up the phone and rushed to the shower, feeling better with every second as the steaming water washed away the film of developing chemicals and the dull ache in her shoulders. She washed her hair, letting the hot water flow from her head down her back for a while. It was past one in the morning and she was only just beginning to feel awake and alive. *Probably*, she thought, *my days and nights will be mixed up for a while—like they were when I first came over from America.* After all, it was the middle of the afternoon back home. Her folks would be listening to all the news about the Middle East right about now and thinking about her as they wrapped Christmas presents to mail to faraway Palestine. For a moment Ellie felt a twinge of homesickness as she pictured her mother sitting on the living room floor busily boxing what she referred to as "Ellie's Red Cross packages." One arrived at least twice a month containing safety pins or squashed chocolate chip cookies. Ellie made a mental note to write her mother for Kleenex. It was easy to write and ask for needs like that. What Ellie found difficult was telling her folks how she really felt about David. Maybe it was because she was so unsure herself about what she felt or what she really believed. Her folks had always been so certain of everything. The world was full of right and wrong, justice and injustice, truth and falsehood. There were no gray areas, no maybes. Ellie had felt exactly as they had until she had fallen in love with David. Then there was no more right or wrong, only him and their love—or what she had thought was love.

Ellie stepped from the shower and dried briskly, wiped off the mirror and looked closely at the wild red hair on the ghost gawking back at her. No one could tell by looking how changed she was. Her mother and father mailed the packages to someone who really no longer existed, thinking all the time that she was still their "little girl." She didn't begrudge them that; she simply did not see any reason to tell them any different. No one needed to know what she carried in her soul. Those secrets were hers. And maybe God's, if He still happened to be interested. She wasn't even sure she believed that anymore, either. And maybe it didn't matter, anyway. Nothing could ever give her back what she had lost. Nothing could take the gray away from her life.

Ellie towel-dried her hair in front of the popping radiator, then braided it into a damp rope hanging down her back. She dressed quickly, pulling on dark blue slacks and a gray sweater, a favorite from college days. Then she padded back down the hall to the photo lab for one more look at the scroll.

Partially unrolled, it lay on the stainless steel counter top, looking fragile and ancient next to the shining surface. Ellie touched the leather and put her index finger gently on the faded ink of the strange squared letters. She wished she could read their message, decipher whatever secret they held.

"If Moshe were here," she said to the scroll, "you wouldn't be so secretive."

Then she gathered a few tiny fragments that had crumbled from the edge and carried them back to Uncle Howard's study. Opening an unlocked drawer, she pulled out an envelope and brushed the fragments into it. Then she dated it and wrote the words, "Secret Code," on the outside before she placed it carefully on the desk blotter. She looked up to see Miriam standing at the door with a disapproving look on her face.

"Where is your nightshirt, Miss Ellie?" she shook her head. "You are not going out now to street dance—except over my dead body, maybe."

"I'm okay. Fine. Wide awake, really."

Miriam's voice started at a low rumble and got louder with every word. "The professor will not like to have his sick niece out dancing the hora with the rabbi's daughters, and Miriam will not let you out the door tonight when every Muslim is counting his bullets for tomorrow's party!"

She was interrupted by the arrival of the group of rather boisterous students at the front door. "Ha!" she shouted at them. "Go to bed where you belong!" She grabbed a fire poker and brandished it menacingly as she moved toward the door. Ellie beat her to it. "We won't need that, Miriam," she laughed. "I think these troops are on our side." She pulled open the door and was greeted by a group of seven young male students and Darla Makewith wearing a ridiculous pith helmet and a bright blue dress.

"Trick-or-treat!" they shouted with glee. Laughing uproariously, they pulled Ellie out the door, drowning out Miriam's protests with a rousing chorus of "We're Off to See the Wizard!"

Ellie looked back just long enough to see the silhouette of Miriam and the poker in the open doorway. Ellie waved a cheerful good-bye, then walked toward King George Avenue where throngs of people had all but halted the flow of automobile traffic. It was Mardi Gras and New Year's Eve and, as Darla had said, V-day all rolled into one. From sidewalk to sidewalk the broad Avenue was jammed with singing, dancing, laughing human beings. In front of her a black-coated covey of orthodox Jews hefted a British soldier high above their heads and spun him around as he roared with delight, "God save the Jews!" The joy was infectious. The brightly embroidered kaftans of the Bukharian Jews bobbed beside the khaki-clad Sabra Jews who were more at home on the kibbutz than in the synagogue. It was a night to remember. *A night to be recorded on film*, thought Ellie as she watched the British soldier, still on the shoulders of the Jews, bob down the street toward the Municipal Park.

In a moment Ellie and Darla were sucked into a whirlpool of dancers. Linking arms they hummed a song that even without words breathed joy into the night air. Faster and faster they spun in a great human wheel until, exhausted from the effort, Darla fell away and Ellie, too, let go of the shoulders of the strangers on either side of her. She spotted a red-faced, puffing Darla several yards away from her and began to inch her way back to her.

Suddenly she caught a glimpse of a tall, sandy-haired man across the street. Her heart stopped, and she gasped for breath. *Surely*, she thought, *he can't be here, so far away from home! Surely it's not David!* She stood on her tiptoes, craning her neck to see the man again. Through the living tide, she saw briefly only a quarter of his profile and the back of his head.

"David!" she called as loud as she could, barely hearing herself above the din. "David!" she called again, almost certain this time.

A short, balding man turned and put his arms around her. "Did you call me, pretty lady?" he asked, smiling.

Ellie struggled to free herself, still straining to see over the crowd; but the tall man was gone, leaving her heart pounding. *What a dope I am*, she thought, feeling foolish. David was back home in San Francisco, and now she was in love with another man. Possibly in love, at any rate. Regardless, she could not follow every sandy-haired stranger who resembled David Meyer.

Darla tapped her on the shoulder. "What's wrong? You look like you saw a ghost."

"Yes, well, I did, kind of." Ellie took Darla's arm and pushed through the crowd toward the park.

David Meyer zipped up his worn leather flight jacket and patted his wallet and passport for the hundredth time that evening. Michael Cohen had warned him that the streets would be full of pickpockets, and he did not want to take any chances when it came to his American passport.

He turned around twice, looking for the balding head of Michael amid the crush of human flesh. David gazed with a detached amusement at the mixture of weeping and laughing, with Michael in the middle of it embracing every young woman heart and soul. He felt as though he had, like Dorothy from Kansas, been swept away to the political Land of Oz where little Jewish Munchkins battled wicked political witches against incredible odds. Maybe he was the Tin Man, rattling around with no heart, a mercenary in the truest sense of the word. Only there wasn't really enough money in this assignment for David to call himself a mercenary. Americans were called volunteers, and most of the guys David had come over with the week before didn't have much of an idea what it was all about.

"Yeah, my grandfather was Jewish," David had told Michael three months before. "But my dad's a preacher. So what's that make me?"

Michael had looked at him with that deadly serious gaze of his and said, "The grandfather in your family tree would have been enough for Hitler, David. Maybe it ought to be enough for you, too. You're the best there is. We need you with us."

So, here he was, feeling about as foreign as a fortune cookie in an Italian deli. A room and all the kosher lamb he could eat was about the extent of his pay. And, of course, the possibility he might run into an old friend of his. He stopped and scanned the crowd, looking for Ellie's red head and wondering if she were here tonight. Feeling foolish as he fought off the hopeful excitement that pushed against his chest, he thought about the other possibilities of this adventure—for instance, the chance that after four years in a world war fighting Nazis, he could end up getting his tail shot off over a piece of real estate no bigger than Rhode Island. And all for the fun of it, for the adventure! He was a fighter with no wars left to fight until this little skirmish came up. To his father, fighting for a Jewish homeland represented some kind of spiritual responsibility, a real honor. David, the Tin Man, simply had nothing else to do with his life.

For a moment he thought he caught a glimpse of red hair weaving through the throng. Then it was gone, and he turned back to Michael just in time to see a grubby little kid in a black coat pull the wallet out of Michael's back pocket and dash away with a shaggy-looking dog at his heels.

"Hey, you!" David shouted, shoving his way through an embracing couple toward Michael. "Michael! Some kid just got your wallet. Get 'im!"

In the midst of a passionate kiss, Michael did not hear him or even look up. David lunged toward him and pushed him away from the young lady, then grabbing the collar of his jacket, he began dragging him toward the escaping criminal.

"What are you doing?" Michael roared in protest.

"The little beast got your wallet!"

Michael slapped his hip pocket and shouted, "Well, where'd he go?" Then he plunged ahead of David, cutting a swath through dancers and drunks, searching for a child he had never even seen.

5 The Attack

Ellie tapped on Darla's pith helmet, wondering where this previously shy, studious bookworm had come across her head gear. Darla turned her head, unable to face Ellie because of the press of human flesh around her. Her face was worthy of a photograph, Ellie noticed—flushed with excitement and effervescence.

"Wonderful!" Darla cried, her voice a high squeak. "Isn't it wonderful?"

"I'm going back!" Ellie shouted to Darla. "For my camera!"

Darla cupped her hand to her ear and looked puzzled, then she was swept away by a wave of dancers. The other students had been lost in the first few yards of King George Avenue. As Ellie worked her way back toward home, she thought she got a glimpse of one of them passionately kissing any female within reach between the ages of thirteen and thirty.

As she neared the corner, an old man in a tattered coat embraced her and kissed her square on the lips, his eyes full of delight. He tipped his hat as she pushed past him and he shouted, "Ve haf a schtate!" Every man she passed wanted a kiss, it seemed.

Ellie moved closer to the storefronts where it was a little easier to navigate through the crush. *Getting my camera might take half the night*, she thought as she inched her way against the flow. She wished Moshe were here to cut a path for her. After a fifteen-minute struggle, she reached the corner of Rehavia, a dark and nearly empty street. Only a few stragglers and late-comers scurried past her toward King George Avenue. She breathed deeply and began to walk toward home.

Her photographer's eye focused on two men strolling toward her through the shadows across the street. As she watched, one of them stopped, leaned against a stair railing and lit a cigarette, the orange glow momentarily illuminating his face. *Grim*, thought Ellie, *nothing like the happy revelers just a few blocks from here*. His features seemed hard as stone, his heavy lower jaw jutting out like that of a bulldog. *He must be English*, Ellie noted; Americans didn't wear heavy overcoats like the one hanging on his massive frame. As she mentally snapped his picture, he looked up—straight at her, it seemed—until his match flickered and died. The other man hung back, his smaller form all but hidden in the large man's shadow.

For an instant Ellie felt the hair on the back of her neck prickle, then inwardly laughed at her foolishness. She remembered the way she had felt as a kid listening to Basil Rathbone playing Sherlock Holmes on the radio. She was silly, she knew, but she quickened her pace to the front steps of Uncle Howard's large, white stone home. Remembering Miriam's weapon, she gingerly inserted the key and prayed the old woman wouldn't hear the squeaking hinges.

The house was still and dark as she retraced her steps through the walnut-paneled parlor to the hall that led first to her quarters, then to the photo lab.

The light was on in her bedroom and she glanced in. There sat Miriam, fast asleep in a chair by her bed, her chin resting on her chest and her gray hair falling in wisps around her face. The old woman had waited up for her, like a worried mother waiting for her child to come home from a date. Ellie paused for a moment, then tiptoed into the room.

Gently she shook the old woman's shoulder. "Wake up and go to bed, Miriam. I'm home—you can go to bed now."

Miriam sat up with a start then launched into another Arabic tirade, sprinkling in a few English words for good measure.

"You're right, Miriam," Ellie said soothingly. "It's too rowdy for me." Then she sat down on the bed and began to remove her shoes.

Miriam appraised her sleepily and rubbed her hand across her eyes. "You are for bed then?"

"Right, Miriam," Ellie assured her sweetly. "Thank you for waiting up."

"Huh," grunted Miriam shortly, rising from the chair with difficulty. "You should listen to Miriam," she said, wagging her index finger, then turned down the hall to the kitchen and her own bedroom beyond.

Ellie waited a few minutes until she was sure Miriam had gone to bed. She crept down the hall to the lab with shoes in hand. Switching on the light, she gathered flashbulbs and several rolls of film, and stuffed every pocket full. She carefully loaded film into her large bulky old Leica camera.

It was German-made before the war and had been a gift from her parents at graduation. Even though secondhand, it was in exceptional condition and very valuable. Ellie's pride and joy, its wide-angle lens had already captured the best of her feelings for the streets of this strange jumbled city. Tonight she would record the moods and the faces of the rebirth of an ancient nation. She inserted the flash attachment, snapping a bulb into place.

Searching the room for anything else she might need, her eyes fell on the stainless steel counter where she had left the scroll. *It was gone.* She put the camera down and moved quickly across the room, touching the surface of the counter as if to make certain she was not imagining that it was empty. Quickly she scanned the room, then jerked open the door to her darkroom, relieved to see her photographs still hanging on the drying racks. Surely the old woman had simply put the scroll in what she considered a safe place. Leaving her shoes and camera, Ellie padded back through the hallway and kitchen to Miriam's room.

"Miriam," she whispered softly knocking, "don't go to sleep yet." Without waiting for an answer, Ellie cracked the door and poked her head in. "Miriam?" she said again, louder this time, aware of the heavy tick of an ancient alarm clock and Miriam's steady breathing. "Miriam? Where is the scroll? Where did you put the scroll?"

Ellie's eyes adjusted to the dim light, and she could see Miriam's form beneath the blankets of her small bed. "Miriam?" she tried again. For a full minute Ellie stood in the doorway, wondering if she should shake the old woman awake. Probably even King Richard and the looting Crusaders couldn't stir her. She glanced around the room. On a plain bureau she could make out the clutter of two dozen framed pictures of Miriam's family. On the wall above her bed hung an olivewood cross and on the opposite wall a painting of Jesus with His arms outstretched. On the nightstand was a thick book bound in cracking black leather with a gold-leaf Arabic title in large print on the front. *Must be her Bible*, thought Ellie as she pulled the door shut and left the old woman to sleep. There was nothing she could do about the scroll now, anyway. Miriam simply must have put it in a safe place.

Ellie pulled on her shoes and retrieved her camera, no longer bothering to tiptoe.

She locked the front door behind her, smiling broadly at the sounds trumpeting over the housetops from King George Avenue. She skipped down the steps, worrying briefly that the flash bulbs in her bulging pockets would be smashed if she got trapped in too many joyful embraces. She crossed the street at a slow jog, anxious to join the celebration.

Again, she noticed the two men standing opposite her. On impulse she raised the camera and snapped the shutter. The pop of the flash caught a wild and angry expression in the taller man's eyes, and for a moment Ellie felt a sense of panic. What had she done? *Stick to happy faces tonight, old girl*, she told herself as she quickened her pace down the dark, deserted street. To her dismay, the men fell in step behind her, following through the dim light and dark shadow of the street like determined hounds through the brush. *They can't be following me*, Ellie comforted herself, walking faster toward the light and sound of King George Avenue. She heard one of the men cough, and the sound of their footsteps quickened to match and then exceed her own.

Fear welled up inside her and suddenly the noise and crowds just a few short blocks ahead seemed light years away from her. Three blocks in front of her a group of women danced on top of a military sedan while the driver roared out the window in frustration. *Only three blocks.* Ellie ejected the spent bulb and inserted a new one as she walked. She glanced over her shoulder, certain now that her fear was justified; she was being pursued. Suddenly she whirled around and faced the men who were a mere ten yards behind her.

"What do you want?" she shouted.

The men stopped in surprise and stood facing her with their hands in their coat pockets. Ellie imagined she could see the outline of a gun in the pocket of the large man. The smaller man stayed where he was as the large man took a step forward.

"Mazel Tov," he said in an oily, heavily accented voice. *Definitely not British*, noted Ellie. "Mazel Tov, young woman. We celebrate, no?" He stepped nearer and put a large hand out, palm up in a gesture of harmlessness.

"Leave me alone," Ellie warned, "or I'll scream." Just then a burst of squealing laughter floated down from the celebration and a woman's scream echoed in the street.

"And who will even notice you?" His voice became harsh and menacing. He took another step, and Ellie felt frozen to the pavement, as if she were in the midst of a nightmare. "Give me the camera," he warned. "And I will not hurt you."

Ellie clutched her camera to her. "You want the camera?" she gulped, her words pushing past her throat with difficulty.

"Just the camera." The oily voice returned as he took another step. He stood now a little more than arm's length away, his huge hand outstretched.

Slowly Ellie raised her camera toward him, and as she did he lunged for her. She snapped the shutter; the flash bulb popped in the darkness just inches from the man's eyes. He reeled back and clutched his face as if he had been stabbed. Ellie wheeled around and, holding the bulky Leica, ran toward the lights and safety of the mob. It took the big man only moments to regain his vision. Shouting, "Get her!" to the other man, he ran hard after her. She could hear his tweed overcoat flapping behind him. For her every step he seemed to gain two, the slap of his feet keeping time to the clapping rhythm of the street dancers. The night air stung her nostrils and her chest ached. She stumbled and nearly fell, grabbing at the wall of a rough-sided building. The big man rushed on, fast closing the distance between them. Only a block and a half ahead was the safety of the mob, but it was too far.

The heavy slap of footsteps on the pavement echoed and drowned out the happy cheers of the street ahead. He was three yards behind her now. Ellie whirled and swung the heavy Leica at his head, and he slammed into her like a lineman in a football scrimmage. She heard him grunt as he hit her full force, knocking her clear around and down on the pavement. Ellie felt the glass from the flash bulbs in her pockets smash and pierce her thighs. The skin on her hands and elbows skidded away as she tried to brace herself against the fall. The Leica clattered out of her grasp and littered the sidewalk with broken bits of lens glass. She had no breath to cry out. Blood was thick in her mouth and a warm sticky ooze formed beneath her hands as she lay on the sidewalk among the litter of broken bulbs and small metal cans of film. She remained still as the man picked himself up and walked past her in the darkness. He stooped and picked up the camera; then, as Ellie watched with half-opened eyes, he ripped the back off and tore out the film.

"You should be careful whom you photograph, Miss Warne," he said in an amused voice. Then he threw the camera down with a crash and walked toward her.

"She's out," said his companion, sounding frightened. "Leave her. She's out."

The big man stood with one foot on either side of Ellie's head. She did not move, but felt her body tense against further violence.

"The girl is more stupid than they said," growled the big man. "Stupid. And lucky." Then he laughed and nudged her with the toe of his shoe. He turned and the two men walked slowly toward the busy intersection.

———————

Yacov pushed Shaul down behind the stair railing as the two men approached. The hair on the back of the big dog's neck bristled, and Yacov heard a low threatening rumble deep in Shaul's throat as the men passed, near enough to touch. Yacov nudged his shaggy companion into silence as the small man glanced furtively in their direction.

"It is nothing. Nothing," said the big man. "We could have killed her. No one would have seen."

But Yacov had seen. From his hiding place in the cellar entrance of an apartment, he had watched with shameful excitement, first the pop of the bulb, then the pursuit of the pretty American lady by the two thugs. They had not seemed to Yacov to be ordinary street hoodlums; they had not searched her for money. And strangely, they had seemed to know who she was.

Yacov watched as the men disappeared into the bright lights and clamor of the celebration; then, seeing the lady stir in the shadows, he bounded up the stairs and jogged toward where she lay. He stopped ten feet from her and watched cautiously as she struggled to pick herself up.

"Dumb," she muttered between sobs, "Dumb. They broke my Leica." She stood amid the shambles, her hands limply at her sides.

Yacov did not know what the American word "Leica" meant, but this lady had a broken one, and was undoubtedly in great pain.

"You need help, lady," Yacov said. It was more a statement than a question.

Ellie looked up at the small dark figure of the little boy and wailed. "Did you see it? They chased me and beat me up, and— Oh! They broke my Leica!"

"Yes, lady, I saw them. Very bad fellows. You know them?" He moved toward her to help her stand. Perhaps her leg was a "leica."

"Know them!" she exclaimed, crunching through the broken glass toward the shattered black box that had seemed to cause all the trouble. She stooped with difficulty and retrieved the camera. "My poor Leica," she moaned again.

"It is broken," repeated Yacov, a smile of comprehension crossing his face.

"Smashed. Ruined. Destroyed." She hobbled toward some steps and lowered herself onto the second step as Yacov and Shaul stood before her watching in fascination. "You better watch your dog, son, unless he's wearing combat boots. There's glass all over the place," she said miserably. "Even in me."

"You should go home, lady," Yacov said, picking up the little cans of film. "They might come back." Hoping that there might be a reward in it, he picked up the last roll of film and said, "Yacov will help you, lady." Then he gestured toward his dog. "Shaul will let no harm come to you."

"Yes, well. Good dog." Shaul whined softly and tried to lick her bloody hand. "I could have used you a few minutes earlier."

Yacov felt a stab of guilt. He could have easily sent Shaul to help, but he had hung back from the drama eager to see just what would happen next. "We will take you home," he said quietly.

Ellie stood with difficulty as the boy took the broken camera from her. Then he put his arm around her waist, and she leaned heavily on him.

"You say they did not know you, lady? I thought perhaps the big one said your name."

They limped along a few paces in silence. "Did he? Maybe he did," Ellie answered in a puzzled tone. "I've never seen them before in my life." Ellie replayed the entire event in her mind and tried to remember if anyone had said her name, or if she had only imagined it. But only the phrases "stupid girl" and "lucky" echoed in her mind. She would call the police when she got home and this little boy could tell them what he saw as well. For the time being, she felt little pain. The rage that seethed inside her overshadowed everything else. "Whoever they were, we'll get them. I'm going to call the police, and we'll find them."

Ellie felt the little boy stiffen at the mention of the word "police," and a sense of panic rose in Yacov at the thought of talking at length with the very constables who had only an hour before pursued him and his dog for petty theft.

"I cannot talk to no policemen, lady," said Yacov. "I got to take you home and go. Me and Shaul, we have to go to the Rabbi's house with a message. In the Old City."

"You're a long way from where you're supposed to be."

"I wanted to see the party."

"I'll pay you to stay a while. It won't take long."

"Pay?" Yacov adjusted his skull cap, which had begun to creep down over his forehead as Ellie leaned against him. "Okay, maybe for a few minutes I can stay," he said, attempting to sound nonchalant. Everyone knew that Americans were rich and always overpaid for every service and item they purchased. There was a saying in the souks of the Old City marketplace, "Americans pay for one olive when they could have taken the whole tree." The few Americans that Yacov and his friends had seen in the Old City were remarkably unlike their British counterparts. The British had an air of detached superiority as they wandered through the Jewish Quarter in search of interesting sights. They gazed upon the ancient dress and customs of the

Orthodox Hasidim and muttered words like, "quaint," and "positively medieval."

Americans, on the other hand, stared with open curiosity and sniffed around for souvenirs like puppies in search of bones. From them, Yacov had learned important expressions like "oh, boy," and "jeepers, Fran, what d'ya know!" They were like children, Grandfather said. Most Americans who came were Jewish, but they were somehow very different. The rabbis warned that men who do not study Talmud forget to grow up. Americans must have never studied Talmud. Yet Yacov liked them. Their generosity was rarely condescending, unlike that of the conquering British; it was naive and, for the merchants, as amusing as it was profitable. So, Yacov decided, he would stay. God provided for him and Grandfather in strange ways, and such a story he would have to tell the old man!

"How much will you pay me?" asked Yacov without pretense.

"You're no 'Good Samaritan,' I can tell that," muttered Ellie as she limped up the steps to the front door. "A little mercenary, aren't you?" she asked, a tone of amusement in her voice.

"What is this mercenary?" asked Yacov as she unlocked the door and they stepped into the lighted alcove.

Ellie noticed for the first time the boy's ragged clothes. His long black Hasidic coat was badly patched and two sizes too small. His cuffs were frayed and the soles of his shoes were beginning to separate from the cracked leather uppers. "Hmmm," she said thoughtfully. "Mercenary, in your case, means hungry, I think." She held the door for a moment as Shaul padded in after them and sat calmly beside his young master. "Would you like to come to the kitchen and have something to eat while I call the police?"

To stand in the home of a gentile American for the first time is enough excitement, thought Yacov. *To eat the food of the unclean would be sinful. Who could say if it would be kosher?* Though his stomach rumbled in protest, Yacov shook his head, preferring to stand where he was, poised for flight into the night. He lowered his eyes to the parquet floor, not daring to look at the many pictures that hung on the walls around him. From the corner of his eye he saw the stone statue of a man on a horse. He had indeed stepped into a den of iniquity and impiety! He would not tell Grandfather that he had actually gone into the house.

"Come sit down, anyway, will you, Yacov?" Ellie urged with a strained voice, feeling her scraped elbows beginning to stiffen.

"Thank you no, very much," Yacov answered, still not looking up. "Shaul and I will wait here, if you please."

Ellie shrugged and limped back to Uncle Howard's study to call the police.

Yacov stood in the alcove for what seemed an eternity. He could hear the blood pumping in his ears as he waited, careful not to look at the Gentile art. He gazed intently at the top of Shaul's rugged head, then traced the pattern of the wood on the floor with his toe. Only once did he cast a quick glance at a picture that hung on the right above him—a pretty red-headed girl in a yellow dress sitting on cushions and reading a book. Yacov squinted and strained his eyes, trying to see the title of the book she was reading. As he moved closer, Ellie appeared at the doorway and stood silently watching him until he noticed her with a start and jumped back.

"You like that, do you?" she asked. "What do you think it's called?"

Yacov shrugged, his eyes again downcast with shame. He did not want to know the name of the painting.

"It's called 'Young Girl Reading.' Original, isn't it?"

Yacov shrugged again, feeling very uncomfortable and wishing that he had not seen the young American lady or her assailants, even for money.

"The police can't come tonight," Ellie continued without stopping. "They've got enough to handle out on the streets, they said. I guess every thug and petty thief in Palestine is out tonight."

Yacov felt the tingle of fear in the pit of his stomach. Did his avocation of crime show on his face?

"I want your name and address. Someone will come out here tomorrow and get the details. I want to know where I can find you if I need you."

"You will pay me tonight?" Yacov raised his eyes to her and wondered seriously if he should give her his address which she in turn would give to the police.

"Yes."

"Okay," he said happily. "But you must not tell the police my address. If you want I should come talk, you come fetch me. Grandfather would not like the Palestine Police coming to our home. It will look not good, you know?"

"All right," Ellie agreed, and got him a one-pound note as he scribbled down his Old City address on the back of an envelope.

"I am so sorry you broke your Leica," he said, snatching the bill from her and hustling out the door with Shaul trotting along behind. "Shalom."

Ellie watched them until they disappeared in the shadows of the street. What a strange city this was, that one so young would be roaming the streets among the thieves and bullies lurking in the night! She bolted the door and slowly headed back down the hall to the bathroom to clean and dress her wounds.

Yacov almost skipped through the darkness. He was the happiest of all boys in Jerusalem. He had a few coins in his pocket, stolen from a drunken man's nearly empty wallet and a one-pound note as payment for a good deed. Surely God had smiled on him! He reached under his skull cap for the note Grandfather had written to Rebbe Akiva, the mayor of the Old City. For a moment he chided himself for not going directly to the mayor's house, but he had been caught in the excitement of a band of revelers and had instead followed them out the Old City gates and into the New City of Jerusalem. He could clearly see the hand of God in all of it. For if he had not gone to the New City and picked the pocket of the man and been chased, he might never have been the American lady or received his reward.

"God in His wisdom is great," sighed Yacov, winding his way along the outside of the Old City Wall toward Zion Gate and the crooked corridors that would take him to his destination.

The craggy hand-hewn stones of the wall seemed to glow even in the darkness as the towers of Zion Gate loomed above him. As he passed beneath its massive brow, the feeling of exuberance left him. He had to go a hundred yards through the alleyways of the Arab Quarter before he reached the section of the Old City he called home. In sharp contrast to the light of the Jewish Quarter, this narrow, twisted street was dark and shuttered. Yacov wondered what plans were being laid behind those locked and bolted doors. And he wished for daylight and friendly faces as he passed through the gloom. Before, the quarter had always seemed friendly enough, but tonight it seemed full of threats and an air of foreboding.

With Shaul at his heels, he ran the last few yards to the archway that marked the beginning of the Jewish Quarter. Lights still burned in nearly every house, and music drifted through the streets from the great Hurva Synagogue. A sense of relief washed over Yacov as he passed a group of three Hasidim who shouted "Shalom!" and "Mazel Tov!" as they returned from worship. The deeper he walked into the cobbled heart of the Jewish Quarter, the more faces he recognized. And to his surprise, most seemed happy at the news.

"Shalom, Yacov!" exclaimed a group of Yeshiva students, each reaching out to pat his head. "And how is your grandfather Rebbe Lebowitz taking the news?"

"He is not dancing," Yacov replied, feeling that he was somehow a party to disloyalty to speak to those of his own kind who were, in fact, dancing. These were Grandfather's very students; shouldn't they be mourning this night instead of joining the new Jews in their celebration across the wall? "Tell your Grandfather we have been this night to pray for the peace of Jerusalem," they instructed. Then they patted him again and sauntered off. Even at his young age, Yacov knew that Jerusalem was in need of prayer; Grandfather always said that God enjoyed the joyful prayer of a good Jew. He put away his misgivings and began to answer back enthusiastically, "Shalom!" and "Mazel Tov!" He skipped down the last few steps to the house of Rebbe Akiva, with Grandfather's note clutched tightly in his hand. Boldly, he unlatched the gate to the courtyard and, commanding Shaul to stay, approached the massive door. He lifted the large brass knocker and let it fall three times. Light seeped from the window, and from the second story he heard the harsh monotone of the radio. After a full minute, Yacov heard the soft voice of Akiva's sixteen-year-old daughter, Yehudit.

"Who is it?"

"Yacov Lebowitz. I have a note from my grandfather," Yacov said, feeling very important.

The great door cracked, then swung wide. Yacov touched his fingertips to his lips, then slid his hand over the mezuzah that hung on the left doorpost and entered the house.

In her long black dress, Yehudit looked pale and drawn.

"Shalom," said Yacov.

"Shalom," Yehudit returned the greeting, her eyes downcast. "Wait here," she instructed, swishing out of the entry way.

Now, this is a house, thought Yacov, contrasting it to the home of the American lady. There were no paintings on the thick walls, but the furniture was heavy and massive. A solid silver tea service sat on a dark walnut buffet in the dining room to his right. Silver candelabra graced the heavily oiled table, and Yacov imagined the most wonderful and wealthy guests sitting in the high-backed chairs. He stood on a thick oriental rug, studying the patterns of deep red and blue that swirled around his feet. Rebbe Akiva was a wealthy man: one of two in the Old City with the luxury of a telephone.

Yacov heard Akiva's footsteps at the top of the stairs and glanced up to see his slippered feet as he began a regal descent. He wore the finest black suit of any Hasidim that Yacov had ever seen. A heavy gold chain stretched across his vest, adorning his expansive belly. His long beard was as black and heavy as the wool of his coat and his eyes glowered from beneath his heavy brows and seemed to pierce Yacov's very soul.

"Shalom, Rebbe Akiva," Yacov said timidly.

Akiva continued his descent. "Shalom!" he boomed in his powerful voice.

Then as he neared the bottom step, Yacov ventured a half smile and said hopefully, "And Mazel Tov!"

A controlled fury swept over Akiva's heavy features as he glared at the boy. Yacov felt his stomach tighten and twist with the certainty that he had said the wrong thing.

"Mazel Tov? Mazel Tov, is it?" Akiva sneered. "And what is it you congratulate me for?"

Yacov looked quickly away from Akiva's legendary wrath. "Forgive me, Rebbe Akiva. I mean I—"

"Are you one of them?" Akiva gestured toward the streets with his broad head. "Do you dance in the streets of our doomed city, too?"

"No, sir," Yacov stammered. "I pray for the peace of Jerusalem." Akiva rocked back on his heels and turned his head to regard Yacov with one eye squinted in suspicion. "You answer well for one so young, boy. So should we all pray for the peace of God's Holy City of David. And for what else do you pray?" he asked, raising his chin in challenge.

Yacov frantically searched his mind, then plunged into an answer that would be right regardless of what the rabbi wanted to hear. "I pray for the coming of our Messiah, Rebbe Akiva."

The rabbi's features seemed to relax and a half smile danced across the hard line of his lips for an instant. "Well said, boy. Well spoken. Your grandfather teaches you well."

"Yes, Rabbi." Yacov sputtered with relief.

"And does he also teach you that there is no nation without our Messiah to lead us? That those who declare a state now shake their fists in the face of God and deny His chosen one?"

"Yes, Rabbi," Yacov answered, uncertain if Akiva's pent-up fury was somehow directed at him.

"What does he say of those Jews who seek to come to Palestine illegally? Without regard to the legal, God-given authority of the British mandate?" asked Akiva, enjoying the game.

Yacov himself had entered the country as part of the Aliya, which had smuggled Jewish children into Palestine. Akiva's question was almost too difficult for Yacov to answer. "I suppose . . ."

Akiva narrowed his eyes. "Yes? Yes?"

"That it is by God's grace if they reach these shores." He looked straight at Akiva and thought of his own family, wishing that they had lived to run the final blockades of the mandate.

"Well?" Akiva relaxed. "And what do you believe?"

"I would pray that every Jew could come home," he answered without fear.

"I see. At the expense of and in exchange for the lives of those of us already here?" Akiva scowled, and Yacov regretted his boldness. "My family has lived here for many generations, Yacov. Yours for only a relatively short time. The Mufti and I know one another well, and both of us believe that no good can come of this Partition business."

Yacov did not raise his eyes, but stood in silence.

"So, boy, will you join these traitors to God? This Haganah? This secret organization of Jews who subvert the goodwill of the government?"

"No, sir," Yacov answered, holding the note out to Akiva in hopes of ending the interrogation. "But I wish that Jews could come home."

"Home!" snorted Akiva, tearing the seal off the note. He read it in silence then glared at Yacov. "So go home, boy," he said sarcastically. Then he turned on his heels and stomped up the stairs.

Yacov let himself out, thankful to breathe the cold night air as he walked slowly home.

6   Rescue

Moshe held the young woman firmly as the breakers caught their bodies and swept them toward shore like driftwood.

"We made it!" he shouted above the roar.

The woman could only nod her head in exhaustion as she struggled to find footing on the shifting sand.

"Hold on to me." Moshe stood in the shallow water and pulled her out of the waves. She was crying, he noticed, as they stumbled the last few yards to the beach. Quiet little sobs shook her slender shoulders as she fell in a heap on the dry sand. The warm salt of her tears mingled with the cold drops of the Mediterranean.

"You're home," he said gently, stroking her head like a child. "Home, little girl."

She shivered still, but gradually the sobs diminished and she slept. He scooped dry sand over her like a blanket, then he, too, began to drift into sleep. *Surely*, he thought, *Ehud has spilled his cargo onto this same beach hours ago. The Ane Maria would have chugged on to another destination.* Moshe hoped that the refugees had not been met by a patrol of immigration officers and carted back to Tel Aviv for deportation. He also hoped that the two of them would not be spotted by the British soldiers who checked the beach regularly for illegal immigrants. Right now, though, he was too tired to think. For an instant he wondered what the woman's name was. Then they both slept quietly where they had fallen.

A hazy sun cracked the horizon to the east, pushing back the darkness and bringing with it the fresh memory of the night before. Moshe opened his eyes and lay very still on the sand next to the woman, examining her sleeping features as if he were seeing her for the first time. Her head was turned away from him and her long dark hair was thrown back from her face, revealing a graceful neck and slender shoulders. Her white cotton camisole clung wetty to her slender figure. As he gazed at her, Moshe felt a stirring that made him turn his eyes away and sit up suddenly, spilling sand into the breeze that skimmed the beach. Her soft white arms were folded across her waist, and as she moved slightly Moshe caught a glimpse of the numbers tatooed on the inside of her left forearm. During her imprisonment by the Nazis, she had been 7645–8927, and beneath the number was the jagged black scar of an S.S. lightning bolt and the words "NUR FÜR OFFIZIERE." The mark of a prostitute assigned to brothel for Nazi officers. Moshe turned away as a sense of revulsion and deep sadness overcame him. "FOR OFFICERS ONLY." He wondered if this young woman still remembered her name.

Slowly she stirred with the awareness that he was awake. She opened her eyes—a deeper, clearer blue, Moshe thought, than the sea from which they had just come. Almost as if by instinct, her right hand moved to cover the tatoo on her left arm. She seemed to have no shame at sitting in her underclothes with a strange man on the beach. Her shame was that he would know that there had been other men, many other men, and each had left within her soul a gaping wound until, perhaps, there was no part of her own soul remaining. Moshe pretended not to notice her gesture, instead looking out to sea.

"Good morning," he said quietly.

She sat up and began to brush the sand from her body, careful to keep her left arm from view.

"Are you well?" he asked, still not looking at her directly. She continued to brush away the sand almost angrily. "I know you can speak," Moshe said impatiently. "I heard your voice last night."

"Am I well?" she snapped. "And how do you suppose I am, half frozen and covered with sand?"

"Well, you're alive!" Moshe bellowed, losing all patience. "No thanks to that stupid stunt you pulled last night. We could have been warm and clean right now if you hadn't jumped— you all snug at a kibbutz and me on my way back to Jerusalem. I should have let you drown."

"Yes," she said with resignation, "perhaps you should have." She stopped brushing then and sat quietly, hugging her knees to her chin as she gazed out at the lapping waves.

Moshe felt a rush of shame at his anger. For this young woman, perhaps death would have been more merciful. *What guilt and memories she must have to face each day of her life!* he thought.

"Look," she said like a small child. "The tide is out." Then she looked at him uncertainly. "Isn't it?"

"Yes." He looked back at her and smiled apologetically. "The tide is out."

"I thought so. All the shells along the sand. I read about tides and beaches once when I was a child. But I never sat on one." She tried to make up for her unpleasantness.

"Sometimes bits and pieces of old wrecks wash up on shore."

"Like us, eh?" She smiled at him and raised her eyebrows as though the two of them shared a secret.

"What is your name?" he asked after a long moment.

Her eyes clouded once again with the pain of a memory and sadness washed over her features. "I was . . ." she began slowly, "I am Rachel. Rachel," she said again, as if the name sounded foreign to her.

"A beautiful name," he said, thinking how well it fit her. " 'And Jacob served seven years for Rachel; and they seemed unto him but a few days, for the love he had for her.' " The young woman looked amused. "It's from the Bible," he finished lamely.

"Oh," she looked away again. "Then I will tell you now I have nothing in common with her." She tucked the tatoo tighter against her.

"Rachel," Moshe began haltingly, wishing to comfort wounds as gaping as the crevices near the Dead Sea. "You are free now. No one here will hurt you."

Her eyes grew dull and sullen. "There is not enough of me left to hurt," she said flatly. "I brought my prison with me."

Uncomfortably Moshe cleared his throat and sniffed. *I certainly put my foot in this one,* he thought. "It is cold, isn't it?" He shivered as he looked down at his undershirt and boxer shorts and black socks.

"Where are we?" she asked. "Do you know?"

"Tel Aviv is about two miles down the beach, unless I miss

my guess." He stood and stretched in the morning breeze.

"You won't get far like that," she remarked in amusement, scanning his lanky form.

Moshe did not reply, but instead strained his eyes in the direction of the sunrise. He stood motionless for a full minute, and Rachel shielded her eyes against the glare to see what captured his attention so.

"What is it?" she asked finally.

"A patrol. Coming our way fast."

Rachel stood, looking about desperately for a hiding place. "Oh, no!" she cried. "Not when we are so close!"

"Sit down," he commanded. "Just keep your mouth shut and let me do the talking. Act calm." Moshe spotted his trousers, soaked and knotted on the water's edge. With seeming nonchalance he walked across the damp sand to retrieve them. Rachel heard the sound of an approaching army jeep before she saw it and remained huddled on the sand as Moshe had instructed her.

As the jeep roared across the sand, three hundred yards from them, Moshe waved his arms in an attempt to flag the soldiers down.

"What are you doing?" Rachel asked in alarm.

"I said, let me handle this, will you?" Moshe said through gritted, smiling teeth. "Keep your mouth shut."

Two men manned the jeep—one driver and a passenger. The driver steered the vehicle so close to the water that a wall of salt spray shot up and drenched the passenger. As the passenger shouted obscenities, the driver would weave out to drier ground for a moment, then return to the water and repeat the scene again and again. It took a while to divert them from the game, but once they spotted Moshe waving to them, they roared straight as an arrow to them, skidding to a halt right in front of Rachel.

"Well, what 'ave we 'ere, blokes?" cried the driver as he set the handbrake and leaped out of the jeep in one smooth move.

"It's a mermaid." The young officer hopped out and marched toward Rachel, who tucked her head down on her knees. She had felt the gaze of men on the prowl before.

Moshe stepped quickly between them and Rachel and spread his hands in a gesture of harmlessness. "We're so glad you chaps have come along," he said in a crisp British accent that shocked Rachel into peeking out to be sure it was the same man. At the sound of his refined accent, the whoops and stares ceased, and the men suddenly assumed an attitude of deference.

"Right, sir," said the baby-faced officer, as he trudged toward Moshe at the front of the vehicle. He had obvious difficulty concealing his amusement at the man in his underwear stranded so far from civilization. "Having a bit of difficulty, I see?"

"Thank God someone in authority is here," Moshe growled. Then he snapped at the leering driver. "Get the lady something to put around her, will you? Can't you see we're in distress here?"

The smirk slid off the driver's ruddy face and he snapped to attention, rushing to the jeep to retrieve an Army issue blanket.

"You can do better than that, Wilkes!" barked the officer. "Get her your overcoat!"

Moshe snatched the blanket from the driver and wrapped it gently around Rachel's shoulders while the driver rummaged through the back of the jeep for a heavy overcoat.

A frown creased the brow of the officer. "He's still not calmed down from last night's celebration, sir."

"Indeed." Moshe found himself wondering if the celebration had been for the defeat of Partition or its victory.

"The chaps can't believe we'll be going home, y'know."

"Hmmm." Moshe took the coat from the driver and helped Rachel put it on as the soldiers turned their backs. "That's no excuse for this sort of behavior toward British subjects obviously in distress," he spat, leading Rachel to the jeep. "Sit here, my dear," he said, gently helping her into the officer's seat. Then he wrapped the blanket around his own shoulders, inwardly warmed by the news that the British would be going home. Partition had passed.

"Robbed, were you sir?" asked the officer, now suitably humbled. "You and the lady? At the celebration, I'll wager."

"Well, see for yourself, man!" Moshe growled in mock outrage.

"I said it wasn't safe on the streets last night for a British subject. Sir, you and your, er, wife?"

"My wife is back at the Embassy, Captain," Moshe lowered his voice in confidence.

The officer winked slyly. "Quite. A ticklish situation for you, sir. Did you say 'The Embassy,' sir?" he asked, clearly intimidated.

"You heard me!" Moshe roared. "Gads, man. Can't you see *this*, in that cursed Jewish rag of a paper? The honor of Britain is at stake! Take your clothes off."

"Wha . . . what?" The officer stepped back a pace.

"Well, you can't expect me to go back to Tel Aviv like this, not possibly."

"Why, no. No, sir."

"I'll send a driver back for you. We'll have *his* clothes as well." Moshe stared down the now-humbled driver who immediately began unbuttoning his tunic. "For the lady," Moshe added.

"Right, sir," stammered the driver.

"Now see here—" the officer protested with bravado.

"We're looking at a major political incident, Captain, when a member of the Embassy is kidnapped, robbed, stripped, and left on the beach with a young woman. Now the Jews, you may be sure, will make something of the fact that the woman is not my wife. I intend to make the incident as pro-Britain as possible, and you will assist me. As far as you are concerned, you never saw this young woman, is that clear?"

"Yes, sir!" the officer saluted.

"Well, then, let's have your trousers!"

Without another word the officer removed his uniform and meekly handed it over to Moshe who rubbed himself briskly with the blanket, then dressed, down to the shoes, which were a tad small. The dejected officer stood to the rear of the jeep in his undershorts and gartered socks with the likewise undressed driver.

Rachel quickly pulled on the driver's uniform, then tucked her hair under his hat. With final triumph she put the overcoat back on and, looking like a very effeminate British soldier, winked at Moshe.

Moshe knotted the tie with difficulty, asking assistance from the stripped captain. "There you are, sir," said the captain, giving the knot a final pat. "No one will know the difference."

"Quite," Moshe said crisply, placing the cap on his head at a jaunty angle. "I'll need a few pounds as well, Captain."

"Money, sir?" the officer clutched his wallet uncertainly. "Certainly man," Moshe said in a disgusted tone. "Of course you can expect to be repaid immediately. I'll give you my personal note, if you like."

"All I have is two pounds six, sir." The officer rummaged in his wallet and pulled out two worn bills with a few coins. "Your personal note is quite unnecessary, sir. Between gentlemen, as it were."

"Right you are. You're quite a decent fellow, Captain. We'll have someone back to pick you up shortly, then. Well, we're off." Moshe hopped behind the wheel and started the engine.

"Thank you, sir."

"And if you're ever at the Embassy—"

"Thank you sir! I'd be delighted." He waved cheerily as Moshe roared away, kicking up a cloud of grit and sand.

For the first time, Rachel laughed. Throwing back her head in delight, she tore off the cap and let the wind blow through her hair. Moshe cast a sidelong glance at her as they bounced over the dunes; then he, too, whooped with delight at the thought of the two soldiers waiting in their stocking feet on the beach.

Rachel shook her head in wonder. "Where did you learn to speak English like that?"

"Grew up around it all my life." Moshe shifted gears. "And I went to Oxford University for a while before the war."

"And did you study the gentle art of dramatics there? You are a convincing actor."

"No, I learned that during the war. Smuggling Jewish children out of Europe with the Aliya," he added with a smile, "one must be convincing."

Rachel touched his arm. "You are that." She laughed again. "The Embassy?" Delight and admiration filled her face. "And what is *your* name, Ambassador?"

"Moshe Sachar, dear lady," he stuck out his hand and they shook as though meeting for the first time.

"So pleased to meet you," Rachel nodded her head, then saluted. "Sir." The jeep rocked and bolted over the sand so that Rachel held tightly to her seat. "Where are you taking me?" she asked.

"How do you feel about breakfast?" Moshe pushed harder on the accelerator and topped the dunes to a stretch of a ragged paved road that would take them to safety.

7   The Scroll

The policeman clasped his hands behind his back and paced the width of the oriental rug in front of Ellie.

"A big fellow, you say," he mused, with a hint of a British accent tainting his Palestinian speech.

"Big," Ellie answered. "The other one was about your height. But I didn't get a good look at him."

"You can describe the big fellow, though?" He stopped in front of her chair and rocked back on his heels. "If you saw him again you would recognize him, eh?"

"Yes, easily." Ellie felt vaguely as though she were the one being interrogated. "Large, jutting jaw. Hawkish nose and a rugged face. Maybe about forty years old. Dressed like a European. Or an American. Only he wasn't."

The policeman frowned and leaned toward her. "Wasn't what?"

"American."

"How can you be sure of this?" he asked brusquely.

"He just wasn't, that's all. He didn't *sound* American." She surprised herself at the certainty with which she said the words.

"He spoke to you, then? What did he say?" The policeman's eyes narrowed and bored through her.

"He must've said something. I remember something, you know, but I don't remember exactly what it was."

The officer pursed his lips thoughtfully and began to pace once again. "Could you describe his accent, then?"

"I remember something like it in a war movie." Ellie hesitated. "Like the Gestapo. Maybe German. I would say it was a German accent."

The policeman ran his hand over his lips as he glared down at Ellie doubtfully. "Are you certain perhaps you did not have a bit too much to drink last night, young lady? You fell and hurt yourself, broke your camera and . . ."

"Too much to drink?" Ellie stood indignantly. "The man chased me down and tried to steal my camera. He ripped it open and took my film and smashed it to pieces. I've got a witness. A boy. He was hiding in the..." Ellie's voice broke off sharply as the policeman stepped back as though he had been struck.

"A witness?" he said gruffly. "Someone else saw this?"

"Yes. And I know where to find him, and he can tell you the whole story. Maybe even what the other man looked like too!" she snapped.

The policeman seemed to blanch for an instant; then he regained his composure. "Then we must speak with this ... witness. A boy, you say? Where shall I find him?"

"I've got the address," said Ellie, suddenly feeling cautious in the presence of this man. "I'll get him and bring him to the station if you like. He said he didn't want policemen nosing around his house."

The man's demeanor became sympathetic and kindly, causing Ellie to forget her vaguely uneasy feeling about him. "That is understandable, certainly." He smiled, revealing a gap between his front teeth and deep lines around his eyes. "Is four o'clock this afternoon suitable? And perhaps the boy would be more comfortable meeting someplace besides the station?"

"Probably. I would think so, yes."

"Shall we meet here, then? It is quiet and less hectic than the station."

"Fine." Ellie walked toward the front door, sensing a need to terminate the interview. "And officer—I'm sorry, I have forgotten your name."

"Rausch." He stuck out his hand. "Officer Rausch."

Ellie shook his hand and again a feeling of uneasiness settled hard on her. She quickly opened the door and stepped aside as he brushed past her onto the steps. "Four o'clock then, Officer Rausch. We'll see you then."

Rausch put on his cap and strode down the street as Ellie leaned on the doorjam and watched him until he was out of sight around the corner. There was something about his manner that made her uncomfortable. She shrugged off her doubts and closed the door behind her.

It was nearly nine a.m., and only now did Ellie hear Miriam stirring in the kitchen. The old woman's late night vigil had undoubtedly caused her to sleep later than she had ever slept in her life. Ellie pulled on a sweater to cover her bandaged elbows and, feeling a little guilty, peeked into the kitchen. Fully dressed, with every hair in place, Miriam stood grinding coffee beans and humming to herself.

"Good morning!" Ellie walked in and tried to take the handle of the grinder from Miriam. "Let me help."

Miriam held tightly to the grinder. "Sit," she commanded. "For twenty-seven years I grind coffee beans in this house every morning. You want me to take pictures for you?"

Ellie plopped down at the table in resignation. "Rough night last night?"

Miriam glanced at her and shook a few more beans into the grinder.

"How did you sleep?" Ellie asked cheerfully.

"After Miss Ellie realize the error of her ways and come home to bed, I slept well. Our Lord Jesus watched over you last night. It is a shame that a young woman go out in the streets to dance like a harem girl," she chided.

"Yes, well—" Ellie changed the subject. "Miriam, where is the scroll? I looked for it last night and couldn't find it. Did you put it away?"

"Ha!" Miriam exclaimed, grinding a little harder. "You left it in the lab, lying on the counter. It is something holy. I know that, you will see when the professor comes . . ."

"Where did you put it?" interrupted Ellie, relieved that it had not simply disappeared in the night.

"In the professor's study. Away safely in the case."

"Good. I want to have another look at it." Ellie started to rise.

"Sit!" Miriam commanded. "You need your breakfast. It is some days since you eat, and now that you are up, you will have a good breakfast."

"Just coffee."

"Coffee!" Miriam rolled her eyes and threw up her hands in despair.

"I've got some business in the Old City today. I want to take the scroll over to one of the Yeshiva schools. Maybe a rabbi can give us a clue, since Uncle Howard and Moshe are gone."

"It is not safe today in the Old City. The Mufti has called all Muslims to a general strike. I will make waffles and you will stay home, Miss Ellie," Miriam turned to the refrigerator for eggs and milk.

"Just coffee. Miriam, I really want to know what this thing is; I need to know."

Miriam shook her head at Ellie and replaced the eggs. A sharp knock came from the front door; Miriam retreated down the hall to answer it without another word.

Ellie poured herself a cup of coffee and leaned on the counter, inhaling the steam from her cup. Miriam poked her head in the door.

"They are here—those desert goatherds. They say they want money or the scroll back now."

Strangely disappointed that they had returned so early, Ellie set her cup down and padded out to the front hall to meet them.

The two men stood before the picture of the Young Girl Reading, discussing the merits of her figure with great animation as they waited for Ellie. She cleared her throat and they turned to her, eyeing her with great interest.

"Salaam." They bowed with elaborate courtesy as Ellie stood beside Miriam.

"Salaam," she repeated, extending her hand to the tall young man. "And good morning."

He returned her handshake. "Not such a good morning, I fear. The vote last night makes it necessary that we leave Jerusalem now."

"I would very much like to show the scroll to someone else before I give you my answer," Ellie said.

"You have the photographs, no?" said the young man. "We must go. The scroll please, or two hundred pounds, eh?" He held his hand out palm up.

"When will you return to the city?" she asked, feeling uneasy about allowing the scroll out of her possession until Uncle Howard had seen it for himself.

"Two weeks, if it be the will of Allah." He repeated her question in Arabic to the old man, who nodded enthusiastically.

"And you will bring the other scrolls as well?"

"You will have the money?"

Ellie turned to Miriam. "Go get this man his scroll," she said with resignation. Then she said to him. "If only we could keep it here safely until you return."

"There will be no safe place in Jerusalem anymore. No, lady. We must go."

Miriam returned, reverently bearing the scroll in both arms like a baby. Ellie took it from her and handed it to the old man who stuffed it back into his leather bag.

The old man smiled his broad, toothless grin and looked Ellie over from head to foot, jabbering to his son in a stream of Arabic. Miriam threw up her arms in exasperation, opened the front door and firmly escorted them both out onto the street.

"What did he say?" asked Ellie as Miriam slammed the door behind her and bolted the lock.

"He says that you would make a nice addition to his wives, and wonders if you are the same girl in the picture hanging on the wall there. He says you are created to suckle many little lambs."

Ellie felt the color rise in her cheeks. "I'm a long way from UCLA, eh?" she asked with a smile.

"Yes, but I think maybe you will go home soon, and you will be much safer there than you are here."

————————

Hassan cleared his throat and spit through the gap in his teeth. From his post across from the Moniger home, he watched as the old Arab woman pushed the two Bedouins out the front door. They stood for a moment, then turned toward the wall of the Old City and walked rapidly away. He hesitated a moment, wondering whether to follow them or wait until the young woman emerged and follow her as he and Gerhardt had followed her and Moshe Sachar for the last several weeks. In the uniform of a Palestine police officer, the Bedouins would not question his right to search the leather pouch that they carried into the house empty and brought out full.

He sniffed and crushed out his cigarette, conscious that it was Gerhardt's cigarette last night which had gotten them into trouble with the girl in the first place. If Gerhardt hadn't lit the match, chances are she never would have seen them. *Ah, well,* he thought, *if it hadn't been for the witness, it would have all been water under the bridge anyway.* Perhaps Gerhardt had been right. Perhaps they should have killed her and been done with it. There was still time for that—after they located the witness. There would be time and opportunity to kill them both.

Without more thought, Hassan started out after the two Bedouins. If the uniform did not convince them to stop, then most certainly the gold symbol of the crescent moon that he wore around his neck would. No faithful Muslim in Jerusalem would dare to deny or refuse the authority of one of the Mufti's secret police.

He quickened his pace as the Bedouins turned the corner of the residential district and, jabbering too much to notice him, turned up the long sloping road that led into the Arab Quarter of the Old City. As they passed through the gate, he was only a few yards behind them. Almost immediately inside the Old City, the two ducked into a darkened coffeehouse and inched their way back through the crowded tables to an empty space in the back corner.

Every eye turned in hostility toward Hassan, now painfully aware that the uniform he wore was out of place in the midst of keffiyah-clad warriors preparing for a Jihad against the infidel Jews. He reached into his shirt and pulled out the crescent moon medallion, a sparkling announcement of his place among the Arab political structure. He was in the "Gestapo" of Haj Amin, Mufti of Jerusalem. As he passed through clusters of men, heads nodded in recognition of his importance. Salutes and quiet salaams echoed throughout the coffeehouse as the warriors set their small cups of bitter coffee on the table and waited in respectful silence for him to pass.

The two Bedouins gazed in astonishment as Hassan passed by all the other tables and chose instead to sit at theirs.

"Salaam," the two Bedouins stood and bowed to their un-invited guest.

"You have been to the home of the infidel Zionist woman this morning!" Hassan snapped in Arabic without returning their greeting.

Smiles instantly faded as father and son exchanged fearful looks.

"But, sir," began the old man, "we went simply to transact business."

"Quite simply," repeated the young Bedouin.

"Sit down," Hassan motioned with a barely visible movement of his index finger.

Slowly they sank to their cushions, horrified that they had somehow offended the Mufti, Haj Amin, who with a wag of *his* finger could end their lives—indeed, the life of anyone in Jerusalem's Arab Quarter who offended him. "The gentleman is fond of antikas, or so we have heard, having never done business with him before. We have this to sell." The young Bedouin hastily pulled out the scroll and laid it on the table in front of Hassan.

Hassan glanced at it with only minor interest; then he peered back at the two grimly. "The Mufti is not pleased," he said softly, watching the color drain from the faces of the Bedouins. "What is this you have shown to the Zionists?"

"An ancient scroll, your excellency. Very old."

"And what did the American professor say?"

"We did not see him. But the woman seemed interested— quite interested. She wishes us to return so that her uncle might examine it."

Hassan pursed his lips thoughtfully and toyed with the crumbling edge of the scroll. "Perhaps this might be of interest to the Mufti," he said solemnly.

"We would be most honored," exclaimed the old man, "if the Mufti would accept this most humble gift!"

"Then you two will disappear into the desert to tend your flocks?"

"Exactly. With great joy, if Allah and the Mufti will it so!"

"Then go." Hassan raised his finger once again, and the two jumped up from the table and scrambled from the coffeehouse in relief.

Hassan threw a coin onto the low table and took a sip of the young Bedouin's coffee as he stared thoughtfully at the scroll before him. Perhaps the Mufti would be interested in something so obviously of interest to these Jew-lovers, these Americans. Perhaps there would even be great reward in it for himself.

He gathered the scroll up under his arm and walked through the crowded room and into the streets of Jerusalem.

———

Ellie took the photographs of the scroll from the drying racks one by one until they lay in numbered order in a neat stack in front of her. She pushed away the feeling of disappointment that she had returned the original scroll, telling herself that at least she had the photographs and would know soon enough what the content of the scroll was. She shoved the pictures into a large padded envelope and flicked off the light to the darkroom.

She found Miriam peeling potatoes in the kitchen.

"I fear that we should not have let the scroll go," the old woman sighed.

"It's probably just junk, Miriam. You know how much of that stuff is floating around here. We'll know what it says soon enough, anyway." Ellie dipped her finger in the sugar bowl as Miriam washed off the counter.

"We shall hope that those two return with the other scrolls, Miss Ellie. My heart tells me that this is something of great importance, though I do not know just why."

Ellie wondered about the strange inner voice that the old woman seemed to have. Miriam had heard that whisper of truth on several occasions. But she was, after all, only an old woman who worked in the home of an archaeology professor. She had no knowledge of archaeology itself—yet there were times that Uncle Howard had consulted her about the location of this or that biblical story, and she had seldom been wrong.

"You must not take these photographs to the Old City today," Miriam chided when she saw Ellie's package. "I tell you, this Mufti has called for a general strike. It is not safe to travel in the city today, I think."

"You think there will be violence?"

"Probably yes. It is not safe."

"I ought to take a camera, then. I might win a Pulitzer if I get a couple of good pictures—who knows?" Ellie retreated quickly back to the lab for a camera, regretting once again the loss of her Leica.

"If you win a prize you will collect it after you are dead!" Miriam shouted down the hall after her. "And if you are killed, somehow I am thinking I should have stopped you. But if you are so foolish . . ." Her voice trailed off as Ellie rushed past her.

"Not foolish, Miriam. I'm a journalist."

"You are a girl. I will pray to Jesus that you do not get your head shot off!" Miriam turned back to her potatoes as Ellie loaded her camera and headed out the door to the Old City.

Yacov's directions were plain enough for those who had lived in Jerusalem all their lives. Ellie studied the scrawl on the back of the envelope and wished for the thousandth time that Moshe were there with her. "Of course, if he were here," she muttered as she walked briskly toward King George Avenue, "I wouldn't need to show this to anyone else." She patted the envelope and searched the street ahead for one of the ancient taxis that rattled through the city. A taxi was the only way she would get where she wanted to go without Moshe. Even then, a taxi would take her no farther than the entrance to the Old City's crooked streets.

As she stood on the corner of King George, ten taxis dashed by within a minute, leaving a swirl of last night's trash in their wake. Confetti carpeted the sidewalk, and fragments of the morning's special edition of the *Palestine Post* proclaimed the passing of Partition. It was the morning after the celebration, yet Ellie could not see any signs that Miriam's prediction of violence would come true. Life appeared to be resuming a normal pace in this part of the city—if perhaps a bit hung over. As she flagged a taxi and stuck the directions under the nose of the non-English speaking driver, she did not notice the man stepping out of the tailor shop just behind her.

Jerusalem is an old city, thought Ellie, *but there is also so much that is new and hopeful about it.* As her driver turned left onto Julian's Way, she noticed the sapling trees that lined both sides of the road. Whoever planted them—the British Mandatory Government or the Jewish Agency—had hopes of being around long enough to watch them grow and enjoy their shade. *Somebody was surprised by last night's vote,* she thought as the taxi passed the two quonset buildings that housed the British Officers' Club.

Just beyond the officers' club on the left was the large stone Y.M.C.A. building and directly across from it the King David Hotel. Neither building showed any scars from the deadly explosion set off the year before by Jewish terrorists, killing many of the British Mandatory Government's staff as it ripped apart an entire wing of the hotel. The Irgun, a renegade collection of militant Jews, had claimed responsibility for the tragedy, and every Zionist, however peaceful, had suffered for their bloody deed. The bodies of clerks and typists had been hauled from the rubble, bloodstains cleaned from the surrounding buildings, and the King David rebuilt. The mandate itself continued to crumble, however, until the British government had called for help from the fledgling United Nations. But they had never expected the outcome of the vote to be in favor of the Zionists; and Ellie guessed that this morning the government workers were in a state of shock. Unless the U.N. revoked Partition—and everyone knew that could still happen—they would be out of a job.

The driver took the longest route to Jaffa Gate, passing the triangular shaped post office building and turning on Jaffa

Road through the business district in the great shadow of the rugged wall. The castle-like structure of the Citadel loomed ahead with Jaffa Gate just below it. The taxi screeched to a halt in front of the gate and turned to Ellie with his palm up for payment. She placed the coins in his hand without a tip, aware that the route he had taken had pushed the fare up considerably. Smiling at his frustrated expression, she hopped from the back of the taxi into the human tide that surged into the Old City.

She had entered the Old City and joined the crowd of Christians who were flocking to Sunday worship in the dozens of holy sites of the Christian Quarter. This place, too, was a minor political battleground; each of the Christian sects and nationalities argued over whose ground was the most sacred and which was the proper mode of worship. Each claimed to have cornered the market on truth and righteousness and God. Ellie paused to stare up the street as a procession of incense-bearing priests passed by. To her left rose the towers of the Church of the Holy Sepulchre where Jesus was said to have died. Ellie wondered what He would have said if He could see Jerusalem now. Splintered into a hundred fragments, each block was a deadly time bomb of self-righteousness. *And where is God in all this?* Ellie wondered. *If He was ever really here,* she decided, *surely He has given up on this contention and moved His headquarters somewhere else.* She raised her camera and snapped the shutter as smoke from the incense curled around the cap of a bearded Eastern Orthodox priest.

Directly ahead was the Street of the Chain which led to the Jewish Wailing Wall and the Muslim Dome of the Rock. The golden dome shone dully today beneath the overcast skies; still, it outshone anything else in Jerusalem for majestic architecture. Ellie couldn't help but believe that those who worshiped there had an advantage over the poor shabby Jews who stood in front of the ancient stones of the Wailing Wall and prayed.

To her right was the Muslim Quarter, spiked with Minarets for calling the faithful to prayer. *They would also make terrific posts for snipers,* Ellie thought as she noticed how they looked down over the rooftops into the streets of the Jewish Quarter. And as she gazed down the alleyways of the Arab section of the city, she noticed that something was very wrong indeed. Unlike other days in the Old City, when Arab vendors hawked their wares and pursued pedestrians down the street while dickering over a piece of unwanted merchandise, today was sullen and quiet. In the Arab Quarter, merchants sat inside closed little shops and warmed themselves near the rattling primus stoves while they talked of the Mufti's speech and brooded.

Conversations ceased as Ellie passed by, and angry eyes followed her as she passed through the gloomy alleyways toward the home of Yacov. She felt more like an infidel trespasser now than she had at any time since she had arrived in Palestine. Thinking that perhaps her camera had aroused hostility, she tried to tuck it under her flapping jacket. For now, at least, she had no motivation to take pictures of anyone who wouldn't smile back at her. Not after last night anyway.

A veiled woman carrying a water jar on her head passed her and stared fearfully with liquid brown eyes as if to ask, "What are you doing here today?" For a moment Ellie was tempted to turn on her heel and run back the way she had come, back to the relative safety of the New City. Instead, she stopped at the open entrance of a tiny shop filled with brass pots and candlesticks and bravely handed the envelope with Yacov's address on it to a harmless-looking old Arab man.

"Can you tell me . . ." Ellie began, as the old man turned the envelope upside down and studied the scrawl that held no meaning to him. "Is there someone here who can read?" she continued.

"Read?" The old man smiled, revealing only two yellowed teeth. He reminded Ellie a bit of a jack o' lantern. "You American?" he asked.

"Yes, American," she took the envelope from him.

"You like to buy candlesticks, eh? Very cheap," he rubbed his hands together.

"I need this address." She pointed to the envelope and talked a little louder as though raising her voice would help him understand what she wanted.

The old man picked up a pair of dusty candlesticks and held them out to her. "Very fine, very fine."

Ellie was about to pocket the envelope when she heard a deep resonant voice from the darkest corner of the musty little shop. "What is it you need?" A man dressed in a black robe and checkered keffiyah stood up and walked from the shadows. Ellie saw the blackness of his eyes before his craggy bearded face came into the light. There was only a hint of a smile on his thick lips, but it was not a kind smile. It was amused at the foolishness of an American woman in the Arab Quarter on a day like today. A golden crescent moon medallion glinted on his chest.

The black-robed Arab was no taller than Ellie, but his presence seemed to fill the room. Hesitantly, she smoothed out the wrinkled surface of the envelope and held it out to him as he approached. Studying her face, he took the envelope from her, and only when she began to feel the color rise to her cheeks did he look at the writing on it.

"Why do you go to this place today?" he asked, his eyes boring through her once again.

Ellie swallowed hard. "I have a friend there. A little boy I want to visit."

"You would be well advised to stay away from the Jewish Quarter," he warned.

"I have to go, you see, I . . ." her voice faded as she watched the strange smile creep back to his lips.

"You are going to take pictures?" He pulled back the hem of her jacket to reveal the camera. Instinctively Ellie took a step back toward the door.

"Maybe. If you don't know where the place is, I'll ask someone else," she said in a rush.

He took a step nearer to her, his steely eyes roaming from the top of her red head to her feet. "I will show you where it is," he said finally. "Come."

He pushed his way past her and strode majestically into the cobbled street. Ellie followed self-consciously in the wake of his flowing robes. *Is it my imagination*, she wondered, *or do I glimpse fear and respect on the faces of Arab men as he passes?* It didn't matter: she felt somewhat protected and was grateful for the escort to the archway that marked the end of the Arab Quarter and the beginning of the Jewish Quarter.

"There," he pointed into an alleyway teeming with black-coated Hasidic Jews. "Take many pictures, young woman, for soon this shall be no more. Salaam." He bowed and touched his forehead in salute, then turned and was gone.

The street was so narrow in places that Ellie could almost reach out and touch the houses on either side. Streets were built that way to keep the sun from beating down unmercifully during the hot months, Moshe had told her. Today, especially, Ellie felt as though she had entered a maze peopled with men and women from another century, and she did indeed begin to snap pictures as she made her way up the steep slope of the alleyway to Yacov's tiny apartment.

———

Hassan leaned against the entrance of the brass shop and lit his last Lucky Strike cigarette as he waited for Kadar to return from escorting Ellie. He inhaled deeply, wondering how long it would be before he could lay his hands on another pack of American cigarettes. They were a luxury enjoyed only by the very wealthy, or the privileged and feared. He was both privileged and feared by the general Arab population. And so was Kadar. It had most certainly been the will of Allah that the stupid girl he followed had stopped in the shop of Kadar's father to ask directions.

Kadar nodded briefly as he approached. A self-satisfied smile tugged the right corner of his mouth slightly upward. Hassan followed him into the shop and they both sat in the darkened corner by the stove.

"Allah is kind to us, Hassan," Kadar toyed with the medallion.

"You recognized her from the photograph, then?" Hassan leaned back against the wall and inhaled deeply, then flicked his ashes into a brass bowl.

"Surely many of our number on the streets today recognized the red-haired companion of Moshe Sachar. The truth is, even if we were not following her every move, I would have escorted her."

"Straight to your bedroom, eh?" Hassan laughed loudly.

"A beautiful woman, is she not?"

"Such a shame that we will have to kill her."

"Perhaps," Kadar smiled and narrowed his eyes, "she will not have to die quickly. Not before we learn all of her Haganah secrets."

8   On Eagles' Wings

The smell of hot apple strudel and cheese blintzes drifted into the dining room from Fanny Goldblatt's tiny kitchen. She poked her head out the swinging door and trilled, "Starving by now, eh? So don't rush me. Strudel takes time!"

"It's worth the wait, Fanny." Moshe rubbed his hand over his newly shaven face.

Fanny wagged a wooden spoon at Rachel. "I expect you to eat everything," she stated. "Then I will make more."

Rachel nodded and smiled in appreciation, trying to remember the last time she had cheese blintzes and strudel.

"We need to get a little meat on your bones," Fanny added, pulling her majestically plump figure back out of sight.

Moshe shrugged. "Fanny thinks every woman should at least *look* like she knows how to cook."

"And eat, too?" Rachel sipped her coffee, feeling clean and comfortable for the first time in days. Her slim figure was lost in Fanny's deep blue dressing gown, but Moshe noted how it highlighted her black-rimmed cobalt-blue eyes. Her freshly shampooed hair bore a sheen like black satin. *In broad daylight, clean and groomed,* he thought, *she is perhaps the most beautiful woman I have ever seen.* He looked quickly away as her eyes caught his.

"So, tell me," she said softly, circling the rim of her cup with her index finger. "What do you do when you don't do . . . this?"

"You mean when I am not eating breakfast at Fanny's?" he countered, noticing that her nails were chewed to the quick.

She set the cup down and leaned her chin in her hand. "No, when you are not pulling foolish girls from the sea."

"Actually I lead a rather dull life." Moshe evaded her question. "It would not interest you, I am sure." The less she knew about him the better. Most certainly after this morning they would never see one another again, and there was no sense in revealing his civilian identity to anyone who did not absolutely have to know. "You will stay here with Fanny for a day or so. I'll arrange for your papers. Someone will pick you up."

"Like they picked up the two soldiers?" she smiled.

"They will not have far to walk."

"And where will they take me?"

"There is a kibbutz not far from here. Probably there. It is where the others from your group . . ."

"It doesn't matter. I told you last night. I *have* family in Jerusalem. That is where I belong."

Moshe smiled at the insistence in her voice. "Family is important," he said. "It is important to belong."

"You are going to Jerusalem. May I not travel with you?"

Her voice had dissolved into the pleading cry of a child, and for a moment Moshe thought it would be heartless not to take her with him. He hesitated, staring hard into his coffee cup. "And what would you do if the British caught wind of us? Would you jump from the jeep like you did the boat? I can't take you to Jerusalem. Not now."

Rachel began to protest as Fanny burst through the swinging door carrying a tray heaped with steaming food. "So, am I interrupting anything?" she asked as Rachel drew back from Moshe and looked away. "Such a pretty girl, Moshe! Your mother, God rest her soul, should have lived so long to see you sitting here with such a pretty girl!" She transferred cheese blintzes onto Moshe's plate. "So eat already," she instructed, then turned to Rachel. "Grandchildren. That's what every mother wants. And a nice Jewish girl for her son." She smiled as Moshe and Rachel shifted uneasily in their chairs.

"Come on, Fanny, sit down." Moshe took a bite of strudel and rolled his eyes in delight.

"No, no, I'll leave you children to yourselves. Lots to do in the kitchen, you know." She clanged back through the door humming a Yiddish love song as the two tried not to notice.

Finally Rachel looked up and said softly, "Is she always . . . like this?"

"You mean trying to marry me off?" he shrugged. "You are not the first, but you are certainly. . ." his voice trailed off.

"What?"

Moshe toyed with his fork, then glanced up into her eyes and again at his plate. "The most . . ." he paused again, wanting to tell her how beautiful she was. He could not force the words that surely she had heard a thousand times before. "You are the most hungry," he finished lamely, then quickly took another bite.

Rachel threw her head back and laughed. "That is true! I have not eaten like this since before the war."

Fanny came back with seconds and spooned more blintzes onto Moshe's plate in spite of his protests. "You know, Moshe dear, everyone will think you are dead by now. Such a worry having you fall off the boat like that. Maybe you should call somebody, eh? So we're not saying Kaddish for you and someone is maybe dying of grief?"

Moshe excused himself and stepped into a tiny bedroom that adjoined the main room. He dialed the number of the red house and let the phone ring twice before he hung up and dialed again. The rough voice of Ehud Schiff answered on the fifth ring.

"Ehud," Moshe said quietly. "Did you get the catch to market?"

"Is it you?" Ehud growled in disbelief.

"In the flesh," Moshe laughed.

"Then I'll kill you myself for giving us such a scare!" Ehud was jubilant. Moshe heard him shouting to others in the house that he was alive, and the background rang with delighted cries and insults. "Such a windbag is too full of air to drown!"

"I landed a very nice flounder as well, Ehud," Moshe said, referring to Rachel.

"It is a miracle," Ehud chuckled. "I like miracles. Now, where are you?"

"Eating the best strudel in Palestine, where else?"

"Quit wasting time, will you? The Old Man wants to see us right away. Right away," he emphasized. "I'll be by for you in a few minutes, then."

Ehud hung up and Moshe sat on the edge of Fanny's bed, tempted to pull back the blankets and climb in. It would be so nice, he thought, just to go to bed and forget the whole thing. Let somebody else worry about refugees and Arabs and British gunboats. Right now the only thing that sounded worthwhile to him was a few days to sleep off Fanny's breakfast. Most likely, though, this would be the last free moment he would have to even consider the possibility. A meeting with the Old Man meant only one thing: hard work and only a couple of hours of interrupted sleep a night for the next few weeks. He listened to Fanny's animated conversation and Rachel's quiet replies from the next room, wondering if he would ever see her again after today. Then he wondered why he wanted to see her again so badly.

The forty-mile trip from Tel Aviv to Jerusalem had been frantic and rough, to say the least. Ehud might have made an excellent ship's captain, but on the highway he was a deranged lunatic. Gripping the wheel with his hairy hands, his eyes seemed to wander to every sight but the road.

Military traffic en route to Tel Aviv seemed to be especially heavy, and as they passed a British troop transport, Ehud would shove the accelerator to the floor with his size thirteen foot, then hang his upper body out the window and shout, "God Save the King!" as they careened only inches from the vehicles. The soldiers would then thunder in response, "God Save the King!" Ehud would finish the line with, "and keep him far from here, Amen!"

More than once Moshe had the impulse to stomp down on the brake, and several times he actually noticed his foot searching the empty floorboard for the pedal.

When at last they entered the Old Man's book-lined study, Moshe quipped, "Make Ehud chauffeur to the Mufti, and we have won the battle!"

Unsmiling, David Ben-Gurion peered at Moshe from beneath bushy white eyebrows.

"The Mufti may well indeed be our first battle." He paused and glanced around the crowded little room for effect. Respectful silence settled over the dozen men who had gathered there to discuss the strategy of the next few hours and days. The Old Man tapped a pencil on an open map of Jerusalem on his desk, the lead dotting the courtyard of the Dome of the Rock. "Even now as we meet here, he is addressing ten thousand Muslims in the courtyard of the mosque. His speeches have always had the immediate effect of filling Jewish cemeteries. That, of course, has been his goal."

Moshe glanced around the room at the unsmiling faces, and wondered how many were recent arrivals. Many, he knew, had never experienced the fury of the mobs Haj Amin had aroused over his years as Grand Mufti of Jerusalem. From Moshe's earliest childhood, Haj Amin had been the shadow over the lives of Jews in Jerusalem. His name was spoken in whispers or in loud political discussions around the dinner table, and once, in the strained voice of grief after the body of Moshe's older brother had been lowered into the grave. Haj Amin, Grand Mufti of Jerusalem, with his bright red hair and flashing blue eyes, became Moshe's midnight ghost; the terrible specter lurking in the darkness of his childhood nightmares. Only once had Moshe seen him; surrounded by his six black bodyguards, he had emerged from his armor-plated Mercedes and disappeared into the residence of the British High Commissioner as Moshe's bus passed by. He had not taken his eyes off the flowing red and blue robes until the door closed the Mufti from view. Even then he stared at the Mercedes and wondered what hateful thoughts were directed toward the Jews from that vehicle.

The silence of the men in the office was grim and heavy now. Ben-Gurion coughed and leaned back in his chair. "When, and if, the British do indeed give up the mandate, they will leave in their wake a vacuum—not a vacuum of promises or pronouncements, but a vacuum of military power." His eyes searched the faces of the men. "No doubt Haj Amin Husseini will be first in line to fill that vacuum with his own power. It is my guess that he will not wait until the British pull out to begin chipping away at the territory granted to us for a Jewish homeland."

He stood and pulled down a map on the wall behind his desk. Outlined in red were the boundaries of the future state. Yellow boundaries marked the Arab state, and deep in the center of Arab territory lay the city of Jerusalem. He tapped at the pinpoint that marked the Holy City. "The United Nations is under the illusion that Jerusalem will belong to neither state. It will be, as they say, an International City, eh?" He arched his eyebrows and shook his head slowly. "Whoever dreamed that up must be some kind of meshuggener. A crazy man!" Uneasy laughter rippled through the group, and some of Moshe's tension lifted. "The U.N. does not know the Mufti like we do. Here. This city of Jerusalem must be our first line of defense." Moshe looked at his hands as a surprised murmur rose from the Old Man's captive audience. "Any questions?" The Old Man sat down and began to tap his pencil as every man shouted a question. "One at a time. Where do you think we are? An Arab bazaar?"

Ruggedly handsome Shimon Devon fired the first question. "With what will we defend Jerusalem? Sticks and rocks? We

have no more than a few hundred ancient rifles hidden throughout the entire Yishuv, and precious little ammunition. Not to
mention larger weapons or artillery. We will be hard-pressed to
defend the ground within our own territory, let alone this place.
I say we pull out the Jews in Jerusalem and defend the rest."

Ben-Gurion ran his fingers through his white, unruly hair and
grimaced. "Technicalities, Shimon." He gave a half smile. "A
problem, yes, but if we read the Book, Jerusalem is part of the
State of Israel. Always. Every problem we face here must have
a solution." He ran his hand through his hair again and said,
"So. We start with Jerusalem. There is a problem. Our position
here is precarious and indefensible. What is the answer?"

A short, balding man standing next to a tall fair-haired man
in a leather jacket spoke up. *His accent is decidedly American*,
thought Moshe. *So is his conquer-all attitude.* Instantly Moshe
liked him. "Before the war there was this American film director
named John Ford who used to shoot western movies on an isolated Navajo Indian Reservation, see?"

The Old Man nodded his head but seemed unclear as to the
meaning of the man's story. "Yes, Michael," he said politely,
"continue."

"Well, back in '40 it snowed a blizzard up there. I mean there
was no way in or out. No way to feed the Indians. The rest of
the country had just pulled out of a depression, and no one
much cared that these people were starving to death out there.
But this guy Ford organized benefits, you know, dinners and
stuff. He educated people. Turned public opinion and—"

"I fail to see what this has to do with Jerusalem, my American friend," Shimon interrupted with disgust.

"Shut up for a minute, will you? I'm getting to it," Michael
snapped as the Old Man nodded his head for him to continue.
"Okay, so people got interested. And they raised a lot of money.
Then they bought food and hired transport planes and we air-
lifted rations to the Indians." He nudged his tall friend. "Me and
David here flew for that one. And in terrible weather, too. Plenty
of ice."

"We haven't got even one plane large enough for that kind
of operation," Shimon insisted as the Old Man listened and said
nothing. "And Arab bullets are a bit more formidable than bad
weather."

"Yeah? Says who?" Michael challenged. "A real optimist we

got here! I bring America's top war ace to train fliers—right here, David Meyer—and bring him to his first meeting, and all we hear is a crybaby saying we don't have planes!"

Shimon's lip curled and Moshe watched as his fists clenched and unclenched. "I simply believe we would be better off concentrating our efforts on our strengths!" he retorted angrily. "Not trying to salvage a hopeless situation."

David Meyer cleared his throat then, and all eyes turned to him as he took a deep breath to speak. "You might be right," he began. Shimon's scowl changed to triumph. "But you know, if all this talk has meant anything, Jerusalem might be worth hanging on to. For a while, anyway."

The Old Man leaned forward with interest.

David cracked his knuckles. "If this Mufti is so intent on winning Jerusalem, he's going to concentrate his troops there, isn't he?"

The men nodded thoughtfully and Moshe spoke up. "Legally, we will not be able to purchase arms until after the mandate ends," he said to Ben-Gurion. "I see what he is driving at. Perhaps, if nothing else, Jerusalem can buy us some time while we arm the new nation."

"Right," said David with a smile. "Any of you guys ever heard of the Alamo?"

The Old Man nodded and pursed his lips. "Our heritage is full of Alamos, Mr. Meyer—last stands and sieges and fights to the death. But it will all mean nothing if we cannot supply the people of Jerusalem with food and water."

"If the water mains are blown—" Shimon interjected.

"Then we have the cisterns. We will ration," Moshe interrupted.

"Water, we can't help you with." Michael rubbed his balding head thoughtfully. "But we did it with the Navajo as far as food goes."

"Not in Piper Cubs, you did not!" Shimon snapped. "You will be wasting time and energy."

"Hey, fella, me and David can do it in sail planes. Back off, will you?" Michael snarled sarcastically.

"And with a little money," David added, "we can find all the planes you need. And train the fliers to man them."

The room was still again and all eyes focused on the Old Man. "A little money, eh? A little public opinion on our side.

97

Every nation should have an air force, Shimon. Even if Jerusalem were to fall—and it will not, but regardless—the nation of Israel must have an air force." Then he turned his gaze on Michael and David, "You find the men and the planes. I'll handle public opinion and the money, eh? For now we will hold the Holy City, and if God wills, we will hold it forever." The Old Man spoke with finality, silencing Shimon. Then he picked up the large black Bible that always accompanied him everywhere, and he thumbed through the pages until he came to his favorite book, the book of Isaiah. Drawing out each word, he began to read, "They that wait upon the Lord shall renew their strength; they shall mount up with wings as eagles . . ." He paused and looked up at the men around the room. "The Lord knows we cannot wait any longer. Let us pray that He will guide us and give us strength. As for the rest, we each have a job to do. We shall work together for 'Operation Eagles' Wings.' "

9   The Home of the Rabbi

Grandfather carefully lifted the kettle from the kerosene stove and poured the hot water through the tea strainer as Ellie and Yacov looked on. Yacov knew that Grandfather was trying his best to be hospitable because the tea leaves he used were fresh, and the cups were those used only for special guests. He set them on an olive wood tray and moved over to the table where Ellie sat. She smiled at the old man as he held the tray down to her.

"Drink, drink," Grandfather urged. "It is the day after Shabbat, and we have not been to the bakery yet today. We have no cakes for you, I fear."

"That's fine," Ellie said. "Really, this is very nice of you."

Yacov wondered if she knew that they never had any cakes in the house regardless of what day of the week it was. She sipped the tea while Grandfather watched and nodded in approval. Then he set the tray down and took a cup himself before he sat on the edge of the bed next to Yacov.

"You are lucky you are not badly hurt, young lady. Yacov told me of the assault. A terrible thing."

"I was very grateful that your grandson was there to help me." Ellie sipped her tea and smiled at Yacov who felt a blush begin on his cheeks.

"He is a good boy," Grandfather nodded. "A comfort to an old man."

Yacov wished that the talk would focus somewhere besides his character. "You brought another camera!" Yacov interjected.

"So you must like to take pictures, eh?" Grandfather asked.

"That's how I make my living," Ellie volunteered, running her hand over the package that contained pictures of the scroll. *I hope he can tell me what the scrolls contain*, she thought. "I am staff photographer for The American School of Oriental Research. Archaeology."

Grandfather nodded politely. "Ah, yes, the study of ancient things. Lives that are dead and gone, is it not?"

"I guess you could put it that way," Ellie chuckled, remembering endless hours of cataloging jar handles at the site of Gibeon.

"I, too, study the ancients. The living word of Him who lives forever, Amen."

"Amen," Ellie repeated, feeling foolish when the old rabbi looked at her in amusement. "I mean, uh, sometimes we get things like that too. Old writings and . . ." she began to open the envelope as Grandfather feigned interest and continued nodding his head as she spoke. Ellie pulled the stack of pictures out onto the table, and the old man's eyebrows arched with surprise as he reached out and lifted the first numbered picture of the scroll. "A couple of Arab herdsmen brought this by the place. I don't know really what it is all about, because the man who normally interprets is out of town. But, I thought maybe you know someone who could tell me what this says . . ." she babbled as Grandfather studied the words on the scroll.

His mouth curved up in a smile, then he began to read: "Come now, and let us reason together, saith the Lord: though your sins be as scarlet, they shall be as white as snow; though they be red like crimson, they shall be as wool." He looked up at her and placed the photograph back on the stack.

"You can read that!" Ellie exclaimed in delight.

"Of course," the old man shrugged and smiled, amused at her surprise. "You have the writings of the Prophet Isaiah there, young woman."

"Is it very old?" she asked, leaning forward eagerly.

"Hmmm." Grandfather tugged on his beard thoughtfully. "The words of Isaiah are very ancient. Your scroll? Maybe old, maybe not. The scribe had an interesting hand, but probably not so old. We have a scroll at the Hurva Synagogue over seven hundred years. Now that is old, eh?"

A surge of disappointment flooded Ellie as she sat back and shoved the photographs back into the envelope.

"Wait," Grandfather reached out. "So what's the hurry? Maybe you got something else in there?" He paused for a moment and thumbed through the stack, then again he began to read aloud: "How beautiful upon the mountains are the feet of him that bringeth good tidings . . . Hmmm," said Grandfather. "Today everyone in Jerusalem should read this, eh?" He continued solemnly. ". . . that saith unto Zion, Thy God reigneth. Thy watchmen shall lift up the voice; with one voice together shall they sing: for they shall see eye to eye, when the Lord shall bring again Zion. Break forth into joy, sing together, ye waste places of Jerusalem: for the Lord hath comforted his people, He hath redeemed Jerusalem."

The stones of the tiny basement room seemed to echo with the voice of the old rabbi. "Whoever wrote that must have loved Jerusalem," Ellie said finally.

"Yes," he smiled and placed the stack on the table. "You could say that. God wrote it."

"God? What about Isaiah?" Ellie asked.

"Oh, he held the pen, but God told him what to write, eh?"

"After so many thousand years of men copying the words, don't you think it has been changed?" Ellie toyed with the edge of the stack.

"You ask too many questions." The rabbi winked at her. "It is not the age of the parchment that men should study maybe, but the principles within. I will tell you the truth. This that I have read contains the promises of the Holy One of Israel, blessed be His name forever. That has not changed, though there has been no Israel for two thousand years." Carefully he replaced the photographs in the envelope; then he handed it to Ellie.

"Study the words, and the world will be a safer place to live. And smarter, eh?"

Ellie sensed that the words he had read contained within them his every hope and dream. He loved Jerusalem as Isaiah had loved it. *But if there is a God,* Ellie concluded, *this would be the last place on earth He would love. Yosemite maybe; Jerusalem, never.* Nobody here ever seemed to see eye to eye.

"Why did you not bring the scroll itself, young woman?" Grandfather asked.

"I had to return it to the owners. My uncle will be able to analyze some fragments and actually date the scroll; if it's truly ancient, the school will no doubt purchase it. Anyway, thank you for helping me."

"In any language, Isaiah is a smart fellow. So go home and read it for yourself." He patted her head as if she were a small child, and Ellie felt a warmth from the old rabbi that she had not expected. "I wish you good luck. May your scroll be ancient, for then you will see the words are indeed unchanged."

He stood, indicating that the visit was over. "And you want to take Yacov back with you to talk with the policeman?"

"Yes. I'll send him home in a taxi," she promised. Yacov brightened at that, and Grandfather reached out and chucked his chin.

"I've never ridden in a taxi, Grandfather!" he said hopefully.

"Nor have I, Yacov." He smiled into his eyes. "What's the matter—a bus isn't good enough anymore?"

"It's fine but . . ."

"Such an expense!" The old man looked up at Ellie. "The bus is fine. Home before dark, eh?"

David stood across the street from the Moniger home and continued the long debate with himself. "You should have called her first, dope. He looked up at the windows in the square stone house and wondered which window was hers. If she looked out now, she would see him sweating and pacing as he worked up the courage to go to the door and knock. "So what are you going to say to her? 'Hi, I was in the neighborhood; thought I'd just drop by'? That won't make it, David," he muttered. " 'I've got this old Jewish buddy who happened to mention they needed somebody to fly planes over here. It's a legitimate job. You said I ought to quit barnstorming and settle down.' " Somehow, nothing sounded right to say. The truth of the matter was simply that David had accepted the job because he knew that Ellie was in Jerusalem and he wanted to see her again. He just couldn't figure out how to tell her.

David took a deep breath and ran his fingers through his tousled hair. He unzipped his flight jacket, then zipped it up again nervously as he crossed the street to the front steps. He raised his fist to knock on the door, then hesitated, waiting for the knot in his stomach to smooth out. "Good grief," he mumbled, "I've been up against crack Nazi pilots and wasn't this scared." As if he were forcing the control stick forward into a fatal dive, David forced his hand to knock on the massive white door. For a few moments, to his relief and disappointment, it seemed as though no one would answer, then, as he was about to turn and retreat down the steps, the knob clicked and the door creaked open a few inches. Miriam poked her face out and surveyed David.

"What do you want?" she demanded.

"I . . . uh, is this where Ellie Warne lives?" He plunged his hands into his pockets.

"And if it is?" the old woman asked.

"I'm an old friend of hers. I mean I—" He noticed that his voice sounded much higher than usual. "I'm from the States and I brought this letter from her mom. Can I see her?"

"Miss Ellie is not home."

"When is she coming back?"

"I will give her the letter and tell her you have come here to see her." The old woman put out her wrinkled palm.

"That's okay. I want to surprise her." He stuck out his hand then and shook hands with her. "David Meyer is the name."

The old woman's face was transformed when she heard his name. "Ah, yes, I hear of you!" she exclaimed.

"You have?"

"Many times. When Miss Ellie is sick she say your name! A very good friend, indeed." The door swung open wide and Miriam stepped aside to let David in. "So come in, young man. I shall fix tea. Such a long way you have come to bring a letter."

Baffled by the reception, he followed her meekly into the entryway and then into a parlor filled with antiquities. "You sure can tell what the professor does for a living," he said, admiring an ancient enameled Egyptian jar on the table beside him. "Kind of like a museum, isn't it?"

"The dust, it is most terrible. Just wait here," Miriam instructed as she bustled off to fix tea, leaving David alone in the room. "So she talked about me, huh?" David mused. "And all this time I figured she wouldn't even think about me. The old lady says she said my name. 'Course she could have been having bad dreams just as easy." The knot inside tightened again and he felt the urge to turn and run.

It had been almost a year since he had seen Ellie. He figured after this much time he should have forgotten not only the color of her eyes, but her name as well. Now here he was, halfway around the world, playing the role of mailman to a beautiful green-eyed woman that he couldn't forget no matter how hard he tried. In a way he hated the weakness in himself that brought him to this place, and he hated her for making him love her so much. Without her he felt like a plane without a rudder, when before he could simply glide with the wind and never care what direction his life was taking. Now he cared. Just like those other dopes in his squadron during the war who had fallen in love and gotten married on leave while he had laughed and sworn that it couldn't happen to him. Then he had met her.

From the beginning he had known that their relationship was important to her, but he had denied what he felt, pushed aside the noose that would fit too tightly around his neck. He denied that he loved her even as he whispered to her and held her gently against him. Even when thoughts of her crowded out the laughter of every other girl he spent time with, he had refused to admit that there was something special about Ellie.

He knew he had hurt her. And she realized what he was doing to her soul, so finally she had told him to shove off, to go stall his engine in a power dive. *She has a way with words*, he thought, smiling at the memory. With a shrug of his shoulders he had gone, pretending that he didn't care—the big tough war ace, too hard to care anymore. They called him Tin Man in the squadron because everyone said he had no heart, and he had almost come to believe it about himself. Now here he sat like a teenager in love for the first time, following his girl from one end of the world to the other. Jerusalem was sure enough the far end of the world!

He took a deep breath and caught the sweet scent of lilacs

that he recognized as her perfume. The first time he had buried his face in her neck, he had told her that she smelled just like his grandmother. Some compliment. He inhaled again, aware that this was the place she had lived for six months. He looked around the room, wanting to touch the things she had touched. Mostly he wanted to see her face and tell her he had been wrong. Wrong about everything. He wanted her to know that he wasn't running away anymore; he was searching for a missing piece of himself, searching for his heart, like the Tin Man.

Miriam brought tea. It was hot tea, which he didn't like, not without lots of lemon and a couple of spoonfuls of sugar, but he sat on the edge of the chair and held the dainty little china cup awkwardly in his big paw.

"Shall you like to wait, young man?" Miriam asked. "Or perhaps you will rather go find her? I worry so on a day like today. Lately any woman alone in the Old City is not safe."

David set the cup down with a clatter. "She's where? Alone?"

"With her camera, no doubt hoping murder will be done so she will be on hand to photograph the deed, no? I say this because you know Miss Ellie." She was only half joking.

"Right. Looking for the Pulitzer." He stood. "Do you know where she is? The general area."

"She leaves an address here." Miriam retrieved a piece of paper from the long sideboard. "The Jewish Quarter. The home of Rabbi Lebowitz. Go by way of Jaffa Gate."

The Mufti's orders to his men had been simple: the riot was to serve a twofold purpose. It would show the U.N. and the world how foolish they were to think that Jews could ever hold their ground against the tidal wave of the Faithful who surrounded them. Surely when they saw what bloodshed they had caused with their foolish vote, they would consider ways to change it. And, of course, violence would provide an excellent cover for the murder of the Jewish boy, the witness, and the disappearance of the red-haired woman.

The riot must appear to be spontaneous and without any connection whatsoever to the speech he had given that morning in the courtyard of the Dome of the Rock. All the Arabs of Jerusalem feared his power, but the majority did not approve of his politics or his methods. Men would not murder for the sake of politics; they must be moved by passion and revenge. This demonstration must begin as a spark that would ignite all of the Arabs against the Jews, and no one must ever suspect that it was the hot wind of the Mufti that blew the fire where he willed.

"Our leader is inspired by Allah," commented Hassan as he and Kadar moved quickly from Arab shop to Arab shop.

The lie united men and boys into one raging, avenging mob that swept through the souks repeating the lie until hatred simmered, then boiled over into the adjoining quarters of the Old City. When at last the lie surged through Jaffa Gate and into the Jewish commerical district, no one bothered anymore to ask if it was true. It was shouted from the lips and written on the heart of every Arab in the city.

"Did you not hear?" Kadar asked the quiet coppersmith. "A gang of Jews raped two young Arab women only this morning at Jaffa Gate."

10   The Riot

It was nearly noon by the time Ellie passed through the gate with Yacov and his dog. The smells of roasting chicken and grilling lamb drifted through the air of the New City Jewish commercial district, and Ellie felt her stomach rumble. She wished she had taken Miriam up on her offer of Belgian waffles that morning.

"Are you hungry?" she asked Yacov as he and Shaul in unison lifted their noses to the aroma and inhaled deeply.

The boy nodded his head vigorously.

"Me, too—starving!" Ellie said. "So where's a good place to eat around here? Lunch is on me."

"There is a falafal shop not far." He licked his lips at the thought. "The best in the New City." Then he added, "You have falafal in America?"

"Something like it." She smiled and put her arm around his shoulders. "Back home we call it a hamburger, but it's not half as good as falafal, Yacov." The image of the round, flat pita bread stuffed with lamb and rice made her mouth water. If there was one thing Ellie could write home about, it was the Jewish food.

The cafe was a tiny place wedged between a tailor shop and a linen shop. It was crowded with black-coated merchants and shop girls shouting their orders over a tall counter to the harried couple behind. Two men seated at a rickety table in front of the window stood up as Ellie and Yacov entered. Quickly Ellie sat down and pushed the empty plates and wadded napkins into a heap at the edge of the table. Yacov pulled up the chair opposite her and sat down, then looked out the window at Shaul waiting patiently by the door.

"Looks like everybody in Jerusalem but me knew about this place," Ellie shouted over the din of clattering plates and bantering customers. "What is good to order?"

"Everything," said Yacov enthusiastically as a stoop-shouldered old waiter scraped the dirty dishes onto a tray and bustled off. He returned a moment later with a pencil behind his ear and a small pad of paper to take their order. He spoke kindly in Yiddish and Ellie said quickly to Yacov, "Order for me."

When Yacov finished, the old man bowed politely and said to Ellie, "Sehr gut, liebshen," as he replaced the pencil behind his ear and plowed through the standing customers to deliver their order.

"What am I having?" she asked Yacov.

"Chicken. And I, lamb. And do you know about a drink called Coca-Cola? A new invention in Palestine."

"Pretty good stuff, is it?" asked Ellie wryly.

"I have had it but one time," assured Yacov, "but it is most wonderful."

Outside the window, Shaul leaped to his feet suddenly and began to bark. Yacov craned his neck to look at the dog, who seemed to be eyeing someone across the street.

"Is he hungry, too?" Ellie asked.

"No. It is something else he sees," Yacov watched him with disturbed interest. "Or hears."

For a few moments Ellie searched the faces of the pedestrians that passed in front of the window, then turned her interest to the strange menu before her. Without Yacov, she would not have had the slightest idea what to order. When she looked up again, Yacov was standing at the window with a deep frown on

106

his face as he scanned the street then turned his eyes to the barking dog.

"Sit down, Yacov," she said. "Lunch will be here in a second."

"But look," he said, almost in a whisper. "Do you not see?"

With alarm, Ellie gazed in the direction he was staring. Far up the street, people seemed to be running toward them. A man on the sidewalk directly in front of them stopped to stare at the same time. Ellie watched his face fill with horror and fear. He turned on his heel and crashed through the door of the cafe, knocking another man down.

"It is a riot!" he cried. "The Arabs have taken to the streets. Close your shops! Everybody return to your homes."

A woman screamed. Men cursed in Yiddish as they pushed through the door en masse. Ellie and Yacov jumped from their chairs and crowded back in the corner, still able to see the panic in the street. Ellie pulled out her camera and began snapping pictures as Jewish men and women rushed past. A plump older woman in a blue flower-print dress ran past with her arms raised high in the air and her mouth open in incomprehensible screams.

"Come on," Yacov said as he jerked Ellie's sleeve. "We must run." Yacov pulled her toward the door. The cafe owner pushed her from behind, while his wife stood weeping and wringing her hands behind the counter.

For an instant Ellie stood on the sidewalk in the midst of the confusion and gawked. Everywhere, anxious merchants cranked down the heavy metal shutters over the doors and windows of their shops. Only a block away the thunderous cry of "Jihad! Jihad! Jihad!" mingled with the cries of the Jews as they fled before the mob or fought the fires that engulfed their shops. Then, as the merchants ran past her and the angry mob approached, Ellie saw the figure of the same Palestinian police officer that had interviewed her only that morning. He stood nonchalantly leaning against a wall with his arms folded, watching with indifference. Three young Arab men stood a few yards away from him, just out of her view. All of them gazed steadily at her. With a nod of his head, one of the three pointed at her and began to cut through the fleeing crowd in a deliberate path toward where Ellie stood. She raised her camera and photographed the policeman, filled with rage that a man with government authority could stand in the midst of such carnage and never lift a finger. Then she turned to Yacov, whose pleas for her to run with the others had been made in panicked Yiddish.

A few minutes after the howling mob had entered the district, Princess Mary Avenue and Mamillah Road were littered with injured Jewish shopkeepers and the loot from their shops. Ellie stood riveted to the sidewalk, helpless to stop the violence exploding around her. The smoke that swept along the street like a thick gray fog stung her eyes and engulfed everything in a dreamlike darkness. Her cheeks were wet with tears. Shaul's frantic barking mingled with the sounds of crashing glass and anguished cries. Workers, peasants, and adolescents in black and white checkered keffiyahs swung clubs and iron bars in frantic and inhuman rage.

"Come on, lady!" urged Yacov. "Please!" He pulled hard on her arm; then he was pushed into the flow of the crowd, still reaching and calling for her.

"It's a nightmare!" she shouted. "God, a nightmare!"

The three Arabs shoved their way toward Ellie as she tried to reach the boy. Just in front of her a sobbing tailor cranked down the shutter of his shop. The three men emerged from the crowd near him and stood in a defiant line waiting for Ellie. The tailor lunged at them and was cut down by a blow to the back of his head with a pipe. Then, as Ellie raised her camera with trembling hands and snapped the shutter once again, the tallest of the three Arabs plunged a long curved knife deep into the tailor's back. Ellie screamed as the man's life ebbed away on the sidewalk. She felt her stomach revolt at the sight, and turned aside to be sick. The world spun violently around her; she braced herself against the half-closed shutter of the tailor shop and stared blankly at the three Arabs that stood before her. Then her eyes fell to the knife of the murderer; blood dripped from the point of his knife onto the toe of his shoe. Then they took another step nearer to her. For the first time, Ellie saw the leer on the face of the man with the knife as he reached out and grabbed the collar of her shirt; then he pressed himself against her, pinning her to the wall with his weight and the force of his rage.

Yacov turned and through the undulating flow of the mob saw Ellie pushed against the shutter. "They will have her!" he cried. "Shaul!" he screamed to the dog. "Stop them!" He pointed toward the men and Ellie as he fought his way back toward her.

The murderer tore at Ellie's blouse, ripping away the buttons as he shoved her to the sidewalk and under the shutter into the darkness of the shop. If two Arab women were raped, then a thousand Jewish women would pay. He would begin the retribution with this red-haired woman before he turned her over to Hassan and the Mufti.

The dog dodged and ran through the legs of Jews and Arabs, then, lips curled back in a snarl, he leaped at the face of the murderer as he ducked into the shop. Shaul's wolflike teeth tore a jagged hole in the man's cheek, and he screeched curses and flailed wildly against the force of the attack. Startled, his companions stepped back long enough for Yacov to slip past them and the body of the tailor into the shop where Ellie scrambled to find a place to hide.

"They will come for you, lady. Come on!" Yacov grabbed her arm and ran toward a stairway at the back of the shop.

Just as suddenly as he had attacked, Shaul turned away from the whimpering man and followed Yacov and Ellie as they dashed toward the stairs.

Watching the event from an alcove across the street, Hassan left his post and started after Ellie and the boy as his henchman struggled to his feet, wiping blood from his face.

As Ellie and Yacov bounded up the dark stairway, the cries of the riot seemed unreal to her. Her ears were filled only with the sounds of her heart beating and short sobs that she knew must be her own. Yacov held her arm and led her, stumbling, toward the door at the top of the stairs. She clutched at the camera still dangling around her neck.

"It's okay, lady," he said softly. "We will make it." Then as Shaul bumped his heels, he ordered, "To the butcher shop, Shaul!" In instant obedience, the dog turned and ran back toward the street, ramming into the legs of Hassan and the three men as he passed beneath the shutter.

"I shall kill the dog!" screamed the murderer as Shaul disappeared into the crowd.

"Forget the animal!" Hassan snapped. "It is the woman and the child we need. They have no way out. Set a fire and let us be done with it."

Hassan took a can of gasoline from a teenaged boy, sloshing

the volatile fluids through the open door of the falafal shop. The three Arabs poured a stream of gasoline into the tailor shop and struck a match. With a roar, hot flames devoured the fabrics and suits that filled the tiny cluttered shop. Yacov turned the door-knob and threw himself against the door at the top of the stairs. As heat and light rushed toward them, they fell into the tailor's apartment. With a sense of unreality, Ellie noticed the dead man's lunch still on the table. A half glass of wine waited where he had left it.

Deftly, Yacov found the narrow ladder that led to the rooftop. "Come on, lady. They will roast us like chickens!" he yelled as he pulled her toward the ladder.

"What's up here?" she asked, feeling trapped and panicked.

"It is the only way!" he cried, shoving her up toward the trap-door, then onto the flat roof as flames crackled behind them. Black smoke followed them as the fire quickly devoured the interior of the shop and then licked the apartment. Yacov slammed the trapdoor closed and ran to the edge of the roof. Peering over, he saw the police uniform of Hassan and the three Arabs who had pursued them.

Hassan looked up and glimpsed Yacov; then he pointed as his view was obscured by the smoke of nearly one hundred fires.

"There is a policeman standing by the men!" he shouted to Ellie. "Come see. Perhaps he will stop them."

Crouching low, Ellie scrambled toward Yacov and looked over the edge as smoke began to pour from the under rim of the closed trapdoor. Wafts of black smoke drifted by as Ellie tried to make out the features of the policeman. In one clear instant she recognized the upturned face of Hassan. "It's the same one we're supposed to talk to this afternoon. I saw him a while ago, too."

"Come, we must go. The fire." Yacov tugged at her arm and led her to the edge of the roof closest to another building. Although the space between the two buildings was only four feet, to Ellie it looked like a yawning chasm. "We must jump." Yacov climbed to the lip of the roof.

"I can't." Ellie looked down at the rough earth thirty feet below her as the fire burst through the trapdoor. "Now!" Yacov jumped to the opposite roof, rolled a few feet then jumped up. "It is not too far, lady! Jump!" he urged.

The fury of the fire raged behind her, warming her back as she teetered on the edge of the roof trying to gather the courage to jump. Below her she could hear the crash of timbers as the second floor of the apartment began to fall through.

"Hurry!" Yacov cried. "Please, lady. Please jump!" He held his hands out toward her.

She focused on his hands. Such small hands, yet she somehow felt as though they were trying to lift her over the gulf that stood between her and safety. Her knees felt like water; she turned in time to see the tar of the roof catch fire and race toward her. Then she crouched and jumped with all her might, reaching out toward Yacov's outstretched arms. She landed on her feet, holding tightly to the boy as the roof of the tailor shop collapsed where she had stood only seconds before.

Hassan and his men followed their progress as Yacov led Ellie to yet another rooftop leap and still another. A volley of gunfire ripped through the crowd below, silencing the screams of nearly a dozen Jews. Ellie recognized the body of the woman in the blue-flowered dress who had run in front of the cafe. Slouched against the side of a building was the Yiddish-speaking waiter who had taken their order. His white apron was drenched with blood, but Ellie saw the pencil still lodged behind his ear. And always, Hassan and the three Arab men followed them, their eyes turned upward as if the death and destruction around them were an everyday occurrence.

"The policeman is one of them!" Ellie shouted. "He's leading them right for us."

Suddenly a bullet ricocheted off the dome of the roof, just inches from Yacov's head. Plaster sprayed his eyes as the force creased the wall. He dropped to his knees, crying out, clutching his face.

"Are you hurt?" Ellie cried, rushing to his side. She pulled his hands away. His face was pitted with plaster and his eyes were swollen shut.

"I can't see!" the boy sobbed. "My eyes!"

Another bullet ripped into the structure behind Ellie. "Yacov, is there another way off these roofs? We're like ducks in a shooting gallery up here."

Still unable to see, the boy nodded. "Do you see just down the block? A large building? It is the theater. We can get to the balcony from here. Inside the theater. But you will have to help me."

"God, help me!" Ellie glanced back as the flames from the tailor shop raced from building to building and threatened the structure where they waited now. Never had she felt such fear, and yet as she remembered the boy's small hands reaching out to help her, she wrapped his arms around her neck and swung him onto her back. Crouching, she ran to the edge of the building and leaped onto the next, spilling onto the rough tar roof. "Are you okay?" she asked, gathering him onto her back once again.

He nodded, then clung tightly to her. "Tell me when you are jumping, lady."

"You scared or something?" she asked, running a pattern across the roof like a football quarterback.

"Yes," he answered.

"Me too," she replied, staring over the edge of the roof to the top of a building several feet below them. "Ready?"

The jump was at least a foot farther, but Ellie hoped that since the roof was below them they would make it. Just beyond was the theater, and Ellie could just make out the fire-escape ladder that led to the balcony. "Ready?" she repeated, not sure that she was.

"Yes."

Ellie took a deep breath as though she were plunging off a diving board into deep water. Then she jumped, her feet landing on the very edge of the building. She fought to regain her balance, but the weight of the boy pulled her backward. Yacov fell from her back as she lurched forward, his hands barely catching the ledge. He cried out, sensing death below him if he lost his grip.

Ellie clambered toward him on her hands and knees, and reaching him just as his hands began to lose their tenuous hold. "I've got you, son!" she cried, grabbing his wrist and pulling him up to her. "We almost got it that time."

She hauled him up, then fell back, exhausted as he sat heaving, cradling his face. Smoke swirled through the sky above her, dancing to some unheard melody, while below, the staccato of gunfire was punctuated by screams.

David fought his way inch by inch up Princess Mary Avenue trying to reach Jaffa Gate. Somewhere, he knew, Ellie was in the thick of this. A knot twisted tight in his stomach as he watched men and women fall around him. Had she fallen, too?

He wanted to shout her name, to keep on calling until she heard and answered, but he knew that shouting would be futile in this din. His eyes searched for the copper glow of her hair amidst the bloodstained rabble that surged against him, pushing him back. And on he pressed, straining against the current, hoping to find her before it was too late.

Piles of goods were everywhere being set on fire and no one, it seemed, had raised a finger to stop the mob. He heard the roar of an engine and with some relief watched as two dozen British troops piled out of the canvas-covered truck bed onto the street. His relief soon evaporated, however, replaced by anger as the troops simply stood ready in the street as the brutality raged around them. A man in a Palestine police uniform stood gawking at the roof of a burning building doing nothing to help, nothing to stop the bloodshed. David saw him gesture to three grim Arab men; then his eyes followed the gesture toward the rooftop. A girl's copper hair bobbed across the roofline. But it couldn't be—she was carrying a small boy on her back! *But if it was Ellie, and those men*—Horror and hope rose up in David's heart as the girl plunged over the edge of the roof onto another building across a gulf five feet wide and another six feet below her. She fell, and the boy slipped from her grasp and clung to the edge of the roof. Then she turned, grabbing the boy by the wrist, and David caught a glimpse of her face as she leaned over the building. "Ellie!" he shouted. "Hold on!" he yelled. "Don't let go! Hang on!"

As she hauled the boy to her, one of the Arab men pulled an ancient revolver and took aim as the policeman simply looked on. David yelled again and charged at the man, knocking him to the ground as he pulled the trigger. "Ellie!" he cried again. "Run for it!" The gap-toothed policeman smiled and kicked David hard in the groin, and darkness circled around him.

———

Ellie pulled herself up and pulled Yacov onto her back once again. She sprinted across the rooftop, and without looking at the ground, she reached out for the rickety metal ladder on the side of the theater building.

"Hang on now," she warned. "It's just a short hop to the ladder. Just hang on." Her fear had given birth to a courage she had not been aware even existed in her. "I'm no Errol Flynn," she muttered, "but I can do this." She grasped the ladder and jumped, both feet catching the rungs with ease. She looked over her shoulder and down, watching as Hassan and his thugs attacked a man in the street. "At least they're not watching us," she said, climbing as quickly as she could to the small wrought-iron railing around the fire-escape entrance to the theater. She carefully placed Yacov's hands securely on the railing and helped him climb up to the platform. Even before she joined him, he had the splintered wooden door open and was crawling into the theater. She climbed in after him and shut the door, hoping that their pursuers had not spotted them.

"I sneak into the movie this way," Yacov leaned against the cool cinder-block wall behind a heavy velvet curtain. "My eyes," he said softly. "They hurt."

Ellie peeked out from behind the curtain. The place was nearly dark and totally deserted. Outside, the popping of machine-gun fire filtered through the thin, wooden door. Ellie felt as though they had, indeed, just come through a war movie complete with genuine bad guys. But a moment later she heard a dull systematic thudding. "The theater doors!" she cried. "They've found us!"

The boy reached out for Ellie as the steady cadence slammed against the building. For a moment she thought he was afraid; then he said, "It is all right, lady. We will be okay. But we got to go." He patted her hand comfortingly. She wondered if he had forgotten that she was the adult, and he was the child.

A barrage of gunfire accompanied the final crash of the doors. The theater filled with murky light and the sound of Hassan and his men ordering rioters to slash and soak the seats with gasoline. Ellie peered out from behind the curtain at Hassan as he stood in the center of the reeking chaos and scanned the theater for signs of their presence. Then he raised his chin in grim pleasure, secure in the fact that his quarry would die in the fire or be caught as they tried to escape the inferno.

"Lady, I smell petrol. They are going to burn us up, too. Let's go!"

With one last glance around, Hassan ordered everyone out, then threw a match, turning the interior into an instant hell of smoke and flame. The floor beneath them began to heat up and Ellie knew that they had only seconds before they, too, would be trapped. And even when they escaped, the fire would pursue them through the opened exit. "We've got to jump for it the instant we open the door," she coughed.

Yacov climbed onto her back and wrapped his arms around her neck once again. She shoved hard against the door and jumped for the ladder even as the flames roared after them and licked the sudden flow of oxygen at the door.

Ellie glanced below them and saw Hassan and his men waiting at the entrance of the alley with their arms folded. "We've got to go up!" she cried. "They're waiting for us." As the flames pursued them up the ladder, Ellie fought her way through the dense, strangling cloud of smoke. The boy was nearly unconscious, yet still he clung to her. She was aware of her camera banging against the rungs of the ladder as she painfully pulled herself and the boy up.

Hassan sprinted to their only other hope for escape—a ladder on the far side of the theater.

As Ellie pulled herself onto the roof, already spots were beginning to smolder. She carefully set Yacov on his own feet and surveyed their precarious situation. "Roast chicken or sitting ducks," she said after a moment. Flames lapped up the side of the building behind them, and below waited Hassan and the man who had tried to rape her. She grasped the rail of the ladder that led down to them and stared bleakly at Hassan.

Hassan cupped his hand around his mouth and yelled above the roar of the rapidly encroaching flames, "Come down, Miss Warne. You will not be injured." Her eyes went to the gun in his hand, and the still leering face of the murderer beside him. In an instant she made up her mind. There was no easy way to die, she knew, but to become the main course in a barbecue was not her idea of a noble demise. There was always a chance she could escape. She hefted the boy once again and began a careful descent down the ladder to the waiting grip of Hassan.

Then, with a howling scream, the windows on that side of the building burst and flames licked out all around them, engulfing the middle ten feet of the ladder. Rungs and rails became hot to the touch. Hassan stepped back with a shrug of his shoulders. Well, he had tried to talk them down, at least. This would certainly solve the problem of how to dispose of them.

11   Deliverance

Clutching himself in agony, David dragged himself to his feet and leaned against a lightpost as he surveyed the destruction around him. He caught sight of Hassan and the man who had kicked him as they ran around to the far side of the burning theater. He limped after them in time to watch Ellie begin her climb down. To his horror the windows exploded and fire closed in on them. *They haven't got much time*, he thought. Suddenly he saw the canvas-covered troop carrier standing deserted. With a war whoop, he ran to it. As he climbed aboard and cranked the engine, a British sergeant stuck a muscled arm through the window and grabbed his throat. David drew back his fist and struck him full in the face, knocking him onto the ground. Without looking back, David pushed the accelerator to the floor and ripped toward Hassan and the waiting men below the ladder.

Hassan turned in disbelief at the approaching truck, screaming and jumping clear just before the vehicle slammed into the murderer at his side. The dead Arab lurched onto the hood of the truck, his face pressed against the windshield. David slammed on the brakes, stopping the truck just below Ellie and the boy.

The flames licked higher, reaching out to where Ellie waited, frozen in terror, on the ladder. "Ellie!" he cried at the top of his lungs. "Jump, girl! Jump onto the canvas top!"

She looked down, in shock and disbelief, certain she recognized David's voice, but certain it could not be him.

The fumes had choked her almost to unconsciousness, and in only a moment the ladder would be too hot to hold. She tried to focus on the top of the truck. If the canvas would hold against the force of their weight, perhaps there was a chance. "God—"

she whispered. It was all the prayer she knew. "We're going to jump now, Yacov. Hold on, boy, hold on."

She leaped into the open air, grasping the arms of Yacov as they fell for what seemed a long time. The boy screamed with Ellie, who expected to miss her target and die. When indeed they did hit, the canvas broke their fall, but it tore away and they crashed to the metal bed of the truck. The world grew dark, and Ellie gasped for breath.

When she came to, the ping of bullets dented the tailgate of the rumbling truck. She stayed down and shielded the boy with her body as the vehicle careened wildly through the streets. The sounds of the riot died behind them, and after a few minutes Ellie dared to raise up and look through the torn canvas. A tight spiral of smoke rose above the commercial district and the wail of sirens echoed off the peculiar pink stone that comprised most of the buildings of the city. Behind, a military motorcycle with a sidecar screamed toward them, manned by two British soldiers who glared in deadly earnest through their goggles. They whipped around the troop transport and pulled up alongside the driver of the truck. Only then did Ellie remember the voice that had sounded so much like David's calling for her to jump to safety. *It must have been my imagination*, she thought. But she couldn't help wondering who was driving the truck and where she and Yacov were being taken. She did not have long to wonder. The truck began the ascent to Hadassah Hospital with the screaming siren of the motorcycle alongside. Ellie lifted the canvas on the side of the truck and peeked out at the British soldiers. They had their guns trained directly on the driver of the truck. She craned her neck to see the driver, but saw only a leather-clad arm hanging out the window. *Flight jacket*, thought Ellie, her heart pounding. *Could it truly be David?* She pulled her head back and clutched at her torn and gaping blouse. If she ever expected to see him again, this would not be how she had envisioned the meeting.

The truck screeched to a halt outside of the emergency entrance to the hospital. The two soldiers were immediately on the driver of the truck, prodding with their guns as the door swung open slowly and a pair of lanky Levi-covered legs extended and jumped to the pavement. In disbelief, Ellie watched as David was whirled around at gunpoint and slammed face down onto the hood of the truck.

117

"David!" she screamed.

"Ellie, I . . ." he looked toward her, only to be slammed down once again on the truck.

"Y' can't steal a troop transport and expect t' get away wi' it now, mate," said one of the soldiers.

"I didn't steal it!" David insisted.

"There is an injured boy back here, officer!" Ellie cried out at the top of her lungs.

The soldiers looked at one another, then at David suspiciously. "I'll go see," said the driver of the motorcycle as the other shoved the muzzle of his rifle against the back of David's neck.

The soldier sauntered back to the bed of the truck and peered in at Ellie, who was cradling Yacov. He was still unconscious and his face was swollen and distorted.

"You don't look s' good yourself, ma'am," he said, scanning her smoke-smudged, torn clothing.

David said loudly, "I'm telling you, if I hadn't taken this truck, they'd be dead. For goodness' sakes, get the kid into the hospital, will you?"

The driver nodded at the soldier holding David, who reluctantly pulled the gun away. David straightened himself, then rushed back to pick up Yacov. For a moment his eyes met Ellie's. They were full of emotion as she handed the limp body of the boy to him.

"Are you all right?" he asked quietly.

Emotion flooded her. Tears pushed at her throat as she tried to hold herself. She grasped her blouse and lowered her head, then fell against him. "Oh, David!" she sobbed. "David."

Suddenly the truck was surrounded by medical attendants. David handed the boy to a team who placed him carefully on a gurney, then raced into the building.

"It's okay, Ellie," he whispered. "It's okay, honey. I'm here." He folded her in his arms; then, oblivious to the nurses standing by with a second gurney, he lifted her out of the truck and carried her gently through the doors into the safety of the hospital.

————

The gray smoke of the commercial district gradually disappeared as dusk fell over the city. Moshe ran up the steps of the hospital and burst through the doors. The lobby was crowded with small clusters of people awaiting word about friends or relatives who had been caught in the riot. Policemen and British officers seemed to be everywhere, taking depositions and moving back and forth among the bustling doctors and nurses.

Moshe felt angry at himself for not having called Ellie when he first got to Jerusalem, and angry at Ellie for having been so foolish as to go out alone—today, of all days! When he had finally called, he had learned that Howard Moniger had returned and was at the hospital with Ellie. Miriam had no more details than that.

Gently, Moshe pushed past a weeping woman at the information desk. A harried-looking receptionist glanced up from the buzzing switchboard.

"What is it?" she asked impatiently.

"I need the room number for Ellie Warne. Maybe it's under Michelle Warne." Moshe clenched and unclenched his fist nervously.

She scanned a list and without looking up said, "Room 312."

Moshe did not wait for the elevator. Instead, he ran up three flights of dimly lit stairs. Ignoring the posted visiting hours, he strode quickly down a long corridor. Near the end he spotted Howard's portly form next to a tall, middle-aged British officer with a handlebar mustache. The officer scribbled notes as Howard spoke with deep concern. Worry clouded the professor's usually cheerful face, and he was still dressed in his khaki clothes and field boots. Moshe wondered if he felt as exhausted as he looked.

Howard glanced up and saw Moshe, raising his hand in greeting.

"How is she?" Moshe asked as he walked up, interrupting the officer.

"She's going to make it, Moshe," Howard put a hand on his arm. "A concussion. Smoke inhalation. A few scrapes and bruises. They'll keep her here a couple of days."

"Can I see her? Talk to her?" Moshe started toward the door.

"She's sedated."

"Oh." Moshe felt disappointed and wanted only to see that she was alive. He noticed that the British captain was holding Ellie's camera. "What's this?" he asked abruptly.

"Moshe, I'd like you to meet a friend of mine. Captain Luke Thomas." The officer nodded and extended his hand.

"Ellie took a photograph of her assailants," the captain explained.

"Assailants? You mean she . . . was she . . ."

"No, Moshe, she escaped," Howard said solemnly. "She was with a little boy, it seems, and he led her away."

Moshe turned and without waiting pushed the door open and walked into the half-light of the hospital room. A small lamp was lit by the bedside, and her damp hair glowed like dark copper against her pillow. He stood for a moment and watched her chest rise and fall with her deep and even breathing; then he stepped quietly to the edge of her bed and took her hand.

There were dark circles beneath her eyes, but she slept as peacefully as a child. His anxiety melted away and was replaced by tenderness. He placed her finger tips against his lips. "My silly girl," he said softly. "My darling, foolish girl."

She sighed and turned her face toward him and gently squeezed his hand. He wanted to take her in his arms, but was afraid that he would hurt her, so he stood for a full minute gazing at her as she slept. He leaned down to kiss her, but as his lips were about to brush hers, he heard a sound from a darkened corner of the room.

"Ahem." Startled, Moshe whirled around and stared into the darkness, just barely able to see the dim features of the man who had cleared his throat.

"Moshe Sachar, aren't you?" The voice was clearly irritated.

"Who is there?" Moshe asked grimly as he stepped between Ellie and the man in the corner.

"I saw you at the meeting this morning. With the Old Man. What are you up to? I want to know. And what have you got her involved in?" The voice seemed angry now.

"She is involved in nothing." Moshe felt anger welling up in him.

"Is that so?" The hostility turned to sarcasm. "Those jokers weren't chasing her and that kid for nothing, you know. They were after something."

"Look," Moshe demanded, clenching his fists, "what business is it of yours?" The dim figure stood up then and stepped out into the light. Moshe instantly recognized the American flyer from the meeting, his face now rigid with fury, his eyes hard and piercing as they glared at Moshe.

"I happen to be in love with her," David answered fiercely.

Moshe smiled sarcastically. "Then you have my condolences, Mr. Meyer. David Meyer is the name, is it not? I thought I recognized the name at the meeting this morning. Ellie told me all about you." He continued to smile as though he were in on some great private joke. David glared back at him, then blinked hard and looked at Ellie sleeping quietly. A trace of tenderness passed across his face and Moshe stepped to the side, blocking his view. "At any rate," Moshe said with finality, "you have been out of the picture a long time."

"Well, I'm back now. And whatever political garbage you've got her involved in—"

"She is involved in nothing," he interrupted. "She knows nothing of my work; she must not."

"Good. Because as soon as she's on her feet, she's going back to the States. Understand?" David strode to the door and walked out, leaving Moshe alone by Ellie's bedside. He turned to her and stroked her forehead, smiling at the trace of freckles across her nose. "He is right, you know, dear one. Because I love you, I must send you home."

———

Hassan bowed low before the presence of Haj Amin Husseini, Mufti of Jerusalem. He hoped that the trembling of his hands would not show as he handed the package of the young woman's photographs to the chief bodyguard. In turn, the package was given to the Mufti who opened them without expression, then thumbed through them with perfunctory interest before he lifted his gaze to Hassan.

"Well?" said the Mufti, as if amused.

"The girl dropped them as she ran into the tailor shop. Surely they must be of some importance to the Haganah. Perhaps the scroll is some sort of code."

"Unless we have the girl, we have no way of knowing, is that not so, Hassan?"

"Yes, Haj Amin, it is so. If it be the will of Allah—"

A spark of anger flashed across the Mufti's placid expression. "It is the will of Haj Amin, Grand Mufti of Jerusalem, Hassan!"

Hassan bowed low again, fearful of the slightly raised voice of his leader.

"I beg your forgiveness, Haj."

The Mufti smiled graciously and raised an eyebrow. "Our friend the Führer had the proper attitude toward the Jewish problem. Such a pity he had not the opportunity to finish what he started. Gerhardt would have killed her had you not stopped him."

"But the boy. . ."

"He still lives as well, does he not?"

"He is still at the hospital. It seems there has been some damage to his eyes."

"His eyes? Poor child. He is blind, then."

"Only in one eye, they say—the right."

The Mufti pressed his fingers together thoughtfully. "An excellent idea, Hassan. Perhaps you will redeem yourself after all."

Hassan stood in dumb confusion, trying to think what idea he might have had that would so please the Mufti.

"If the boy is blinded, he shall not be able to identify our top agent, shall he?" The Mufti continued. "A pity you could not have taken his left eye as well, but we shall hope that you will prove yourself worthy of our trust."

Hassan nodded eagerly. "Anything you request, Haj Amin."

"Well, then," the Mufti leaned back against a cushion. "Bring us the boy's left eye as well. Or his body. It makes little difference, although the eye of a Jew would be more amusing for us. And the girl. Kadar says she is beautiful. It would please us."

"As you say, Haj Amin."

The Mufti leafed through the stack of photographs. "As for these, we shall take them to that fool of a Jew in the Jewish Quarter, Rabbi Akiva. Perhaps he can shed light on their meaning."

PART 2

The Awakening
December 1947

"In the end days it is said that the lion and the lamb will lie down together. I think even then I would rather be a lion."

David Ben-Gurion

12   The Truth About the Scrolls

Seven days had come and gone since the British officer had come with news of Yacov. A lonely Shabbat had passed, and there had been no further word on his well-being. Grandfather rose stiffly from his chair and stood silently surveying the tiny apartment. "Too large it seems without you, Yacov," he muttered to no one. "Too empty. Too bleak."

He wandered past the boy's iron cot and paused to touch the pillow. How he longed to touch Yacov's brow and speak to him of the Torah! But the Old City was cut off from the New. The gates were blockaded by angry Arabs called in by the Mufti to guarantee that Jews who passed beyond the gates of the quarter did not return to their homes. The Mufti, it seemed, would starve the scholars and the rabbis from the Old City even though they, like him, were against the Zionist radicals who sought a homeland without the Messiah. "Come let us reason together..." Grandfather hummed. But he feared there was no reasoning left. He could only hope that Rebbe Akiva would be able to reach some sort of agreement with the Mufti that would enable life to resume some normality in the quarter. Then he would be able to travel to the hospital where Yacov lay.

Grandfather took his coat from the peg by the door. Slowly he pulled it on, feeling the fragile thinness of the worn fabric. His heart, too, was becoming thin and fragile. Yacov was all he had left, all he lived for—that and the hope of Messiah.

Ellie held Yacov's small, pale hand and toyed with the wrist identification bracelet. His head was swathed in bandages, and he had been silent for a long time after she told him why his grandfather was unable to come to visit him. She wondered if he had fallen asleep. Then he sighed and said quietly, "What about Shaul? Did you find him?"

Ellie looked painfully up at Moshe who stood at the foot of the boy's bed. Moshe cleared his throat and answered gently, "Perhaps he returned to the Old City. To your home."

"No," Yacov answered with tears in his voice. "I told him to wait at the butcher shop. He would wait."

"He could have gone back to your grandfather," Ellie interjected hopefully.

"He is most certainly dead if you did not find him where I said." The boy turned his head on his pillow and pulled his hand away. "I cannot see to read my prayers or the Torah," he said finally. "Shaul was just a dog, I know, but I will say Kaddish for him when I am well."

"You and Ellie were very lucky." Moshe reached out and touched Yacov's foot through the covers. "The Eternal was with you."

Helpless in the face of the boy's grief and loneliness, Ellie sat back in her chair and stared bleakly at his bandages. She could not tell him that perhaps he would never see clearly again; that almost certainly he had lost the vision of one eye and that the other was an uncertainty at this point.

"Mr. Sachar," said Yacov. "They say that you studied in Yeshiva. That you were almost a rabbi?"

"Who told you this?" Moshe smiled.

"The doctor who checks my eyes says that you are a great professor of the ancient languages for the Hebrew University."

"Ye'he sh'lomo rabbo min sh'mayo, ve'chaim oleynoo ve'al kol Yisroale, ve'imroo Omaine," said Moshe, then winked at Ellie.

"Omaine," repeated Yacov. Then after a pause he asked, "Then it is true? Will you help me say Kaddish for Shaul?"

"We do not know that he is dead, Yacov. Wait, boy. We do not know."

Yacov's small shoulders seemed to sink into the bed and the eagerness of his voice seemed to fade. "Will you help me with my prayers, then, before you leave? I cannot wear my yarmulke."

"The bandages will do for a head covering," Moshe sat beside him and patted his hand. "We will pray together."

Ellie stepped back and leaned against the windowsill and bowed her head self-consciously as Moshe and the little boy recited words that had been uttered by Jews since the days of

Moses. *Maybe it was not such a big step for Moshe from rabbi to archaeologist*, thought Ellie. As she listened to the ancient Hebrew tongue she felt vaguely uncomfortable and somehow distant from Moshe. This was a part of him that she was completely unfamiliar with. What other things about himself did he hold from her, she wondered, watching his broad shoulders rise and fall with the cadence of the prayers, and listening to his confident but tender voice. He belonged here in this land; she did not. She had begun to wonder if she belonged anywhere.

————

As Rabbi Lebowitz stepped into the chill of the evening air, he began to cough, the pain in his chest growing fierce. Tonight he would speak with Rebbe Akiva. He would ask him if it was not possible for such an old man to receive special permission to leave the confines of the quarter and return after a visit to his grandson. Perhaps Akiva could negotiate with the Mufti. Then he would see Yacov and be comforted.

Heaps of sandbags had begun to grow in front of homes and shops. The fear caused by the commercial district riot had boarded the windows and blockaded the streets of the Jewish Quarter. Grandfather had seen it before and remembered with a spark of hope, *Those bad days passed. Soon, so will these.* For now, though, bread would have to be rationed and the ritual baths closed for fear of a water shortage.

The gate into the courtyard of Akiva's residence was closed and locked. Grandfather rang the bell and waited for one of his daughters or a servant to answer. Only seconds passed, but the old man rang the bell again impatiently. From the far side of the thick stone wall, he heard a woman's voice call loudly, questioning what fool would be out alone on the streets at this hour. He recognized the voice of Yehudit, Akiva's daughter.

"It is I, Rabbi Lebowitz," he called. "I have urgent business with your father."

The hinges of the gate creaked as it swung slowly open.

"Shalom, Yehudit," he greeted the girl.

"Shalom, Rebbe Lebowitz. Are you well?" Her tone reflected genuine concern that the old man was out in the cold after dark.

"Well enough, thank God, amen," he answered, moving past her purposefully. "Your father is not engaged?"

"He is in the study, Rebbe Lebowitz. He studies the Prophets tonight." She opened the door and let the old man pass.

"A worthy pastime. Perhaps we shall find our answers there."

Yehudit knocked softly on the door to her father's study. "Father, Rebbe Lebowitz has come."

Grandfather heard the sound of a drawer closing; then the door swung open. Akiva's grim face and massive frame blocked the old man's view of the study. Akiva nodded his head and stepped aside, revealing bookshelves against every wall and a large desk with papers stacked like piles of fallen leaves.

"My friend," Akiva said without feeling as he took his arm and led him to a large leather chair. "Have you any word on your grandson? Are you well?"

"I have been better, Rebbe Akiva. And as for Yacov," the old man coughed. "Still no word on his condition."

Akiva circled around the desk and sat down in his chair, folding his hands across a stack of photographs that lay before him. "What can I help you with?" Akiva asked without warmth.

The old rabbi stared first at Akiva's sausage-like fingers, then at the photographs they rested on. With a start, he recognized them as the pictures of the scroll that the red-headed woman had shown him the day Yacov had gone with her. He tugged his beard a moment, then gazed at Akiva with astonishment.

"Forgive me, Rebbe Akiva," he said finally. "You are studying Isaiah, I see. You do not have a scroll of the prophet?"

Akiva leaned back and tapped at the stack of Ellie's scroll photographs with his fingers. "It is nothing. I have been asked to examine these. Photographs of a scroll possibly stolen from a genizah. The scroll itself is in the possession of an important citizen. Interesting, but hardly of merit."

"I have seen those very photographs, Rebbe Akiva. They were in the possession of the woman with whom my Yacov left. They are—"

Grandfather stopped speaking as he noticed Akiva's expression change to acute interest. "Go on, friend."

"Hardly of merit, as you say. . ." the old man finished, feeling vaguely uneasy. *How*, he wondered, *had Akiva come by them?*

"Exactly what I shall tell the owner of the scroll. Without merit . . ." he shrugged. "Well," he said, abruptly changing the subject. "We are making some headway in our negotiations, Rebbe Lebowitz. The Arab High Command and the British seem willing to help us if we are willing to make some minor concessions."

"That is what I came to speak with you about," said the old man, leaning forward in his chair. "Perhaps if I could see Yacov—"

"If we agree to forbid weapons in our quarter," Akiva interrupted, "the British will escort our people through the Arab Quarter. "Soon," he smiled, "you will be able to see your grandson, Reb Lebowitz."

Relief filled the old man and he raised his right hand slightly, "God be praised," he whispered.

"The Mufti knows that we are but poor scholars here," Akiva sniffed and tugged at his vest. "We have no need of Haganah or weapons in these streets."

"Well said, Rebbe Akiva. Well spoken. Come, let us reason together," Grandfather nodded.

"The Muslims are a reasonable people on the whole," Akiva said with authority. "The Mufti and I have dealt with such passions before. As always, the passions will die and we will live in peace." Akiva rose and walked to the door. He called loudly for Yehudit then and she came quickly, her eyes downcast. "Yehudit, can you not see that our friend is in need of tea?" he demanded. Yehudit nodded and disappeared down the hallway. Akiva turned to the old man then, his curiosity about the scrolls once more rising to the surface. "Now, about these photographs?" he smiled broadly.

Grandfather buried the suspicion he felt, instead telling himself that Akiva had given him good news and perhaps he would do well to return favor for favor by giving him information. "The shiksa, the red-haired woman brought them. She works for the American School of Oriental Research. They are goyim, and she had no knowledge of the Hebrew language. I read the passage to her from Isaiah—"

"What of the scroll itself?" Akiva interrupted, his eyes narrowing, and again Rabbi Lebowitz felt a vague uneasiness.

"She thought that perhaps it was ancient. She spoke of another as the owner. Possibly that the school might purchase it. I told her only what you have concluded: that it is taken from a genizah and probably worthless. Nu?"

"Just so." Akiva stared thoughtfully at the photographs, then looked up and smiled at the old man again. "Ah, but if it were indeed written by the hand of the ancients . . ." he paused. "A chest the size of this desk filled with pounds sterling would not touch the value of such a find."

"An unusual script, Rebbe Akiva, but I think the only thing of value would be the words that are written, not the scroll it is written upon."

"Perhaps." Akiva paused. "That is the view of a true scholar, Rebbe Lebowitz."

Yehudit brought a steaming pot of tea and served it in delicate china teacups. Grandfather gratefully drank the strong brew, feeling the warmth return to his body. *Rebbe Akiva is a truly great man*, he thought as they discussed the Torah together. *Who else could walk in the ways of peace and find an answer to the terrible threats that surrounded the quarter?* When at last the candle burned low and the old man threaded his way back home, thoughts of Ellie's photographs were dim in his mind. The anticipation of seeing Yacov kept him warm.

————

Howard Moniger adjusted the focus of the large microscope on the table. Carefully he examined a fragment of the scroll from the envelope Ellie had marked "Secret Code." Tiny rivulets and pores on its yellowed surface caused him to draw a deep astonished breath.

"What is it?" Moshe asked, drawing nearer.

Howard looked up, raised his eyebrows, and stepped aside for Moshe to take his place at the lens. "Have a look for yourself."

Moshe sat on the stool and peered in at the magnified fragment. "It is leather," he said simply. "It is leather, not parchment. Howard, do you know what this could mean?" He could hardly take his eyes away from the microscope, and when at last he looked up, Howard was trembling with excitement.

"She said that the old rabbi told her it was the complete book of Isaiah." Howard shook his head in amazement. "If it means what I think it means . . ."

"It could well be the most important find of our century, Howard!" Moshe finished. "Thank God she has the negatives of the photographs. When she feels well enough, we'll have her make up another set, eh?"

"She's at it right now, Moshe," Howard laughed. "Back in the lab."

Eerily surrounded by memories of all that had transpired since she had first developed the pictures of the scroll, Ellie watched the strange letters appear on the blank paper in the developing tray. She rinsed the final prints and hung them carefully to dry, then went to work on the roll of film she had taken on the day of the riot.

From negative to print took only a few minutes; print by print she retraced her trip through the Old City to Yacov's door, then out the Jaffa Gate. The face of Hassan glared back at her from the tray, causing her to shudder involuntarily; finally, the anguished tailor cried out as the curved blade of the murderer's knife plunged into his back.

She rinsed the prints and tried to look at them with the objectivity of a professional photographer. "The policeman is a bit fuzzy. Forgivable with all the smoke and jostling. But the murder—an incredible shot," she said. Then a sadness swept over her and she looked away quickly and snapped on the light. It was all reality, not simply an act staged for the benefit of her camera. The memory of the screams crowded into her mind, and once again she felt a wave of nausea. She groped for her stool and sat down, dropping her head to her knees. Her stomach had just begun to settle when there was a soft knock on the door.

"You about finished?" Uncle Howard called through the door.

"Almost," she said, trying to sound cheerful. "Don't open the door for a second." She sat up and took a deep breath, careful not to look at the tailor. "Okay, come in," she said, forcing a smile.

Like excited children on Christmas morning, Moshe and Howard opened the door, then froze dumbfounded at the rows of photographs.

Howard let out a low whistle and put his arm around Ellie, who sat pale and shaken on the stool next to him. "What do you think?" he asked Moshe who caressed the images with his eyes.

"Beautiful. The letters drip like honey from the rule lines. I have not ever seen anything quite like it." He looked up at Ellie in admiration. "You have done well, my little shiksa." He touched her face tenderly and bent to kiss her forehead, but

131

she stiffened and stood suddenly, moving back to her worktable and the prints of the riot in the rinsing tray. Moshe stood behind her, his hand on her shoulder. His jaw tensed with anger as he took in the face of Hassan and then the tailor as he screamed and died. Smoke and fire and cries of anguish seemed to fill the room. Howard's gaze followed Moshe's as Ellie turned away and gazed blankly out the door of the darkroom into the lighted lab beyond.

"You saw this," Howard said heavily, feeling as though he had been kicked in the gut. "Dear God, Ellie! You were in the middle of it!"

"I thought I'd send that picture someplace." She struggled to sound matter-of-fact, trying to dismiss their concern as if the riot had been an everyday occurrence. "Maybe *Life* magazine or someplace." She pushed past them both and stalked out of the lab, leaving them to stare at the photographs.

"Are you okay, my friend?" Howard sensed how deeply Moshe seemed to be affected by the pictures. Moshe did not answer; instead, he turned away and followed Ellie into the lab.

"You are right," he said, gently touching her hair. "These pictures must be seen. We are sending fragments of the scroll to New York for analysis. Your photographs must accompany them." He lowered his voice. "Truly you are a remarkable woman." He kissed her trembling lips, then walked down the hall to the study.

Uncle Howard leaned against the stainless steel table and fixed a steady gaze on Ellie. "Are you all right, child?" he asked tenderly.

Ellie nodded. "Sure."

"Sure?" he asked again.

"I guess I just . . ." she began haltingly, choking back a flood of tears that wanted to escape. "I feel so empty. I've been living in some kind of fairy tale, Uncle Howard. I never watched a man die before, you know. Death is so—" She stopped, unable to find the words.

"Real."

"I saw it. I felt it follow me from rooftop to rooftop. It chased me. It scared me. I'm not ready for it, and nobody who died down on that street was ready for it or expected it."

Howard walked toward her and put his arms around her. She leaned her head against his chest and tears began to flow silently from her eyes. "There, there," he wiped the tears away.

"Aren't you scared, Uncle Howard?" she asked in a little girl voice.

"No, dear. Every day I piece together the fragments of someone's life. No matter that they lived in the first century—they were alive, like you and me. I live with death's reality, but I'm not afraid of it. God says our lifetime is not much more than a breath of wind. In all of eternity we are a tiny second, the blink of God's eye. Still, He sees us and cares for us. And He's got a reason for our being here."

Ellie pushed herself away. "How can you believe that? What possible purpose could that little man's death serve? And what difference could it make that I be there?"

"I don't know, Ellie. And I'm not saying that God caused this to happen. Men did. But I'm going to pray that somehow what seems so wrong and senseless now will be used for some purpose." He rubbed his forehead wearily. "It all sounds so trite, doesn't it?"

She looked away, avoiding his gaze. "I don't know. I just have to think where I fit in all of this."

"I'm sorry, honey. I wouldn't have asked you to come if I had known you'd have to see any of this. I'll see to it that you get back to California as soon as possible."

She laughed sarcastically. "Back to the real world?"

"Back where you are safe. I think it's best."

"One thing about me, Uncle Howard, I've always managed to play it safe. I just didn't know there was any other game."

"I feel responsible," he said, shaking his head.

"It's nobody's fault but my own. But I can't believe that God or somebody has some kind of plan for my being here, either. I'll make my own plans and learn to live with them, that's all." She walked slowly out of the room, the face of the tailor vivid in her mind.

13 Moshe and David

Moshe did not look up from the microscope when Ellie entered the study. He continued to gaze with unseeing eyes at the pattern on the leather fragment. Everything else seemed of little importance after seeing the face of Ibrahim Hassan staring up at him from Ellie's developing tray. He only hoped that the rage he felt did not give away the fact that he did indeed know the identity of the gap-toothed policeman. But why had Ellie been the target of his brutal pursuit?

He sighed deeply, inhaling her fragrance as she stood silently behind him. Her association with him had brought her under the scrutiny of a man like Hassan, and that realization made her seem suddenly more dear to him, as vulnerable as a child.

A dull ache throbbed between his shoulder blades and crept up to the back of his head. He sat up straight and moved his head from side to side, trying to loosen the tension that gripped him.

"Headache?" Ellie asked, rubbing her fingers gently on his temples.

"Hmmm," he answered. "The back of my neck."

"Are you okay, Moshe?" she asked, sensing his uneasiness.

"I think you should return to the United States," he said to her as she massaged his neck with her fingers.

"You too?" she smiled. "Why?"

"It is not safe for you here." He turned and lifted his eyes to hers.

"There's that lovely word again. Safe."

"Anyone would be a fool who did not value safety, Ellie."

"And you're no fool, are you, Moshe?" There was an irritated push to her voice that startled him, then made him smile. "That's what I like about you, you know," she continued. "You're so in focus, so safe. I mean, you've grown up around stuff like this, haven't you? Riots? Beatings?"

"It has been a fact of life here in Jerusalem."

Something clicked inside Ellie and her irritation swelled to disdain. "And what do you do about it?"

"I simply live."

"With your books and scrolls and precious clay tablets. While people are suffering and dying, you're safe!"

Moshe smiled. "As long as it does not affect one's life, is it necessary to be anything else?"

"I don't know," she said angrily. "I have to figure that out. But I'll tell you, Moshe, you're a Jew. You grew up here, and never once have you talked to me about politics or this Mufti or the Jews coming out of those horrible places in Europe. All you care about is that I got pictures of that scroll, and that I'm safe. I can't figure out how you can grow up here and not care at all. At least I have an excuse. I mean, I'm from Los Angeles." He laughed at her final sentence, and she wished she hadn't mentioned L.A. "Go ahead and laugh," she said.

"What are you saying?" He reached out and took her hand. She pulled it away and sat down in the chair farthest away from him.

"I don't know yet. But maybe my idea of what I respect in a man is changing. Maybe what I can respect about myself is changing."

"Ellie, I . . ." Moshe wanted to tell her of his other life; about the *Ave Maria* and his years with the Haganah. But he remembered his sacred vow of secrecy and paused, frowning as he turned back toward the microscope. "The work you did on the scrolls is very fine," he said finally.

"Is that all you care about?" she asked quietly. His silence was her answer. She stood abruptly and glared at his back as he sat hunched over the microscope. *He is a man without conviction,* she thought, *without courage.* "Maybe we shouldn't see each other for a while, Moshe. Socially, I mean. Not until I decide what I'm going to do."

Moshe gripped the edge of the table, wanting to grab her and hold her to himself and tell her everything he felt and believed and that the depth of his convictions forced him to silence. Instead, he nodded and said quietly, "Whatever you think is best."

Ellie stalked out, certain that Moshe did not even care for her. She went straight to her room and slammed the door loudly behind her as if making some final statement. Then she threw herself across her bed and took her alarm clock off the night

135

table. It was only seven in the evening, and she suddenly felt like a jailed prisoner. She could not leave the house, and with Moshe out there, she did not want to leave the room. If she had to look at him too soon, her anger and resolve might melt away beneath the steady gaze of his ebony eyes. She wanted to enjoy her anger, to hate him for his apathy, to blame him for his complacency. It was much easier than sorting through the other emotions that assaulted her, pushing and crowding out all the self-images she had clung to so fiercely.

She thought about David then. Where had he gone? He had been with her at the hospital, she remembered that. What comfort she had felt as he stroked her hair! It had not been a dream or a hallucination; after she had awakened she had asked Uncle Howard about him, and received a note scrawled in David's cramped handwriting. Ellie took it from the nightstand and read it for the hundredth time:

Wish I could be the first face you see when you open your eyes. I'll be back in a few days and we'll go dancing. D.

The certainty of his words had frightened her. She was not at all sure that she should see him when and if he did call. After all, she had only just begun to walk through a day without thinking of him.

———

Ellie sat up at the soft knock on her door.

"It's open," she said, winding her alarm clock. Miriam poked her face through the door and frowned.

"You are for bed?" she asked. "That young man who comes the other day is here for you. I shall tell him you are for bed."

"Don't tell him that!" Ellie shot back, imagining David's response to Miriam's broken English. "Do you mean David Meyer, Miriam?"

"Yes, yes," Miriam repeated. "The very same David. You will see him when Professor Sachar is here?" she whispered hoarsely.

"Yes. Tell him I'll be out in a few minutes."

Miriam shook her head in disapproval and ducked back out, muttering in Arabic.

Ellie freshened her makeup, feeling a vague sense of satisfaction that her two suitors would meet. "It never hurts to keep a man guessing," she murmured, running a brush through her hair. She smiled her most winning smile into the mirror, then, spraying herself with lilac, went to greet David.

He was standing as she entered the parlor, hat in hand. Inhaling deeply, he took a step toward her and reached out to take her in his arms. "Gee, you smell terrific," he said.

She stepped out of his grasp and said coolly, "It's good to see you again, David. What brings you to Jerusalem?"

"Don't play games with me, Ellie," he demanded, stepping toward her. "Not after the other day."

"I don't know what you're talking about." She sat down and crossed her legs. "Have a seat." She pointed to a chair on the other side of a coffee table from hers.

He plopped down angrily. "That smoke must have given you brain damage. You don't remember all the stuff you said to me?"

Ellie felt a blush color her cheeks. "No, David, I honestly don't. That was hardly the time or the occasion." She stopped. "Listen, I'm glad you came along when you did. I'm grateful. But my life is not the same as it was before. I don't know that I want to be involved."

"It's that other guy, isn't it?" he demanded.

"Things are not the same, David. I don't know why you're here, but I'm grown up now. If you're looking for a good time, I'm sure there are plenty of—"

"I wanted to see you—that's why I'm here. You're not the only one who can change, you know. Let's go home, babe. Let's get out of here and back to where we belong."

"Where *do* we belong?" Her response carried a trace of irritation. She didn't like being called *babe*, and she was put out by his possessive attitude.

"I don't know about you, but I'm kind of partial to Frisco. We can work out the details later. I just want to get you out of here, okay?"

"Why?"

"Because I—" He wanted to tell her he loved her, but the words stuck in his throat. He had been able to say it to that Moshe fellow as she lay unconscious in the hospital. *Why,* he wondered, *is it so hard with her sitting up wide awake and beautiful across from me?* "Listen," he changed his approach, "I could use a few laughs tonight. How about my offer?"

"You mean the note? About taking me dancing? I thought it was a summons," she said coolly.

She always had a way of making him irritated faster than any other woman he had ever been with. "No. It was a question. Do you want to go dancing or not?"

Moshe walked by in the hallway behind David and looked in as he made his way to the front door. Ellie caught his eye, then turned back toward David. "I'd love to go dancing with you, David."

Moshe stepped quickly out of her view, hoping that she did not see the pang of jealousy on his face.

"Great!" David exclaimed.

"Just a minute," she said a bit too loudly as she rose and walked toward the hallway. "I'll let Uncle Howard know we're going. Where are we going? The King David?"

David couldn't understand the sudden change of heart, but he was relieved all the same. "Sure. They've got a nice little band there," he called after her, unaware that she had followed Moshe.

"Going so soon, Moshe?" she asked, stepping out the front door? "I would have thought that you and Uncle Howard would be up all night talking about the scroll."

Moshe did not answer her, but reached around and closed the door behind her. He searched her face and raised his hand to her cheek. "I can understand your lack of respect for me right now. But it is not like you to toy with a man's heart. Be careful, my love—things are not always as they seem."

Ellie felt a rush of shame at the game she was playing with this gentle and loving scholar. "Moshe," she said haltingly, "I . . . we need to talk. Will you call me?"

"I am leaving the city for a while. University business. We are sending the fragments out—along with your photographs." He held a package up. "Your friend . . . David, is it not? He will likely be flying me to Tel Aviv in the morning."

"You know him?" she asked, astonished.

"We met briefly at the hospital," Moshe answered, careful not to mention the first time he had met David in the Old Man's office.

"When will you be back?" She looked him full in the face, noticing the way the streetlamps cast shadows that emphasized his rugged good looks. She suddenly did not want him to go.

"A week, possibly. I hope no more than that. We shall talk then, my little shiksa." He bent low and kissed her on the lips, gently at first. Then he pulled her tight against him and searched her face with a passion in his eyes that she had not seen before. "Perhaps you are more Sabra than you know," he whispered; then he kissed her again with a force that left her feeling weak against her will.

"That felt more like hello than good-bye," she said breathlessly, pushing away from his embrace.

"I will bring you a surprise when I return." He turned and strode briskly toward the lights of King George Avenue as she looked after him from the front step.

David and Uncle Howard were talking quietly together when she returned to the front room. Uncle Howard looked up at her, then stood with the politeness of a man raised in a more courteous age. David, she noted, remained seated. A frown creased his brow and she guessed that Uncle Howard had told him Moshe had been here only moments before.

"Seeing Moshe out, were you, child?" Uncle Howard asked. "David thought you had gone in search of me."

"Moshe is leaving in the morning," she said, ignoring the pout on David's face. "I didn't know."

"And did he tell you where he was going?" Howard cast a quick glance toward David, who did not look up.

"Something about the university," answered Ellie, wondering about the tone of Uncle Howard's voice. "Didn't he tell you?"

"Yes, he told me." His eyes were still fixed on David as if waiting for a reaction.

David stood and zipped his flight jacket. "If we're going to have any time before curfew, we'd better get going," he abruptly changed the subject. "Good to see you again, Professor."

"Of course, of course. You'll be at the King David Hotel, then?" He walked them to the door. "Things seem quiet enough tonight, don't they?" The jovial tone had returned to Uncle Howard's voice. "I'll wait up for you," he said as he helped Ellie on with her coat.

"Don't do that, Uncle Howard," Ellie protested.

"Nonsense. I have work to do, regardless." Then he turned to David and said solemnly, "I expect you will not want to be late either, seeing that you will be flying early tomorrow." Uncle Howard seemed to search David's face knowingly. Ellie felt as though she were on the outside of a conversation in which every line had a double meaning.

"For heaven's sake," she kissed Uncle Howard lightly on the cheek and took David by the arm, "let's get going."

David led her to an old green Plymouth parked across the street and opened the door for her. As she stooped to get in, she was met by a barrage of wet and lavish dog kisses on her face. There, in the front seat, whining and shaking with delight, was Shaul.

She wrapped her arms around his shaggy ruff and pulled the big dog onto her lap, laughing with surprise and joy. "Oh, Shaul!" she cried, "you mutt! Where have you been?"

David slid in behind the wheel. "He's been sharing a one-room apartment with me and Michael," he said wryly, cranking the engine. "I'm evicting him. Think you can put him up?"

"Where did you find him?" She squealed in amazement as Shaul nuzzled closer to her.

"At the butcher shop. Just where you told me he'd be. I'm so glad this is the right dog. I thought maybe I'd picked up the wrong mutt or something. I had a terrible time getting him into the car. It took me and Michael both. I almost gave up on him, but I looked at him and I thought I had seen him someplace before. 'You know,' I said to Michael, 'that looks like the same mutt that ran off with your wallet at the celebration. And I bet Yacov is the kid that picked your pocket!' So Michael went into the butcher shop and came out with some corned beef, put it into the backseat, and the dog went for it. I think he hopes the boy will give him back his wallet if he gives back the dog."

Ellie stared in wonder at the wide grin on David's face. "But how did you find him?" she asked again.

"You told me where he was. At the hospital. You don't remember?" He turned onto King George Avenue and headed toward the Hotel.

"No, I really don't."

David pursed his lips and frowned. "You said a lot of other things to me, too. I guess I'm going to have to remind you."

Her eyes filled with tears of joy as she thought of Yacov in the hospital and how happy he would be to hear that his shaggy friend was safe. Ellie reached out and put her hand on David's arm. "You are wonderful. Wonderful."

"Yeah, now it's coming back to you," he smiled at her. "Remember anything else?" He raised his eyebrows in happy expectation.

Ellie felt her heart swell with tenderness for David. He was, as he had always been, so eager to be loved and admired. And it was not difficult for her to do either. "I remember," she began haltingly, "that you were there. Somehow it was your voice I heard in the darkest moment of my life."

He cleared his throat self-consciously. "Yeah, well, I'd like to be part of your happiest moments, too, y'know?"

Ellie stroked Shaul's head and weighed each thought and emotion carefully. "You have already been that, David. I love you," she said softly. "But I don't know if I am *in* love with you anymore."

"I can take care of that." His voice was husky and his words full of memories.

"That's what scares me. I don't know if I want to go back, David. I've had time to think about us and there was so much that wasn't right. I have been happy here."

"It's that Moshe guy, isn't it?" The joy dropped from his voice.

"Partly—maybe. I just don't know." She glanced up in time to see that they had passed the massive stone structure of the King David Hotel. "What are you doing?"

"Just driving," he answered, turning back past the Jewish Agency building and then onto Ellie's street in Rehavia. They passed the Moniger home without stopping, then drove on another five minutes in silence until David passed two men on guard near a pile of sandbags. He stopped the car at the edge of what appeared to be a plowed field across from the Monastery of the Cross, set the hand brake, and sat staring straight ahead into the darkness for a moment. Then he turned toward her. "I want to tell you something," he said awkwardly. Then he stopped as if choosing his words carefully. In the darkness she could hear the ticking of his wristwatch.

"David, I think we should go," she said finally.

"Not yet. Please. Come with me." He got out of the car and came around to open her door. She continued to sit, feeling uncomfortable at the air of mystery in David's voice. "Please, Ellie." She got out reluctantly and he led her by the hand across the field to a small shed. He unlocked its double doors and swung them wide, then flicked a switch, dimly lighting both the shed and the field. Inside was a tiny blue and white airplane.

"Help me push her out," said David, grabbing a wing.

"Why? What are you doing, David?" Ellie allowed the irritation she felt to creep into her voice.

He rolled the plane onto the field as she stood and watched. "Come on," he opened the cockpit door for her. "I want to show you where I live." He smiled in the soft light, and against her better judgment she climbed in. David started the sputtering little engine and taxied a few feet before rattling down the bumpy runway so slowly that Ellie did not believe they would ever get off the ground. Suddenly, in a rush that flipped her stomach, they lifted off and began the slow climb that took them over Mount Scopus and the now-sleeping Hadassah Hospital. David banked the plane and swept over the King David Hotel, then continued to climb until the lights of the city winked up at them like tiny stars. Ellie gazed out the cockpit window at the millions of stars above them. David looked at her and grinned.

"This is where I live," he said finally. "Here I am King David. How do you like my kingdom?"

The soft glow of the instrument panel shone on his face, and Ellie realized that there was something different about his expression. She had never seen him like this before. "It is very beautiful," she said matter-of-factly. "You know, you've never taken me flying before."

David pointed to a tiny cluster of lights on the black velvet below them. "Bethlehem," he said. "The way the angels must have seen it the night Christ was born. No guns. No anger. Nobody hating anybody else. Peace on earth. At least that's the way it looks from up here." He turned to her with tenderness lighting his eyes. "I wanted you to see the world like that tonight because I want to tell you, Ellie—" he paused, groping for the words. "I want you to know, I want to spend my life with you." He gulped, then quickly looked away from her steady gaze.

"You've never said that to me before. Thank you," she said, privately wondering if he had said it too late, if it really mattered anymore. "You can say it up here, where the world is so distant. It all looks so beautiful. But it isn't. The reality is that down there people are standing in line to wipe each other off the face of the earth." She motioned toward the broad glitter of the Milky Way. "This is beautiful, David, but you can't live up here. Sooner or later your little plane has to come down. If this is the only place you feel really alive, then I can't join you. If you can't tell me you love me when we are both standing flat-footed on the asphalt, then maybe what you feel for me isn't real love." She turned her head away from him and stared at the tiny lights of an automobile as it crept through the streets of Jerusalem. "I'm sorry," she said feeling suddenly confused and foolish. "I don't understand what's wrong with me. I've wrecked your big moment, haven't I?"

"It's okay," he answered quietly. "I had it coming. Things haven't exactly been normal for you the last few days."

Ellie wondered if anything would ever be the same for her again. "It's just that I never knew before . . ." Again a rush of sadness choked off her words.

"It's okay," he reassured her, furious at himself that he had not waited until the shock of her ordeal had worn off. "I don't know what I expected, coming to Palestine like this."

"Why did you come, David?" she asked, as the plane dipped low above the city.

"I came for you," he said simply.

———

As Ellie climbed beneath the cool sheets she thought about Moshe hiding from commitment behind his ancient writings and David trapped between the Milky Way and the tiny twinkling lights of earth. Maybe she had been trapped, too. The reality of life simply did not measure up to her hopes and illusions. Hot tears ran down her cheeks, and she wished that somehow the soft, peaceful lights of the heavens and the winking stars of Jerusalem could melt together as one heaven and earth. "But that's not going to happen," she whispered into the darkness.

She thought about Uncle Howard then—so full of peace and joy; so certain of his life. "God," she said at last, "can you see me?"

Somewhere in the distance, the popping of gunfire raked the stillness of the night. Ellie reached down to stroke the head of the big dog, then slipped into an uneasy sleep.

14   The Hadassah Plot

Silently Hassan nursed the short brown stub of his Turkish cigarette. He inhaled the harsh smoke and tapped his cheek lightly, watching with satisfaction as a string of tiny smoke rings popped from his lips, then drifted into the lobby in ever-expanding O's. It was a trick he had learned from a tall blond lieutenant when they attended Nazi S.S. Commando school together. Hassan glanced at the face of his German-made watch. It was already 6:15; Gerhardt was late. Residents of the Hotel Semiramis, in the suburb of Katamon, scurried through the lobby on their way to and from dinner.

From the worn red-velvet chair in the corner, Hassan studied their faces as they stopped at the mahogany desk to check with the small, bespectacled manager for messages. Some, he guessed, were Arabs who had lived in the second-story flats above the shops of the Jewish commercial district. When the district had burned, they had fled to the safety of Hotel Semiramis with its potted palms and worn red floral carpets and cheap monthly rates. Here, in the heart of a pleasantly mixed Arab and Jewish neighborhood on the outskirts of the raging fanaticism of the all-Muslim quarters, and the burning Zionism of an all-Jewish district, no doubt they felt safe. There was moderation in Katamon. After all, Jews and Arabs lived side by side here.

Hassan smiled to himself at the innocence of these Christian Arabs. Haj Amin had marked the peaceful neighborhood of Katamon for his own. Soon Gerhardt would come, and the hotel would become the assembly plant for his packages of TNT and the clever letter bombs that tore the hands from anyone unfortunate enough to open one. Then there were the big surprises that Haj Amin and Gerhardt had planned for Jewish Jerusalem. In a small, neatly furnished suite overlooking the street, every detail would be planned to perfection. Far from being the refuge of the Christian Arab middle-class, the hotel had become the headquarters of the Mufti's terrorist activities.

A large group of men and women burst through the double

doors, two old women bundled tightly in shawls followed by grown sons and daughters and a host of little ones. A tall stoop-shouldered man in a tweed suit stopped and rang the desk bell, then leaned on the counter as the rest of the group clustered in front of the wrought-iron grate of the elevator. Two small boys haggled over the right to push the elevator button as the two old women talked above their heads. Hassan had no illusions that the battles about to be fought would be fought for their benefit. No, all would be won for the glory of Haj Amin Husseini, Mufti of Jerusalem and future ruler of the united land of Palestine. Haj Amin was a name these people feared, and in the end, they would be the ones who would lose. They were Arabs, yes, but their kind would be gone before the final line was written. In the end it made little difference.

Hassan gasped and turned as he felt an iron grip on the shoulder. The grim face of Gerhardt stared down on him. He wore the same heavy tweed coat he had worn the night they had been seen by the girl and the little boy. A broad-rimmed fedora was pulled low over the cruel steely gaze of his ice-blue eyes. "Well, my friend," he said softly. "Are you ready to finish the job you left undone?"

Casually, Hassan inhaled the cigarette one last time, then flicked the ash onto the carpet and crushed out the red-hot tip with his fingers. He dropped the remaining stub in the shirt pocket of his police uniform. "The boy is still at Hadassah—an easy target. I thought perhaps we might have a bite to eat before we finish him."

"You can eat later," Gerhardt growled.

"Why the impatience, my friend?" Hassan rose and faced him as he pulled on his coat.

"It is the impatience of Haj Amin that I should worry about, were I you." Gerhardt smiled grimly and turned toward the stairway leaving Hassan without an appetite.

The night was cold and the stars hung like fragments of ice against the sky. Hassan pulled the collar of his overcoat up around his ears and wished that he had stolen an enclosed vehicle rather than this open jeep.

He passed through the Arab neighborhood of Sheikh Jarrah at the foot of Mount Scopus. He felt a sense of satisfaction as he looked at the blazing lights of Hadassah Hospital atop Scopus. He would be able, he was sure, to finish his assignment, then fade into the anonymity of Sheikh Jarrah before the last drop of the boy's blood had spilled onto the floor.

He shifted into first gear as he rounded the last curve before the climb up Mount Scopus. Commanding the highest ground in the area, the hospital and the Hebrew University would certainly be a Jewish stronghold in the days ahead. But, Hassan noted with satisfaction, their locations deep inside Arab suburbs would make them easy enough to strangle. He would mention it to the Mufti when he reported the final disposal of the little Jew witness.

He glanced at his watch—nearly seven o'clock. He pulled into the parking lot of the hospital and parked in a restricted area reserved for official cars. No one would notice the army jeep there among so many others. He set the brake, then ran his hand quickly along the side of his leg to his boot top and the narrow handle of the dagger hidden there. *All in all*, he thought, *this should not take more than a few minutes*. He hopped from the jeep and strode purposefully past a British guard who saluted smartly when he touched the brim of his hat.

It was still early when he passed through the doors of the hospital's main entrance. Perhaps there was even time for a quick cup of coffee in the cafeteria to warm his hands after the drive through the chill night air.

The crowd in the first floor hospital cafeteria had thinned considerably. Hassan sat in the far corner across from a group of three buxom nurses who gossiped and giggled throughout their break.

Hassan took a last bite of strudel and slurped down his coffee, cursing Gerhardt for the urgency with which he had sent him to finish off the little Jew. *I would have had time*, he thought glumly, *to eat a good meal*. The lights in the rooms were only now winking out as shifts of doctors and nurses came and went. He scraped the tasteless cafeteria food to the side of his plate and stacked the silverware and coffee cup on top. Then he left the sterile room for the now nearly empty lobby. He considered taking the elevator to the fifth floor, but thought better of it, certain that some sharp-eyed nurse would stop him at her station.

He pushed a heavy swinging door marked "STAIRWAY" and began the slow climb to the pediatric ward, room 529, where the boy rested. His footsteps echoed loudly in the stairwell; once a nurse pushed open a door on the floor above him and skipped past him on her way down.

"I hate waiting for that elevator," she said cheerily.

Hassan nodded and tipped his hat but said nothing in reply.

He hoped the boy would be sleeping soundly. It would certainly make his task easier. A quick slash of the knife and, like the Jewish butchers said, Yacov Lebowitz would be dead the kosher way—his blood draining painlessly and silently from his body.

———————

From a small glass porthole reinforced with wire, Hassan watched as a nurse rattled down the dimly lit corridor with a metal cart full of medication. He stared at the large red numbers and the arrows on the wall pointing the way to the little Jew's room. Rooms 520 to 529 were to his left opposite the direction the nurse had taken. He smiled at the wave of excitement he felt; then he bent and touched the handle of his knife once again.

He pushed the door open a crack and watched with satisfaction as the nurse disappeared around a corner. Soft light reflected on the shiny floor in front of the nurses' station. Hassan was out of the view of the nurse who sat behind the large desk flipping through the pages of a magazine.

He slipped from the stairwell into the corridor, careful not to let the leather soles of his boots squeak on the freshly scrubbed tiles. He walked close to the wall, passing rooms smelling of antiseptic and urine, cursing the fact that 529 was at the very end of the hall. A child swathed in white moaned as he passed the open door of room 525. He glanced in at the bars around the bed and imagined first the red blood of Yacov Lebowitz soaking the sheets and then panic that would echo through this hallway when the deed of Ibrahim El Hassan was discovered with the first light of morning. He wished that he could be on hand to watch, and even toyed with the idea of returning to the hospital in the morning.

The wooden door of room 529 was closed. Hassan gingerly pushed it open, knowing that the boy's eyes were bandaged and that he would not be awakened by the light. A cruel smile danced across his lips, and he felt intoxicated as he slipped the knife from his boot top and tiptoed into the room.

Then his smile faded. There before him in the darkness was not the bed of one small Jewish child, but twenty beds occupied by twenty sleeping children. He turned with a gasp, bumping his arm hard on a large metal crib. His knife clattered to the floor, and a child cried out at the noise. Hassan backed up behind the door in anticipation of a nurse scuttling into the room. Beads of sweat formed on his brow and trickled down his temples into his collar. Slowly, his eyes began to adjust to the semidarkness, and when no nurse appeared and the only sound was the steady breathing of the children, he allowed himself to relax and step forward. He would, he decided, simply search the sleeping faces.

He tiptoed to the first bed, then turned away immediately as he noticed a small leg encased in plaster and raised upwards in traction. The next bed held a little girl whose long dark hair fanned over the pillow. As he peered down at her she moaned and thrashed as if sensing something evil was near. He stepped away, brushing the foot of her bed with his fingers. "Two," he counted wordlessly. Then he lowered his face close to the pillow of the next child, his breath causing the little one to turn away. There were no bandages on this child's eyes, and Hassan crept stealthily to the next. Before him was the tiny form of a child whose head was swathed in bandages. He was in luck, he felt, and toyed with the blade of the knife before he raised the limp arm to check the identification band.

"I want a drink of water," said a sleepy voice. Hassan dropped the arm and raised his knife to strike.

"What is your name, boy?" Hassan whispered softly.

"Michael. I want a drink."

"Shut up," Hassan whispered menacingly. "Where does Yacov Lebowitz sleep?"

"On the end," came the whimpered reply.

Hassan straightened himself and, touching the foot of each bed as he passed, stole to the bed on the end, nearest the window. There in the light and shadow of the city lights, he could make out the dim figure of Yacov.

"I came for you," he said with a cruel edge to his voice. Then he touched the neck of his victim and raised his knife to strike.

The child he had awakened cried out loudly, and Hassan hesitated a moment.

Then Yacov awakened with a start and bolted upright. "Shaul!" he cried loudly. "Shaul!"

In an instant the ward was a mass of crying children. Hassan backed against the window, then as the door was flung open and the harsh lights of the ward flicked on, he smashed the window and lunged onto the fire escape. He clambered down the tiny steel ladder to the second floor balcony, then opened the window and slipped into the darkness of a deserted room. He sprinted toward the door and into the hallway, then ran to the emergency stairs, smashing into the same nurse who had greeted him only a few minutes before.

As he reached the lobby floor, he paused barely a second, then strode out quickly. "There's a terrorist on the fifth floor!" he cried to a group of British soldiers. As they ran toward the stairs and elevator, he walked calmly out to the stolen jeep and disappeared into the streets of Sheikh Jarrah.

15 The Haganah

Moshe paced the length of the Old Man's office, glancing from time to time at the white head bowed over the stack of photographs.

"And you think the girl is trustworthy?" Ben-Gurion said at last.

"Beyond doubt," Moshe said without hesitation.

"An American journalist as a member of the Haganah would be helpful, to say the least." He took his glasses from his nose and rubbed a hand across his eyes. "Then approach her. Cautiously. But do speak with her. There is only one way the world will hear our voice, that is if someone else shouts our cause." He thumped the photographs. "I see your old friend Ibrahim Hassan was a part of the riot."

"You are surprised?"

"Perhaps we should take you out of Jerusalem for a while?

Another assignment? How would you feel about a few weeks' travel in Europe? Arms Procurement."

"Leave the travel to Arazi. I am Palestinian; even more, I am from the dust of Jerusalem. I can deal with Hassan."

"What about the woman, Miss Warne? Have you considered her safety?" The Old Man leaned back in his chair and eyed Moshe knowingly.

"I have thought of nothing else for days." Moshe sat heavily in the chair opposite him.

"You feel strongly about her, then?"

Moshe nodded, "Unfortunately. I am certain to lose her if I do not tell her of my involvement." He stared miserably at the map of Palestine hanging behind the Old Man. "She has become committed to the cause, you see, and suddenly holds the Moshe Sachar she knows in contempt."

"Well, then, she would find a way to stay even without you, wouldn't she? Of course you could lose her. As she could lose you; as we have each lost someone in this bitter struggle. But that is a chance you must take."

"She is not yet sure what it is that has changed in her heart. She does not know what has awakened, but I saw it in her eyes: She has become one of us."

"Then you must let her be what God has made her. You must accept the risk or destroy what you feel in your heart for her. Listen to an old man, my young friend. There is always risk in love, nu?"

"I have not spoken to her of love," Moshe said, looking down at his shoes, then back at the unrelenting gaze of David Ben-Gurion.

"Ha!" the Old Man exclaimed. "And you are worried that she will think you lack commitment!" he said sarcastically. "Perhaps she is right, eh?"

"I had not thought of it like that." Moshe scratched his head and stood. "Perhaps you are right."

"Perhaps." The Old Man waved his hand. "And as for these other matters, which seem less important than the heart"—he passed his hand over the piles of papers that cluttered his desk—"they are in God's hands. I know that God promised all of Palestine to the children of Israel. I do not know what borders He set. I believe that they were wider than the ones proposed. If God will keep His promise in His own time, our business as poor humans who live in a difficult age is to save as much as we can of the remnant of Israel. That means that for now, Moshe, we must smuggle in a different cargo than we have in the past. We will not last a week without defense to hold our ground." He gazed seriously at Moshe, who had begun to pace once again. "Sit down, will you?" He sounded irritated. Moshe resumed his seat and stared at a smaller map of Jerusalem to the right of Ben-Gurion. "You are reading my mind, maybe? What about Jerusalem?"

Moshe smiled grimly. "I have spent the week speaking with area commanders. We have a very short supply of weapons and ammunition hidden in the New City. The Old City seems hopeless. Hopeless," he said again.

"The very word Shimon used. So what is the situation?"

"We have ten men inside the walls. Yeshiva students—determined but untrained. There arc only fourteen rifles, antiques from the First World War, hidden in a cellar wall there, with enough ammunition for possibly three rounds each, if the boys even know how to fire the guns."

"And the civilians?"

"Already the Mufti has made it impossible for them to pass into the New City. There are 2,500 ultra-orthodox inside those walls. They depend on this agency for their food, but there is no possible way that we can deliver anything to them," Moshe frowned.

"Are you suggesting then that we begin by evacuating the Old City?"

"They are like lambs in the midst of lions."

"In the end time, lambs will lie down with lions. Even then I will want to be a lion, I think. I am asking you for an opinion. What is to be done?" The Old Man glared at him.

"Strategically, the Old City is a waste of time. We will have enough difficulty holding on to Jerusalem as a whole. But spiritually it is the center of our being. Even those who do not believe in God recognize the value of the Old City."

"Yes. It has changed little over the centuries. And now that the synagogues and ghettos of Europe have been wiped off the face of the earth, what else do we have but Jerusalem?"

"Then I say, somehow, we must make lions of the lambs behind those walls. Do what you can do. Talk with the British High Command before that vulture Akiva strikes some sort of bargain with the Mufti. If, on humanitarian grounds, you can get permission to convoy food to the Old City Jews . . ."

"You think you can smuggle in the necessities of survival?"

"Well, it is certain that Arazi and the others must transport the weapons we need into Palestine first. But once they get them to the New City, I can find a way to mix bullets and beans. I believe that we must try to save the Old City for the sake of our spirit."

"It is certain," the Old Man said with an air of finality, "that the eyes of the world are focused on the Faithful City. And Moshe—" He tapped the photographs. "Your friend Miss Warne may well capture the image that they see."

Moshe bit his lip thoughtfully, realizing the danger that she would be placed in if she recorded the struggle. He wondered once again if he could ask her. "That square mile of earth and the Wailing Wall are what we had left after Titus destroyed everything two thousand years ago. How can we lose that without a fight?"

"Good," the Old Man nodded. "I am glad you do not agree with Shimon. And now, what about these scrolls of yours?"

"Are you asking Moshe the archaeologist, Moshe the Jew, or Moshe the Zionist?" he laughed.

"All three."

"I believe that they, too, may be the last remnant of Judaism of two thousand years ago."

Ben-Gurion drew an astonished breath. "You believe they date from before the Diaspora? Incredible."

"If that *is* so—and I must say *if*—their discovery at this time in history, when our people return from the four corners of the earth, is significant. Somehow I cannot help but believe that these ancient fragile writings may be as important as the Old City itself. They, like us, have been hidden from our legacy for these two thousand years. And today when we most need hope, God has reminded us of His ancient promises."

"This is Moshe the Jew speaking?" The Old Man smiled strangely as he looked at the photographs of the scroll. "And what does the Zionist say?"

"We will know shortly if Professor Moniger's and my belief about their authenticity is correct. If it is, then we have on our side a powerful weapon. We have the Word of God. There are some who will listen; we should let the world know what has been found."

The Old Man straightened the stack and handed it back to Moshe. "We need everyone we can muster on our side right now, my friend. Especially God, nu?"

Moshe leafed through the pages once again, skimming the words of Isaiah. "As well as His friends."

"Does Professor Moniger share your enthusiasm over the significance of the scroll?"

"It was he who first mentioned it to me last night. He has lived in Jerusalem for twenty-eight years. He is a Christian, but also a Jew at heart. He is a good man, at any rate."

The Old Man looked at his watch. "You have a plane to catch? And a ship to catch tomorrow night, I believe?"

Moshe nodded, rose, and shook his hand. "Shalom."

"And shalom to that hairy ape, Ehud, eh?"

Moshe left his office, filing through a crush of men and women waiting to see Ben-Gurion. *If there is truly to be a nation of Israel*, Moshe thought, *surely this will be its Prime Minister*. The Old Man's door was never closed, nor was his heart.

For the first time in days, Moshe felt lighthearted. He was at least clear as to the course of action he would take with Ellie. Once she knew the truth about him, he felt sure, she would tell the American flyer good-bye.

As he approached the makeshift landing strip next to the Monastery of the Cross, he saw David and the other Haganah pilot, Michael, peering at the engine of the little blue Piper Cub.

"I'm a fighter pilot!" he heard David exclaim. "Not some kind of pansy chauffeur for an archaeologist, y'know? When do we start training pilots, anyway Michael?"

"As soon as we get the planes. This is it, David. This and twelve others like it. Eliahu bought twenty of these things for scrap, and we pieced these together."

David rattled something in the engine. "Good grief," he said in disgust. "We can't just fly these tin cans over the Arab Legion and drop rocks on their heads. Somebody might get mad and shoot us down."

"Be patient." Michael clanked against the engine with a wrench.

"Patient? Isn't that somebody in a hospital?" He nudged Michael hard, causing him to raise up and bang his head.

"Watch it, will you?"

"Did you get it, *patient*?"

"You think I'm dumb or something, Meyer? Holy cow!" Michael rubbed his hand on his balding head, leaving a streak of grease. David pulled out a handkerchief and rubbed the spot.

"Yeah, I think you're dumb. Look what you're doing. We could be eating crab down at Fisherman's Wharf in Frisco right now. Instead, you're in Jerusalem tryin' to hide your bald spot with engine grease from one of the twelve existing planes in the Jewish Air Force. Right?"

"I didn't say these were the only existing planes. I said they were the only ones that can fly."

"Okay. Right. Don't tell me you're not dumb, Mike. Dumb Jew."

"Yeah? Well, you're here too, you dumb half-Jew."

"Quarter. My grandfather is the one who got me into this, remember?"

Moshe laughed out loud and thought of the last Abbott and Costello film he had seen at the Arab-owned Rex Theater, the week before it had been blown up by the Irgun Jewish terrorist organization. Then he laughed again at the absurdity of life. "You are right," he said, as David and Michael looked up at him. "We should all go to this Frisco and have crab."

"There, y'see? He agrees with me, and he doesn't even like me." David glared at Michael, then climbed into the little plane without ceremony. "You coming or not?" he called to Moshe, who stood wondering how to respond to David's comment.

The truth was that he really didn't like David much, but that was simply because of his involvement with Ellie. More than likely, this zany American was not such a bad fellow. Moshe swallowed his uneasiness and climbed into the cramped passenger seat in the cockpit next to his rival. As the propeller spun to life, Moshe gripped his briefcase with white-knuckled intensity.

"Sorry you don't have a seat belt, pal," David said with a wry smile. "You'd better hang on. This little sardine can gets a little bumpy."

Moshe placed his case under his feet and clutched the edge of his seat with both hands. Beads of sweat formed on his brow as he noticed how close the end of the runway was to a row of apartment buildings.

"You fly much?" David probed as the Piper began to taxi.

"Hmm," Moshe nodded. He had flown only once before, and he had not liked the sensation.

"Know how to use a parachute?" David asked as he kicked the engine to a roar.

"No." Moshe hoped that his terror did not show on his face.

"That's okay." The little plane rattled over the field, "These buckets only carry one parachute, anyway—and it's mine." David smiled brightly as the plane lifted off, its wheels barely clearing the tops of the apartment buildings. He took a particular delight in watching Moshe close his eyes and mutter a prayer of deliverance.

Moshe opened his eyes and looked down as the plane began a steady southward climb. Below him he could make out the stone buildings of the Monastery of Saint Simeon that bordered the wealthy suburb of Katamon; until now, a pleasant mix of middle-class Arabs and Jews had lived there in harmony together. Soon, Moshe knew, Katamon would become a battleground between the Mufti's hired bullies and the Haganah as each struggled for one more foothold in Jerusalem.

David began a slow turn to the east, and to his left Moshe could make out the tiny forms of British soldiers at Allenby Barracks. Just beyond, a sliver of road climbed the Hill of Evil Counsel where Judas had received payment for his betrayal of Christ. *How ironic*, thought Moshe. *Some misinformed Englishman with a desire for a good view chose to build the office of the British High Commissioner atop that very hill.* In spite of good intentions among those Britishers who had governed Palestine since the collapse of the Turk-Ottoman Empire in 1910, there had been very little besides Evil Counsel from that hilltop fortress. Moshe felt pity for the man who now held the office of High Commissioner. Sir Allen Cunningham was personally sympathetic toward the cause of a Jewish homeland, but his policies were set by Foreign Secretary Bevin, a man known for his antagonism to the Jews and a desire to see the Partition plan fail before it was even implemented. Nothing would assure that failure quicker than continued armed uprisings by the Arabs. Bevin hoped that Britain then would be asked to step back in, playing a role more to his liking. *What words of evil counsel*, Moshe wondered, *are being passed from London to Sir Allen today*? He would know soon enough, as would the Old Man and the Jewish Agency. Many Jewish sympathizers within the British Mandatory Government were willing to pass along those top secret dispatches for no more than a handshake and a thank-you.

The tiny Piper continued to sputter and putt in a slow turn back over the Mount of Olives. Like ants on an anthill, a black-clad caravan wound slowly up the Mount toward the Jewish cemetery—yet another scene in the drama being acted out in the streets below. Sniper fire had claimed the lives of six Jews since Partition night. Only six more among the six million who had died in the death camps. Only six from among the hundred thousand who lived in the city of Jerusalem.

And yet Moshe knew the grief that was borne up that hillside. He remembered the face of his brother Eli, and looked away from the funeral procession toward the rugged walls of the Old City and the golden Dome of the Rock. Such a tiny remnant of Jews lived in the shadow of the Mosque of Omar, yet they were a thorn in the flesh of the Muslims who surrounded them. The Mufti's holy strugglers, the Jihad Moqhades, had marked the synagogues and Yeshivah schools for destruction first. Somehow they must hold on to those ancient stones.

It will be easier, he thought, *to hold the modern facilities of the Hebrew University and Hadassah Hospital to the north of the city*. Although pine-covered Mount Scopus, the hill on which they were built, was deep behind Arab lines and surrounded by Muslim neighborhoods, the structures had the advantage of height. It would be difficult for even an army of irregulars to capture as long as the hospital was properly supplied. That would be the Haganah's main problem.

Moshe gazed down at the road that led through Arab-held Sheikh Jarrah to the university and the hospital. At the base of the long incline was a curve in the road. *The perfect place for an ambush*. He made a mental note of it as they passed over the heart of the Jewish section of the New City, then completed their turn to the northwest toward Tel Aviv.

Below them lay the artery that would carry the lifeblood of Jerusalem from Tel Aviv. This slender ribbon of highway was Jewish Jerusalem's one link with the sea and the supplies needed to survive the approaching tidal wave of the Mufti's fury. Moshe knew how easily that lifeline could be cut. Below them the road descended for twenty miles through a narrow gorge called in Arabic *Bab El Wad*, the Gate of the Valley. Soaring pines and rocks covered the hillsides on either side of the gorge. It was an ideal place to attack any convoys headed for Jerusalem. No doubt the soldiers of Haj Amin knew every outcropping and hiding place where one man could do the work of one hundred.

Finally David spoke, as if reading Moshe's mind, "Down there's where you fellas are going to have your problem. There's not much going to come up that gorge without a fight. I've been looking it over this week as I've flown this run. Here, let me show you." He pushed the stick forward and the plane dropped steeply toward the tops of the trees along either side of the road. Moshe gulped and held tightly to his seat as he stared straight ahead.

"Well, stick your head out the window, pal. You can't see anything that way!" David exclaimed.

Obediently Moshe shoved the window open and stuck his head out into the wind. Just below him were treetops. *Without much effort*, he thought, *I could gather eggs from the birds' nests.*

"Watch this!" David yelled as they came to a small clearing. There among the rocks was a small group of Arab peasants, rifles and bandoleers full of bullets slung over their shoulders. Their faces were so distinct that Moshe could make out missing teeth in the gaping mouth of one of the men. As David buzzed their little squad, they whipped their rifles into action and began shooting with a menacing pop at Moshe's head. He jerked it back inside as a bullet punctured the wing, and David swept the plane quickly skyward and out of range.

"You idiot!" Moshe cried angrily. David raised his eyebrows in mock concern.

"Gee, are y' hurt, pal?" he grinned.

"We could have been shot down!" Moshe slammed the window shut, noticing a neat round bullet hole through the glass.

"Nah," he sniffed. "These little cans will take a lot of flak. Practically indestructable, according to my friend Michael. He says we're going to bomb the Arab Legion with 'em."

"I could have been killed!"

"That would have been a real shame," David said in amusement.

"You are a madman." Moshe combed his fingers through his hair and resumed his survey of the road through Bab El Wad.

"Ah, come on," David said at last. "Don't take it so hard. Most

157

of these Arabs are lousy shots. Chances are if they aim at you they hit each other."

"Counting on that, were you?" Moshe glared at David. "Just why did you come to Palestine, Mr. Meyer?" he asked.

"Ellie asked me the same thing last night. Sitting right where you're sitting." David grinned again.

"And how did you answer her? I am curious."

"I said I came for her."

"And what did she say to that?"

"She asked me if I would have joined the Egyptian Air Force if she had been in Cairo. I told her maybe."

"I fail to see what it was she ever saw in you."

"Funny thing, that's what she said." David scratched his head. "But you know, she doesn't think much of you, either. She thinks you've copped out on your own people, you know." David paused long enough for his words to sink in. "Of course, the professor is wise to us both, I think. He's got you figured for a Haganah man, and I don't know what he thinks of me."

"No one quite knows what to make of you, Mr. Meyer."

"I'm driving this plane, aren't I? I've got my reason for being here. And until I get my reason safely home, I'm going to do what I can to help this two-bit operation. That's what counts in my book."

"We live by different books, apparently."

"Maybe. Maybe not. You're worried about a lot of people. I care about one."

"Yourself?"

"Make that two. Me and Ellie. Maybe a few more on the fringe like Michael. But that's the lot."

As they swept down from the gorge, David dropped the plane several hundred feet in elevation. Just below them lay the barbed-wire encircled blockhouse of a British police station and the red tiled roof of the Trappist monastery of the Seven Agonies of Latrun. *How many agonies will our people face*, Moshe wondered, *before the prejudice and suffering come to an end*? Every foot of this territory had once belonged to the ancient nation of Israel. Just beyond them was the Valley of Ayalon, where the sun had stood still for Joshua. Then the road twisted through the Valley of Sorec, where Delilah was born and Samson destroyed the crops of the Philistines by turning loose foxes with burning tails. The ruins of Gezer lay beneath a bald hill just beyond, dowry of the daughter of Pharaoh when she married Solomon. How he loved this land and hoped in the promises! "We are people of the Book," Moshe said at last. "Millions have been murdered beneath the apathetic gaze of men looking out for themselves. Saving what is left, making sure it never happens again—that is my concern."

"Yeah," David said quietly. "I wish you luck. And for as long as I'm here, I'll do what I can. But I've got a future, and I just spent four years fighting a bloody war. And I'll tell you, pal—" David paused and frowned, leaning forward to stare intently at a small black form that crept slowly forward like an ancient beetle along the road.

"What is it?" Moshe asked. "The bus from Tel Aviv?"

"Yeah. Look back about half a mile. There in all those rocks beside the road—"

Moshe strained his eyes to see what David's sharp eyes had picked up moments before. Far below them, like a swarm of crawling insects, were at least a hundred keffiyah-clad warriors waiting for the bus from Tel Aviv. Just beyond them, hidden from view in the bend of the road, stood a roadblock of stones and timbers. Behind the bus, out of sight behind a small hill, an armored vehicle waited to cut off escape. As they watched from their high vantage point, the bus passed an Arab sentry on an outcropping, who then signaled the armored car to pull forward and block the road.

"Hold on!" David cried, pushing the throttle forward. "We're going down for a better look."

Moshe braced his feet against the floor and gasped as the ground and the Arab band loomed before them until he could clearly see the patterns of the checkered keffiyahs and the startled expressions of terror as the men ran for cover. "Pull up!" Moshe shouted, certain that they were about to plow nose-first into the earth. "Pull up!" he shouted again as the stubble of an Arab's beard became clear and the shrieks of the men louder than the roar of the engine. David's hands remained firmly forward until the ground loomed only feet from their faces, then with a suddenness that hurtled Moshe backward, he pulled up, thumping the head of a scrambling bandit with the landing gear.

"Eeeeeeee-haaaaaaaaa!" David shouted as Moshe scrambled to regain his seat. "Did you see that?" He climbed steeply, then banked the fragile little craft for a better look at the chaos below them. "That's the way, darlin'," he cried, patting the instrument panel.

For a moment Moshe was reminded of Ehud stroking the *Ave Maria*, and he wondered at the madness of the men in this war. He looked down at the Arabs, who were pointing their rifles at the little blue Piper. Small explosions from their barrels showed that they were indeed firing at the plane as they struggled to pick themselves up from the dust. Spotting the piper's hawklike swoop, the bus had halted momentarily, then seeing the armored car move in behind, it had lurched forward toward the band and the roadblock. "They can't see the barricade!" Moshe cried.

David circled the plane, barely noticing each time the dull thud of a bullet tore through the fuselage. "We gotta go again," he said, pushing the throttle forward and plunging into a dive steeper than the last. "Break up that little tea party," he said through gritted teeth as he struggled to control the tiny plane.

Again the ground and the enemy rose to meet them as they plummeted toward the rocks. The rattle of a machine gun burst from the armored vehicle, spraying the air around them and shattering the windshield. Dust filled the cockpit as David pulled up at the last possible instant, leaving the ground littered with screaming, cursing Jihad Moqhades, searching for their guns.

The bus inched toward the barricade; as it rounded the corner, the dull thump of two land mines blew out its tires. David climbed out of range of the shower of bullets and quickly surveyed the damage. Wind was streaming into the cockpit and he had a deep gash over his eye. Below them, the bus had crept to a lopsided halt, and the Arabs rushed toward it with their rifles raised in rage. To David it looked like a scene from a western movie when the hostile Indians circle the wagon train.

"Use the wireless," urged Moshe. "Call Tel Aviv for help."

"Are you kidding?" said David. "This thing barely has wings, let alone a radio. We'll have to try and make it to Lydda and hope they can hold out long enough to get somebody out here."

"Dive again! Chase them away!"

"The plane won't take it. We'll end up in pieces." David struggled with the rudder and set course for Lydda Airfield as Moshe slumped in the seat beside him. Once he looked back and glimpsed a tight pillar of black smoke rising from the horizon.

They flew the last fifteen miles in silence, Moshe certain that he could have run the distance faster than the crippled little aircraft was flying. He felt sick with the certainty that any help that could reach the bus would reach it too late.

That afternoon, the tiny waiting room at Lydda Airfield was crowded with British officers and Jewish civilians waiting for word on the fate of the Jerusalem bus. David sipped coffee as Moshe paced and listened to the crackle of the wireless on board the British armored car. When at last the news came, a bearded man beside David crumpled in silent sobs. "No survivors. Thirty-two dead, as near as we can make out."

16   Kibbutz

Rachel stared at the slats of the bunk above her. Outside a child threw a ball against the wall of the barracks with a steady thump, thump, thump. She stopped counting after one hundred and eleven. A small group of women, Dachau survivors, sat at the far end of the room near the stove and lowered their voices as they cast furtive looks in her direction. Words like "traitor" and "whore" drifted down to her, and she wondered why they bothered to lower their voices at all. She knew she was the topic of their conversation. They had survived their ordeals and kept their lives without defying the law that called for death before loss of chastity. Rachel had saved her own life, but had sacrificed her soul in the bargain.

She sighed and glanced around the bleak interior of the makeshift kibbutz housing. It was clean, certainly—a far cry from the displaced persons camps or the filth of the concentration camps. But Rachel wondered if she would ever again sleep in a real bed or set her own table for supper. Would she ever comb her hair in front of a mirror that did not reflect the images of a dozen other women jostling in line? Netanya Kibbutz was clean, and the food was good, but it was not home. For Rachel it could never be home—not as long as others spoke in hushed tones about the brand she bore on her arm. They called her a whore and turned their backs on her. Even those Sabras, the native Palestinian Jews, who smiled or spoke kindly to her did so only out of pity, never seeing the person who lived beneath the indelible mark of the S.S.

She got up and walked slowly, her eyes downcast, past the group of whispering women. "Oh, look," one said just loud enough for her to hear, "the whore is finally out of bed." The group snickered and passed the comment from one to another. Numb, Rachel glanced up and smiled sadly at a thin, frail young woman bouncing a baby on her lap. A sneer crossed the woman's face and she called out to Rachel, "Business is bad since you came to Palestine, eh?" The group roared with laughter as Rachel turned her head away and hurried outside. But their mockery followed her into the sunlight.

Small children ran through the neat rows of quonset-hut barracks, enjoying a game of tag. One small boy fell headlong into her legs as he dodged his pursuer. He hit his chin on the ground with a thud and wailed loudly for his mother.

Rachel knelt to help him up. "Are you hurt?" she asked, brushing the dirt from his ragged trousers.

"Mama!" he howled. "I want my mama!"

"There, there." She touched his curly hair and looked at his chin. "Only a scratch. Just a little scratch. You'll be all right," she smiled.

From behind her she heard a high-pitched shriek from the door of her barracks. "Samuel!"

Rachel turned to see the thin woman hand her baby to another woman and run toward her and the little boy. The boy saw his mother and wailed even more loudly. "Mama! She knocked me down. This lady tripped me and knocked me down!" As a small group of angry women gathered about her, Rachel began defensively, "The boy fell into me as he was playing—"

"Get away from my son!" shrieked the mother. "Get your filthy Nazi hands off my son!"

"But I . . ." Rachel tried to speak, but the woman charged at her, knocking her to the ground, then spit on her. Grabbing the still-whimpering boy by the shoulders she scurried back into the building.

Rachel wiped the spittle from her cheek and blinked hard to hold back the tears. A dozen other curious camp members looked on silently as she rose from the dirt. Then one by one they turned their backs on her and walked away with their arms about their children's shoulders; they must not speak to her or even let her shadow fall upon them. Only one, a thin, timid girl of eighteen or nineteen, dared break the silence. Brushing strands of dark hair out of her face, she stared at Rachel with wide brown eyes and whispered, "In the camp, we all did what we must to survive." Her glance traveled, unbidden, to the tattoo on Rachel's forearm. "But never that—never that."

This place is still a death camp, Rachel thought, *and I am one of the living dead*. Selling her body to the enemy in exchange for life, she had died to her people and lost her soul. She had only one hope left, that her grandfather was still alive and in Jerusalem where she had last heard of him. She was not like the rest of these survivors, she told herself as she raised her chin and returned to her bunk and the tablet of writing paper beneath her pillow. She had family in Jerusalem. She had a family, and the Jewish Agency would help her find her grandfather, a Yeshiva schoolteacher in the Old City. Then she would go home.

———

David had taken off, heading for Netanya Kibbutz, Haifa, and then Jerusalem, barely two hours before, leaving Moshe at the airfield. The bullet-marred hulk they had flown in had been quickly shoved off to a small metal hanger at the edge of Lydda. Then a new plane, identical down to the I.D. numbers, had been pushed out onto the runway for David to complete his run. Ten other identical planes, all numbered *VAL 572*, were stored in shacks bordering the dirt airstrips near kibbutzim around the country. "If the British ever see two of the planes at the same time, they'll think they are seeing double," Michael had explained. "We don't want anybody to know we've got an air force, y'know—even if it is just made up of Piper Cubs."

The sun had just touched the rim of the horizon as the Swiss-Air DC-4 taxied onto the runway at Lydda. *Now, that's the kind of plane we need*, thought Moshe as he watched Flight 442 lift off over the orange groves and head slowly toward the sea beyond Tel Aviv.

By air, Moshe knew, it was only seven hours from Tel Aviv to Paris, and another fifteen to New York. This time tomorrow, the priority mail pouch he had sent to Zionist headquarters in New York would be in the capable hands of men who could make best use of its contents.

Fragments and photographs of the scroll would be shuttled off to Johns Hopkins University in Baltimore for dating. And Ellie's snapshot of the dying tailor of Princess Mary Avenue would be on the desk of the editor of *Life* magazine with a full explanation. The press would know what to do with it; he hoped that within the week the world would begin awakening to the fact that the death camps were not the end of the Jewish struggle for survival.

"God," Moshe whispered as the airplane became a tiny speck in the darkening sky, "speak for us."

———————

Captain Luke Thomas tugged at his waxed handlebar mustache, then rubbed his forehead as he studied Ellie's snapshot of Hassan during the riot. He cleared his throat finally and laid the picture down on Howard's desk. "Is there nothing more you can tell me about this fellow?" he asked, glancing around the room at Howard, Ellie and David.

"We figured *you* ought to be able to tell *us* something." David's eyes flashed with impatience.

"We have run a thorough check, Mr. Meyer. The man is not and never has been a member of the Palestine Police Force."

"But the uniform . . ." Ellie began, leaning forward in the large leather chair.

"Unfortunately, Miss Warne," the kindhearted captain tugged on his mustache again, "a uniform is a guarantee of nothing but a skilled tailor."

"Is that so?" snapped David. "So who are you?"

Howard gave him a sharp look, then said to the captain, "Luke, I called you in on this simply because we are not sure what it is all about. Frankly, before we were confident that the man was not a member of the mandatory government, we didn't want anyone else involved."

"I understand, Howard," Luke nodded. "These days it's hard to know whom to trust. The entire command is split down the middle. Just between us, the Foreign Minister has made a dreadful mess out of the whole thing."

David interrupted, "So who was this guy, and why was he after Ellie? I mean, why her?"

Luke leaned back in his chair and pulled out a large dark briar pipe, filling it carefully from a black leather pouch. "Miss Warne," he began, ignoring David's aggressiveness, "I have shown the man's photograph to several of the Hadassah Hospital staff. No one remembers seeing him the night the boy was attacked. But Yacov himself says the voice sounded familiar. I have a hunch that the fellow in the ward and the man who followed you are one and the same." Luke smiled at her and tamped his tobacco. "There is a connection."

"But I told you I met the boy only on Partition night."

"And the kid's a pickpocket, not a government agent," David interrupted again.

"We are not sure what he is at this point," said Luke. "But at any rate, the children's ward is under guard." He struck a match and drew deeply on the pipe. "Perhaps you, too, should have a guard?"

"We are making arrangements for Ellie to leave for the States within the week, Luke," Howard volunteered, casting a quick look at Ellie as she frowned unhappily and shifted uneasily in her chair. "Until she leaves, perhaps it would not be a bad idea."

"But I—" Ellie protested.

"Miss Warne, it is no secret how your uncle feels about the establishment of a Jewish homeland here in Palestine. I must confess that I share his views, and I am not alone among the British officers here. This fellow"—he waved his smoking pipe at the photograph of Hassan—"we know is not one of us. We do not know, however, what he could possibly gain by following you. Is there anything you have not told us? Any political involvement during your stay in Palestine?" Then he glanced up at Howard. "Or perhaps I should ask you, Howard? If this fellow is an Arab agent—and I suspect that is the only answer as to his identity—why would he be trailing your niece?"

"I am simply an archaeologist—right now, anyway. My political activism can be translated into nothing stronger at this point, if that's what you are getting at. I am not a member of the Haganah. However, if you ask me again after the mandate ends . . ." his voice trailed off, and he smiled broadly.

"You and a quarter of the British soldiers stationed here, I'm afraid," said Luke. "And another half will join the Arab Legion."

165

He turned his gaze full on David, who was not smiling. "And how about you, Mr. Meyer?"

David grunted sardonically. "You know good and well I'm a pilot for the Jewish Agency," he answered belligerently. "There's nothing illegal in that."

"No"—Luke struck another match—"nor in my asking." Then his face grew serious and he stared intently at David. "You were the fellow who spotted the ambush of the bus yesterday. I read the dispatches. Ghastly!"

"You could say that," David glared. "Listen, I don't know what is going on with Ellie, but until we get her out of here . . ."

Ellie felt a flash of resentment at David's mention of her leaving. "I haven't had contact with anyone even remotely connected to the Haganah, Captain Thomas," she said, "but from what I have seen the last few weeks, I can tell you that if I had half a chance of doing anything to help them, I would not be returning to the States."

"What's your point?" David asked Luke.

"The point is," the lean, sun-burned captain answered, "that for some reason, this young woman is dangerously of interest to the anti-Zionist faction in Palestine. I don't believe they have picked her at random. Certainly there is a motive behind their actions."

"Could it be the scrolls?" Ellie asked.

"Not possible." Uncle Howard toyed with a pencil thoughtfully. "They would have no concept of their political importance at this point."

"You are seeing a fellow," Luke probed. "Moshe Sachar. Are you romantically involved?"

Howard yawned and stretched. "A cold trail there, Luke. Moshe is interested in the politics of ancient Assyria."

"Thought I'd ask," Luke said, puffing cheerfully on his pipe and casting a quick look in David's direction.

David was staring hard at Ellie, noticing the blush that colored her cheeks at the mention of Moshe's name. A rush of jealousy filled him and he stood up and walked over to the bookcase, pretending to read book titles as the conversation continued behind him.

"Whatever you might think," Ellie tossed her hair and lifted her chin, "Moshe is the last person in Palestine to be a threat to anyone. Especially the Arabs. As long as he can continue his work, the world can fall down around him. He'd no doubt leave notes on clay tablets for archaeologists digging around in another couple thousand years."

"And where is Professor Sachar now?"

"University business," said Howard, his eyes fixed on David as though he were trying to see into his mind. "Isn't that right, David?"

David turned and leaned against the bookcase. "I don't know," he stated. "I just drive the bus." David was certain now that it had indeed been Ellie's association with Moshe that had brought her so near to death. He clenched his fists and turned back toward the bookcase. Ellie's ignorance of Moshe's Haganah connection would insure that she got on the plane for home five days from now. In the meantime, he would keep his mouth shut and let Moshe deal with the Arabs when Ellie was safely on her way. "Sachar seems like a real egghead type to me," he said. "No offense, Professor. All he wanted to talk about was archaeology stuff. When the Arabs attacked the bus, it scared the stuffing out of him, poor guy." He turned and winked at Ellie, who looked away, feeling ashamed and embarrassed for Moshe.

"You see, Captain," she said. "That avenue is a waste of time."

Perched on a large rock, Rachel shielded her eyes against the late afternoon sun and searched the skies in the direction of the faint drone of the airplane engine. She shifted her weight and nervously chewed her nails. Today was mail day again, and as she scanned the horizon for the tiny blue-and-white airplane, her pulse began to race in anticipation that perhaps this was the day that she would hear news of her grandfather in Jerusalem. *By now*, she hoped, *the Jewish Agency must have located him; by now he knows that I am alive and searching for him.*

As the small speck in the sky grew larger, so did her excitement, although she attempted to mask it behind a placid exterior. She had learned too late that the others in the camp merely mocked her hopefulness; most doubted that she did indeed have a family.

Two women with whom she shared a small corner of the barracks walked by and snickered as they eyed her from head to foot. Rachel quickly looked at the ground.

"Still waiting for your precious letter, Rachel dear?" one of the women sneered.

Rachel did not answer. The other jibed, "No, she's waiting for the pilot. Maybe he's a paying customer."

Rachel stood quickly and walked to the kibbutz mess hall, listening as the steady buzz of the engine grew louder. Just as she reached the heavy double doors of the building, the airplane passed low over the grassy square, touching Rachel with its shadow. She whirled around and looked up at its bright blue under-belly, then she stood blinking in the sun as it slowly turned and landed on the kibbutz's makeshift landing strip. Everyone except the armed guards on duty around the settlement's perimeters dropped their work and ran to greet the fragile little craft and her pilot. But Rachel turned her back instead and entered the empty mess hall to wait alone for mail call.

The sounds of her shoes on the concrete floor echoed hollowly. She poured herself a cup of coffee, then pulled out a long wooden bench and sat down. On top of the white table, two lovers had scratched their initials and a heart. Rachel traced the heart wistfully with her finger and wondered what it must be like to love and be loved by a man. Then the doors clanged open and the crowd pushed in behind David Meyer, the tall American pilot. Quickly, as if to hide her thoughts, Rachel placed her coffee cup over the initials.

David was laughing loudly, the mailbag slung over his shoulder as he made his way to the center of the room. He dumped the mail on the table and sprawled out on a bench.

"Hey, how about some coffee for the mailman!" he shouted playfully.

One of the Sabra girls filled a cup and set it down in front of him as two men began to sort through the bundle of letters and call out names of those gathered for mail. Rachel continued to stare at the rim of her cup. She tapped the handle nervously with her index finger.

One by one the names were recited and whoops of delight filled the room as first packages and then letters were handed out. Rachel swallowed hard as the last name was read and hers had not been called. She sipped her cold coffee and listened to the snatches of conversation that floated around the room. "Looks like the Mufti's going to strangle the Old City first," she

168

heard David say to the leader of the kibbutz. "Then the Arab Legion will go for the city's jugular. I don't know how much longer we'll be able to get in and out freely."

A wave of panic swept over Rachel. Not to be able to reach Jerusalem would mean she had no reason left to live. *There must be some oversight*, she thought. *Maybe the letter is still in the bottom of the mailbag. Perhaps it has been overlooked.*

She rose from the table and jammed her shaking hands down into her pockets. She hesitated a moment, then slowly walked to where David sat talking and sipping coffee with several other men and two young Sabra women. She stood quietly at his right elbow until the conversation died and the attention turned to her.

"Pardon me," she said haltingly. David turned to her brusquely; then a smile danced across his lips as he drank in her beauty for the first time.

He gave a low whistle and nudged a man beside him. "You guys have been holding out on me," he laughed. "Where have you been hiding all the gorgeous dames? What are you doing tonight, honey?" he joked.

The two women at the table exchanged glances and the men looked self-consciously at their hands. David noticed the change of mood. "What's up?" he smiled.

"Excuse me, please," Rachel turned to go. "I should not have interrupted."

"Whoa now, pretty lady!" David jumped to his feet and grabbed her arm.

Rachel continued to look down at a crack in the concrete floor, aware now that nearly every eye in the mess hall had turned toward her and the pilot. "Please," she said quietly, pulling away from him. "I am sorry."

He lowered his voice then and held on to her wrist. "No, I'm sorry. I mean, I . . . I was just kidding, you know?"

"It's all right," she answered.

"Can I help you with something?" he asked kindly as he pulled her to a bench. "You want some coffee?"

Still not looking at him directly, she searched for words. "I am waiting, you see. For a letter from the Jewish Agency in Jerusalem. About my family."

David nodded. "It didn't come today?"

Rachel looked into his eyes. "I thought perhaps it might have become lodged in the mail pouch."

"Sure," David said hopefully, filled with pity at the anguished hopefulness of the girl. "We'll have another look. What's your name?"

"Rachel Lubetkin." She spelled the name slowly as he opened the bags and rummaged inside them.

"I'm sorry," he said, holding the bags upside down. "That's it."

She looked at her hands again and tried to smile. "Yes," she said stiffly fighting back tears of disappointment. "Thank you very much." She started to rise but David again touched her arm.

"Maybe next time, huh?" he said, trying a smile to cheer her up.

"Maybe."

"Yeah, uh, well, is there anything else I can help you with?"

Rachel clasped her hands tightly in her lap. "Could you . . ." she began haltingly. "Would you take a letter to the agency for me by your own hand? Perhaps if you brought it to someone's attention. I have family there. In Jerusalem, you see, a grandfather in the Old City," she explained in a rush.

"Sure. You got it? You got the letter with you? I'll take it."

"It's in the barracks," Rachel stood and walked quickly to the door. She turned and gazed gratefully at David before she ran to the barracks and her bunk, pulling yet another sheet of paper from her note pad and stuffing it into an envelope addressed to the Jewish Agency.

"Another letter, Rachel?" one of her barracks companions said in mock sympathy. "Don't tell me—still no word from Jerusalem?"

Rachel licked the seal and glared back at the woman. Then she turned on her heel and dashed back to the mess hall. She opened the door and stood self-consciously for a moment watching as the two women at the table filled David in on her peculiar past as an S.S. prostitute. One of the two looked up and saw her at the door, then nudged her companion to silence. They both stared awkwardly at her. David turned, his eyes full of pity as he gazed at the beautiful young woman.

Rachel's heart went numb, and she simply stepped back and closed the door. She clutched the letter to her and walked bleakly across the square, feeling totally alone. But she had felt alone before, and still she had lived—or at least survived.

The sound of footsteps came from behind her. "Hey, Rachel Lubetkin," came a cheery voice. She did not turn or stop until David caught her by the elbow and spun her around. "Hey," he smiled into her eyes, "haven't you got a letter for me to deliver?"

Moshe watched in amusement as Ehud finished his third helping of cheeze blintzes then wiped his mouth on his red flannel shirt sleeve and belched loudly.

"It warms my heart, Ehud," cooed Fanny Goldblatt lovingly, "to feed a man who likes to eat." She poured another round of coffee for Ehud, Moshe, and Dov Yori, chief of Haganah intelligence, who had gathered in her Tel Aviv apartment.

"Someday I am going to marry you, Fanny." Ehud belched again and pushed his plate away from him.

"Only you would eat yourself to death in a week," Moshe laughed.

"She feeds you free now, Ehud. Marry, and you pay the grocery bills," Dov quipped, ducking as Fanny reached out to whack him on the top of his shiny bald head.

Fanny plopped down at the large dark oak table and folded her hands in front of her. "And what makes you think I would have such a gorilla as this?" She stuck out her lower lip in a mock pout. "King Kong would eat my cooking and not smell half so bad."

"That is why he went to sea," Moshe added with a grin. "The sardines don't notice."

"But the refugees do!" Dov howled.

"At least I get them safely to shore," Ehud mumbled.

"Which reminds me, Moshe darling," Fanny broke in. "Have you heard from Rachel Lubetkin, hmmm? Such a beauty." She raised her eyebrows.

Moshe looked at her with surprise, then shrugged and changed the subject. He had not allowed himself to think of the beautiful young woman since he had last seen her. Now, at the mention of her name he felt suddenly embarrassed as though someone might sense the thoughts he had had about her. "So," he said, "are we going to discuss the delivery, or what?"

"All right, all right," Dov pushed his chair back from the table. "Let's get to it."

"This might be my last ride for a while. I will be in Jerusalem." Moshe sipped his coffee, then added a little sugar, wondering how difficult it would be within a few weeks for the Jews of Jerusalem to find either sugar or coffee.

"Then tonight we shall make it a good trip, my little darling and I," Ehud promised.

Dov cleared his throat and pushed on the edge of the table, balancing his chair on its back legs as Fanny glared in silent disapproval. "We are bringing in a large group of young males this trip," explained Dov. "Military age. As soon as they are off the boat, we begin their training."

Moshe nodded in approval. "How many?"

"As many as you can squeeze on board, eh?" said Dov. "There is one problem we have encountered," he paused. "Some of our passengers may be plants."

"British?" growled Ehud, and Moshe imagined his hackles standing up like the ruff of a fierce dog.

"Some," said Dov, a frown creasing the deep lines of his plump face. "American Army intelligence has been able to help us with this a bit. Don't ask me why or how. But there is one man in particular we need to watch for. They themselves have been searching for him for eighteen months." Dov reached into his pocket and pulled out a faded photograph. He stared hard at it, then tossed it across the table to Moshe. "He is a Nazi S.S. Commando, an explosives expert until he murdered another officer over a girl in a brothel. His mother was Muslim Arab and his father German. This fella grew up hating Jews. No wonder, with a combination like that, eh?"

Moshe studied the craggy face and the jutting jaw. The ice-blue eyes seemed cruel even in the picture. The only evidence of the S.S. officer's Arab heritage was a large hawkish nose. Moshe had the vaguely unsettling feeling that he had seen the man somewhere before. "So why should we be looking for him?"

"He is a terrorist—trained and bred for it. The Americans think he's responsible for a number of atrocities. They would have liked to have had him as a defendant in the Nuremburg trials. Unfortunately, after he sliced up his fellow officer, the Nazis threw him into Ravensbruk."

"Ravensbruk?" gasped Ehud. "With Jewish prisoners?"

Dov nodded. "Poetic justice, eh? There he rotted until the

172

end of the war. Five months among his avowed enemies."

"And now?" Moshe asked, the feeling of uneasiness growing.

"He was traced heading south through Yugoslavia. The Americans believe he may try to pass himself off as a Jew to get onto one of our ships and smuggle himself into Palestine. Not that it matters, because he's sure to take an alias, but his name is Fredrich Ismael Gerhardt. Tattoo number 346686. If you see anyone resembling him, check the tattoo."

Moshe passed the photograph to Ehud, who studied it closely, then grunted and pitched it back to Moshe. "How do you know he is not already in the country?"

"We don't. But we are assuming he will make for the heart of Jerusalem and the Mufti's good graces. He had a friend, an Arab that he attended commando school with. I am certain you must remember him from the '36 uprising, Moshe."

Moshe leaned forward and rested his arms on the table. "Who is it?"

"Ibrahim El Hassan."

17 Ellie's Decision

Yacov felt tears of joy burn his eyes as Ellie told him about Shaul. ". . . and Miriam scolds him, but I see her sneak scraps of meat to him when she thinks no one is looking."

"Like Grandfather!" he said with a delighted laugh. "Always he scolds, but then he pats him and scratches his ears." A wave of homesickness flooded the boy, and all he wanted was to see Grandfather and Shaul once again. Just to see.

"It won't be long, you know, and you'll all be together again. The doctor ought to be here in a while, and you can get the straight story from him. He told Moshe and me that it's looking good."

A balding, white-coated English doctor with a thin moustache pulled the curtain back and said cheerily, "Quite good, actually."

Yacov turned his head in the direction of the crisp British

173

accent. "They found Shaul, Doctor!" he said excitedly. "He is at Miss Ellie's house."

"No doubt eating you out of house and home?" he asked, switching the overhead light off and turning on a dim bedside lamp. "Today we change the bandages and give you a few minutes to look about while we check your progress."

Yacov grimaced at the sharp pain he felt as the doctor gently cut away the bandages covering his eyes. "Relax, my boy," said the doctor. "Things may be a little fuzzy at first." Ellie reached over and took his hand. "It's okay, Yacov. I'm here."

He squeezed her hand tightly, fearful that when the bandages were finally taken away, he would see only darkness. It was, he thought, God's punishment for his sin. "I am afraid."

"The room will be dark," intoned the gentle voice of the doctor. "A little later we will lighten your surroundings so you will have a chance to read just a bit at a time."

"If I am blind, it is God's punishment," he said quietly.

Ellie drew her breath in sharply. "Don't say that, Yacov," she gripped his hand tighter and kissed his fingers. "God didn't do this to you." She heard herself echo Uncle Howard's words. "Men did."

"And very evil men at that," added the doctor as he unwound the bandages.

"But I looked at the graven image. I sinned against the law of Moses."

Ellie exchanged concerned looks with the gray-haired physician as he took away the last of the long bandage, leaving two cotton pads over the boy's eyes.

"What do you mean?" she asked, feeling the same sense of isolation she had felt when Moshe had prayed with Yacov.

"The picture—Young Girl Reading. I looked upon it and have broken the law. I have thought through these days that it must be my punishment to be blind."

The doctor paused and stroked Yacov's pale cheek. "I would think that if I were God, Yacov, I would do everything possible to give you sight. I am only a doctor with the heart of a man, and have I not done everything I could to help you?"

Yacov nodded slowly.

"It is now most certainly in the hands of God," said the doctor. "But do not judge His heart until I lift the bandages." He smiled and winked at Ellie, and she felt grateful for his sensitivity and understanding.

She patted Yacov's hand and remembered the story of Jesus healing the blind man. For the first time since she had been a child, she prayed that the tender heart of God had worked through the hands of the doctor.

Gentle hands lifted a corner of the gauze pad. "Do not open your eyes until I say you may." He switched off the bedside light, leaving the room in a soft gloom as he removed the final layers and dropped them into a metal pan. As he washed away a layer of crust covering the eyelids, Ellie stroked Yacov's arm and silently prayed.

"All right then, young man, open your eyes."

"But I have sinned in other ways as well," he said, beginning to panic.

"Open them slowly. It may be a bit painful."

As if they were too heavy to lift, his eyelids fluttered, then opened a crack. The doctor held a tiny pencil of light above his eyes and moved it slowly to the right and left.

"What do you see, Yacov?" he asked. "Tell me what you see."

"A little light. A small candle moving in the darkness very far away."

Ellie sighed with relief.

"Excellent!" exclaimed the doctor. "Perhaps God has a tender heart even when we sometimes have sinned?" he asked, medicating Yacov's eyes, then covering them with fresh bandages.

"Grandfather says He is slow to anger and ever merciful," Yacov smiled.

"Your grandfather sounds like a wise man."

"He is a rabbi. At the Polish Yeshiva in the Old City."

The doctor glanced quickly at Ellie. "And has he been to visit you, Yacov?"

"They say the Old City is cut off. I should like very much to talk with him about all that I am learning."

"Soon, perhaps. And do you have family in the New City with whom you could stay if we were to allow you to leave?"

"No one," he answered sadly. "Except Shaul."

"Ah, yes," the doctor nodded. "The dog?"

Ellie caught the doctor's eye. "We could help make arrangements, Doctor. Don't make him stay here any longer than is necessary."

"I would say by Christmas, anyway." He squeezed Yacov's shoulder. "Hanukkah for you, eh?"

"I should like very much to spend Hanukkah with Shaul and Grandfather." Yacov turned his freshly bandaged head toward Ellie. "Hanukkah is called The Festival of Lights, you know. It shall be good if I can see the lights, will it not?"

The broad headlight of the ancient Harley-Davidson cracked the cold darkness before Moshe, illuminating the road back to Jerusalem and Ellie. The motorcycle would have to do; he would not wait for the Jewish Agency's sputtering Piper Cub to lift him over the danger that lurked by the roadside—not since he had heard about Gerhardt and Hassan. His uneasiness about Gerhardt's photograph had transformed into the brutal awareness that he knew the terrorist's face not because he had seen him, but from Ellie's detailed description of the man who had broken her camera and knocked her to the sidewalk. Gerhardt was not, he had realized, on his way to Palestine; he was already in the service of the Mufti and walking freely about the streets of Jerusalem.

Three times he had tried to reach Jerusalem by phone, only to learn that the phone lines were down. He had sent Ehud and the *Ave Maria* out alone for the pickup, and borrowed Dov's motorcycle for the midnight trip back to Jerusalem. He did not know how much danger Ellie was in at this point; he could only guess that Gerhardt and Hassan had followed her because of his relationship with her. Undoubtedly they had sought to locate Haganah bases throughout the city and had marked them as targets. At any rate, no Jew was safe in the Holy City now, not with the likes of Gerhardt working for Haj Amin. That was, after all, the nature of terrorism: strike where least expected, mutilate and murder the innocent until, in the end, terror defeats the morale and determination to stand and fight. Jerusalem, Moshe feared, stood on the brink of another kind of holocaust.

The biting wind tore at Moshe's face and fingers as the heavy cycle roared past the ghostly white stone of the ancient village of Beit Dagon, named after the ancient fishing god of the Philistines. Six miles farther along, an icy rain fell, soaking through his jacket and trousers as he passed Sarafand, Palestine's largest British military base. Just beyond Sarafand, a tall minaret marked his passage into the hostile Arab territory. *All the kingdoms and governments that have sought to possess this land,* he thought—*where are they now?* As the cold numbed his cheeks, he remembered a saying he had learned from the old rabbis when he was a child skipping through the streets of the Old City: "As dust outlasts iron, Moshe, so Israel shall outlast her oppressors. Someday our Messiah will come, and once again we shall have a nation. Then we shall be truly free."

Moshe could not remember when he had stopped looking for the Messiah. Perhaps it had been the day the British officer had come with the news that his older brother Eli had been killed by the men under command of Ibrahim El Hassan. "There must be another way for Jews to live in freedom," he had told his grief-stricken mother. "If God will not send the One to bear our burdens, then maybe we must learn to bear them ourselves and make a homeland that is a refuge for every child of Abraham." Thus the establishment of a nation of Israel had become his dream, his Messiah.

It was a dream, he knew, that would be purchased with the blood of many. As he neared Latrun, he passed the burned-out hulk of yesterday's bus from Tel Aviv, the coffin for thirty-two precious lives. *Was it only yesterday,* he wondered? Already their blood had been washed from the road by the rain. Only thirty-two more Jews, the world would say—what was thirty-two compared to millions? A sense of despair filled him as he realized that each life lost would soon be washed from the world's memory. "They don't know," he said to their ghosts as he passed, "that each of you had a name."

Ahead lay Bab El Wad and the twisting, contorted agony of mountain gorge that led to Jerusalem. Moshe gripped the handlebars as the cycle reared back and he began the ascent. By now he was completely soaked to the skin, but still he thanked God for the rain that slashed against him. The cold brutal night had driven the Arab peasants who guarded the pass into the warmth of their villages. The smell of rain-soaked pines filled his nostrils, and he found it hard to believe that danger lurked so near to him.

Five miles outside Jerusalem the friendly lights of Kibbutz Kiryat Anavim glistened from the hillside to his left. Just beyond on the right stood the medieval remains of a Crusader castle, and ahead the lights of Jerusalem sparkled a welcome.

It was hours past curfew when, at last, Moshe passed the dark, squat building of Egged bus station and then the brightly lit building that housed the *Palestine Post*, where printers were setting tomorrow's news. For once, the headlines would be tame when the morning paper hit the streets. *But*, Moshe thought, *that couldn't last long*. He turned on Ben Yehuda Street and roared past the Atlantic Hotel, where David Meyer shared a room with Michael Cohen, and where half a dozen other members of the Haganah lived. Moshe wiped the rain from his goggles and looked up at the third floor where the lights of several rooms still burned. When at last he turned onto King George Avenue and passed the Jewish Agency building, he could see that the Old Man's office was still lit up. He was tempted to stop and share his information with him, but there would be time enough for that in the morning. Right now, all he wanted was to see Ellie's face smiling up at him, to hear her say she understood why he had not been able to tell her of his secret life. He turned onto Rehavia and idled up the street, his eyes searching the shadows for someone who might be watching the Moniger home. The street seemed to be silent and empty. Every window was dark.

Moshe turned off the engine and coasted on the heavy machine, balancing with his legs as the cycle rolled to a stop in front of the Moniger home. Moshe lifted off his goggles and hung them from the dripping handlebars; then he stiffly dismounted and set the kickstand. He stood for a long moment staring up at the sleeping house; then he slowly walked toward the front door.

Suddenly, he felt the hair on the back of his neck prickle as he heard the rapid scuffing of feet rushing toward him from behind. He whirled around to face two unidentifiable black forms. They instantly leaped on him, hurtling him to the wet sidewalk. Moshe swung a hard right, knocking one of his assailants away. The other hit him hard with the butt of a pistol on the side of his face.

The world seemed to swim around him, but still Moshe fought, placing a well-aimed kick into the man's groin. He fell back with a groan and rolled in agony on the sidewalk as his comrade rushed forward again and jumped on Moshe. Moshe felt cold wet steel against his temple and heard the hammer of a pistol lock into place.

"One word mate, and you're a dead man," said a menacing voice. "Get your 'ands behind your back, and roll over on the sidewalk."

Without another word, Moshe complied, feeling a sharp stab of pain as the man kicked him in the back. Then handcuffs clicked firmly onto his wrists. "Are you okay, Smith?" the man called to his companion. "Did 'e 'urt you, lad?" The accent was decidedly English.

Smith groaned, climbing to his feet with the aid of the wrought-iron stair railing. "Kill 'im!"

"Forget that, lad. Rouse the professor and we'll call H.Q. with word we've captured someone lurking about." The man pressed the gun to Moshe's temple once again. "Get up," he growled.

Awkwardly, Moshe struggled to his knees, the handcuffs biting into his wrists as Smith limped up the steps and knocked hard on the door. After a moment the porch light came on, revealing that Moshe's two assailants were, in fact, two miserably wet British soldiers. The door burst open and a disheveled Howard Moniger peered unhappily out the door.

"What is it?" he snapped.

"We got your man." Smith snapped to attention—with some difficulty, owing to the pain he still felt—then turned his gaze on Moshe.

" 'e gave us quite a fight, you might say, but 'ere 'e is. We got 'im." Pride filled the voice of the man behind the gun.

Howard blinked in disbelief. Then rage clouded his face and he rushed down the steps, pushing the startled young soldier to the side. "Idiots!" he exploded. "You have just arrested Professor Moshe Sachar of the Hebrew University!"

Thirty minutes later, behind the closed door of the study, Moshe nursed a cup of tea as Ellie held an ice bag to his cheek. He was wrapped in Howard's red plaid robe and looked for all the world like a man with a very bad hangover.

"And so you can see, Howard—" he looked sorrowfully at Ellie—"and Ellie, why I felt I must come back. I know that my words will not pass beyond these walls. But it is most important that you understand the seriousness of your association with me now. Perhaps it is I who have placed you in danger."

"Oh, Moshe," said Ellie, her voice full. "I am so sorry. All this time I thought you were—"

"It is I who need your forgiveness, my love," said Moshe. "Also yours, Howard."

Howard sat in his massive leather chair, his fingers pressed together at his lips. He had listened to Moshe's story without comment. He drew a deep breath. "I have suspected as much for some time," he said gently. "There is no need to ask for forgiveness from this quarter, my friend. My heart is fully with you—surely you know that." He picked up a pencil and tapped it on his desktop. "If there is any way that I can be of help, Moshe. Please . . ." his voice trailed off as Moshe reached across the desk and took his hand.

"My dear friend," he said quietly.

"We both have Ellie to consider now, of course. Next Wednesday the students from the school will be leaving for the States. She is going with them," explained Howard.

"If you are staying Uncle Howard—" Ellie interrupted.

"Nonsense," Howard responded gruffly.

"I'm over twenty-one," she argued. "I can make the same offer, Moshe. If there is anything . . ."

Moshe put his hand on her cheek. "I had a lot of time to think on the ride from Tel Aviv. I think perhaps your uncle is right. Your skill as a photographer would be of great benefit to publicize our plight. But, Ellie, in case you have not guessed it by now, I love you. You must go home."

———

Miriam knelt with difficulty among the packing crates that littered the floor of the professor's study. Ellie watched as the old woman carefully wrapped an ancient clay bowl in newspaper, then placed it in the crate before her.

"Ah, I remember when the professor finds this one!" she said. "I do not think he will ever have to leave Jerusalem. Even in the riots when my beloved husband is killed, the professor stays and makes a place for me here." She sighed sadly.

"He'll be back, Miriam. And Beirut is not so far away. He asked you to go there until this thing blows over. Why don't you go with him?"

"I am too old. Too old. And if we all go, as the Mufti would wish of us Christians, who then shall be left in Jerusalem? Only the Mufti. Miriam will stay here, thank you. My son, he finds me a nice room at the Semiramis Hotel in Katamon. Not so far away."

"Your son will be staying with you?" Ellie asked, carefully wrapping a clay tablet.

"Oh, yes," she replied brightly. "And my young grandson. But I will tell you the truth, Miss Ellie. Miriam shall miss you with your strange ideas. And shall pray daily for you as you return to your home."

"And I'll tell you the truth, I wish I weren't going. If I thought for a minute I would be anything but a bother and a worry—"

"Ah, yes, but now the America government says that those who stay and help will lose their . . . what do you call it?" she asked.

"Citizenship," Ellie finished in a disgusted tone of voice. "Somebody's making a bad decision over there, if you ask me."

"Without the help of America I fear gravely for my Jewish friends," the old woman sighed. "But our Lord, He sees it all, does He not?"

Ellie did not answer, instead continuing the work with renewed vigor. Her bags were packed and standing at her bedroom door, waiting for the flight that would take her home the next morning with the other students and most of the school's staff. Her heart felt heavy as she thought about leaving Moshe and David, who had decided to stay in spite of the U.S. Embassy's warning to American citizens. She looked around the room at the half-empty bookshelves and wondered if she would ever be back again. *If only there were something I could do*, she thought miserably.

"Soon the Jews celebrate Hanukkah, the Festival of Lights. This year will be most sad and quiet, I fear," the old woman shook her head. "And Christmas!" she threw up her hands. "We must celebrate in our hearts Christ's birth. If others knew Him, I think that then there will be no need of packing and talk of armies and killing. This old woman has seen too much." Miriam pulled herself up and left the room without another word, leaving Ellie alone with her thoughts.

After a few minutes Miriam returned. She held her hands out of sight behind her back; then as she neared Ellie, she pushed a brightly wrapped package into her face. "Here," she murmured. "Take it. I buy it especially for you. You are sometimes a very foolish girl but also—" her old voice broke—"very dear to this old heart."

Flabbergasted, Ellie took the bright red package from Miriam's gnarled hands. "But it's not Christmas yet," she protested.

"Just so," Miriam responded. "Well, then, you have to pack it, and when you are happy in Los Angeles, you will think of us here and pray for the peace of Jerusalem, eh?"

Ellie clutched the package to her, then stood and embraced the old Arab woman who for a lifetime had lived in the hope of peace and the threat of war. "You know," said Ellie, gazing tearfully into Miriam's faded brown eyes, "I feel like I'm running out on something I'm supposed to do. I feel . . . bad."

"May the Lord hold your life in the palm of His hand, child." Miriam patted her cheek, then turned and left to work away her emotion with some task in a distant part of the house.

Ellie sat on top of a large sealed crate and cradled her Christmas gift. She was tempted to find Miriam and open the present now so that the old woman could share the joy of having her gift appreciated. *But maybe she will be happier thinking of me on Christmas Day, just as I will feel sad thinking about the ones I am leaving here,* Ellie thought.

She had just returned to her task when she heard a loud, insistent knocking at the front door. Uncle Howard walked quickly past the study and answered the door. Ellie strained her ears to hear but could only hear muffled words of a very short conversation, and the solid closing of the door.

Still in his pajamas, robe, and slippers, Uncle Howard padded into the study and plopped down on a crate next to her. His face was grim and serious and he held two envelopes in his hand.

"Now child," he began. "I am sure this is nothing serious . . ."

He sounds serious, thought Ellie with alarm.

"What is it?" she eyed the envelopes suspiciously. Both were telegram envelopes, and telegrams usually brought only grief with their brief messages. "What?" she asked again.

Uncle Howard held them out to her. "They are both for you. One from L.A. and the other from New York."

She took them gingerly from his hands and sat staring at the envelopes as if trying to guess their messages. "They are addressed to me."

"That's what I said," Uncle Howard leaned forward impatiently. "So open them, child!"

Carefully, Ellie tore the flaps first of one and then the other. She handed the one from Los Angeles to her nervous uncle. "Here, you read that one," she instructed, pulling out the contents of the envelope from New York. She didn't know anyone in New York, and felt certain that whatever message it carried would not be news of a death or some other tragedy.

Uncle Howard read aloud the message from Los Angeles as relief flooded his weary face.

"ELLIE:
DADDY AND I FLYING TO MEET YOU IN NEW YORK STOP WILL CELEBRATE CHRISTMAS IN BIG APPLE STOP PRAY FOR YOUR SAFE RETURN STOP KISSES FOR HOWARD MOM"

———

Shaul lay stretched out in the middle of the parquet floor of the study, reveling in a patch of warm afternoon sunshine. Fifteen minutes earlier, Ellie had sent her parents a wire that would stop their trip to New York. Unshaven and clearly distraught, Uncle Howard followed her into the study.

"I am responsible, ultimately, for your safety, Ellie." He clasped his hands behind his back and paced to and fro in front of the now-empty display cabinets. "If anything ever happened to you, I would never forgive myself." He stopped before his desk and picked up a rumpled telegram. "Worse than that"— he waved it under Ellie's nose—"your mother would never forgive me."

Ellie reached down and patted Shaul's broad head, then scratched him under the chin, pretending not to hear Uncle Howard's stern voice. "If I leave now," she said with an amused smile, "*Life* magazine will never forgive me." She pulled the New York telegram from her trouser pocket and rattled it at him. "You can't argue with the power of the press, Uncle Howard. Neither can Mother." She unfolded the paper and began to read deliberately:

". . . LIFE EDITORIAL VERY IMPRESSED WITH PALESTINE PHOTOGRAPHS . . . HOPEFUL YOU CAN ACCEPT ASSIGNMENT . . . ALL EXPENSES, etcetera, etcetera, etcetera," Ellie finished triumphantly.

"Ellie, if you take that assignment, there's no telling what you'll get yourself into. Haven't you had enough? Haven't you heard enough and seen enough to know that no one is playing games here?"

"You're right. Nobody's playing games. Least of all me. You remember what you said to me about everything having some kind of plan? Well, maybe you're right. Maybe this crazy mixed-up mess I call my life is meant to be lived right here, at this exact moment. Maybe I can be just a tiny part of some kind of miracle." Excitement rose in her voice.

"That's not what I meant, young lady," he scowled.

"You don't think God can watch over me, Uncle Howard?" She lifted her chin defiantly, having sprung a trap he could not maneuver out of.

"God is not some kind of bulletproof vest, Ellie." He frowned down at her. "Take a look at Yacov—"

"That's right. What about the boy? He'll be getting out of the hospital in a few days. He can never get past the Arab blockades into the Old City. Where's he going to stay?"

"You're changing the subject, Ellie Warne. You remind me more of your mother every day." He sighed with exasperation and plopped down in his chair. "I had already considered staying here myself," he said absently. "But you—"

"I didn't change the subject. Yacov has no place to go, and I think he ought to stay here with us." She sat back with finality and glared at his frowning face.

He slammed his fist on the desk and leaned forward angrily. "Not with *us*. You, my dear, will be back in sunny, nonviolent California in time for Christmas. And regardless of my decision to stay here or wait it out in Beirut . . ."

Ellie raised her eyebrows in defiance. "Take another look at my telegram. *Life* has offered me all expenses, a room at the King David Hotel. Go ahead and close the school. Pack up your jar handles and move to Beirut. Either I stay here with you and work for them, or I stay at the King David and work for them. It doesn't matter. I'm taking this assignment."

Uncle Howard leaned back in resignation. "I should have you shipped home, you know."

"Crate me up like a mummy and send me back out of harm's way, is that it?"

"I had considered it." He rubbed his hand across his bald

184

head and gazed around the room. "I'm sending these treasures to Beirut for safekeeping, regardless. They're worth more than I am," he mumbled. Then he looked up at Ellie, a light of humor flickering in his eyes once again, "You think God can use the likes of us, child?"

Ellie rolled her eyes as if to comment on the seeming impossibility of it. "Who knows?" she laughed.

"Well, then, you better call Moshe and find out where we begin."

18   The Sacrifice Lamb

David rubbed his stockinged feet together under the makeshift poker table in his hotel room. Wearily he toyed with his dwindling pile of matchstick chips as Michael Cohen leered from behind a miniature lumberyard of winnings.

"Good grief," drawled cherub-faced Benny Rothberg as he shuffled the dog-eared cards, "don't you get sick of winning?"

"Yeah," David chimed in, "if he gets any more matchsticks over there, the whole table's gonna collapse."

"Shut up and deal already!" snapped Bobby Milkin, a coarse-featured New York born Jew. His large green cigar clouded the room with a thick reeking haze.

"Why don't you put that thing out?" Benny wrinkled his nose and fanned the air with the deck of cards.

"Nah," snarled Bobby, "I gotta fumigate the place. Get rid of the bugs from that stinkin' dog."

"He didn't have fleas," said Michael defensively.

"He had a terminal case of mean." Bobby chewed the cigar.

"He just don't like cigars." Benny dealt the cards.

"Or people that smoke." Michael nonchalantly picked up his cards one by one.

"Or people that smell like Milkin." David smiled as Bobby blew smoke over in his direction. Then he began to cough and choke as he looked at his cards. "It's not the cigar that stinks, fellas; it's this hand!" He pitched his cards to the table. "I'm out."

Michael's eyes remained cool as he picked up two match-sticks and tossed them onto the ante. "It'll cost the rest of you guys two to stay."

David scraped his chair back from the table and stood and stretched. He walked slowly to the windowsill and looked out over the rain-soaked stillness of Ben Yehuda Street below. *Never,* he thought, *has the Street of the Jews housed such a motley crew as the American Haganah volunteers.*

"Has it stopped raining yet, David?" Michael asked, as he triumphantly laid his full house on top of Bobby's three nines.

"Just a little drizzle," David answered. Milkin groaned, and the others laughed.

"At least it don't smell like wet dog in here no more," growled Bobby as he counted his meager ration of matchsticks.

"Guess that cigar's good for something," Michael agreed. "But it's a good thing for you, Milkin, that we weren't playing for cash."

Benny straightened the cards carefully before replacing them in their worn-out box. "So what'd you guys do with the mutt, anyway?"

"David had him made into a fur coat for his girl," Bobby guffawed.

"Nah, he took him over to her house and left him. She said she'd keep the dog, but David had to go. Right, Dave?" Michael added up his winnings.

" 'Bout the size of it." David smiled and plopped down on his bed, which sagged and groaned under his weight. "I better go to bed so you guys can get out of here." He lay back on his pillow and put his hands under his head.

"We can take a hint," said Benny. He filed out the door after Milkin, who continued to mutter about the evening's entertainment as he disappeared into his room down the hall.

"See ya in the morning," Michael called after them, no doubt rousing most of the residents of the Atlantic Hotel. Then he shut the door and rubbed his hands together, gloating. "What a night! You'd think Bobby lost his life savings, the way he acted."

"You got X-ray eyes, or were your cards marked?" asked David dryly.

"You're jealous, Meyer." Michael kicked off his shoes, then opened the window and inhaled the blast of cold air that flooded the room. "You gotta have heart to play this game right, y'know?" He slammed the window shut again and threw himself down on his bed.

"You call that heart? You went after Milkin like you wanted to beat the socks off him," David laughed.

"Didn't want his socks or I would've had 'em. The man is such a schmuck. I'll take that dog over him any day."

"Don't be so hard on him." David eyed Michael's toes sticking out of his socks. "You might have heart, but if you had a brain in your head you'd have played him for his socks."

Michael wiggled his toes. "Scarecrow, right? Scarecrow and Tin Man, that's us."

David leaned over and switched off the light. "Michael?" he asked as he unbuttoned his shirt and threw it into the darkness.

"Yeah?" Michael's voice sounded sleepy.

"If we had brains we'd be back in Kansas with Aunt Em." David closed his eyes.

"Don't forget Dorothy and that shaggy mutt Toto over there in Rehavia," Michael muttered. "I'm not so dumb that I don't know why you came to Palestine, y'know."

"Yeah, well, she's going back to the States."

"You staying on?" Michael asked after a long pause.

"After what I saw on the road yesterday, I get the feeling I ought to hang around and help out."

"Great," Michael yawned. "Can I borrow a pair of socks tomorrow?"

———

Gerhardt leaned against the building across from the Atlantic Hotel and peered up through the pouring rain at the brightly lit windows on the third floor.

The red-headed woman's escape, as it turned out, had been a windfall for him. It had brought yet another young suitor under his ever-watchful eye. The tall American flyer had not come to Palestine simply for his pleasure; he too, then, was a member of the Haganah, as were those men who stayed with him at the Atlantic Hotel on Ben Yehuda Street.

What better place, thought Gerhardt, *than this Street of the Jews, to celebrate the Jewish Festival of Lights with a little gift from Haj Amin?*

He studied the structure of the building, making mental note of its weakest points. Then he scanned the building on either side and smiled at the simplicity of his plan.

The staff of the King David Hotel at least maintained the pretense of opulent normality. The red-coated doorman, complete with medals and epaulets and a hint of gray hair peeking out from beneath the black cap, looked more like a retired general than a doorman. As David pulled up to the main entrance in the battered green Plymouth, the doorman stepped forward and effortlessly opened Ellie's door and helped her out in one movement. She stood staring up at the leaded arched windows until David joined her on the broad red carpet that led to the plush interior of the hotel.

David was angry at the news that Ellie would not be joining the other students and staff of the American school for their flight home tomorrow. "You know this was supposed to be your good-bye dinner," he said gruffly as he took her arm and passed into the lobby.

"Well, can't we make it a hello celebration?" she smiled coyly. "Come on, David, I thought you'd be happy for me. After all, this is *Life* magazine!"

"It's *your* life I'm worried about," he remarked sullenly.

Dark-skinned Arab bellhops scurried to and fro about the walnut-paneled lobby. Aristocratic looking gentlemen reading the *London Times* sat slouched in deep red leather chairs, while waiters served them Glenlivit whiskey or gin and tonic with twists of Palestine-grown limes. The carpet, a rich red floral, swirled around the well-polished shoes of British officers and government staff who spent their spare hours relaxing and reliving the latest events. All in all, the establishment bore remarkable similarity to the Savoy Hotel in London. Brass lamps on tables near the chairs gave the feeling of an English manor house, and in the bar adjacent to the lobby Ellie glimpsed paintings of horses soaring over jumps and galloping across the broad meadows of England.

Why, Ellie wondered, *if they are so in love with the atmosphere of Great Britain, are they so eager to stay here?*

Dressed in a tuxedo, the headwaiter stood at attention near a small desk as they walked into the high ceilinged dining room. White tablecloths and gleaming silver graced the delicate Queen Anne tables, and waiters gracefully moved from one table to another, bowing slightly and seeing to the needs of the diners before needs were even realized.

Ellie had a strong sensation that she had walked into a Cole Porter comedy where everyone was droll and witty and the world was simple. She tried to forget the military guards stationed outside throughout the grounds. For tonight, she decided, she would pretend that this charade was the real world and that the world outside did not exist.

"Sir?" asked the headwaiter with a heavy British accent.

"We have a reservation for two. Meyer. I stopped by this afternoon. Your phones are all messed up."

The headwaiter smiled slightly—uneasy, Ellie thought, at the reminder that the real world touched even the King David. "Quite," he said. "Meyer. Ah, yes, this way."

He took two leather-bound menus from a rack and led the way to a small corner table for two almost hidden behind a potted palm. He pulled Ellie's chair out for her, then lit a tall white candle and with a bow was gone.

David searched the menu without seeing, angrily skimming the pages. Ellie looked over the top of hers and watched him, a tolerant smile on her lips. "Would you rather take me someplace else?" she asked.

"Yeah. How about the Copper Kettle on the corner of Gower and Sunset?"

"My mind is made up."

"Your parents are going to be worried." He glared at her.

"I'm a big girl. And I can take care of myself."

"Like you did in the riot? They'd have been shipping you home in a box if I hadn't—"

"I know that." Ellie laid her menu down. "But something has happened to me."

"You could say that." David pretended to read the menu again.

"I mean inside. Something is going on in me," she tried to say calmly.

"You're on overload, that's what."

"There might be some way that I can help here." As she picked up the menu, she felt a surge of irritation.

"Who do you think you are, Joan of Arc? Saint Ellie? You're going to get yourself killed for the noble cause of journalism. Even people who fought their way across Europe are going to

189

get blasted in this thing. Walking down the street can be fatal. If we—you and I—have any future at all together—"

"You're assuming an awful lot, David," Ellie interrupted, "just like you always did. I told you I'm not the same."

"How do you think Moshe feels about you if he asked you to stay?" David's voice got a little louder.

"I think he loves me."

"Not as much as he loves this stinkin' little piece of real estate, he doesn't."

"I'm a journalist. This is my job."

"Two days ago you were an archaeologist's flunky on your way back home. Now all of a sudden you're a journalist!"

Ellie noticed a couple casting sidelong glances at David as his voice got progressively louder. "Lower your voice," Ellie said too loudly. "I've had it with you, David. If that is all you think of me—"

"I don't care if it means you're going to win a Pulitzer, do you hear me?"

"Yes, and so does everybody else in the room."

"You want to be a journalist, go ahead. But do it without me. I want a woman, okay? This is it. We're finished!"

The shadow of a waiter fell over the table. Angrily Ellie and David glared up at him.

"Is there anything I can get for you?" he asked, feeling uncomfortable under their gaze.

"Yes." Ellie stood up. "A taxi."

Moshe stared blankly out the window to where the sun shone on the glistening surface of the Dome of the Mosque of Omar. Only once had he stood on the soil of the sacred spot where Abraham had offered his son on the altar he had built with his own hands. A tall, lanky boy of fifteen, Moshe had donned the stolen uniform of a British soldier and had walked past the Muslim guards at the gates of the mosque. No Jew could openly visit the site without fear of reprisal or arrest. Sweat had formed on his brow and his heart had beat faster as he strode into the courtyard. He had imagined how Abraham had felt, knowing that he had come to this place to offer his son as a sacrifice. His mouth tasted of iron and the pit of his stomach churned.

And yet God had been faithful, Moshe remembered. God had provided a ram for the sacrifice, so Isaac had not died. Moshe had raised his eyes toward the Western Wall, which stood as the last remaining edifice of the Great Temple which had been destroyed along with the nation of Israel nearly two thousand years before. Moshe had not entered the mosque, but instead had visualized the ragged band of Jews who prayed just on the other side of the wall. They, too, prayed for a Savior who would one day deliver Jerusalem. Only a thin wall of hand-hewn stones separated those Jews from the Muslims he had walked with in the courtyard. But it was a line that marked the hardness of men's hearts, he had thought.

Moshe turned from the window and sat down heavily at his desk. He toyed with the photographs of the scroll: the book of Isaiah as it was written when the Great Temple stood where the Muslim shrine now glistened. Not one word had been changed. The promises remained the same. The destruction of Israel and the wanderings of her people had all been foretold. Now her people were returning. But what of the Messiah? He had long since turned his back on the belief of the Holy One of Israel. And yet, the Orthodox Jews who prayed at the wall still denied that there could be a nation again unless the Messiah came personally to govern and redeem. There were so many different beliefs among the Jews of the world. Surely there must be one truth in it all. Had the Messiah come to Israel once already, as Howard believed? Had God provided the Holy One as a lamb of sacrifice to redeem and restore in a different way than the way they had always expected?

The small brass lamp on Moshe's cluttered desk illuminated the glossy photographs of the Isaiah scroll. Moshe reread the confirmation from Johns Hopkins University:

"Congratulations. You may well have uncovered the most significant find in recent history. The material confirms the scroll to be of first-century origin . . ."

For what seemed like the hundredth time, Moshe leafed through the photographs, amazed at the clear, precise lettering of the ancient writings. He opened his most recent edition of the Hebrew text of Isaiah and scanned the pages for any variation of wording between the scroll and the modern printed page. Letter by letter the words read the same; the message was the same. Moshe flipped to Isaiah 53 and frowned as he carefully reread the words.

> But he was pierced through for our transgressions,
> He was crushed for our iniquities;
> The chastening for our well being fell upon him,
> And by his scourging we are healed.
> All of us like sheep have gone astray,
> Each of us has turned to his own way;
> But the Lord has caused the iniquity of us all
> To fall on him . . .

Moshe's eyes fell on the modern rabbinical commentaries below the text: "The Prophet refers to the nation of Israel . . ."

Although the text has remained unchanged over two thousand years, the interpretation of the scripture had, indeed, changed. He leaned back and scratched his head, trying to remember the ancient commentaries he had come across on this passage so many years before. He stood and searched his bookshelves for the Aramaic translation written in the second century by Rabbi Jonathan ben Uzziel, a disciple of the great Hillel.

"Targum Jonathan on Isaiah 53," he muttered, pulling the dusty volume from the shelf. He opened the book to the fifty-second chapter and began to read the Aramaic. "Behold my servant Messiah shall prosper . . ." He frowned at the word Messiah: then he laid the book down and with a feeling of urgency searched for a ninth-century prayer book on the topmost shelf. He carefully removed the crumbling book and leafed through its pages until he found the paraphrase of the fifty-third chapter of Isaiah written for recitation on Yom Kippur: "Messiah, . . . Our iniquities and the yoke of our transgressions he did bear, for he was wounded for transgression: He carries our sins upon his shoulders, that we may find forgiveness for our iniquities . . ."

"And so," he said aloud. "The interpretation was changed, although the words have remained the same. The ancients knew the prophet spoke of the Messiah. How inconvenient truth can be at times!" He half smiled, staring down at the photographs washed in light. "Especially when for so long the one you thought to be your enemy is, in fact, your Savior. This is truth, Moshe Sachar," he said aloud to himself. "So what will you do with the Messiah? The one they call Christ?"

19 Haganah Woman

The Old Man flipped through the pages of the December 15th issue of *Life* magazine, pausing at an advertisement showing Santa Claus puffing away on a Chesterfield cigarette. "Hmmm," he said, turning the page, then peering at Ellie from beneath his bushy white eyebrows, "Your photograph sells the magazine, and Santa sells cigarettes. Not exactly full of Christmas cheer, your photograph, eh?" He folded the cover back and lay the magazine face up. Ellie gazed at the shot of the tailor grasping his heart as the murderer's knife plunged deep into his back.

"No, sir. It was like a nightmare," she said softly.

"Moshe tells me how you saved the boy." Moshe cleared his throat and shifted his weight from one foot to the other. "You have a commission now from the publication to stay in Jerusalem and cover the story?"

"Yes," she nodded, still staring at the tailor, remembering his choking cry.

"That is good. Very good. Perhaps you can help the world see what we are up against here. That is very important, Miss Warne. We are alone and outnumbered, we Jews. We have been around quite a while, and I hope that when the dust clears we shall still be here. But we will not do it without public opinion."

Ellie looked into his eyes. "I was right in the middle of that, you know. I saw what was going on. I still can't figure out *why* it happened, but it happened. So what do you want from me?"

Ben-Gurion looked first at Moshe, then back to Ellie. He frowned and pursed his lips thoughtfully. "If it is pictures you want, we can make sure you are right in the thick of it. Moshe says you are made of pretty tough material."

"He says that, does he?" She looked at Moshe, who shrugged and grinned self-consciously. "I'm not running for the first freight back to America, if that's what you mean." She sat back in her chair.

"Good. If you can take it, we will have all the story you can use."

"I know you're worried that *Life* isn't sending some big tough war correspondent to Jerusalem for this. I know I'm a woman and—"

"On the contrary. The agency has no qualms about your ability, or the ability of any dedicated woman. I would ask a man the same questions. Where you'll be going, the other side will be shooting real bullets in your direction. You have to understand."

"You think after what happened to me two weeks ago I am not aware of the danger? Jerusalem is a keg of dynamite with the fuse lit. And I'm lucky enough to have plenty of film and an assignment to be here when it blows."

"Lucky?" The Old Man repeated.

"That's the word." She held her chin up.

Ben-Gurion rocked back in his chair and tapped the photograph of the tailor's murder. "Luck is not a word many residents of Jerusalem are using right now." He sat silently.

"Then it's settled." Moshe rubbed his hands together. "You are staying!"

"You'd have a terrible time getting rid of me, Moshe," she said.

"Perhaps we should begin with the *Ave Maria*?" The Old Man asked Moshe.

Moshe grinned and nodded, then turned to Ellie. "How would you like to take a little Mediterranean cruise?"

"Romantic?"

"And dangerous."

———

Fumbling with excitement, Ellie stuffed a heavy cable knit sweater and a pair of Levis into the blue canvas duffle bag on her bed. As an afterthought she tossed in an extra pair of wool socks and two changes of underwear. *Moshe said we would only be gone overnight, but*, Ellie thought, *it never hurts to be prepared*.

Her bedroom door squeaked on its hinges and Miriam entered carrying a small brown paper sack. "I don't know where you are going or why, but you will need to eat, eh? Chicken sandwiches and zucchini bread. The bread is frozen but will thaw soon. Also two oranges." She tossed the sack onto the bed and stood with her hands on her hips, shaking her head in disapproval. "You are wearing this?" She squinted at the Levis and denim shirt, then shook her head again.

"This is not a picnic, Miriam. I could get dirty."

"What is this?" The old woman picked up Ellie's stocking cap and held it between her thumb and forefinger as though it were something contaminated. "You will wear this?"

"Probably." Ellie continued to pack, wishing Miriam would go away.

"Ah!" she pitched the cap into the duffle bag. "You will look like a sailor."

"I guess so," Ellie avoided answering the question in Miriam's voice.

"So, you will not tell this old woman where you are going?"

"I can't." Ellie put her arm around Miriam's shoulders and gave her a quick hug.

"Well, then, our Lord knows and may He be merciful and keep you safe." She sighed and turned to leave. "And take a warm sweater."

"I will."

"And if you are going to sea, take extra woolen socks."

"I did."

The old woman smiled broadly. "And stay dry," she said finally, chuckling as she left the room.

Ellie rolled her eyes in exasperation and tied the duffle bag, then followed Miriam and called after her, "Take the day off. Go visit your son." Miriam raised her hand in acknowledgment and disappeared into the kitchen. *There is no use in the old woman staying home and worrying*, thought Ellie as she grabbed her camera bag and skipped into the study to kiss Uncle Howard good-bye.

He sat among the empty shelves and cases, scribbling notes as he studied copies of the scroll photographs. When at last he looked up, his eyes were rimmed with weariness. "Leaving, child?" He put his hand out to her.

"On a convoy to Tel Aviv. They say Arabs don't bother convoys leaving the city."

"Only coming in. When will you return?"

"Tomorrow night. David will fly me back. It's all arranged." She stood over the desk and stared at the photographs. "I'm sorry the Bedouins didn't come back with the scrolls."

Uncle Howard leaned back in the chair and stretched, "To

195

be expected. It is, after all, dangerous for them as well. Perhaps when it is all settled here, quiet again."

"When will that be?"

Howard shrugged and smiled. "God knows."

"I'm glad somebody does." She leaned down and kissed him lightly on the forehead.

———

Ellie sat across from Moshe on a small metal jumpseat inside the heavily armored transport. The morning light streamed through the narrow slits just above their heads. They shared the car with four others, two men and two women on their way to Tel Aviv and destinations unspoken but somehow understood. Ellie recognized one, a man with thick glasses in a rumpled business suit carrying a bulging briefcase. He and the slim, muscular Sabra man in khaki had been in the waiting room at the Jewish Agency building. She could only guess at their assignments. The two women looked equally intent. One was thin, almost frail. *Probably not yet twenty*, Ellie thought. *How much like a high school girl she looks!* The other was heavyset and thick-featured. Her kindly brown eyes smiled from behind a very large nose. Her graying hair was pulled back in a bun and she wore a plain blue wool dress and black low-heeled shoes that looked like they had walked many a purposeful mile. She smiled and nodded at Moshe and called him by his first name, but—as if by some unwritten law—no one asked the others the reason for their travel on the road to Tel Aviv.

"The weather seems to have turned for the better," said the heavyset woman, turning her eyes toward the streaming light as the vehicle lurched into motion.

"It is warming up," said the bespectacled man, clutching his briefcase to him. "This morning my long underwear didn't need defrosting."

"Much better for the roads, eh?" said the Sabra man. "We are less likely to get bogged down if it's not raining."

"Hmmm," agreed the first. "Less mud for politicians to sling," he said with an impish grin.

The descent from Jerusalem to Bab El Wad was much slower and more uncomfortable than Ellie had remembered it. Rocks and ruts seemed to jostle the travelers every few feet, and the monotonous drone of the engine soon was the only sound in the armored vehicle. Twenty minutes down the road, the Sabra began to hum a sad-sounding melody and soon Moshe joined in softly until everyone was singing but Ellie, who could not understand the words. The tempo increased, filling the faces of the travelers with joy as they clapped and stamped their feet in time.

"That is beautiful," Ellie said when at last the song ended. She reached out and took Moshe's hand. "What does it mean, Moshe?"

"It is called *B'Shuv Adonoy*," he answered quietly. Then he frowned thoughtfully and began to translate:

"When the Lord brought back those that returned
to Zion, We were like them that dream.
Then was our mouth filled with laughter,
And our tongue with singing;

"Then they said among the nations;
The Lord hath done great things with these,
The Lord hath done great things with us.

"Turn our captivity, O Lord,
As streams in the dry land.
They that sow in tears shall reap in joy."

"Will you teach me?" she asked brightly.

"Oh, there are many songs to learn," the Sabra chimed in; then he burst into song and the others joined him once again and the grinding miles seemed to melt away. After each song Moshe would translate and then the group would sing it again more slowly so that she could sing along.

Occasionally the small convoy would pass an Arab riding a donkey as his wife walked along behind. And once, when Ellie raised up to peek out the slit window, she glimpsed three silent Arab peasants standing on top of a boulder by the roadside, their battered rifles plainly in view. "They will not attack trucks coming out of the city," Ellie said to herself. "They are waiting for the convoy into Jerusalem." Somehow the thought was not reassuring.

Moshe tugged on her sweater. "Sit down. Sometimes there are snipers in the rocks. They can see movement through the windows."

Instantly, Ellie planted herself on the seat and remained there until at last the road seemed to level out and the curves became less difficult.

"A few minutes to Latrun now," the driver called back over his shoulder.

"Latrun?" Ellie felt her mouth go dry. "Isn't that the place where the bus . . ."

Moshe nodded and closed his eyes for a moment at the memory. Then the vehicle slowed as the driver downshifted and leaned forward to peer intently out the slit. "Roadblock ahead," he said apprehensively. "British."

The frail woman shifted uneasily and fear crossed her face. The older woman reached out and touched her arm reassuringly, then pulled herself up very straight. The vehicle ground to a halt and Ellie heard the accents of British soldiers shouting orders, then a loud banging on the doors at the back.

"Open up!" a harsh voice demanded.

"Bus fare," quipped the little man. "Exact change or death." He sliced his finger across his neck, but no one laughed.

"By whose authority?" shouted the Sabra man.

"By the authority of His Majesty's Mandatory Government of Palestine." The soldier pounded on the doors again. "Open up."

The Sabra unlocked the doors and shoved them open hard, causing the soldier outside to fall back. Three other soldiers stepped forward with guns in hand.

"It is our information that this convoy is carrying armed members of the Haganah as guards. Step out please. Everybody step out."

"I must protest!" snapped Moshe. "Arab territory is hardly the place for unarmed Jewish civilians to climb out of an armored transport."

"Maybe not, mate," growled a portly sergeant, "but them's our orders. Ladies first." He extended his hand and helped the heavyset woman out first, then the thin, frightened-looking girl. "You too," he pointed at Ellie who stood and inched her way through the tangle of legs to the back of the vehicle. She jumped down, feeling unwilling to accept the help of this intruder. He eyed her with interest, taking in her casual dress and heavy field boots. "Goin' campin', are y' miss?" he sneered. "We'll start with you then. Get your 'ands on the truck."

Angrily, Ellie turned and placed her hands on the side of the vehicle. She closed her eyes and gritted her teeth as the leering soldier frisked her. A wave of disgust and humiliation passed over her as the man ran his hands over her much too slowly for the purpose. "That's enough!" she demanded, whirling around and looking straight into his smirking face.

"Got any luggage?" he asked. "'and 'er bags out 'ere, mates," he called as Ellie's camera bag and duffle were passed out to the waiting soldiers. The sergeant pawed through her clothes, then unzipped her camera bag.

"A tourist are you, miss? 'ardly the place to take pictures."

"I'm a journalist. *Life* magazine. You've heard of it?"

He blanched and zipped her bag back and handed it to her. "American, I take it? Just following orders. Weapons check." He seemed eager to explain. "We can't 'ave Jews carryin' weapons about the country no more'n the Arabs, now can we? Carries a death sentence, y'know, carryin' a weapon." He sniffed and grinned obnoxiously. "You can get in now, miss."

"No, thanks," Ellie's eyes narrowed with controlled anger as she remembered the Arabs and their rifles back up the road just twenty minutes. "I think I'll watch."

The old woman was quickly frisked, and did not utter a word of protest. The thin woman grew paler by the minute and hesitantly complied with the order. Ellie thought she detected tears welling up behind the thin woman's thick glasses as she turned and placed her hands on the truck. The sergeant quickly ran his hands over her, then shouted, "Ah, ha!" as he touched her just above the knee. "Let's 'ave it, darlin'," he said triumphantly, extending his hand.

The woman raised her skirt and pulled a loaded revolver from a leather strap on her thigh. She raised her eyes defiantly.

"You don't expect us to travel these roads without protection, do you? Not after what has been happening?"

"I don't expect anything!" he snarled. "I'm just doin' a job." He handed the gun to a cocky private and led her by the arm to a waiting car.

Ellie pulled out her camera and began snapping pictures as the men filed out of the transport one by one to be searched.

"I wouldn't do that!" the sergeant snarled at her.

"And who's going to say I can't?" Ellie focused on the thin girl in the British car and snapped the shutter.

The sergeant backed off and chewed his lip, then rubbed his

hand over his cheek nervously. "I told you I'm just doin' as ordered." Then he looked the group of travelers over. "You can get back in now. And that goes for you, too," he said to Ellie.

Then the heavyset woman stepped forward and asked with dignity, "Where are you taking the girl?"

"Latrun. Headquarters," he answered curtly. "Now get in."

"No," said the heavy woman. "I shall go with her to your headquarters. That is in Arab territory. We shall see what your superiors have to say about this." Then she turned solemnly to Ellie. "Would you like to photograph our arrest?" She smiled and climbed into the British car as Ellie snapped several more pictures.

"Suit yourself." The sergeant slammed the door. "If you're with her and she had an illegal weapon, then I ought to arrest the whole lot of you."

Ellie snapped his picture, then smiled a bit too brightly at his irritated expression before she waved at the woman and the thin girl and climbed back into the transport. The doors clanged shut behind her as she took her seat, still furious over the search. Each of the men patted her back as she passed them, and chorused congratulations.

"What will happen to the women?" she asked in dismay.

"Don't worry," Moshe smiled knowingly. "They'll make it to Tel Aviv."

"How do you know that? They're being taken to Latrun."

"Didn't you recognize the lady who went with the girl?"

"No."

"You just shot a roll of film covering the arrest of Golda Meir, Ben-Gurion's right-hand man at the Jewish Agency. That ought to make a cover story," he laughed. "I'd hate to see what they do to the sergeant when she pulls out her papers."

"What about the girl with the gun?" The transport lurched forward.

"Golda will not leave her alone. And the British are usually pretty proper when it comes to women. That's why there are women guards on our convoys. A Jewish man caught with a weapon even for defense would be hanged."

Ellie nodded, still enraged at the unfairness of the policy. "That was Golda Meir?" she asked, hardly able to believe that such a high-ranking member of the Jewish Agency would put her life on the line so readily. "She seems so—"

"Like a nice Jewish grandmother?"

"Uh-huh."

"And so she is. Jewish grandmothers like her have helped our people survive two thousand years," he grinned.

"I can see why." Ellie shook her head in amazement.

The occupants of the transport began to sing once again as they passed through Latrun and Sarafand. It seemed to Ellie that they bellowed even louder as they drove along the outskirts of the British military base. The tune they sang was called Hatikvah, "The Hope," and though Ellie could not understand the words, she *felt* them in the voices of her companions. There was one hope they all lived for—a homeland.

When at last they arrived at the Tel Aviv bus terminal, Ellie had learned most of the words of Hatikvah and was harmonizing with her clear alto voice as Moshe sang bass and the little man joined with the Sabra to sing the melody in tenor.

"Just like singing in the shower," Ellie laughed. "Sounds terrific."

"Maybe we should sing on Broadway in *South Pacific*, eh?" grinned the little man with an accent decidedly that of a New Yorker.

"Maybe you should just make your homeland in the South Pacific somewhere. It would sure be easier than this." Ellie gathered her belongings as the Sabra opened the doors and the interior flooded with light.

"I always thought Tahiti would have been a nice place for a Yeshiva school." Moshe jumped out and extended a hand to help her down.

"As long as it was for Hassidim," the little man followed. "So when the Yeshiva boys saw the girls in grass skirts they could say, 'Ha see dem!' " Everyone groaned and the Sabra tapped his finger to his temple and shook his head.

"You are a meshuggener, Arazi. A crazy man," he said.

"That's why I'm here with you, right?"

Moshe whispered loudly into Ellie's ear, "An old joke."

"After four thousand years, how many new Jewish jokes can there be?" The little man guffawed and punched Moshe on the arm; then he extended his hand, "Good luck to you both. Mazel Tov." Then he winked at Ellie. "I'll buy a copy of your magazine." He turned and followed the Sabra across the lobby of the bus station.

Ellie watched their retreating forms, then gazed up at Moshe. "Crazy people in this thing," she shook her head.

"It helps to be something of a lunatic. It could get depressing otherwise." He put his arm around her shoulder. "And now you will meet the biggest meshuggener in Palestine." He led her out onto the street and scanned the bustling, frantic traffic until he spotted a battered, rattling black hulk of an automobile weaving wildly through the other cars. It screeched to a halt at the curb and Ehud climbed out of the window on the driver's side, shouting curses at another car that passed and turned the corner.

"Maniac!" he yelled, shaking his hairy fist. He stuck out his lower lip and seemed to growl, then, still glaring at the last spot he had seen the car, he stomped toward Moshe and Ellie muttering, "Must have worked for the Führer."

"This," Moshe said sheepishly, "will be your host, Ehud Schiff."

Ehud saw Ellie standing next to Moshe and instantly his demeanor changed. "Ahhhhh!" His eyes lit up and he took her hand and bent to kiss it. "You are the Miss Ellie Warne we have heard so much of. Ah, yes, Moshe, she is beautiful. Beautiful indeed, as you have often said."

Laughing, Ellie shook his meaty hand and said, "Well, Moshe has not even told me about you. Until now, that is." Then she looked wonderingly at Moshe. "We are riding with Ehud?"

"I am afraid so," he said with mock seriousness.

"Ah, that," Ehud gestured toward the now-vanished enemy automobile. "That car you saw? Refused to move when I wanted to change lanes," he explained.

"Ehud thinks the highways are like the seas." Moshe took Ellie's bags and threw them through the window of Ehud's car. "That is why the doors of his automobile will not open. They are crushed shut. I shall drive, Ehud. This lady is much too important for me to lose her on the streets of Tel Aviv."

Ehud pouted for a brief instant, then tugged his beard thoughtfully and climbed into the car through the window. "As you wish, Moshe. So get in already; my darling waits for us at the waterfront."

Ellie climbed in awkwardly after him and sat wedged between his massive frame and the door of the car as Moshe pulled into traffic.

"Are you all set?" Moshe asked.

"Oh, yes, I am. But my darling Maria, my love; she is not feeling well."

"What seems to be the matter?" Concern was etched on Moshe's face.

"She is simply at that age, you know. I fear I shall have to someday get rid of her."

Ellie tried not to register shock. She leaned forward to see Moshe's expression as Ehud spoke about his beloved and her potential demise. To her dismay, Moshe did not seem to think that there was anything unusual about Ehud's conversation. "Has anyone checked her?" she asked, trying to be helpful.

"To be sure," Ehud nodded solemnly. "But he was such a greasy fellow. Lacked the sensitivity a lady requires, so I myself have taken care of her. An occasional kick in the right place when she becomes contrary—"

"Don't you think you should call someone more qualified?" Ellie asked as they rounded a corner and pulled onto the dock.

"I have been her master these twenty-five years!" Ehud exclaimed. "Sweet Maria would have no one but me. Who could know her half so well?"

"But you can't just get rid of her!" Ellie protested. "Not after twenty-five years."

Moshe began to chuckle as he set the brake and climbed out onto the wood-planked dock. "Ah, there you see her. Is she not a vision?" Ehud pointed out the window of the car as he waited for Ellie to climb out.

Ellie searched the waterfront and saw no one but two old fishermen scraping barnacles off a dry-docked hulk, and another young man mending nets on the deck of an old trawler. "Where?"

Moshe poked his head in the passenger window. "Do you need help getting out?" he asked Ellie.

She rolled her eyes and made a face as if to ask which asylum Ehud had escaped from. "Where is Maria?" she asked. "I don't see anybody female out there," she said to Moshe as Ehud climbed out the driver's side.

"I suppose it depends on one's perspective." He pointed to the ancient, weather-scarred trawler moored in a row with several others. "That," he said, "is Ehud's beloved."

Ellie squinted and puckered her face as she read the barely visible red letters on the chipping white paint, *Ave Maria*. Relief flooded her voice and she rubbed her forehead as a flush of embarrassment crept to her cheeks. "I thought . . ." she whispered hoarsely.

Moshe laughed and offered Ellie his hand. "An easy mistake to make."

Ehud joined them and gazed dreamily at the little ship. "She was so beautiful in her younger days—my little darling." Then he hastened to add, "But surely not half so beautiful as you, sweet lady."

"Watch out, my friend," Moshe warned. "Maria will be jealous."

Ehud put a thick finger to his lips, "Quite so, quite so. She is so sensitive." He walked toward the little trawler.

Ellie leaned close to Moshe, tugging on his shirtfront until he leaned his ear down to her lips. "Is he serious?" she asked with alarm at the thought of going with him.

"Quite so, quite so," Moshe repeated mischievously. "I told you, meshuggener, eh? But there is none in these waters with half so big a heart. Come along." He walked after Ehud toward the deck of the trawler. "We have a long way to go before nightfall."

———————

Sea gulls circled overhead in the clear blue sky, and only a faint breeze ruffled Ellie's hair as she stood on deck, waiting for the ship to get under way. Tiny waves lapped the sides of the *Ave Maria*, and sunlight on the water reflected against her hull. Cables and nets cluttered the deck, and as Ellie looked down the row of moored fishing vessels, she found little about the *Ave Maria* that distinguished her from the other ships at port.

"It is her heart," Ehud nodded when Ellie commented that there was no way of telling that she was not an ordinary boat. "God has been with us, surely." He patted the wheel.

"She carries the children of Abraham well for her age," Moshe had said.

"Like Sarah? Maybe you ought to call your next boat Sarah. She was ninety when she had her first child."

Ehud's face clouded, and he stroked Maria's wheel. "You shall wound her if you speak so. Pay no mind, my love," he had muttered. "Why don't you go on deck until we are under way?"

Ellie left the wheelhouse amused—until the engine refused

204

to turn over and only moaned in response to Ehud's coaxing. "Now see," he shouted down to her from the wheelhouse, "you have hurt her feelings!"

Ehud cursed and clanked down below deck in the engine room, until at last the stubborn engine sighed and turned over with a roar. Ellie sat on a pile of rope and watched as Moshe cast off the lines and the old hulk shuddered in reverse into the harbor, then lunged forward out past the seawall into the serene blue of the Mediterranean. Gulls cried and followed after them in hopes that they would find fish to catch and share. Ehud occasionally glowered down at her, and Ellie felt intimidated enough that she stayed on deck until at last Moshe joined her with two mugs of coffee in his hands.

"I said the wrong thing," Ellie smiled. "He doesn't like me, I'm afraid."

"He'll get over it," Moshe handed her a mug. "Drink this."

"He's a little strange, isn't he? I mean, the boat and everything."

"This boat *is* everything. He lost his own family in the camps—sisters, brothers, and a young wife early on in the war. He's a good man. He has defied the blockade a hundred times. Sixty-seven thousand Jews have been caught trying to get into Palestine in spite of the mandate. The *Ave Maria* has been stopped and searched a dozen times, but never with passengers on board. Ehud is right. There is something special about the old girl."

"What happens to the ones who are caught?"

"They are still behind barbed wire, on the Island of Cyprus. The British keep them there so as not to arouse the wrath of the Mufti."

Ellie inhaled the steam of her coffee, then sipped the warm brew. "Looks to me like the Mufti is plenty mad already." She gazed steadily at Moshe. "What would happen to you if you were caught?"

"Up to now we have only smuggled human contraband. We would be tried and imprisoned. Smuggling weapons means execution."

"They would kill you for that? Weapons for defense?"

"Many of us have died already." Moshe tasted his coffee.

Ellie thought about all the things she had accused him of; then she took his hand and stared out across the sea as the skyline of Tel Aviv began to shrink and disappear. "I said a lot of things to you that were wrong. I didn't know you had put everything on the line for this."

"How could you have known?" he lifted her chin. "I would have been a fool had I let anyone know."

"I'm . . . I don't want to be just anyone to you, Moshe. Would you forgive me for the things I said?"

"Even as you said them you were forgiven, my little shiksa." He kissed her on the cheek. "But in many ways you are still a child—impatient with those who do not see the world your way, at the same moment your eyes have only just been opened."

Ellie lowered her eyes and stared at the coil of rope just in front of where they sat. "You think I am insensitive?"

"On the contrary. I believe you feel"—he waved his hand toward the unbroken horizon—"everything. But there is more to truth than simply feeling. Just as there is more to love than feeling. Do you understand?"

"I'm trying," she said, feeling hopeless and lost in his words.

"Finding the truth involves commitment to search, to be open and work at uncovering the facts."

"You sound like an archaeologist."

Moshe laughed. "I suppose. It is your uncle, after all, who first challenged me to search." He looked away and tried to find words to begin again. "There are so many things I do not understand, and yet I believe that just beyond my understanding lies an answer. God says that we will be a nation once again. I do not understand how we have survived the oppression of two thousand years of Christian and Muslim hatred, and yet stand on the brink of statehood. Therefore, what God said through the prophets must be truth. Perhaps my duty is to find the promises, and in those I will find truth for my existence. Does this make sense?"

"Isn't it funny?" Ellie gulped her coffee. "I've spent my whole life thinking that what I feel is the way things must be. You've spent your whole life thinking about facts and truth. There has to be a place for both of those things: knowing truth in your head and feeling it in your heart. I'm trying, Moshe, really I am."

He squeezed her hand. "And so am I. And Ehud and Howard and your flyer friend David—"

Ellie stiffened. "David? He can't see past the nose on his face."

Moshe kissed her on the nose, then winked, "A common failing in human nature, is it not?" he laughed. "Judgment of another without the facts."

"I sure had you figured all wrong, didn't I?" She smiled up at him. "I'm glad."

"Since you have finally figured that out, my love," he stood and stretched, "I will tell you that I think David seems to be a fine fellow. He was very brave in his little plane."

"He's a show-off, that's all." She put her arms around his waist.

"This may not be the moment to convince you otherwise." He drew her close to him and kissed her gently.

"And what verdict have you reached about me, your honor?"

"Can you cook?"

"Where is the kitchen?"

"You see, you really are perfect."

Ellie followed Moshe down the narrow steps into the hold of the ship where cases of oranges and Coca-Cola were stacked in a corridor that led to a dingy little galley. A small brass-rimmed porthole looked out the bow of the ship, and the roar of the engine nearly drowned out conversation. There was barely room for one person in front of the wide wooden counter where loaves of bread were stacked next to a large round of cheese and several sticks of salami.

"We will rendevous with the refugee ship sometime within the next two hours," Moshe shouted over the din. "They will be hungry."

"How many should I make?" she asked, astonished at the amount of bread and cheese in front of her.

"As many as possible. They will eat it all." He dug a large butcher knife out of a drawer and handed it to her. "Welcome to the Haganah, darling," he kissed her lightly.

"What is this? Some kind of initiation or something?" She touched her finger to the dull edge of the knife blade.

"If you can survive this"—he inched his way past her and out to the corridor—"we shall make you sergeant in charge of pots and pans."

She waved the knife in the air. "I feel like a pirate."

"The British would agree with you on that point." Then rubbing his stomach, he said, "If you get a free moment bring us a couple sandwiches, eh?"

"What else have I got to do?" She took the first of twenty thick-crusted loaves from the stack and began to saw on it. Moshe laughed, then returned to the wheelhouse.

The knife barely dented the crust of the bread and tore each slice into ragged chunks. Ellie rummaged through the drawers of the galley but found nothing sharper than a butter knife among the mismatched collection of silverware and utensils. She attacked the cheese with frustrated fervor, until, two hours later, uneven chunks of cheese lay in piles next to mounds of torn bread. She slapped the sandwiches together, grabbed two warm Cokes and headed for the deck, exhausted.

"Don't you guys believe in knives that have blades?" she asked without ceremony as she presented two thick sandwiches to Ehud and Moshe.

Ehud gripped the wheel with one hand, his other encircling the sandwich as if it were a baseball. "Now this is what I call lunch!" He attacked the dripping sandwich. "She is generous, this girl of yours!"

Moshe studied the ragged facsimile of a sandwich, then attempted to find a side thin enough that he could take a bite. "Hmmm. Generous."

"If you don't like it, Moshe"—Ellie crossed her arms and glowered—"you can use it for bait. Dough balls and cheese work great off the Santa Monica pier. Maybe you'll catch a swordfish, and you can cut your own bread!"

"I did not say a word." Moshe pulled a piece of cheese from between the bread and munched contentedly.

"I shall eat his!" exclaimed Ehud. "It is good and plenty big."

"Thank you, Ehud," said Ellie. "Back in the States we would call this a delicacy. Sort of, anyway."

"You see?" Ehud opened his Coke with his teeth. "The girl has made us American sandwiches, and we are meeting the SS *America*. This is a good omen. Not to worry, Moshe."

"Have I missed something?" Ellie paused with concern. "Is there something to worry about?"

Moshe looked up and studied the horizon to the north. "The ship is late, or we've missed her somehow."

"What will we do?"

"We shall wait." Ehud swigged his Coke. "She shall come."

20   Checkmate

It was past four o'clock. The cry of the muzzein had already echoed across the Old City, calling the faithful to prayer. Haj Amin, Mufti of Jerusalem, rose from his prayer rug and slipped on his shoes. Then he entered the patio where Hassan and Gerhardt waited.

"My friends," he said serenely, taking a seat across from them. He clapped his hands twice and a servant brought a silver pot of strong coffee and three tiny cups. Haj Amin poured the coffee himself and handed it to the men. "Have you seen the photograph in the American magazine?" he asked.

Hassan nodded, his eyes downcast.

"You are responsible for this, Hassan?"

"Your excellence—" he began, his cup clattering on the saucer.

"We appear as murderers to the world, do we not?" The Mufti snapped his fingers and another servant brought a copy of *Life* to him. He thumbed through the pages until he found the photograph of the tailor. "And the world weeps in sympathy for the Jews?" He laughed as Hassan squirmed uneasily in his chair. Haj Amin turned his gaze on Gerhardt. "Have you prepared our gift for the Jews of Ben Yehuda?" he inquired.

Gerhardt nodded.

"Good. But I fear we must prepare another first."

Gerhardt frowned and leaned forward, intently eyeing Haj Amin.

"It is a small thing." Haj Amin flicked his fingers and smiled slyly. "Hassan has told me he has seen the old woman, the housekeeper from the home of the red-headed woman. She visits your hotel frequently. Her son lives there, I believe?"

"Yes," Hassan broke in, "and several other members of the family since the commercial district—"

Haj Amin cast a withering glance in his direction. "Quite enough, Hassan." He coughed slightly. "It is, of course, the plan of the Jews to gain the sympathy of the world, to castigate us publicly in the press with pictures such as these. I need not tell you, Gerhardt, publicity and terror go hand in hand. We must, I fear, delay our gift to Ben Yehuda Street until the world has opportunity to weep with us over the loss of Arab lives."

"What do you mean, your excellence?" asked Hassan.

"When the Jews bomb the Semiramis Hotel, who will say that we are unjust when we repay them an eye for an eye?"

"But the Jews have not—" Hassan began, only to be cut short by a glance from the Mufti.

Haj Amin smiled knowingly at Gerhardt. "It is but a few Christian Arabs, more or less. Would tonight be too soon, my friend?"

"Inch´ Allah, Haj Amin," he answered. "If Allah wills."

"Allah and the Mufti." Haj Amin threw his head back in laughter at his cleverness.

————

A late afternoon breeze ruffled the water and the *Ave Maria* bobbed in the swells. Chin in hand, Moshe stared at the chess-board propped on a rope coil between Ehud and Ellie.

"I think she has you, Ehud, my friend," said Moshe, gulping down the last of Miriam's zucchini bread.

Ehud scowled. "The game is far from over. The day will not dawn when Ehud Schiff shall be beaten by a woman."

"The sun may set, however." Moshe scratched his chin.

Ellie smiled sweetly at Ehud, then moved her queen. "Check."

"Ha!" exclaimed Ehud in disgust, slapping his fist on his knee.

Ellie batted her eyes. "And a Gentile woman at that!"

"It is not yet checkmate!" he protested.

"Give it up, Ehud." Moshe patted him on the back, then looked out on the horizon for the hundredth time.

As thick heavy clouds gathered to the north, the tiny swells of the early afternoon had become broader and deeper.

"If they don't arrive soon," Moshe frowned, "we may be in trouble with the weather."

"Like the last time, eh?" said Ehud with his eyes still intent on the board. "When you pulled the young beauty from the sea?"

Ellie looked up curiously. "That's one I hadn't heard about."

"A Venus, Moshe told me. She jumped and he saved her.

Some lucky fellow will thank him one day, eh, Moshe?" He nudged Moshe, who pretended not to hear as he raised the field glasses to his eyes and search the horizon for the thin trail of smoke that would announce the arrival of the *SS America*.

"Did you pull her back into the boat?" asked Ellie, no longer interested in the chess game.

"Oh, no," interjected Ehud, ignoring the dirty look Moshe cast in his direction. "He swam all the way to shore with her. They spent the night on the beach and then he took her to Fanny's—"

"Moshe, why didn't you tell me you were such a hero?" Ellie asked, feeling a rush of jealousy.

Ehud rubbed his hands together delightedly and moved his only remaining rook. "It is your move," he instructed Ellie.

"It is just a part of this job," said Moshe, still staring through the field glasses.

"Ah, now, admit it, Moshe." Ehud crossed his arms. "You would not have jumped in for an old hag!" He narrowed his eyes with satisfaction as Ellie's concentration disintegrated.

"Shut up, Ehud!" Moshe snapped. "Play."

Ehud shrugged innocently, "It is her move, is it not?"

"Was she really that pretty, Moshe?" Ellie absently fingered her knight.

"A dream made in heaven, Moshe told me," Ehud stared hopefully at Ellie's fingers. "So move, already."

"I suppose she was," Moshe answered irritably, "somewhat beautiful."

Ellie moved her knight without thinking, and Ehud clapped his hands together as he made the final move of the game. "Checkmate!" he cried triumphantly. "So, my sweet Gentile lady, you lose!"

"You did that on purpose!" Ellie protested.

"I do not understand," he grinned, gathering the chess pieces into an old shoe box.

Moshe stood and walked to the bow of the ship, then peered through the field glasses at the thunderheads. There, in a thin line against the dark gray clouds, he saw a faint wisp of smoke. "There she is," he called over his shoulder. "Looks like she's just ahead of the storm."

"That is not good," Ehud handed the box to Ellie. "We are

late as it is. After we transfer the passengers, we shall perhaps not land them until dawn."

"I'll bet the sandwiches are stale too," said Ellie miserably as she wondered about the beautiful woman Moshe had rescued.

"No matter," said Moshe. "Let's get her under way."

The sun was low in the sky when at last the *Ave Maria* pulled along side the rusting hulk of the freighter SS *America*, and one by one the refugees were lowered to her deck. Women and children far outnumbered the men, and Ellie overheard Moshe speaking in low tones to Ehud about the need for men of military age.

"We must make it clear," he said. "This must be the last group until statehood is established. From now on only young men. Or women strong enough to train to fight. It is too dangerous to risk transport otherwise."

Ehud nodded grimly, and Ellie hurried off to photograph the faces that seemed to reflect every argument for the statehood of Israel. Gaunt and hollow-eyed, cradling babies and clutching small children, women were led into the hold of the bobbing little trawler. They carried small bundles of belongings or nothing at all, and Ellie thought of her own duffle bag stowed below deck. She probably brought more for an overnight trip than these people even owned. Grateful but haunted eyes met hers as she helped a mother carry a baby down the steep steps. Ellie fought off a feeling of horror as she remembered the newsreels showing the concentration camps and the faces of men and women as they waited in line for death. *What have these people lived through?* she wondered as they patiently took their places on the *Ave Maria*.

No words were spoken that she could understand, but Moshe talked to each person in a kind and loving way, patting backs and shaking hands in welcome. A thin, knobby-kneed boy in short pants and a ragged sweater smiled up adoringly at her and Ellie noticed that his teeth were decayed. "How will he eat?" she asked Moshe, aware that the boy would not understand her.

"When one is hungry enough—" he answered; then he spoke to the boy in Polish and ruffled his hair affectionately. "We will make sure his teeth are fixed. It is the scars we cannot see that break my heart." He shook his head sadly, then directed the boy to the hold as Ellie snapped their picture together. Moshe's eyes embraced the boy and Ellie thought once again how much Moshe *belonged*. Her heart filled with admiration for him, and she wanted to put her arms around him and tell him how very much she cared.

When the last person was safely loaded and at last the *Ave Maria* pulled away from the SS *America*, Ellie blinked back tears and touched Moshe's back as he stood in the bow with the wind on his face.

"I come here always. Every time after we pick them up. I think I will break sometimes, you know." He gazed down at her and his face was streaked with tears. "There is a poem your uncle told me by a man named Byron. 'The birds have their nests, the fox his den, but Israel has only the grave.' "

"I heard it, but I never understood it before."

"Everyone has a country. Everyone but a Jew. These"— he motioned toward the hold—"they have returned from the grave. It is hardest for me when I think that God has allowed such suffering. And it becomes my suffering because these are my people."

Ellie wrapped her arms around him and laid her head against his chest. "I wondered the same thing after the riot. Uncle Howard said that God didn't do this. People did. And the people who did it don't know God; don't have the slightest idea who He is."

"Perhaps he is right."

"I haven't really known, either—but I see this, and I think whoever God is, His heart must be breaking over the way we treat each other. And, Moshe, it makes me want to know Him and be like Him." She wiped the tears from his cheeks.

"I hope you find what you are looking for. I hope the same for myself, that somehow someone can heal the wounds we cannot see. It is difficult sometimes to be near suffering, is it not?"

"Makes me want to run and hide," she smiled. "But the sandwiches are getting stale."

It was past curfew when Hassan entered the dingy lobby of the Hotel Semiramis. The desk clerk leaned against the counter reading the *Cairo Times* which was spread out before him. He stared intently at the front page, studying the latest pronouncements by Arab leaders gathered at Cairo University to discuss which course to take against the Jews of Palestine. While others talked, the Mufti in Jerusalem translated thought into deadly action.

Hassan's final task at the hotel tonight was only one small example of Haj Amin's political savvy. Nine other members of Haj Amin's staff had already left the hotel for Bab El Wad. Only Hassan remained behind to redeem himself in the eyes of his leader. He would set the detonator on the bomb Gerhardt had packed in the battered leather suitcase he now carried.

Hassan glanced around the lobby. An old man dozed in a chair while another man stood in front of the iron gates of the elevator and argued with an old woman. Hassan instantly recognized her.

"There, you see, Mother." The man pulled a pocket watch from his vest pocket. "You must stay here with me and Sammy."

Hassan started toward the stairs, then hesitated.

"I cannot stay. The professor, he shall worry," answered the old woman.

Hassan smiled and turned back to the elevator.

"And so shall I worry if you leave. My mother, must you be so stubborn? We shall simply telephone in the morning when the exchange is open. The professor would worry more if you were to leave now."

Hassan raised his hand to his mouth and coughed, interrupting the discussion between Ishmael and Miriam. "Tonight is not a night to be out. They say there is disturbance in the Montefiore Quarter."

"You see!" exclaimed Ishmael. "Not half a mile from here."

"One cannot be too careful." Hassan reached past Miriam and pushed the elevator button.

"Huh!" Miriam grunted, crossing her arms in disgust.

"The kind gentleman is right, Mother; now, come along."

"Jews or Muslims?" Miriam shook her head in resignation.

"Most certainly it is the Mufti's men tonight, dear lady." Hassan pulled back the grate of the elevator and stepped aside for Miriam to enter.

"That gangster!" The old woman spat. "Perhaps there would be some hope for peace were the devil not in our midst."

"Mother, please." Ishmael looked furtively around the lobby and gently urged her into the elevator.

"Hoodlums. Ignorant bullies, all of them," Miriam said loudly as Hassan lugged the suitcase into the tiny cubicle and pulled the grate shut behind them. "A little Hitler, this Haj Amin; and the innocent die for his glory."

"Alas, your words are so true," said Hassan earnestly as the elevator lurched into a slow ascent. "Second floor?" he asked as it ground to a stop.

Ishmael shook his head, "No thank you. We are on the fourth."

Hassan stepped out into the darkened hallway of the second floor and closed the iron grate. "Pleasant dreams." He smiled broadly and nodded farewell. As the elevator groaned and whined away, he entered the room just to the right of the shaft. Switching on the light, he glanced around, then carried the suitcase to the wall that bordered the shaft as Gerhardt had instructed him. Carefully he unlatched the locks and lifted the lid to reveal the simply-wired bomb that contained enough TNT to demolish the hotel and shatter windows for half a mile. He wound the clock that would trigger the detonator and set the time for six o'clock the next morning. At that hour, people would just be waking up, though not yet out of their rooms. He regretted that they would have no warning of their impending death; it was those last expressions of fear on the faces of his victims that he most liked to imagine. Ah, well, they would not die in their sleep, at any rate.

He closed the lid of the suitcase, switched off the light and locked the door behind him. Then he skipped down the stairs, happy in the knowledge that, indeed, the innocent would die for the glory of Haj Amin, Mufti of Jerusalem.

———

Throughout the night, the *Ave Maria* raced just ahead of the storm. A little past midnight, Ellie wadded up her jacket for a pillow, lay down in the galley between the counter and the icebox, and tried to sleep. Seasickness had begun to take its toll among the refugees in the crowded hold, and Moshe had resumed his post in the bow of the ship, watching for signs of a British gunboat.

Just past four-thirty the little trawler shuddered and lurched. Ellie was suddenly jolted and rolled against the icebox. She struggled to sit up, bracing herself against the counter while she looked at her watch. For a moment she could not remember where she was or why, and a feeling of anxiety swept over her. She stood slowly, clinging to the countertop to keep from falling with the bucking of the *Ave Maria*. The ship, Moshe, the faces— all came back to her with a rush. She reached for a thermos of coffee that rolled across the galley floor and bumped her foot. Then she pulled on her jacket and made her way through the galley, past sick and sleeping refugees, and up the steps to the deck.

The night was black as pitch and the rain fell, slanted and hard in the wind, stinging her face. She groped her way to the wheelhouse with the thermos bottle tucked under her arm. When she opened the door, Moshe stood at the wheel as Ehud took his turn with the field glasses.

"I brought coffee," she said cheerfully.

Neither Moshe nor Ehud answered; instead, Ehud took the wheel and handed Moshe the field glasses. "She's got us all right," said Ehud.

"Yes," Moshe answered grimly. "And she's signaling another."

"Sun will be up within an hour; then we're done for," Ehud growled as he stroked the wheel. "This may be our last voyage, old girl," he said gruffly.

"It is not yet checkmate, my friend." Moshe laid a hand on Ehud's arm.

Ellie stared bleakly out the window of the wheelhouse, watching as the running light of a British destroyer cut through the water on a direct course toward them. "They are going to catch us?" she asked. "Can't we get away?"

"We have been trying since two." Moshe rubbed his forehead wearily.

Ellie opened the thermos and handed the coffee to him. He took a swig, then handed it to Ehud. "We are not far from Naharia." He wiped his mouth with the back of his hand.

"There is no other way, I fear." Ehud's voice was filled with a sad determination. "Use the wireless. Call the kibbutz. We'll run her aground on the beach. Just let the British try and follow her up a sand bar! They will drag their bellies three hundred yards out from shore."

"It is your ship, Ehud. Your decision. Are you certain?"

Ehud did not answer, but instead silently stroked the wheel and nodded.

Moshe took Ellie's hand. "Come with me. We haven't got much time."

Ellie followed him down the steps and onto the deck. Over the roar of the wind, she heard the engine of the destroyer. Then searchlights clicked on and slammed against the darkness that had covered the *Ave Maria*. As the light engulfed them, Ellie raised her hand against the glare. She felt curiously like a rabbit caught in the road by the headlights of an approaching car. She wanted to run but there was no place to go. The wail of a siren screeched above the din of engines and storm.

"Come on!" Moshe cried, taking her by the arm and leading her down the steps. He stood on the bottom step and gazed over the pale faces before him. It was a recurrent nightmare, now become reality. "For the past several hours," he explained in three languages, "we have been pursued by a British destroyer. We turned back into the storm in hopes of evading her. It has done no good. Now we will run the ship aground. Crews will be on hand to help you to shore. Do not fear." He raised his voice as a moan of panic filled the hold. "You will be taken care of. There is little time. Gather your things."

He hurried past the questions and Ellie followed him, feeling helpless as she encouraged, in English, people who could not understand her words. She tried to smile as she pulled her hands away from fearful, clutching fingers. "Are we going to be okay, Moshe?" she asked.

"If ever you have prayed, now is the moment to do so." He strode down the corridor past the galley to a small room in the front of the ship. He struck a match and lit a kerosene lantern, then sat on a wooden crate and began to tinker with the dials of a black radio. Static crackled over the receiver. "It's the storm," he said impatiently as a high-pitched whine answered him. "Mary calling Gideon, come in please," he chanted. "Calling Gideon. Mary calling Gideon."

God, help us, Ellie prayed silently. *Help him get through.*

"Calling Gideon . . ."

The whine slid into a human voice that crackled back over the receiver. "Mary . . . Gideon . . . you're late."

"We've got a wolf on our trail. We're going to bring her in."

"How many . . . repea . . . lambs?"

"Ninety-three. Repeat, ninety-three."

When Ellie returned to the deck, the first gray light of dawn

217

filtered through the thick black clouds and the destroyer had been joined by a smaller gunboat. Ellie could plainly make out the movement of sailors on the decks of the ships and all eyes were turned toward them. The destroyer slid alongside, dwarfing the *Ave Maria*, causing her to shudder in its wake.

"BY ORDER OF HIS MAJESTY'S MANDATORY GOVERNMENT," a stern voice bellowed over a bullhorn, "YOU ARE UNDER ARREST."

Ehud pulled the whistle in response, then turned hard to the port and headed the *Ave Maria* straight into the shore and the breakers. "Get them up here, up on deck!" he yelled to Ellie.

Already Moshe had the refugees standing patiently in line and one by one he urged them onto the deck. Ellie helped with the children, calming them; finally, when a young mother began to sob, she put her arms around her and comforted her without words.

"Sing!" Ellie shouted to Moshe over the wail of the siren.

As the refugees filed on deck along the rail, Moshe began to sing "Be'Shuv Adonoy," and every voice joined him in a hymn of defiance against the giants pursuing them.

"TURN ABOUT!" ordered the bullhorn. "TURN ABOUT STARBOARD, *AVE MARIA*. BY ORDER OF HIS MAJESTY . . ."

The refugees answered by singing louder as Ehud steered his little ship nearer and nearer to the breakers. Ellie could see a group of men and women waiting on the beach ahead. She reloaded her camera and snapped pictures of the defiant faces of the refugees and the armor of the destroyer as the captain bellowed insults and threats and finally turned back from Ehud's suicide course.

The group on the beach launched two wooden lifeboats, pushing them out past the breakers toward the sand bar where the bottom loomed up in anticipation of the *Ave Maria's* final destination.

"Hold on, everybody!" Moshe cried as the little ship chugged steadily on.

Mothers clutched their children to them and held on to one another, tucking their faces down against shoulders and backs. The singing stopped, but the siren wailed on as the destroyer and her companion gunboat stood offshore and waited for the inevitable end.

In the wheelhouse, tears streamed down Ehud's craggy face

and clung to his beard in glistening drops. "You've been a fine lady." He stroked the wheel. "I shall miss you." He shoved the engine into reverse as the bar raised to meet her hull, and she slid onto the sand with a grinding thump and lodged herself securely. Ehud shut down the engine and clambered down the steps to help the passengers who had fallen to the deck.

Strong-shouldered young men pulled against the oars of the lifeboats, moving quickly toward the crushed hull of the *Ave Maria*. Moshe rigged a lifeline from her bow and threw it to a curly-haired young man in a boat below. Calmly, women and children climbed down a rope ladder into the safety of the little boats. The stronger of the group and those who could swim moved to the bow and plunged overboard into the icy water, where members of the kibbutz waded out to help them to shore.

Ellie continued to snap pictures until the last minute, then packed the camera back in her bag and handed it to the little boy who had smiled at her the evening before.

"Tell him to hang on to this," Ellie said to Moshe. Moshe put both hands on the boy's shoulders and repeated her instructions in Polish. "And it can't get wet," she added.

The little boy nodded seriously and clutched it tightly to himself as he clambered down the ladder.

"Okay, this is it," said Moshe as the last of the group plunged into the water and grasped the lifeline to shore. "All out?"

Ehud climbed down the steps for the last time. The water was knee-deep in the hold, but the damage was not so great that she couldn't be floated again if it were not for the destroyer that waited for the last of the passengers to get clear.

"All clear!" he shouted to Moshe and Ellie. He joined them on deck and picked up a bundle wrapped in an oilskin raincoat. "It's her compass," he answered their questioning looks. "She has taken me many places, and I will not leave her."

Moshe turned to Ellie. "Can you swim?" he asked, remembering his encounter with Rachel.

"Sure. I spent half my life in the surf at Balboa," Ellie laughed as she pulled off her field boots and jacket.

"Race me." Moshe stood at the bow as Ellie grimaced in anticipation of the cold water. "So jump," he said impatiently; when she hesitated just a moment longer, he shoved her into the murky gray water.

Cold closed over her head and she came up sputtering and

coughing just in time to see Moshe dive from the bow. "Well, come on!" he shouted as he swam ahead of her with sure, steady strokes. She followed the hundred yards to the sand.

Trucks from the kibbutz had pulled up behind the dunes, and by the time Moshe and Ellie staggered to shore with Ehud just behind them, refugees were already being loaded and driven to hiding places in the area.

Ehud turned to gaze across the breakers to the *Ave Maria* perched forlornly on the sand bar. "Maybe you can float her again," Ellie said hopefully.

Ehud shook his head sadly. "It is not to be."

The three of them stood together and watched as the destroyer lowered her guns and took aim. The scream of the siren and wind was suddenly shattered by the flash and roar of a cannon, and the *Ave Maria* was splintered into a thousand pieces.

"Checkmate," Ehud whispered.

21 Return to Jerusalem

David dumped the contents of the mailbag onto the table, then looked around the room until he spotted Rachel in the far corner, nervously sipping a morning cup of coffee. He pulled the white envelope from his pocket and held it high above his head, "Quiet!" he shouted, calming the din. "I got a letter here from the Jewish Agency that I am supposed to hand deliver." Silence fell over the room and men and women turned toward David. "Seems there is a young lady here who's been waiting for word about her family in Jerusalem."

Eyebrows raised as members of the kibbutz exchanged glances, then focused their attention on Rachel. Rachel remained silent, not daring to look up at David. He pivoted slowly, making certain that everyone saw the letter. Then he cleared his throat loudly, "Is there a Rachel Lubetkin here? Rachel Lubetkin?"

Rachel set her cup on the table and stood shakily, biting her lip to control her emotion. She walked forward through the silent crowd, then stumbled, and a man reached out to steady her. "I am Rachel," she said loudly. "It is my letter." She held her eyes on David's eyes, knowing he must certainly see her gratitude. She reached out for the letter and as he handed it to her she stepped back shyly and lowered her gaze. "Thank you," she whispered. "Thank you."

"Any time," he said, anger flashing across his face as he spotted two women whispering together. "Mazel Tov," he added. "Isn't that what you say? Good Luck."

Without a word, she left the mess hall and tucking the precious envelope into her pocket, walked quickly toward the orange orchard, now heavy with ripe fruit. She sat on the bank of an irrigation ditch and took the letter from her pocket. Clumsily she tore the letter open and held it in her trembling hands.

Dear Miss Lubetkin,

In reply to your inquiry of last week, we have conducted a search and are most happy to report that your grandfather is indeed living and in the Old City of Jerusalem. Under ordinary circumstances we would be pleased to assist you in the reunification of your family. The political situation at this time, however, precluded travel to Jerusalem. It is our hope that at a later date we will be able to assist you in relocation to the city of Jerusalem.

Shalom and Best Wishes,
Freda Moskevitch,
Director of Family
Reunification

She read the letter over again and again. Grandfather was alive! Her heart rejoiced that the old man's heart still beat. The letter did not say if he knew of her. And she was uncertain about the phrase, "precludes your travel to Jerusalem." Was she to leave today? What exactly were they trying to tell her? She puzzled over the words, feeling remarkably stupid and inadequate. And who, in this place, could she trust to help her understand the meaning of the words?

Behind her she heard a gentle knocking on one of the tree trunks, then an orange plopped beside her and she turned to find David standing on the opposite bank of the ditch peeling another.

"Good news?" he asked, jumping across and sitting beside her.

"Yes," she said, emotion flooding her voice. "Yes." She handed David the letter. "But I do not understand many of the words."

Quickly David scanned the letter. "Well, great. That's good, Rachel. The old man's alive, huh?"

"Yes," she nodded again, then pointed to the second sentence. "But what of this? What does it mean, please?"

"Well. I think they're trying to say that things are getting so hot there that you won't be able to get together with your grandfather until things are a bit more peaceable."

Rachel's smile dropped away and she leaned over to study the words once again. "I must stay here, then?"

"Yeah. Looks like it." He watched disappointment wipe away the joy that had only moments before lit up her face. "Only until this political situation gets settled, you know. Don't worry."

"Then I must stay here," she said dully, taking the paper from him. "For how long?" she searched David's face.

He pursed his lips, feeling her disappointment. "It may be a while. Honestly, I don't know what to tell you."

Tears spilled out then. She clutched the letter to her and lowered her head. She made no sound, but David watched as small drops fell on her skirt. He sniffed uncomfortably and patted her back awkwardly. He was once again the Tin Man, clumsy and stupid in the face of emotion. He searched for words to comfort her, but found none. Finally she wiped her eyes with the back of her hand and said, "He is so very old, you know. So very old. And I have no one else."

"I'm sorry." He frowned and threw a dirt clod at an orange peel on the ground in front of him. "I'm really sorry, you know. But the Arab Legion has moved in on the roads from Tel Aviv to Jerusalem. A beauty like you wouldn't get five miles past the blockades. Understand?"

Rachel nodded. "You are the only way into Jerusalem, then?" She looked at him hard.

For a moment he didn't answer; then he stood up. "Sorry. Uh-uh, not me. No way. They've got a list of priority stuff for me to fly in, and you're not on the list, I'm afraid. Besides, once you get to Jerusalem, how are you going to make it into the Old City?

The Mufti's got every way in and out covered."

Rachel continued to gaze at him in silence. David looked away from the question in her eyes. He had never, he thought, seen such hauntingly beautiful eyes. "Don't look at me like that. I can deliver a letter for you maybe, but smuggle you into Jerusalem? No way can I do that. No, ma'am."

She put her hand timidly on his arm. "It is all right, David. You have done so much already. I would never ask you to risk that."

David frowned and scratched his head. "Risk? I don't know that it's such a risk. Except for you, y'know. Jerusalem is hard pressed to feed the folks that live there now. That's the risk. It's no risk for me."

"Then I will find another way to get there. Perhaps I can make it over the roads."

"Wait a minute—just hold it. *That* would really be a risk! You'd be shot or taken hostage or—well, all kinds of things could happen. You're a beautiful woman. Beautiful."

"Do you not think that I know what could happen? I am familiar with what cruel men can do to a woman."

David looked quickly away. "What I meant was . . ."

She smiled sadly at him and took her hand away from his arm. "They told you of my past, David. I am not afraid of anything anymore—except living alone."

David felt an ache of sympathy for her and searched his mind for an answer. "You won't make it to Jerusalem on the road. It's that simple."

"I have to try."

"Ah—" He threw a wedge of orange peel into the ditch. "Have you got a place to stay until we can get you to your grandfather?"

"You will fly me, then?"

"I didn't say that. I asked you where you intend to stay?"

"I do not know. I know no one." She frowned. "I will simply have to find Grandfather."

"You've got to have a plan, Rachel. Do you think you're just going to waltz right up to the Mufti's men and walk through the gates? Listen," he paused thoughtfully, "I know a girl—a journalist. Maybe she can help. She can get into places where sane people fear to go." He laughed at Rachel's questioning stare. "Anyway, I'm supposed to pick her up, along with another guy, in Naharia this afternoon. Maybe you can stay with her for a few days."

"You will fly me to Jerusalem, then? Today?"

David threw down his half-peeled orange, shaking his head in disgust with himself for being such a sucker. "Go get your stuff."

Rachel ran back to her quonset dormitory, clutching the letter tightly to her. She paused at the door and smiled at the women who had just returned from breakfast.

A thin, cruel-lipped woman looked at Rachel as she stuffed a small canvas bag with her few belongings. "Going somewhere, Rachel dear?" the woman sneered.

Rachel did not answer. Instead, she finished packing, then stood erect and squared her shoulders, looking each of her tormentors straight in the eye. "I am going home," she declared at last. Then she turned and walked from the room and across the grassy square to the mess hall.

She pushed the door open and stood for a moment searching for David among the members of the kibbutz. He sat near the far end of the room among a small group of men and women. His plate was heaped high with scrambled eggs and coarse brown bread with orange marmalade, but he had not eaten. Instead, he sat quietly listening to the BBC of Palestine.

A voice announced in frantic, heavily accented English: "This morning just past six o'clock Jewish terrorists attacked and bombed the Arab hotel Semiramis in the Jerusalem suburb of Katamon. The death toll at this time is eleven, with many more believed to be buried in the rubble. The staff of Hadassah Hospital has opened its doors to the injured and dying . . ."

Rachel stepped back and shut the door slowly, then walked toward the plane waiting in the field. She had grown so tired of the talk of death and dying all around her. Just for this morning, she wanted only to think about living, about her grandfather, about the home she had heard her mother speak of so many years ago. She unlatched the door of the little plane and threw her bag behind the passenger seat, then climbed in and closed the door behind her.

Sunlight warmed the interior of the plane and Rachel began to feel drowsy. Leaning her head against the glass windowpane, she gazed across the plowed field into the orchard beyond. A young couple walked hand in hand along the edge of the field and disappeared into the orchard. Tears filled Rachel's eyes as she wondered what loving words were spoken in the shadow of the branches. Such words she had never heard—and never would, now that she bore the mark *Nür Für Offizere*. No man would ever see past that mark to love her.

David pulled open his door with a clang, startling her back to reality.

"There you are!" he exclaimed. "I thought maybe you had chickened out."

"Chickened out?"

"Changed your mind," he smiled.

"No, I have not," she offered, shaking her head.

"Well now's your chance. Another hotel just went up in smoke. Radio says the Haganah did it. Nobody around here seems to believe that, so we got us a real mystery on our hands. Killed a bunch of civilians—Arabs, I guess."

"Terrible," she said. "Sad for everyone."

David climbed in and flipped the ignition switch while two strong Sabra men cranked the propeller. The engine roared to life, and then the plane bounced over the rough terrain and slowly lifted into the air. David circled the kibbutz once and dipped his wings in salute as Rachel gazed, enthralled, at the tiny buildings and trees below her. A feeling of peace flooded her, and for the first time in years she felt unfettered.

"It is wonderful!" she shouted at last over the noise of the motor.

"Ever flown before?" He smiled at her, and Rachel thought she had never seen such a handsome man. She looked quickly away.

"No. But I like it very much, thank you." She sensed his eyes were still on her. She glanced at him. Then as he held her eyes with his own she said, "I know what you are thinking. You must not pity me."

"Pity is the last thing I'd think about. I was just thinking that you must be some kind of lady to have come out of those experiences still sane."

"Sanity is simply a matter of perspective, is it not?"

"I guess that's one way to look at it, especially if you're the one in a straitjacket."

"Everyone, I think, wears a straitjacket at one time or another."

David grinned. "Like I said, that's one way of looking at it."

Rachel sat silently, afraid to say more—afraid to say too much. Finally she asked, "This girl I am to stay with, she is your girl?"

"She'd say that's a matter of perspective," David laughed.

"But you are . . . you love her?"

"Yep." He banked the plane and set course for Naharia.

"Have you known her very long?"

"Three years—since 1944. I met her at the Hollywood canteen. You heard of that?"

"No."

"No, I guess not." He scratched his chin. "It was a terrific place where servicemen could go to dance and meet girls. It was in Hollywood—you know, where they make movies. You know about movies?"

"I have never seen one, but I have heard—"

"Anyway, sometimes movie stars like Lana Turner and Betty Grable would show up—gorgeous dames." David's voice became animated at the memory. "But believe me, they got nothin' on you . . ."

Rachel tried to follow his words and translate them into Polish when a phrase escaped her comprehension, but only bits and pieces of the whole came through.

"And you met your girl there?" she asked, hungry to know stories of love and courtship. "Is she a movie star?"

"No. But she could be. Red hair . . ."

"A shiksa?"

"Whatever. Anyway, I saw her when the band was playing *String of Pearls*, by Glenn Miller. And I said to myself that she was the most beautiful woman I had ever seen . . ." He paused and looked hard and long at Rachel, his smile fading.

"What is it?" she asked.

David looked into her eyes and felt lost for a moment. "Nothing, I just didn't know anybody really had eyes like that. That's all."

"Her eyes are beautiful, then?"

"No. I mean, yes—gorgeous! But I was talking about *your* eyes. They are beautiful."

Rachel looked away, studying her hands clasped in her lap. She felt a rush of embarrassment, even shame, that he had noticed her. "My eyes have seen too much to be beautiful any longer," she said.

"Nonsense. You're still a person, aren't you?"

"I have not thought so for a long time, David."

"Well, you are. And someday the band is going to be playing Glenn Miller, and you'll be standing with a group of girls talking—"

"Like your girl was?"

"Like Ellie. And some guy will spot you across the room and that'll be it. He'll say, 'Hey, beautiful, do you want to dance?'— just like John Wayne or somebody; and he'll sweep you off your feet."

"It sounds like a lovely dream," Rachel sighed. "An American dream."

"Yeah? How do they do it here?"

"The matchmaker arranges for a suitable family."

"Arranges?" David asked, incredulous.

"Oh, yes. My parents had arranged for my marriage with a boy not far from Warsaw. I had not met him, but I spent my days imagining what he must be like."

"How old were you when this all got settled?"

"Nine." Her eyes sparkled. "Quite old. Many are betrothed much younger."

David shook his head in amused disbelief. "You're right. Sanity is a matter of perspective," he laughed. "So what happened to him?"

Rachel looked away nervously and sat in silence for a long moment. "He was—" she paused, searching for words to convey the horror of Nazi occupation: starvation, mass graves, mindless murder. Finally she chose the simplest terms. "He died . . . with his family. And my mother and father and brothers— everyone, even the matchmaker."

David swallowed hard. "I'm sorry," he said quietly. "Dumb question."

"They took me from the line," she continued as if unable to stop the flood of memories. "I was stripped and examined. Then I was branded and used for the pleasure of the men who murdered my family. And I was no longer a person."

"How old were you?"

"Fourteen."

"A child."

227

"Full of dreams." Her eyes were shining with tears. "I am sorry. I have not shared this with anyone. There has been no one who has seen me among so many."

David gripped the control stick hard as he imagined her loneliness. "There must be someone who would understand," he said.

"To my own people I am a traitor. I should have died. I should have . . ." Her voice trailed off. "I had a friend once." The engine droned as Rachel's face clouded with the memory. "She was a year younger than I. She became pregnant, and she knew she would be gassed. It was a rule, you see. So she stabbed a Gestapo colonel." She closed her eyes. "They lined us up in the morning and made us watch her execution. I only wished that I could have been so courageous."

David felt inadequate, groping for words of comfort. "But you lived through it all. In my book that takes a special kind of courage."

"You are kind." She looked at him through eyes that brimmed with pain. "I would have given anything to be that American girl on the dance floor. I am twenty-one now, and my dreams are all buried in the ashes of Auschwitz. At night I lie upon my bed and ask God where He has gone, why I was not allowed to die. He does not answer."

———

Ellie and Moshe stood anxiously beside a truck parked at the side of the Naharia airfield. The radio blared the news of the Semiramis bombing, and Ellie shivered, not from the cold of the day, but from wondering at the fate of Miriam's son and grandson. *The old woman will be frantic*, she thought. The little Arab family had only each other.

". . . the names of the dead and wounded have not been released, pending notification of kin," the radio announcer continued.

Moshe put his arm around her. "Your uncle will be there with her, Ellie. There is little you can do."

"I know that. It's just that she's such a terrific old woman. Moshe, if we are working for and with people who could do such a thing . . ."

"It was not Haganah," he said irritably. "That much I can tell you. Maybe those idiots in the Irgun would do such a thing.

228

Maybe it was an accident. I don't know what to tell you, but it is not Haganah. I would have known. I would not have permitted it."

"Her grandson is a violinist." Ellie imagined broken bodies among the rubble. "A violinist," she repeated. "It just seems so ridiculous that somebody like that could be hurt . . ."

Moshe rubbed his hand wearily across his forehead. "Six million violinists, poets, dreamers, and doctors died within the last six years simply because they were Jewish. Nobody ever said any of this makes sense. Perhaps the story of just one is more moving than the numbers. Perhaps it is too hard to imagine that so many died without cause."

Ellie turned her face toward the gray sky and listened for the faint drone of David's airplane. She switched off the radio and sat forlornly on the edge of the truck running board as the sputtering speck in the distance took shape and finally circled slowly above them.

Moshe looked at his watch. "He's late."

"As usual."

David landed smoothly on the concrete runway, and without switching off the engine rolled to a stop near the truck. He opened his door and dumped out the mail sack for a Sabra woman to retrieve; then he waved to Moshe and Ellie to board.

Moshe opened the door of the buzzing little aircraft and helped Ellie into the back where Rachel sat crosslegged on a mail pouch. Seeing Rachel, Ellie balked and glared suspiciously at David.

"Hurry up," said David. "I'm late."

"We noticed," said Ellie dryly as she took her seat next to Rachel.

As Moshe boarded, David made quick introductions. "Rachel Lubetkin, this is Ellie Warne." Rachel smiled kindly at Ellie and timidly extended her hand. "You must be David's girl."

"A matter of opinion. But I'm Ellie, anyway." She returned the smile.

"And this is Moshe Sachar."

Moshe turned and recognized Rachel in the shadow of the cargo area for the first time. His smile faded as he was once again astonished at her beauty. Then he beamed, "You!"

"It is you!" she exclaimed in delight as she reached out and shook his hand vigorously.

"I see you two have met," said David cheerfully as he taxied out to a much slower takeoff than usual.

"One very dark night, Mr. Sachar taught me to swim," Rachel replied.

A surge of jealousy passed through Ellie as she realized that this must be the woman Ehud had used to win the chess game. Every word he had said about her was true—and then some.

"You have been well?" Moshe asked, his eyes lingering in a way that Ellie distinctly disapproved of.

"David has helped me locate my family." She pulled the letter from her sweater pocket and handed it to Moshe, who read it quickly.

"Mazel Tov," he said sincerely. "So now you are returning home."

"If there is a home to return to," quipped David. "Did you hear we blew up an Arab hotel?"

"In the first place, it was not our men. And Ellie has friends staying there," Moshe shot back angrily.

"Oh—" David's bantering ceased. "Sorry, Els. Open mouth, insert foot, huh?"

Rachel bit her lower lip in concern and gazed sympathetically at Ellie. "I hope no one is . . . injured." She wanted to reach out and put her hand on Ellie's arm in comfort, but instead she crossed her arms and looked away. "I am sorry."

"David, you remember Miriam?" Ellie ignored Rachel. "It's her son and grandson."

"The old woman?"

"Yes."

"Tough as a boot."

"You are a picture of concern!" Ellie snapped sarcastically.

Moshe changed the subject quickly. "Where does your family live?" he asked Rachel.

"It is only my grandfather. He is a rabbi in the Old City."

"Do you have a place to stay until you can get in?"

Rachel looked nervously toward David. "Well I . . . I mean, David thought—"

David chewed his lip thoughtfully. "I figured maybe Ellie could put her up for a few days."

Rachel looked down at the mail sack, pretending not to notice the look of aggravation that crossed Ellie's face. "But if it is any bother . . ."

Ellie glared at the back of David's head. "No bother at all," she said with difficulty.

"Good," Moshe rubbed his hands together. "Then it is settled."

"Didn't I tell you Ellie was terrific?" David yawned.

Ellie turned to stare out the window as Rachel studied her with eyes full of understanding. She hesitantly reached out and tapped her light on the arm. Ellie turned slightly without looking her full in the face. "I'm all right," said Ellie. "A little edgy, maybe. Worried, you know?"

"I can find a hotel room if it is an inconvenience."

"Forget it. Really," Ellie felt ashamed of her jealousy. "It will be all right."

Rachel gazed solemnly down at the road below and the tiny trucks that crawled along toward Jerusalem.

———

Ellie spotted Uncle Howard in the lobby of Hadassah Hospital immediately. He sat at the end of a long row of nearly empty chairs, his face unshaven and his clothes rumpled. In his hands he held the small pocket Bible that he always carried, and as he studied its pages, his face was a strange mixture of sorrow and peace. Miriam's beautiful Sunday shawl lay folded neatly beside him on the chair.

As Ellie hurried toward him, leaving the others to wait by the door, a dark foreboding filled her heart.

"Uncle Howard!" She leaned down and hugged him tightly. Then, picking up the shawl, she sat beside him gazing pensively into his eyes.

Howard drew a deep breath and blinked back tears. "Such a waste. Such a terrible waste."

"Sammy?" she asked.

"He'll live. Broken arm, cuts; that's all."

"Thank God. Ishmael?"

Howard shook his head slowly. "No," he replied simply.

"Oh, Uncle Howard!" Ellie cried, her voice cracking with emotion. "Poor Miriam! Poor old dear!" She glanced around the lobby. "Where is she? Is she all right?"

Howard placed his hand on Ellie's arm. "No. She's gone, child."

"Gone? Gone where? Is she at home?" She clutched the old

woman's shawl to her, afraid of the answer.

A lone tear trickled down Howard's cheek as he tucked his chin and tried to speak. Ellie's eyes filled with painful comprehension as he cleared his throat and wiped away the tear with the back of his hand. "She stayed with them last night," he said finally. "At the hotel."

"Miriam!" Ellie buried her face in the shawl as the emptiness of loss pressed in on her.

"She is safe now, child," Howard wrapped his arms around her. "She has gone home."

"The last of thirty bodies was recovered today from the rubble of the Semiramis Hotel in the Jerusalem suburb of Katamon. Although Haganah sources deny involvement in the bombing, other sources indicate that the hotel was being used as a military headquarters by Arabs. No members of Arab military staff were present, however, and only civilians were numbered among the victims. British High Command called this latest act of violence by Jews against Arabs 'dastardly . . . the murder of innocent people.' "

Haj Amin lowered the newspaper and fixed his eyes on the face of Rebbe Akiva sitting across from him on the patio. "A vile act, do you not agree, Rabbi?" he asked grimly.

Rebbe Akiva shook his head in shame that Jews had resorted to such acts against the innocent population. "My heart is breaking that such as these would call themselves Jews."

"You see our dilemma, then? If we were to allow passage into the Jewish Quarter, what guarantee would we have that the Old City would not be polluted with these Jewish fanatics, these murderers of the innocent among my people?"

"It was my thought, Haj Amin, that perhaps an arrangement could be made. For the sake of my people in the Old City."

Haj Amin's eyebrows raised slightly with interest. "Arrangement?"

Akiva toyed with the watch chain stretched across his belly. "It has occurred to me that we might make a little exchange. There is a possibility that I might obtain something you want very badly."

Haj Amin leaned forward and gazed intently at Akiva. "And what do you have that I could possibly desire, my friend?"

"Victory."

"That is mine, at any rate," Haj Amin shrugged and leaned back in his chair.

"Are you so very sure?" Akiva smiled knowingly.

Haj Amin cleared his throat, then poured coffee for Akiva and himself. "And for this promise of victory against the Zionists, what would you receive in return?"

Akiva confidently sipped his coffee, "The preservation of the Jewish Quarter. For the sake of my people. The places of learning, the synagogues."

"Ah, yes," Haj Amin smiled. "Immortality for the name of Akiva, eh? Savior of the old ways?"

"Just as the name of Haj Amin Husseini shall also be immortal among his people."

"That goes without saying." Haj Amin set his cup on the low table before him. "Immortality. A simple enough request."

"I thought perhaps we would see eye to eye." Akiva tugged at his vest. "And there is one more item I require," he added, certain that such a small request would be honored without question.

"Of much less value than the Old City, I presume?"

"It is but the whim of a poor scholar such as myself," Akiva bowed his head humbly. "A small thing, of little interest to anyone else, and certainly of no importance whatsoever to the world."

"In exchange for victory?" Haj Amin smiled slyly. "What can this small request be?"

"I find the photographs of the scroll quite intriguing, the story of its discovery even more so. I would very much like to study this thing, to have it in my library for reference〞〞"

Haj Amin coughed delicately into his handkerchief, then raised his chin to scrutinize the man sitting opposite him. "Perhaps. Perhaps we may accommodate your wishes, Rabbi." He paused for full effect. "But at present, of course, we have some use for this item. Perhaps later, when it has served its purpose, we shall make it a gift to you."

"What possible use could you have for such old scrolls of our prophets?" Akiva asked curiously.

Haj Amin's face hardened for a brief instant; then he sipped his coffee. "Is it not written in your own holy books that the Word of God draws men unto itself?"

PART 3

The Gift
Late December 1947

"The promised redemption will come to redeem not the Jewish people alone, but all humanity. And the principal object of this divine redemption, which will be brought about by the Messiah, will be to bring blessing and peace to the entire world through the redemption of the Jewish people."

Rabbi Avraham Hacohen Kook
Palestine's Chief Rabbi
December 1929

22　The Passover Hope

Ellie stared blankly into the developing tray as the rubble of the Semiramis Hotel magically began to appear on the photographic paper. Here, a rescue worker stood on a demolished wall. There, another carried a first-aid kit that would be of little use. Two other men pulled yet another body from the heap of stones and brick that marked the end of thirty innocent lives. *How*, Ellie wondered, *can one photograph hope to tell the whole story?*

She rubbed her hand across her forehead in utter exhaustion. From the first hour that she had heard of Miriam's death two afternoons before, she had not slept. Instead, she went to the site with Moshe and wept as she snapped the shutter of her camera, etching her own heartache permanently on film.

The bells had begun their mournful tolling as she had photographed the rescue of a solitary little Arab girl, the lone survivor among a Christian family of thirteen.

Since that moment, the bells of the Old City churches had not ceased to toll out the lives of the dead in solemn, unbroken rhythm. From behind the thick walls of her darkroom, Ellie could hear them still. The hills around Jerusalem, which only a few weeks before had echoed with the joyful call of the shofar, now reverberated with the death knell of reason and sanity.

From the minarets of the Arab Muslim Quarter, the muzzien shrilly called the faithful to prayer and to yet another sermon by the Mufti. And as the Christian Arabs began to dig graves and hastily bury their loved ones, those Muslims gathered in the courtyard of the Mosque of Omar and raised their fists with the frenzied cry of "Jihad! Jihad! Jihad!"

Holy war. Ellie looked down at the photograph once again. All pretense of detached professionalism evaporated. She bowed her head and covered her face with her hands. "Oh, God!" she cried aloud, "this can't be what you want! I've got some kind of war going on inside me! God, I don't want to fight against you anymore," she sobbed. "Miriam knew you. But she's gone, and I'm still down here and I don't know where to look for you." She felt so small and helpless, buried so far beneath the rubble that she could never dig herself out. "Help me!" she cried, tasting the warm salt of her tears. She lay her head on the counter and closed her eyes. She wished the bells would stop ringing. "Find me," she murmured. Then she sighed and drifted into a deep and dreamless sleep.

––––––––

The bells of the churches in the neighboring Christian Quarter tolled mournfully. Grandfather pulled his coat tighter around him and hurried up the Street of the Stairs toward the massive three-story structures of the Warsaw Compound. Here he had walked as a young man. He had come to Jerusalem from the Jewish ghetto of Warsaw, Poland, to study the Torah; he had never returned. Instead, he had grown old and bent teaching the new Polish Yeshiva students in the study rooms and synagogue that surrounded a large, peaceful courtyard. His beard was gray, his hands gnarled from well over half a century of turning the pages of the Holy Books. Only the Warsaw Compound remained unchanged. Many lifetimes before Grandfather had been born, the Jews of Poland had built it as a memorial to the God of their fathers within the Gates of Zion. Generations had sent their sons to study here. Some, like Grandfather, had remained, but most had returned to the land of their birth. Now, there were no new Polish Yeshiva boys. They had died with their fathers in the streets of the Warsaw ghetto as a Nazi Panzer Division had blasted their resistance to rubble. *They died fighting*, Grandfather thought. *Only this small corner of the world remains as a memorial to what once was. Now, we, too, are threatened with extinction.* And all the empty promises of Rabbi Akiva and Haj Amin, the friend of Hitler, made no difference.

The Warsaw buildings stood on the corner of the two most exposed flanks of the Old City Jewish Quarter. The living quarters of the scholars had become like trenches and bomb shelters. Sandbags blocked the windows against gunfire. At night, up-turned tables barricaded the doors. Three residents of the northeast corner of the quarter had been wounded by sniper fire from minarets in the two days since the bombing of the hotel in the New City. Bullet holes marred the faces of several buildings. Members of the Haganah had been denied entrance into the Old City in exchange for Arab promises to Akiva that the Jewish Quarter would be spared. The few meager weapons had been confiscated by the British.

Now, it seemed, those promises had been lies calculated to delay the building of any defense whatsoever. *Perhaps Akiva believed the lies*, Grandfather reasoned. Perhaps he had some other purpose for resisting the help of the Jewish defenders in the New City. Akiva cried out against the Zionists, but that was no longer the issue. Everything had now focused down to the tiny pinpoint of mere survival for the Jewish Quarter.

This morning ten rabbis from among the different sectors of the quarter had been invited to an urgent meeting. *Come, let us reason together*, Grandfather prayed silently.

The Warsaw building loomed just ahead, yet for Grandfather, it seemed almost beyond reach. Pain welled up in his chest and he staggered as he tried to catch his breath. His cough had grown worse over the past few weeks, and even in the brutal morning cold, beads of perspiration formed on his forehead. He leaned heavily on the side of a low, one story structure and closed his eyes. "So, God, are you finished with this old man so soon?" he coughed, doubling up with the force. "A little more time, if you please. For Yacov." For a full five minutes he fought against the pain, feeling it gradually lessen and fade from a hot fire to a dull ache. He stood erect and shakily resumed his walk toward the Warsaw where the other nine members of the group waited to discuss survival. "We will survive," he whispered, gazing at the only corner of the world where the Warsaw of his childhood still remained.

———

Moshe knocked softly on the door of Ellie's darkroom.

"What is it?" came the muffled reply.

"Are you finished? May I open the door?" he asked kindly.

Ellie threw the door open to him, her eyes red and swollen. She sniffed and whirled around, plopping down on the stool once again with her back to him. Moshe stood against the door frame and gazed tenderly at the back of her head.

"Don't you need to sleep?" he asked.

"I was sleeping." Ellie's voice cracked. "You woke me up and now I'm in the middle of a nightmare again." She lowered her

239

head and tears flowed silently down her face. Moshe stepped forward and placed his strong hands on her shoulders.

"Perhaps there is little comfort in my words, my little shiksa. But I know how your heart aches. My heart has been broken, too. For my family. For my people."

"And when will it end, Moshe?" she sighed. "When? And how?" She laid her cheek against his hand. "Miriam was . . . she had such a hope inside her. Why can't I find hope inside of me?"

"True hope, *real* hope," Moshe said, groping for words, "comes from knowing the truth. It comes from seeing what is possible and believing that it will come to pass."

"What are you saying, Moshe?" She turned to him with imploring eyes. "Please help me understand."

"I am only beginning to understand myself. I can only tell you what my heart tells me is true—and my head also."

"I feel so lost. So alone and confused by it all."

"Then I will share my hopes with you."

"There is nothing I want more." Ellie squeezed his hand tightly and then dropped it, gazing up at him.

"Do you remember the day on the *Ave Maria* when you talked about feeling God in your heart and knowing God with your mind?"

Ellie nodded and sat back, wiping her eyes. "Yes."

"And we said that both are important? I will tell you what I know to be true. I cannot tell you what to feel." He rubbed the back of his neck and slid up on the counter, facing Ellie. "The Holy Scripture says that man is sinful and imperfect in his heart because he has turned to do what is right in his own eyes. We have hardened our hearts against the love of God and against our fellowman. Is this true?"

"Of course. Look what they did to Miriam." Ellie's face clouded up again.

"I myself have hardened my heart against others."

"You? Moshe, you are the most tender and—" she objected.

"I have hardened my heart many times. Have you?" he persisted.

Ellie nodded, remembering the day that Miriam had chided her about the clothes in her closet and the hundreds of women refugees who did not even have a thin sweater to shield them against the cold. She remembered the surge of anger and jealousy she had felt toward Rachel.

"Then this much of what the Scripture says is true, is it not?" Moshe said with gentle understanding.

"Where is the hope in that?" Ellie asked dully. "I only wish I could be better. Wish I had done better and loved better. Wish I had never hurt anyone else."

"But wishes are not hope. Hope is knowing the truth and acting on it."

Confusion flickered across Ellie's face. "Then tell me the truth, Moshe. Don't talk riddles to me."

Moshe closed his eyes for a moment and frowned. "In all our seeking and all our trying, there is no way that we can ever reach God, Ellie. The Scripture says that 'all our works are like filthy rags.' They don't change the condition of our hearts or erase our past mistakes. Only God himself can do that."

"How?" Her voice seemed small and imploring, like a child's.

"I am a Jew. You know this. And so I will tell you as I understand it. I have not shared this with anyone," he warned, "so stop me if it becomes confusing."

"I will. Please, go on."

"The prophets long ago wrote that there would be a Savior who would come to my people. Even to the Gentiles. We call Him the Messiah. Always we thought that He would be some kind of political leader. But I believe it is He who was meant to lead us back to God. Do you understand?"

Ellie nodded, unwilling to admit that she was not quite sure what his point was.

"When I was a little boy, each year at Passover I would ask my father the question, 'What makes this night different from the rest?' And he would tell me the story of how God delivered the Hebrew people out of the slavery of Egypt. In sorrow we would remember the Egyptian firstborn children who died in the last great plague before we left that land. They were no different from us, really. They were people, too. Why was it they died and we did not? I used to wonder this and ask God. Then my father told me that even some of the Egyptian firstborn lived because they obeyed the word of God and placed the blood of a sacrificial lamb on their doorposts. Then the Angel of Death passed over them as well. Those who believed God's word were saved. They simply believed and accepted the sacrifice of the lamb.

"All these years I have tried to follow the law and I have watched men of the law live unhappy lives frantically striving to please God. More rules. More laws. They are all broken. And through it all we looked for the Deliverer to save us from persecution and harm from Christian and Muslim nations. We look for the Messiah to deliver bodies while our souls are dying. All through the Scriptures He is mentioned. Then ancient commentaries speak of Him as the final sacrifice for all our sins and imperfections. They speak of His love and kindness and tell us that He alone is the one who can save us from the death that dwells in our hearts."

"Who is He, Moshe? Where is He?"

"He died on the eve of Passover, nearly two thousand years ago. Like the lamb of sacrifice, He took my sins and covered them with His blood. He was perfect and without blemish, and He died in my place like the prophets said He would. Then He conquered death. Ellie, He came to life again and is living still, and He has made my heart alive in knowing Him. That is my hope. My belief in fact and truth."

"Then you are a Christian?" Ellie asked quietly. "Like Miriam? Like Uncle Howard?"

"I am Moshe Sachar, and I am a Jew who believes that the one we call Yeshua is the Messiah. In this I hope with a hope that knows the truth; He will come again to my people and they will know Him for who He is and find pardon and the joy of knowing Him as a loving and merciful Savior. And for you, dear Ellie, I hope that you will reach out to Him. For I know He cares so much for you." His face was full of emotion as he stepped across to Ellie and wrapped his arms around her.

"What do I do, Moshe? How can I know Him too and have hope?"

He stroked her hair and kissed the top of her head. "Just talk to Him, my love. Just ask Him to make you everything you can be. Give Him your heart."

"But it's broken, Moshe; my heart is broken." She buried her face against him.

"He knows all about broken hearts, Ellie. And our King David writes that your broken heart is just the kind of sacrifice He will accept."

Rachel followed the professor into the kitchen, nearly running into him when he stopped suddenly and switched on the light. Blue tiles glistened on the countertops and tiny square mosaics covered the floor. A large gas stove took up nearly one entire wall, and a white refrigerator faced them from the opposite wall. A small white wooden table sat in the center of the room, with a vase of tiny blue flowers just beginning to wilt. The professor's eyes seemed to caress the flowers. "This kitchen is not exactly my domain," he tried to smile. He crossed to the table and broke off one of the blue flowers and stuck it in his shirt pocket. "Miriam was a good cook. You like to cook?"

"My mama taught me at a very early age to cook. It is a pleasure one never forgets," Rachel answered, turning on the tap water in the sink, then shutting it off again. "Do you follow Kashrut?"

"The Kosher diet? Miriam was a Christian Arab," he frowned.

"It is very good food," Rachel said, feeling like an intruder in the old woman's kitchen.

"Yes, very good. And if we bring Yacov home with us, I think it will be very important to him." He turned and opened a cupboard full of clear jars of beans and pasta, all neatly labeled in Arabic. He picked up a jar of lentils and stared sadly at the handwriting, touching the letters with his index finger.

"I am most happy to help out," Rachel said, pretending not to notice the professor reaching out for memories of Miriam. Then she added, "I am very sorry she is gone."

Howard looked up and smiled. "So am I. She was a remarkable woman," he said, still not quite able to believe that Miriam would never rattle another pan or brew another cup of tea. "She knew where everything was kept. I'm afraid I'm a little out of my ken in here. But I get the same feeling looking in these cupboards as I do at a dig. She's still here in a way. At least I know she still lives." He sat at the table.

"Would you like some tea?" Rachel asked, filling the kettle, then striking a wooden match and lighting the stove.

"Yes, thank you," he smiled. "You know, I never had tea in the kitchen. She always brought it to me. In the study, as if she were a servant. But really she was family."

"I understand." Rachel remembered the emptiness she had felt clutching her mother's sweater as they had led her away to a final end. How desperately she had longed for tender arms to fill the sleeves again and hold her close. She had buried her face in the soft hand-knit sweater and wept because of the emptiness that remained in place of her mother. The heart of the man across from her now felt the emptiness Rachel had learned to live with daily. This was still Miriam's kitchen. The stove still hissed and the kettle rattled and shrilled when it was time for tea. But even the old familiar sounds seemed like hollow echoes in her absence.

Rachel searched the cupboards for cups, finding them nearest the sink. She set them on the counter and poured hot water through a tea strainer she found perched on the window ledge. "Milk and sugar?" she asked.

"No, thank you," said Howard, still gazing at the flowers. Silence hung heavy in the room, covering his thoughts like a curtain.

"Has it made you sad to speak of her?" Rachel sat across from him, stirring the tiny fragments of tea leaves floating in her cup.

"Not at all. She always spoke of her death as if she were planning a cruise around the world. I think she very much looked forward to brewing a cup of tea for the Lord."

Rachel curiously appraised his tender smile, then looked down at her cup again. "She was not afraid, then?"

"Never. Joyful is a better word."

"Are you afraid?" she asked, sensing something different about him.

"My mother said that we didn't all come into this world at once and we're not all leaving at the same time either—unless the Lord comes for us. I would prefer to go with all those I love, but no, I am not afraid."

"I wish sometimes . . . many times . . . that I could have died with my family. But I think perhaps my grandfather shall have need of me."

"I am sure, Rachel, that many will have need of your tender heart," Howard slurped his tea. "You are most welcome to stay here for as long as you like. At least until the Old City is safe again. We have need of you." He patted her arm.

"I think perhaps your niece is not happy that I am here. It is a bad time." She wondered if it was possible that he was speaking the truth, and what he would say if he knew her past.

"Nonsense. Ellie can't boil an egg, let alone cook according

244

to Kashrut. And I know the girl loves to eat," he laughed, trying to make Rachel feel needed and comfortable.

The swinging door banged open and Ellie stumbled into the room. In her arms she carried a heap of sweaters and skirts and a pair of walking shoes. Her eyes were red and swollen, but she smiled bravely as she regained her balance and thrust the clothes toward Rachel. "You look about my size. I thought maybe . . ."

Rachel's eyes seemed blank and uncomprehending. "You should like that I iron these for you?" she asked.

"No!" Ellie exclaimed. "I want you to *wear* them. That is, unless they don't fit you or something."

Rachel gazed in astonishment at the beautiful blue and coral sweaters and skirts that lay in her arms. "You mean for me? To wear?" she exclaimed, tears welling up in her eyes. "Such beautiful clothes. Such beautiful things."

"Come on back to my room. I'm trying to reorganize my closet and my dresser drawers. I have a lot of things . . ." She sounded hopeful and friendly.

Uncle Howard's eyebrows raised. He grinned at Rachel. "What were you saying about Ellie?" he asked.

Ellie put her hands on her hips. "Yeah. What were you guys saying about me?"

Rachel ran her hand over a soft, royal blue sweater. "I was saying perhaps I should teach you to cook?"

The floor of Ellie's bedroom was covered by piles of clothes dumped from her dresser drawers and closet. Rachel stood in the doorway and surveyed the mess as Ellie plopped down in the middle of the heap.

"So many things," Rachel smiled.

"Too many. I brought half the merchandise on the Miracle Mile to Palestine."

"Miracle . . . ?"

"Mile. The shopping district in Los Angeles."

"Like the Paris fashion center." Rachel nodded with understanding.

"Not quite. But I still managed to spend my money there." Ellie sorted through a pile of blouses, divided them into two separate stacks. "Have a seat." She indicated a tiny bare patch of floor. "So, I thought, as long as you are here, you might like first crack at these."

"Crack?"

"Yes. I mean—" Ellie pitched a pair of blue wool slacks into Rachel's lap—"these'll look better on you than they will on me."

Rachel stared down in disbelief. "American women wear such trousers as these?"

Ellie quickly scanned Rachel's ankle-length black dress. "Yep. And our grandmothers wear dresses like that. No offense."

Rachel blinked and took the trousers from her lap, then stood and slipped out of her dress, careful not to let Ellie see the mark on her arm. Then she sat on the edge of the bed and pulled the trousers on over her slip. "Where I am from, trousers are only for men to wear."

"In America, women wear pants and build tanks and airplanes. Ever hear of Rosie the Riveter?"

"In Europe"—Rachel zipped up the trousers—"Germans put Jews in the factories so that if they were bombed, only Jews would die. I know some who say that when American planes would pass overhead, they would pray for bombs to fall upon them. When they did not fall, perhaps a Jewish factory worker would put a wire wrong or forget on purpose a screw. So perhaps we have helped America to win the war, eh?" She clasped her hands behind her back and stood shyly in front of Ellie. "So how do I look?"

"You look great." Ellie tossed her a matching blouse. "Try this."

Rachel turned her back to Ellie and pulled on the shirt, shoving her left arm into the sleeve first, quickly covering her tattoo. She buttoned the shirt, then turned around. "Do you wear these when you dance Glenn Miller with David?" She smiled and spread her arms.

"Who told you about Glenn Miller?" Ellie asked in amazement.

"Your David. On the airplane he talked very much about you. I have heard that men and women dance. And how much he is in love with you."

Ellie sat back on her heels. "He told you that?"

Rachel nodded. "You are lucky to have such a one as this in love with you. I must admit I have great admiration for you."

Ellie bit her lower lip and looked down at the floor. "David and I are not . . ."

Rachel tilted her head slightly as if trying to comprehend the unfinished words of Ellie. "You are lucky. So very lucky, Ellie. There is room in his heart for none other but you."

"I thought he was interested in you."

"Me?" Rachel exclaimed.

"And besides, it doesn't matter what he feels anymore."

"You are not in love with David?" Rachel sat down in front of Ellie and crossed her legs.

"He hasn't got a serious bone in his entire body. Absolutely no convictions or commitment whatsoever."

"But this is not true! He has such a heart of kindness. He has done so much for me."

Ellie narrowed her eyes. "I'll bet. Just watch out for the pay-backs. He always wants something in return."

Rachel clutched at her shirt front and sat upright, her face blanching. "I do not believe this of David," she said quietly.

Sensing that she had somehow wounded Rachel, Ellie added quickly. "I'm sorry. I didn't mean that. It's just that I came out of that relationship feeling so used, you know?" she added miserably.

Rachel looked into her eyes and held them for a long moment. "Yes, I know."

"You too? Some guy?"

"Yes." Rachel looked away. "But David and Moshe seemed somehow different to me."

"Moshe? He's wonderful, isn't he? He always makes me feel so loved."

Rachel smiled sadly as the realization of Moshe's relationship with Ellie filled her mind. "Moshe. Yes, he is a good man. I did not know that the two of you were . . ." she swallowed hard. "But he is Jewish. And not an American."

Ellie shrugged and went back to sorting through the clothes. "It doesn't matter. He never used anybody in his life. He is good to me. When I'm with him, he is thoughtful and considerate . . ."

"I see. Yes. You love *him*, then. Moshe." She gazed up at the pictures hanging on Ellie's walls. Among the faces looking back at her was the recent photograph of Moshe on the deck of the *Ave Maria* with his arm around the little refugee boy. His brown eyes seemed to radiate into her soul. "He is a good man." Her words were barely audible. "They are both good men, I think."

23   Brothers

Bonfires burned brightly in the streets bordering El Azhar University in Cairo, and street vendors hawked their wares to the crowd gathered to hear the outcome of the meeting. The leaders of the five Arab nations were cloistered within to decide a unified Arab position on the Palestine problem. Newspaper men and photographers leaned against the polished black limousines parked at the curb. A few men scribbled notes, but most of the group chewed roasted ears of corn and speculated on the outcome of the conference. Without exception, each man believed that the very crowds they mingled with now would become the force by which the Jews would be driven to the sea.

Inside the gleaming marble halls of El Azhar, Hassan struck a match against a pillar and lit the last of his second pack of cigarettes as he waited beside the heavy walnut doors. Across from him stood the bodyguards of King Abdullah of Transjordan, and a few yards from them, the guards of Ibn Saud of Saudi Arabia waited. Hassan noted with amusement how the two groups of men glanced furtively at one another. King Abdullah hated Ibn Saud with the passion of an ancient blood feud. And Ibn Saud, ruler of the vast underground supplies of oil for the world, in turn hated King Farouk of Egypt. The servants of these rulers shared the same Muslim faith, as well as the suspicion their masters bore for one another. There was also one other thing they shared—a mutual and intense hatred of the Jews in their midst. This hatred, Hassan knew, gave his master, the Mufti, power over these men and the policies of their governments. Hassan glanced up as Gerhardt and Kadar walked purposefully up the hallway toward him. Kadar wore the same dark confident expression as the Mufti. Gerhardt seemed more grim and hard than usual. The men of Ibn Saud eyed him curiously as he passed them, each touching fingertips to forehead in respect. King Abdullah's guards, dressed in British-looking uniforms, continued to smoke and talk among themselves.

"Salaam." Hassan touched his head band.

"They have not yet dismissed?" Kadar frowned slightly.

Hassan shook his head. "It is nearly six hours."

"They have much to say," Gerhardt said sullenly. "But in the end Haj Amin will have his way."

Kadar smiled slightly. "If Allah wills."

Gerhardt snorted. "It is the will of Haj Amin. And, after all, short of committing themselves to full-scale war, which each of these braggarts publicly proclaims and privately hopes to avoid, we are their best hope. They will give him everything he asks for. Everything. Even Palestine, eh?"

"That is what this meeting will settle."

"It was settled three days ago when King Abdullah came privately to the mansion to speak with the Mufti. Later Ibn Saud slipped in the back door, and after him came the emissary of King Farouk. I tell you there are only the terms left to settle. Money. Weapons. Men. They will leave it to Haj Amin to decide where to build the last Jewish crematorium. In the meantime, it is our war until the British leave."

"The war of the terrorist." Kadar eyed him coldly.

"Commando," Gerhardt corrected. "Patriot."

"Some would say," Kadar interrupted brusquely, "there is no Arab Palestine yet to be patriotic to. I fear that terrorism will simply turn the world against our cause and in the end defeat us."

"And will the United Nations still support Partition when they realize that they must supply one soldier to protect every Jew in Palestine?" Gerhardt's eyes narrowed and he smiled a cruel, hard smile. "I think not, Kadar. And when the oil of Ibn Saud becomes a threat, they will turn their backs on these Jewish vermin, as they did when the Führer took up this cause." He appraised Kadar contemptuously. "You are too soft, Kadar. It is not neat round bullet holes, draining out Jewish blood like water from a spigot, that will provoke the cowards of the world to appease us. No. It is a blinding flash of light among the crowd in a sidewalk cafe. It is mangled women and children lying in pieces like chunks of raw meat in the butcher shop. All kosher, of course."

Hassan flicked the ashes of his cigarette onto the marble floor and watched the confrontation. "You have a point, Gerhardt," he smiled. "And so do you, Kadar. But in the end, how we wage war is the Mufti's decision. And either way, the Jews will be just as dead. The condition of the bodies does not matter, I think, Kadar."

Kadar shrugged. "My loyalties are, of course, to Haj Amin. I will simply follow his orders." He glanced at the walnut doors and frowned. "Whatever they may be."

———

A single light bulb hung from the ceiling of the basement room at Rehavia High School. It glared down at the nine men seated in hard metal chairs arranged in a semicircle facing Moshe and the detailed maps of the Old City. Behind them, giant shadows imitated their movements against the backdrop of dripping cinder-block walls. *But they are only men*, thought Moshe, *not giants. And this assignment calls for giants.*

Moshe cleared his throat and concluded his instructions. "So you can see, because the synagogues are the most prominent buildings in the quarter, we must make our outposts there." He glanced around at the bearded faces gazing up at him. "Any questions?"

Four hands shot up, their caricatures waving at him grotesquely from the wall. He pointed to a seventeen-year-old boy with a scruffy fringe of beard and angry black eyes behind wire-rimmed glasses. "You say we are to set up posts in the synagogues? You think the rabbis are going to be happy about that? The Orthodox still believe that some mythical ancient God will save us."

Moshe frowned. "With that attitude, Gershon, you will offend the rabbis and no doubt jeopardize what we are trying to accomplish in the Old City. You volunteered for this assignment, but now we will have to find another place for you to serve."

The boy stood angrily. "What do you mean? You are saying I cannot go?"

"That is what I am saying. You might want to fight, but I tell you that you will need the prayers and support of the Old City rabbis if you are to stand. Especially against the thousands of Jihad warriors who flock to the Arab sectors daily."

"You can't do this!" The shadow raised a contorted fist. "It is all arranged."

"It is done, Gershon. You are excused, please." Moshe stared him into silence; then the boy snatched up his coat and stalked from the room without looking back. "Anyone else have anything to say about the mythical God of the Hebrews?" Moshe asked as the basement door slammed shut and the sound of footsteps retreated up the stairs. "You were accepted," he searched each face, "because all of you come from an Orthodox background. If, for whatever reason, you have grown to despise that heritage, you may not defend the Old City. If you feel in your hearts that you cannot any longer be sensitive to the old ways of the rabbis, we shall simply find another place for your services."

"But are the rabbis not against us?" asked a small, frail-looking man of about twenty-five.

"There is division among them since the siege. Akiva has, up until last week, carried the weight of opinion with him. He has controlled the flow of money to the public kitchens and the agency for the poor. That is no longer true, and he is angry. His followers are dwindling. Only a few remain among the Hassidim. The Ashkenazi Jews are sending urgent messages for food and defense."

Heads nodded in understanding and approval. A large, rawboned young Hassidic Jew spoke quietly, "In the Warsaw ghetto, even the rabbis came into the streets on Shabbat to help fortify our barricades and make sandbags. We needed their blessings as well. When at last the ghetto fell, they stood and bravely died with the rest. I escaped. A few others. Very few among the thousands."

"The scene shall not be repeated, Rashi," Moshe said, hoping he was telling the truth. "But there you see how important it is for the sake of working together that you remember who you are and where you come from." He glanced around the room one last time. "You each know what you are supposed to do." Faces gazed pensively back at him. "Well, then, may God go with you. You are our foundation." He nodded, and the men stood and silently filed out of the room and out the door, past the figure of the Old Man, David Ben-Gurion, who stood to the side, a late arrival at the meeting.

When the last man murmured his greetings and shook the Old Man's hand, Ben-Gurion closed the door behind him and plopped down on a chair facing Moshe. He slapped his hands on his thighs. "So. You send them off."

Moshe rubbed his forehead. "Sheep to the slaughter."

"We hope not. We must each find our duty, no?"

Moshe pursed his lips and frowned, then turned to gather the charts and maps of the Old City. "What news have you on the bombing?"

"I thought you would never ask." The Old Man lit up a cigarette. "It was not Jewish dynamite."

"You are sure?" Moshe rolled a map and snapped a rubber band tightly around it. "What about the Irgun? Could they have done it?"

"They could have. Probably wish they had." He blew out a long breath of smoke. "But I spoke with that rascal Menachem Begin and he says it was not the doing of his men. He says he is certainly not against the principle of an eye for an eye, and a tooth for a tooth, however."

"If it were up to the Irgun, we would all have false teeth and feel our way with canes, eh?" asked Moshe. "Well it can only have been the work of Gerhardt."

"And Hassan, Moshe." The Old Man squinted up at him. "There is bad blood between Hassan and you for a long time."

"Between Hassan and all Jews," Moshe interrupted.

"He is a man to be stopped, is he not? Before he stops you."

Moshe did not answer. Instead, he silently cleaned up, stacking metal chairs against the wall. He moved down the row until only the Old Man's chair remained. He put his hand on the back of the chair. "What do you want from me?" he asked.

"He was once your friend."

"The friend of my brother."

"Like a brother, was he not?"

"I suppose so." Moshe took a chair from the stack where he had just placed it, opened it, and sat down across from the Old Man.

"What can you tell me about such a man as this? A man who was once the brother of a Jew who then fled to the Nazis and trained with them in the murder of our people."

"I thought you and Alon had that all on file."

"Facts. Not motives. And you have never spoken of it, Moshe. Perhaps it is time."

Moshe folded his hands and pushed his thumbs nervously against one another. "I don't know where to begin."

"At the beginning."

"We were children together. On opposite sides of the Street of the Chain. From our window above Cohen's grocery. . ."

"I know it well."

"We could see the Dome of the Mosque and from his window no doubt he could see the Wailing Wall. On Shabbat he would come and light the candles for us. At the end of the Muslim fast, we would bring food to his family and he would bring bread and honey at the end of ours. His father and mother were devout Muslims and tolerant, kind people. Ibrahim was not so much my friend as he was a friend and brother to Eli."

"This Eli was your older brother who was killed?"

Moshe nodded. "Yes."

"Hassan killed him, did he not?"

Moshe nodded again, more slowly. "Betrayed him."

"But why did he do such a thing, Moshe?" The Old Man's eyes were burning with intensity now.

"He had a sister. A year younger than Eli. Eli loved her secretly. She loved him as well. Hassan knew of this but felt it was a good thing. That he and Eli would be truly brothers. But . . ." Moshe dug at a crack in the concrete floor with the toe of his shoe.

"But what?" The Old Man urged him on.

"We are Jews." He shrugged, remembering the night Eli had told his father of his love for the beautiful young Arab girl.

Do you know what your marriage to her would mean for you? For all of us?" Eli's father showed no visible anger, but his message was clear. Eli nodded his head silently and went to his room, where Moshe sat reading in an overstuffed chair. He pretended not to notice when Eli stretched out on the bed and tears flowed silently down his cheeks. Finally Moshe asked his brother,

"What will you do?"

Eli wiped his eyes and sat up, wrapping his arms around his knees. "Can I tear out the beard of my father? I must not see her again."

"But why?" Moshe asked. "Can she not become a Jew?"

"She will not. To marry her means that I turn my back on my faith and my family. You"—he looked painfully into Moshe's eyes—"could no longer call me your brother. I would be dead to you. Dead."

"But you love her."

"Yes!" Eli cried. "But we shall not speak of it again."

It was a memory time had not healed. For a long moment, Moshe sat in the metal chair thinking of a thousand things, thinking about Ellie, and what he would have done had he been Eli. His father was dead now and Moshe did not live according to the old ways any longer. And he loved Ellie, loved her as he had never allowed himself to love any woman before now.

The Old Man coughed loudly, pulling Moshe back to the present. "Where are you?" he asked.

"In the past, which sometimes appears to repeat itself," Moshe replied. He looked up at the Old Man. "My brother made a decision I would not have the strength to make. He broke off the relationship with the girl. He would not speak with Hassan when he approached him in the street. He turned his back and walked away when he saw his friend. He turned away in silence from those that he had loved."

"And then?"

"The sister of Hassan was betrothed and married to a member of the Mufti's guard, a fellow named Ram Kadar. She took her own life shortly after. We heard that she had left a note for Eli, but he never got it. A few weeks later, Eli was torn apart by a mob of Arabs in the marketplace who claimed he had defiled an Arab woman. Hassan was at the head of that mob. In the end, you know how many died. Not just Eli. But when it was all finished, this eye-for-an-eye business had killed many innocent on both sides."

"Do you ever fear his hatred?"

"Only when it reaches out for those that I love. Not for myself. I only pity him."

"Your Ellie Warne is not a Jew," the Old Man probed.

"I am not my brother."

———

David leaned his head back against the seat and watched as Michael closed his eyes and nodded and bobbed with the gentle rocking of the train to Prague. He smiled as Michael jerked his head up, then slowly relaxed until his chin once again rested on his chest. As the train rumbled over a trestle bridge, he jerked his head back once again, then, crossing his arms, fell back against the window with his mouth half open. With three days' growth of beard and his hair falling in wisps across his bald dome, he looked for all the world like a skid-row bum sleeping it off. David wished he knew how to use the big camera he had purchased in the Paris secondhand store the morning before.

For a moment he was tempted to pull it out (
attempt to figure it out. Then he remembered
bought film. He sighed and grinned, determin
the sight of Michael with his mouth hanging o
faded plush velvet of their train compartment.

*The generals of the Third Reich prowled Europ
train compartment,* he thought, glancing around hi
was worn thin from the chafing of Nazi uniforms. *L*
The maintenance of luxury and necessity alike ha
on hold as men had gone about the business of blo
another up in Europe. And now that the war had ende
remained was the business of rebuilding.

Rusting steel skeletons of Nazi transports lay along t
road tracks. David stared out the window at the scarred
tryside, then closed his eyes with the memory of German
diers running for cover along these very tracks as he dive
their troop train.

Now, the remnants of Nazi airpower waited on the desertc
airfields of Czechoslovakia to be sold to the highest bidder. H
and Michael were traveling to Prague to meet with Avriel and
examine a flock of ME 109 fighter planes left behind by the de-
feated enemy in their headlong retreat from the victorious So-
viet Army.

The train stopped and started, slowly lurching across the
broken countryside. The gray stone villages all looked the
same—weary, cold, and hungry. The fields, once rich with harvest, seemed blighted; the stubble of the first crops since before
the war poked through the half-frozen mud. As the steady clack-
ing of the wheels slowed to a stop for what seemed like the thousandth time, David fixed his gaze on a peasant man dressed in
a patched brown coat and carrying a basket slung across his
back. His right coat sleeve was empty and pinned up. *In which
war and for what cause,* David wondered, *did the old man give
his arm? And in the end, had it mattered?* David looked down at
his own hands. How he wished that his life would matter; that
he could make a difference in a world whose reality seemed so
barren and hopeless. He thought of his father then, whose faith
seemed to reach far beyond his existence to touch the lives of
those around him. And what of Ellie? His own selfishness had
left wounds in her heart and soul as deep as those on the land
he now passed through. He stared down at the weeds growing

...ged rail lines. The very men who ...task of rebuilding. It seemed ...dless blitzkrieg, and now, ...ssible task of rebuild- ...oped that it was not

...to motion again, passing ...-clad U.S. Army engineers ...ed through the rubble of a ...passed a muddied field, fright- ...no rose and banked against the ...id saw the tall brick smokestack of ...; their thick gray haze now dissipated, ...surrounding them. *The very air of Europe* ...*y*, David thought, *and every human breath* ...*lt of the smokestacks.* "I want to make a dif- ...pered.

...back against the seat and smiled at Michael who ...th the gentle rocking of the train. David reached ...apped him on the top of his head. "Hey, Scarecrow,

...hael opened one eye and scowled. "Yeah? What d'you ...?" He sat up and rubbed his face with both hands.

"I just wanted to say I'm glad I'm here, y'know?"

Michael screwed up his face and rolled his eyes. Then he sighed and settled back against the seat once again. Moments later his head nodded and his chin rested against his chest as the train clacked on toward Prague.

Smoke curled lazily upward, creating misbegotten halos above the heads of the men at Son of Mohammed Coffee House in Latrun.

Hassan smiled disarmingly across the table at the two British Army deserters who leered up at the dancing girl on the small stage before them. Their bloodshot eyes danced with the sound of pulsating music. Hassan hid his contempt for these traitors of their own kind and poured more coffee into their cups, which they fortified with whiskey.

"A drop, mate?" A soldier held out a silver hip flask toward Hassan's cup.

He covered the cup with his hand. "Followers of the Prophet do not drink alcohol."

"Temperance League got to you, too, huh?" the soldier answered drunkenly.

Hassan merely shrugged and sipped his coffee, waiting until the dance ended with a flourish and the two soldiers hooted and applauded wildly. Then they slurped their coffee and wiped their mouths with the backs of their hands. "You like our entertainment, eh?" asked Hassan.

"I ain't seen anything this good since Paris in '45. You think you can introduce me to 'er?"

"This girl or a dozen others, my friend. A few days from now you shall be heroes among my people—as Lawrence who led the Bedouins to victory against the Turks."

"All I say is, where's the money?" The more surly of the two men held out his hand, palm up.

"A minor detail," Hassan assured. "Shall we say thirty pounds now and another thirty when the deed is done?" He reached for his money pouch and counted out thirty pound notes on the table before them.

"So where do you want the stuff delivered?" asked the other soldier.

"I told you," Hassan warned. "You simply keep your mouth shut and drive the trucks. We shall tell you when you have reached your destination."

"Christmas morning, eh? An end to those Christ-killers I say, and good riddance!" The two deserters raised their cups in a toast to death, then drained their drinks in one swallow.

24   Shabbat

Grandfather rocked slowly back and forth among the other worshipers gathered for morning services.

"Accept, O Eternal, our God! thy people Israel and their prayers, restore the service to the oracle of thy house, and the burnt offerings of Israel and their prayers, in love, accept with favor."

His head was covered with the blue and white tallith that had served as the prayer shawl of his father and his father's father in the priestly line of the Cohanim.

". . . And may our eyes behold when thou returnest unto Zion in compassion. Blessed art thou, the Eternal, who restoreth His divine glory unto Zion."

Even as he prayed, an overwhelming sense of sorrow pressed down on Grandfather's stooped shoulders. Today was Shabbat—the day of rest, when a man could not so much as carry a handkerchief to worship, but instead wore it sewn into the sleeve of his coat. This was the day when it was forbidden by law to travel, and yet this was the only day that the Mufti had granted permission for the Jews of the Old City to leave; with the stipulation that they must return before sundown or be shut out of their homes and the sacred places of learning and worship.

Grandfather opened his eyes and gazed up at the dome of the synagogue as the light of early morning streamed through the latticed windows. "Oh, Eternal, ever-merciful God," he whispered, as the men around him continued to bob and pray in uneven cadence. Grandfather tugged his whiskers. "I know that Shabbat is your day. The Mufti knows this too, and he has mocked you by daring us to break the laws of the Torah. But we know better, nu? Today especially it is our mitzah to speak your word. Maybe Yacov has no one who will read Torah to him today, God forbid. So Lord, I know you understand this; today I have to ride the bus."

Voices of the other worshipers surrounded him, reciting the Hallel: *Out of trouble did I call upon the Lord, and the Eternal answered me with enlargement. The Eternal is for me, I will not be afraid, what can man do to me?*

"So. You will go with me today? Even if I ride the bus to the hospital on Mount Scopus? And will you see me safely home again as well?" Tears filled the old rabbi's eyes as he thought about seeing Yacov once again. He sniffed once, then quietly added, "You know, God, the boy is all I got." Just the thought of seeing Yacov relieved the pain in his chest and let him breathe easier than he had in weeks.

Grandfather was ringed about by the final prayer and benediction of the Cohanim. The Great Dome of Nissan Bek echoed with the last "Omaine" of the service, and Grandfather felt in his heart that the Eternal had indeed heard his prayer. He kissed the hem of his tallith and, for the first time in his life, consciously prepared to break the Sabbath.

"Shalom, Reb Lebowitz," a young, scarcely bearded Yeshiva student greeted him as he hurried past.

"Good Shabbat, Yosi," he returned, his eyes avoiding those of elderly Rabbi Eilan, moving toward him through the cliques of worshipers standing in the sanctuary.

"Reb Lebowitz!" came the cracked voice of the rabbi, falling in step behind Yosi. "A word with you please!" he cried. "Oh, Reb Lebowitz!"

Yosi frowned and crowded close on Grandfather's heels, stepping sideways around various discussions and debate concerning the Scriptures. "Reb Lebowitz, I wish to speak with you concerning the laws of hashavat aveida, the return of lost property as we studied in the Talmud and Mishna. Baba Metzi 2. If another's property is found . . ." he began, prepared for a discussion that would normally last for hours.

Grandfather did not slow his pace. "Yes, yes, Yosi. Perhaps another day. Just remember Leviticus 19:18 and all will be well. Now I must hurry, or I shall miss my bus."

The student stopped in his tracks, dumbfounded as Rabbi Eilan plowed into his back. "Your *bus*, Reb Lebowitz?" his voice called after Grandfather as he greeted others and scurried out the massive doors of the Great Synagogue.

The shrill, high voice of Rabbi Eilan followed him into the street where other black-coated men stood about and discussed points of the law as well as the Mufti's edict banning all travel in and out of the Old City except on the Sabbath.

"A word, Reb Lebowitz!"

"Tomorrow! I must not be late!"

Grandfather hurried through the crooked corridors of the Jewish Quarter to the outskirts of the Armenian Quarter where the promised escort waited to take him to Zion Gate and the number two bus. The streets were filled with faces he had known his entire life. Heads nodded and eyes followed him curiously as he raised his hand slightly in greeting.

Just ahead he saw the narrow Mendelbaum Gate that marked the end of the quarter. He looked up and over his shoulder. "So, God, are you coming?" He speeded his pace the last fifty yards until he passed beneath the archway into a small group that waited behind the line of British Highland Light Infantry.

A tall, ruddy-faced officer with a handlebar mustache looked the collection of a dozen Jews over thoroughly. He frowned as Grandfather approached.

"Good Shabbat, Rabbi," he said.

Grandfather looked behind him to see if perhaps the English officer was addressing another rabbi. "Good Shabbat," he said hesitantly. "A beastly thing, this, isn't it?"

Again Grandfather hesitated as the officer lowered his chin and gazed directly at him. "You are addressing me, sir?" Grandfather asked.

"Yes, of course. It is beastly, this edict against leaving the Old City except on the day of rest, and even then you need armed escort. The Mufti's trying to break the spirit of the Old City Jews, and there's an end to it."

"I do not believe I have had the pleasure of meeting you?" Grandfather tugged his beard and inwardly smiled at the indignation of this Gentile against the Mufti.

"Captain Luke Thomas," he extended his hand. "And you, sir?"

"Rabbi Shlomo Lebowitz." He shook hands with the officer, ignoring the nagging pain in his chest.

"I could see you were a rabbi." He twirled his mustache and rocked back on his heels.

"And I could see you were an officer."

"Yes," he cleared his throat. "Quite. Must be urgent business for you to travel on the Shabbat."

"I have a grandson at Hadassah Hospital." Grandfather squinted and adjusted his wire-framed glasses as the officer frowned, then fumbled in his pocket for a small leather-bound notebook.

"I have it here somewhere." He searched the pages. "That would not be a young lad by the name of Yacov Lebowitz?"

Grandfather nodded his head. "The very same. But how could you know that?"

"He's a good lad. I have had the pleasure of speaking with him. He mentioned having a grandfather in the Old City. It could be no one but you."

A feeling of delight filled the old rabbi. This was surely a sign that God was watching. "I have received no word of his condition of late and I felt I must go to his side."

"Quite. Even on the Shabbat."

"It is only men like the Mufti who think God would have such a heart as to keep me from Yacov's side on Shabbat. True? Of course true!"

"Omaine," said a middle-aged woman in a long black wool dress. "And may the Mufti's brains be turned to steam!"

"Omaine," repeated two young Ashkenazi students simultaneously as they spit to emphasize their point. "Well spoken, rabbi."

The captain threw his head back and laughed loudly. "A noble sentiment."

"A worthy prayer," said Grandfather as the group clustered nearer to one another now, drawn by mutual distaste for Haj Amin. "And when do we move to Zion Gate?"

"We still have quite a bit of time until the bus comes." The captain glanced at his watch. "We would not like to leave anyone behind. Five minutes more."

The old rabbi raised his arms. "If this were just any Shabbat, we would now be arriving home from the synagogue, would we not?" Heads nodded in unison. "And we would sing"—he lifted up his voice in the street—"so that the Mufti would hear us:

"When from life's dark dream we awaken
When tired breast God sets free,
Hearts that here with grief were shaken,
Flutter then with ecstasy;

So from the wan brow
All grief is gone now,
For sorrow departs, and joy enters instead . . ."

The dozen travelers sang loudly, their voices echoing off the stone buildings to make a thousand other voices in the canyons. And when they finished and the last echo died out, Grandfather turned to the captain in delight and said, "You see, even the angels have joined us in our celebration of the Lord's Shabbat. The Mufti's edicts cannot steal our joy."

"Well spoken, Rabbi," replied the Englishman with a grin.

"Omaine!" exclaimed the two Ashkenazi as they spit on the ground.

Introductions were made all around, and a bond of camaraderie formed within the little group. Each had his own reason

261

for traveling to the New City, and as they explained to Grandfather, who was the only rabbi in the group, he reassured them with words from the Torah that there were at times special exceptions to the law. Luke Thomas stood a short distance from them, listening to every word. He clasped his hands behind his back, and when Grandfather would make a particularly interesting point, he would nod his head and stick out his lower lip thoughtfully. Finally the old rabbi could stand it no longer.

"You see," said Grandfather to the captain, "the men of Israel sit in the gates and discuss the holy books. You are goyim, Englishmen, and yet you listen like a Yeshiva boy. It is most interesting."

The little crowd of Jews peered intently at the tall Englishman. He twisted the end of his mustache self-consciously as they waited for his reply. "It's just that I find what you say quite similar to, uh . . ." he paused. "That is, you sound like a Christian."

"Ha!" The old rabbi laughed loudly and was joined by the reluctant laughter of those around him. "The thing you say makes me sound like a Christian would make me say you sound like a Jew!"

"I am a follower of Christ, sir." The captain replied as the six English guards clustered around him.

"So! The one we call Yeshua?"

"Indeed. I do believe that He is the Messiah. Fulfilled the prophecies."

Grandfather tugged on his whiskers, conscious that the circle of Jews and Gentiles was closing tighter around him as he pondered his reply. "Many Jews agreed with you, Captain, at one time. Otherwise you would not be standing here telling me you are a Christian. Your ancestors were still praying to trees while this Jesus was teaching from the Torah, and His Jewish disciples were discussing His parables. True? Of course true."

"Well spoken, Rabbi," agreed the two Ashkenazi students as others nodded and murmured approval.

Every eye turned toward Luke then, awaiting his reply. "Yes, I see your point. But does it not say in Isaiah . . . I believe it is Isaiah fifty-two, that even the Gentiles will see the Messiah and believe?"

"Well spoken, Captain," nodded the old rabbi. "But I fear that the Gentiles have made Jesus into a Gentile. And so over two thousand years Jews have been murdered and tortured in the name of Christ. And what does God have to say about that, eh?"

Luke cleared his throat and took a deep breath. "Isn't it written that the character of God remains unchanging and forever the same? No matter what we try to make Him, for whatever reason, Jesus is the same as He was two thousand years ago when the first Jews believed."

"Well put." Grandfather raised his hand to silence the Yiddish discussion that was taking place behind him at the rear of the crowd. Grandfather approved of the gentle, good-natured way in which this Englishman expressed his views. He had discussed before with Christian goyim and usually such discussions involved hostility and hot debate and ended with the phrase, *Christ-killers.* "Perhaps we shall continue this conversation over supper sometime when the followers of Allah and his Prophet allow us poor scholars once again to sup, nu?"

"I should be pleased to bring the bread to such a meal, sir." The captain saluted and turned to his men. "Front and center," he commanded. "Two at the sides and one each front and back. Rabbi, if you will be so kind as to organize three abreast please."

Grandfather pulled his little group together—an unlikely-looking general of the little band. As they marched through the hostile Arab Quarter, the Englishmen scanned every doorway and rooftop shadow that they passed. The captain walked just in advance of the group, his sten gun cocked and ready in the event of an ambush. *He would be the first shot,* thought Grandfather, *if we were attacked,* and he made a mental note that he would indeed invite the captain to break bread with him—if there was still bread to break.

———

It was Saturday morning. Six days had passed since the funeral of Miriam and Ishmael. Along with a thousand other Arab Christians, Miriam's grandson had packed his few meager belongings and gone to the safety of Beirut, Lebanon. Daily the Christian Arab exodus accelerated, stripping the government offices of the cream of the Arab intellectuals, crippling the post office and phone services. Tomorrow, Ellie knew, the doors of the Christian churches would be open to the few who had the courage to openly worship their God. Many of those who stayed on prayed silently behind locked doors and looked toward the Mount of Olives in hopes that the Christ would once again set His foot upon that sacred spot and bring peace to Zion.

Ellie scrubbed the dishes, proud of herself for the cheese blintzes she had made under Rachel's direction. Rachel had retreated to her bedroom—with Shaul following happily at her heels —to prepare for a trip to the hospital to visit Yacov.

Uncle Howard poked his head in the kitchen door. "You about ready hon?" he asked.

Ellie turned off the water and dried her hands. "Just let me get my coat." She switched off the light and led the way toward the door.

Uncle Howard gave a low whistle of approval at Ellie's red sweater and skirt. "You look like Christmas," he said happily.

She stopped and knocked on Rachel's door, "You coming, Rachel?" Ellie called.

Rachel opened the door, wearing a skirt that Ellie had given her and a beautiful royal blue sweater that matched her eyes.

"Not one beautiful girl, but two!" exclaimed Uncle Howard.

"You are kind, Professor," Rachel blushed. "Both of you are kind."

Dry leaves scudded across the nearly empty streets of the New City. Rolls of barbed wire lined the sidewalks like the dying vines of an enormous briar patch. Ellie glanced anxiously at Uncle Howard as they wound around barriers and detours on their way to Hadassah Hospital.

As they passed the headquarters of the Palestine police, Ellie thought how much like a wicked castle in a fairy tale it seemed. Tall electric fences surrounded it, and everywhere the tangled wire seemed to emphasize the policies of the British Government toward a Jewish homeland.

"Is this a prison?" asked Rachel from the backseat.

"Police headquarters. The wire is to keep people out, not in. We call the place Bevingrad, named after the British Foreign Minister who is responsible for all this mess. He is the man who kept you out of Palestine. Blocked immigration to appease the Mufti."

"Seems almost funny," Ellie mused. "All this wire. Fences and guns. They wanted to keep the Jews out of Palestine and now they hide inside a prison of their own making."

She glanced back at Rachel, studying her profile. A sad

smile momentarily crossed Rachel's lips, but she did not look up. *She knows all about prisons*, Ellie thought.

"Does he live here?" Rachel asked, taking in the sight of the armed British guards on duty at the gates.

"No," explained Uncle Howard. "In England."

"Then why has he worked so hard to keep us out? My mother and father tried so hard to come here before the war. If only—" Her words ended, but Ellie heard the anguish in her unfinished sentence. Rachel cleared her throat and began again. "This is such a tiny corner of the world, is it not?"

"Nowadays the British worry about losing their empire and the wealth that goes with it—Egypt, India, Palestine. If they offend the Arab nations, they may not have gasoline to fill up their automobiles," Howard explained.

"So they exchange lives for petrol," Rachel said dully.

"Such things change very little. When Jesus Christ walked these hills, He stood on the Mount of Olives and wept for this city. Later He told His followers all the things that would happen to it. Down to the destruction of the temple."

"And did it happen as He said?" asked Rachel.

"To the last detail. He spoke of the things that are happening today as well. To the last detail," he repeated. "As a matter-of-fact," he winked at Ellie, "I think He even knew how scared a certain archaeologist would be every time we drive through Sheikh Jarrah to the hospital."

"Whomever do you mean, Professor?" Ellie joked.

Rachel leaned forward and rested her arms on the back of the front seat. "What is it like in America, where you come from?" she asked eagerly.

Ellie handed her a copy of *Life* magazine. "This'll give you some idea. Where I live, everything is lit up and decorated right now for Christmas. And Santa Claus is in every store window, and people are shopping like crazy for last-minute presents."

"I shall wait here in the car," Rachel said to Ellie as Uncle Howard pulled into the Hadassah Hospital parking lot and stopped.

"You sure?" asked Ellie. "You might enjoy it. I think the boy can even speak Polish."

"Go ahead. The ride was simply lovely," she said as they climbed from the car.

Rachel sat in the backseat of Uncle Howard's 1932 Plymouth; the ancient reminder of some American diplomat's stay in Palestine. She thumbed through Ellie's copy of the December 22nd issue of *Life* that had come by special courier from the Jewish Agency. On its cover a child stood holding a hymnbook while tiny angels played harps above her head. *It is almost Christmas in America*, she thought, smiling to herself at the memory of Christmas in Poland before the war, when Gentiles had decorated their streets and homes and sung the songs of their religion. Usually their celebration had fallen within a few days of Hanukkah, one of the brightest festivals of the Jewish year. She remembered the last Hanukkah her family had spent together in Nazi-occupied Warsaw. Her little brothers gathered around as she lit the first of the eight candles in commemoration of the eight days of holiday and the Jewish fight for freedom. Gifts had been exchanged and she had saved enough to purchase each of her three brothers a top, even the baby, Yani. In spite of the hunger and hardship of war, laughter and light had filled their house. They had not known that it was their last Hanukkah together as a family. Less than one year later, in the middle of the night, the doors had been broken down by the Nazis and the Jews were herded into cattle cars as men with guns sang:

"Crush the skulls of the Jewish pack
And the future, it is ours and won;
Proud waves the flag in the wind
When swords with Jewish blood will run."

Had it not been for a few good people among the Polish Christian community, all would have been lost. As they had marched through the snow toward the cattle cars waiting at the train station, a Polish woman had taken Rachel's infant brother from her mother with a few tearfully whispered sentences in the woman's ear. Rachel had watched as the woman was stopped by the S.S. guards at the edge of the railway yard, and that was the last she had known of Yani. Her mother had wept silently as she was pushed and prodded onto the train. But she did not turn to look after the fate of the child, fearful that the Nazis would see and know that he belonged to her, that the tiny smiling baby was a hated Juden.

Rachel turned the pages of the magazine, devouring the pictures with her eyes. Everywhere there was bounty. An elderly man stood at a window as an old woman basted a turkey on a wood stove laden with food. A tree stood decorated with candy and popcorn and a brand new shining car was driving up in the snow outside the window. "Here they come, Mom! And Jim don't need the wishbone—they've *got* their PLYMOUTH!" Rachel smiled and looked over the frayed material of the backseat. On the dashboard, the word PLYMOUTH hung haphazardly from the glove box. So, this car she sat in was American too. It certainly did not look anything like the automobile in the magazine, but she had a strange and happy sensation pretending that she was a passenger in the car in the advertisement. She turned another page to a drawing of a large white refrigerator stuffed with food. "KELVINATOR—of course!" the caption read. "You've never seen anything like it . . . never expected it . . . never even dreamed there could be a refrigerator like this. One of America's great new postwar products . . ."

She was filled with wonder at the explanation of the machine's powers. In Poland she had never heard of a machine that could keep food fresh and cold for days. *What a miraculous place must this America be*, she thought, *with its inventions and dance bands and men and women that actually danced together, not only in the same room, but touching one another as well!*

As she flipped through pages containing photographs of parties and the story of the Duke of Windsor, she was shocked when she came to the photograph of the *Ave Maria* perched on the sandbar as refugees straggled to the beach and British gunboats glowered in the background. The caption read, "Refugee Boat in Palestine Beached Intentionally." Somehow the reality of the event seemed detached from the picture, and Rachel wondered if the very eyes that scanned the luscious advertisements would be able to comprehend what had transpired inside the hull of that little ship.

"It was here that I first met Moshe." She pointed to the bow. "And here that we were unloaded from the freighter. And here is where I jumped. But they will see only wet people on the beach and a little fishing boat behind the waves."

She turned the page, startled to read the words, CREATOR AND CREATED titled above EDITORIAL. "The same world," Rachel read aloud, slowly and carefully to practice her English, "which this week celebrates the birth of Jesus Christ is suffering from an inadequate sense of that event's importance." She made a mental note to ask the kind professor what the meaning of these words were. "The right name for our troubles is 'secularism,' which is defined not as the denial of God, but as the practical exclusion of God from our thinking and living. God becomes a remote or merely historical figure lacking contact with the real problems of our day." Rachel repeated the last phrase and looked out over the panorama of Jerusalem spread out below Mount Scopus. "What real problems do these Americans have?" she asked out loud. She ran her index finger down the column of print. "For example, in Europe now. . ." she paused and nodded her head. "There, you see, they write of the problem in Europe, not America." Then she continued reading, satisfied that the bounty of such a land would exclude any problems. "The problem is not so much the ruined bridge, nor the lack of transportation, but rather an illness of the spirit which can only be expressed in the cruel phrase 'the death of the heart.' "

Rachel knew this illness. It was the curse of her life that she still walked among the living while her own heart had died so long ago. She leaned closer to the page, her finger touching every word. "The pathos of it is that many of these hearts have died while half-professing God, seeking in vain to recapture His importance."

And so, she thought with a sense of relief. There was her illness, spelled out in an American magazine. She had never put a name to it before. Somewhere between the first cattle car and the last Nazi officer to abuse her, her heart had died. Even as she had struggled to recapture the importance of God in a life filled with horror and betrayal, she had lost the battle, lost her soul, lost God.

She gazed toward the walled Old City where her grandfather lived, unaware of the fact that she was alive. "Maybe my heart has always been dead," she said aloud, startled at the sound of her own voice. She tried to remember if God had ever been real to her or if He had always seemed remote, simply a historical appendage to her heritage. At Hanukkah or Passover, had He ever been near to her? She closed her eyes and tried to remember the face of her mother at her bedside as they prayed together:

Spirit and flesh are thine,

268

O Heavenly Shepherd mine;
My hopes, my thoughts, my fears, Thou seest all;
Thou measurest my path, my steps dost know.
When thou upholdest, who can make me fall?

The words of her childhood faith seemed to mock her, bouncing back from the ceiling of the car. How she had fallen! Now neither God nor man could lift her up again.

She gazed, unthinking, out the window, watching the approach of an armored car up the long steep slope of Mount Scopus. As she watched, a tall British officer hopped out of the driver's side, then rushed around to open the door on the passenger side of the vehicle. He reached his hand out and stooped to help someone from the car. An old rabbi wearing a broad black fur-trimmed hat stepped from the vehicle onto the sidewalk. He smiled through his long graying beard, then pulled his knee-length black coat tighter around him. He bowed curtly to the officer and turned to disappear through the hospital doors. Rachel smiled at the old man's appearance. *So much like the rabbis back in the ghettos of Warsaw*, she thought. But that seemed another lifetime ago. "Good Shabbat, Rabbi," she said softly, remembering a thousand faces that had gone forever.

———

Gerhardt finished drilling the hole in the dashboard of the stolen British cargo truck. He reached for the three-inch section of pipe on the seat beside him and shoved it into the hole. It fit perfectly. He would have it welded in place before he threaded the fuse through it. Once the fuse was lit, it would disappear into the pipe and no one would be able to stop its deadly path.

He stepped out of the truck, watching with satisfaction as crates of explosives were gingerly hefted onto the truck beds by a chosen crew of Jihad Moqhades. He smiled grimly and wiped his hands on his trousers. Hassan approached him from behind, coughing loudly to announce his presence.

"So," said Hassan pleasantly. "It appears that the will of the Mufti is also the will of Allah."

Gerhardt did not bother to turn around. "Was there ever any doubt?"

"You were correct. Kadar lost the argument, eh? And now kings and kingdoms send us everything we need to do battle while they stand to the side and rage against the Jews. It is only right, I suppose, that we of Palestine risk our lives for the Mufti."

Gerhardt eyed him cynically. "And what position will you ask for in his government?"

Hassan ignored his comment. "Did you hear? The United States government has seized another shipment of explosives being sent to the Jews? A crate fell onto the dock in New York and broke open." He smiled.

"We will share our supplies with the Jews." He waved his hand broadly toward the stacks of crates. "Although they will receive our gifts in slightly different form than you see here."

"Haj Amin has ordered the Jihad Moqhades to cease all action until you have completed the mission."

"A wise decision. That should lull them into sleep long enough for us to deliver the package." He leaned against the hood of the truck and stared in amusement at Hassan.

"I wish I could be part of such a decisive blow against the Zionists." Hassan clicked his tongue in disappointment.

"The Mufti has left other tasks for you on Christmas Eve, has he not?"

"Yes."

"Then be content. You do the will of Allah."

25 Yacov's Release

With a black patch over his left eye, Yacov squinted up at the blurry faces of Ellie and Uncle Howard. Ellie's red hair silhouetted beautifully against the drawn white curtain that separated Yacov's bed from the noisy clamor of the children's ward. The kind English doctor blended in with the sterile surroundings with the exception of a bright blue handkerchief he wore tucked in his white coat pocket at the suggestion of Yacov.

"I am glad you are one of the goyim," Yacov smiled at Ellie's bright red sweater. "You wear such happy colors in your shirts and dresses!" he exclaimed. "In this hospital everything is the same. White. And so I wonder if I am really seeing with this eye after a while." Howard laughed, and Ellie plopped down beside him on the bed.

"I'm so glad you can see me too, Yacov," she said.

"If this were an Orthodox hospital on Shabbat, I would certainly believe that I was blind. For everything would be black—even the beards of the doctors."

"You look like a pirate," said Ellie. "Doesn't he, Uncle Howard?"

"Blackbeard. He was an Orthodox pirate." Uncle Howard mussed Yacov's hair, which had just begun to grow in brown and curly from the Orthodox cut.

"Was he Hassidim or Ashkenazi?" Yacov asked earnestly.

"Hassidim. Like you. And he was rough and tough."

"And he wore a patch?"

"On his left eye. It matched his hat and coat."

"That is good," Yacov smiled. "Then I shall be like this Blackbeard fellow."

The doctor chimed in, "I believe Yacov is feeling lively enough to put to sea."

"I am feeling well," the boy answered eagerly. "And I should very much like to see my grandfather and Shaul . . ."

Ellie and Howard looked expectantly toward the doctor. He tapped his fingers on the bed frame and toyed with the end of his stethescope. "You have been with us for just over three weeks now, and I must say your recovery, considering the amount of damage done, is just short of miraculous."

"Then may I go home?" Yacov pleaded.

"The problem is, Yacov, that you need continuing care. That means that you must come see me at least three times a week. If you return to the Old City, that will not be possible."

The boy frowned and stuck out his lower lip. Ellie took his hand and said gently, "Today is the Sabbath, Yacov, and today is the only day the Mufti has given permission for the Old City Jews to travel out and still return. Every day he makes it more difficult for the Jewish Agency to move food and supplies into the Jewish Quarter."

"This I know. My grandfather will not come out," he said sadly. "He would never break Shabbat."

Howard and Ellie exchanged looks. "You can see how hard it would be for the doctor to care for you, son," Howard placed a comforting hand on his shoulder. "The Old City is not the place for you to be right now."

Yacov nodded again slowly.

"Shaul seems to like our house fine. Would you like to come home and stay with us for a while? We have some other friends as well." Ellie tried to sound cheerful, though her heart was aching for the fragile little boy who seemed so small against the white sheets. "Moshe has promised us a Hanukkah service along with our Christmas. And one of our guests is a very pretty girl. I know how you like pretty girls."

"I would like very much to see Shaul again," Yacov sniffed. "But my grandfather would be very lonely without me during Hanukkah."

Suddenly the curtain behind Howard rustled and moved back along the curved metal bar that held it. "Lonely during Hanukkah?" growled a familiar voice. "And do you think this old man does not have students who will light the candles?"

Yacov drew a deep, astonished breath, "Grandfather!" he cried, jumping up on his knees. He flung himself into the old rabbi's outstretched arms as the tiny cubicle was filled with Grandfather's deep chuckle. "You came! You came on Shabbat!"

"So you thought I wouldn't?" Then he smiled and glanced around. "What is this place? The Holy of Holies? All white. You don't get tired of wearing white, Yacov?" He tugged at his black vest, then looked up at the doctor whose face broke into a wide grin. "And this is the high priest, nu?"

Ellie and Howard stood to the side, delightedly watching the reunion of the boy and his grandfather. "It is a pleasure to see you again, Rabbi," said Ellie.

"So. It is good to see the Arabs did not hurt you. When I saw your photographs the next day, I thought you must have been injured as well." He hesitated at the strange look that crossed Ellie's face. "So, Yacov," he said, tapping the boy on the back, "you are so happy to see me that you have forgotten your manners? Who are these kind goyim who have taken such good care of you while I am locked behind the Old City Gates?"

"Pardon me, Grandfather. I was overcome."

"I see." The old rabbi wiped a tear from Yacov's cheek. "Like David and Jonathan, eh? Sometimes it is good to weep with joy. But never forget your manners."

Yacov sat back and wiped his nose on his sleeve. "Yes, Grandfather."

"So introduce! Introduce! What are you waiting for, the Messiah?"

"You have met Miss Ellie Warne."

"Ah, yes. And the Britisher tells me she has saved your life. For which I thank the Eternal each day. May He bless you in all your ways."

Ellie blushed. "Thank you. It was Yacov who saved me first."

"He is a good boy. A bright boy, my Yacov, and I thank the Eternal for this." He prodded Yacov once again.

"And this is the professor, her uncle."

"Ah, yes, the man with such an interest in the ancients. I thank you for the interest which you have also taken in the very young." He nodded toward Yacov.

"And this is Dr. Brown, whose hands were gentle like an angel to help me."

"Dr. Braun?" Grandfather pronounced the name in a German Yiddish accent. "May God bless you and sustain you with a long and happy life. He who is ever merciful will not forget this act of mercy."

"Thank you, sir. He who is merciful had much to do with it as well, I assure you."

Grandfather bowed curtly. "Of course. Is it not written that all goodness comes from Him alone?"

"Omaine," said Yacov.

Uncle Howard put his arm around Ellie's shoulder. "We will let you two get reacquainted. We'll be out in the hall when you are done."

Dr. Brown nodded slightly. "I have rounds to make. I'll be back in a bit."

They left the boy and grandfather alone then, drawing the curtain to insure their privacy. After they had gone, the old rabbi wrapped his arms around the boy and held him close to him. "Yacov, Yacov. My son."

Yacov snuggled close to Grandfather's vest and let the loneliness of the last three weeks drain away. They sat together silently for a long time, each absorbing the joy of the other's presence. At last Yacov spoke.

"But it is Shabbat. How did you get here?"

"First the Lord and I reasoned together in morning service; then I walked to Mendelbaum Gate after I escaped from that pest Yosi and Rabbi Eilan who no doubt wanted to speak to me

273

about the committee for these young Haganah fellows coming secretly into the quarter. Once at the gate I met a most kind Britisher who is well acquainted with the professor. He escorted our pitiful little band through the Arab Quarter; then noting that the Number Two bus would not possibly bring me through the Arab's nest of Sheikh Jarrah, and that most certainly a lone rabbi walking through the quarter would be murdered and killed and doubtless cause a riot, he offered to bring me to and from the Old City in his armored car."

"But what of Shabbat, Grandfather?"

"You think, Yacov, that the very Lord who made the Shabbat did not know that the Mufti would use it to his own devices? Do you forget so soon the law as written in Leviticus 19:18?" He sniffed expectantly. "So say it. Has this patch caused your tongue to grow dumb?"

"Thou shalt not avenge, nor bear any grudge against the children of . . ." Yacov hesitated.

"Yes, yes, so go on."

". . . of thy people, but thou shalt love thy neighbor as thyself: I am the Lord." Yacov beamed.

"Correct. Did the Lord create Shabbat?"

"Yes."

"And on His day, what does He require of His children?"

"That we keep the Shabbat holy?"

"Is the keeping of Leviticus holy?"

"Yes."

"And what else?"

"It is our duty."

"So. And why did this old man travel to see you, my son?"

"Because," Yacov gulped, "because you love me?"

"As myself," the old rabbi finished. "Well spoken, Yacov. Reasoned as a true scholar and a learned man. Now we must reason other things as well."

Yacov gazed at Grandfather intently and nodded. "Yes, Grandfather."

"It is well we see eye to eye. So, this good doctor has said you must return several times to see him. How shall we best accomplish this?"

"Perhaps we can sneak out at night . . ."

Grandfather shook his head decisively. "Has the doctor not said you must stay in the New City?"

"Yes."

"Why?"

"Because of my eyes. But, Grandfather, I shall be all right."

"Can a man without sight study the Torah and the Talmud? Can he read the stories of the Mishna to his children?"

"No."

"Then is it important that you have sight?"

"Yes."

"Good. We see eye to eye." The old rabbi crossed his arms and peered over his glasses at Yacov. "Where shall you stay then?"

"The professor has offered his hospitality. Shaul lives there."

"Ha!" exclaimed Grandfather slapping his knee joyfully. "I had given the jackal up for dead! Then you must stay on with the professor. When your heart grows lonely, simply send that hairy stinking beast into the Old City with a note. I shall send him back again, and we shall not gaze across the walls and worry away our health, eh?"

"Oh, Grandfather! A wonderful plan! Shaul will gladly run home, and no one would stop him. There are more stray Arab dogs in the Old City than goats in a Bedouin field. They will never notice."

"So. Our hearts can be light. For the Eternal in His wisdom has even made provision in His plan to use the jackal Shaul in His service." Grandfather embraced Yacov again. "And so, I must be gone now. But first—" He felt the boy's arms tighten around him. "He shall bless thee . . ." He began the benediction.

"The Eternal shall bless thee from Zion, the Maker of heaven and earth," Yacov said in a small voice.

"Louder, Yacov," Grandfather instructed. "The Eternal—"

"Eternal, our Lord! how mighty is thy name throughout the earth!" Yacov's voice was stronger; his desperate urge to cling to Grandfather was being replaced with a calmness.

"And preserve thee!"

"Preserve me, O God! for in thee I trust."

Twelve more blessings Grandfather pronounced on Yacov, until at last the boy gazed at him one last time with tearless courage. And as the old man turned from him and slipped from behind the curtain, he felt that Yacov would survive the heart-ache that must surely be before him. He shuffled past the other children in the ward, inwardly blessing each hopeful face. "So, God," he whispered, "this was a good Shabbat after all, nu?"

He paused at the door and glanced back across the ward to the curtain ringing Yacov's bed. Then with a sigh, he pushed the door open and walked into the corridor.

Howard and Ellie stood at the far end, chatting quietly as they looked out a window onto the hospital courtyard below.

"Ah-hem," Grandfather coughed as he shuffled toward them.

They both glanced up at him simultaneously and walked to meet him just in front of the elevator.

"You have room in your home for one very small Jewish boy?" asked Grandfather, searching his pockets for the pound note Yacov had brought home three weeks before. He pulled out the crumpled bill and took Howard's hand, placing the money in his palm.

"Please—" Howard tried to give the bill back to him. "I can't take this."

"It is only a small amount."

"It is a blessing for me if you will allow me the honor of caring for Yacov." The bill dangled limply from his fingers.

"God forbid I should take a man's blessing. So, I cannot pay you. But you know in three days is Hanukkah and I have no gift for the boy. You will take this and buy him a dreidel, eh?" he smiled at Ellie.

"What is that?"

"A top. It is tradition, nu? Don't ask me why. And with what is left, Yacov is partial to rock candy. And let me write him a note in my own hand, eh?" He shuffled to the nurses' station and borrowed a pen and a small piece of notebook paper from a heavyset woman in an overstarched uniform and scribbled a few lines. Then he folded the paper carefully and scrawled Yacov's name on it. He handed it to Howard. "You know what these things mean to such a small boy."

Howard nodded and took his wallet from his back pocket, carefully placing the bill and the note inside. Then he took several clean, crisp, five-pound notes from the wallet and handed them to Grandfather. "For Hanukkah. For you to share with others, if you like. I know things are not easy now in the Old City."

"That is true. True. And daily it seems there are more mouths to feed." He did not take the bills from Howard's outstretched hand. "Suddenly every young man wants to come to Yeshiva.

To study or fight I cannot tell. But with every convoy some new student climbs from beneath a truck or out of a flour barrel." He chuckled.

"So take it, Rabbi. For your students and yourself during Hanukkah. It is a blessing from you to me if you will accept my gift."

"God forbid I refuse to bless you." Grandfather took the money, then slipped it into his pocket, his eyes dancing with humor.

"Thank you," Howard smiled. "Happy Hanukkah."

"And good Shabbat," he returned, peering at Howard over his glasses. "You are such a good man, Professor. Pardon me for saying, but it is a shame such a scholar and a learned man as you is not a Jew." He stuck out his lower lip and frowned thoughtfully. "Now, will you tell me? What news have you got on that scroll of Isaiah? It has often crossed my mind these weeks."

"We received a wire two days ago from the university in America," Howard crossed his arms. "The fragments we dated were around two thousand years. That places their origin sometime around the destruction of the Temple."

"Oi!" Grandfather exclaimed. "So old they are!"

Ellie stepped forward a step and stood close to Howard's elbow. "Did you say you saw my photographs the day after the riot?"

"The very same. Did you not take them to someone else, perhaps, after you left me?"

"No. I lost them when we ran."

Grandfather's eyes narrowed. "As I thought." He paused as if he were troubled. "They are in the possession of one in the Old City whose trustworthiness many have come to doubt. He mentioned to me that he knew who was in possession of the scroll and that it is perhaps of great value. Is this so?"

"It is of great value, yes. The intrinsic value of something so ancient that also proves the accuracy of biblical translations over the last two thousand years is beyond price."

"So. And who doubts that the Holy Scriptures are unchanged?" smiled the old rabbi.

"Not you, perhaps," Howard shrugged. "But there are many. And the timing of their discovery. After two thousand years of the Diaspora, now the Jews are coming home, just like the prophecy in the scroll said."

"You make me a Zionist almost." He tugged his whiskers. "So tell me, Professor. If this discovery is so important for the cause of the Zionists, would it not be most urgent for those who are against the homeland to keep this scroll hidden away? Would it not do harm to their cause as well if the scroll were revealed?"

"I had not thought of the negative aspect, but I suppose that's true." Howard was troubled by the thrust of the conversation.

"Ah, Professor," Grandfather nodded, "you should have gone to Yeshiva school, for there you learn to think through problems backward and forward. As it is written: Gather seven Jews together to discuss a problem and you will have fourteen opinions, eh?" he laughed.

"How did Ellie's photographs come to be in the possession of your friend?"

"Some say that he is no man's friend but his own. I do not know how he came to have them, but if perhaps you would allow me the blessing of helping you retrieve what was lost . . ."

"Most certainly, Rabbi."

"Thank you," he nodded curtly. "You, you care for my lamb, and I shall seek to care for your lambskin. Well spoken? Yes? There are laws written in the Torah and the Talmud concerning lost property. A righteous man will respect your claim. Of course there are the righteous and then there are the righteous, nu? So, now this old man must be gone." He pushed the elevator button, then turned to Ellie first and closed his eyes and placed his hand on her head. "May God bless you and grant you long life with a husband who will care for you and give you many children. Omaine."

"Amen," Ellie repeated, smiling in spite of herself.

Grandfather then faced Howard and repeated the procedure as the elevator clanged open behind him. "And may God bless you in every venture and grant you prosperity and peace. May His blessing be upon your home. Omaine."

"Amen." Howard took his hand and shook it vigorously. "God bless you, sir."

Grandfather stepped backward into the crowded cubicle and bowed slightly as the doors shut. His suspicions about Akiva's sincerity were now confirmed. *So, God,* he prayed silently as the elevator slid down the shaft to the first floor, *maybe this is important, maybe not. But if I can return a kindness to these goyim who care for my Yacov, then I would appreciate a little advice on the matter, eh? And if our little band has been led by a wolf beneath a sheep's fleece, then maybe we should know that, too.*

He stepped carefully from the elevator, his legs feeling shaky from the ride; then he walked slowly across the lobby and into the cold December air. He glanced at the darkening sky to the west. "Another storm, God?" he asked aloud. "Good. We will fill the cisterns of the Old City. At least we shall not lack water." He sighed and turned back to where he had left the armored car and the kind British captain.

"Good Shabbat, Rabbi," he heard a woman's soft voice greet him as he passed a black car parked at the curbside. He adjusted his glasses and nodded.

"Good Shabbat," he replied to a young woman in the backseat. He paused for a moment as her hopeful face smiled up at him. It was as though she wanted to say more—or perhaps that she expected a reply from him. Somehow he felt as though he knew him from someplace, but he did not remember her from the Old City marketplace. For an instant he felt confused by the expression in her eyes. "So," he said again, "Good Shabbat, young woman." Then he resumed his walk to the armored vehicle that would take him home.

———

The red and blue striped turtle-neck shirt lay neatly folded on Yacov's bed. He pulled up the brown wool trousers and buttoned them. Then he stood bewildered for a moment, holding them up at the waist while he searched for suspenders. He found a slim leather belt instead, and for the first time in his life, he awkwardly threaded the belt through the loops of his trousers. His own clothing had been ruined the day of the riot, and so he dressed now in the hastily gathered remnants of the hospital lost and found. "I look like the goyim," he muttered, pulling the shirt over his head.

"What was that, Yacov?" Ellie called from the other side of the curtain.

Moshe pulled the curtain back and peeked in at Yacov; then with a grin he turned to Ellie, "He looks like a Gentile."

"Was that Professor Sachar?" Yacov called.

Moshe stepped into the dressing area again. "I was over at

the university." He sat on the bed. "Thought I would stop by and see how you are. Now they tell me you are going home."

"Not home. To Professor Moniger's home. If I entered the Old City dressed like this, they would take me for a heretic." Yacov tucked the shirt in indignantly.

"Like me, eh?" Moshe flipped the lapel of his brown tweed jacket, then pulled on the open collar of his shirt.

"When first I met you, my eyes were behind bandages. You did not sound like a heretic."

Moshe whispered, "Remember the bandages when you see a man, Yacov. Look with your heart. The Professor Moniger is a kind and good man. I think perhaps God has forgotten he is not a Jew. And so when you are in his home, you must respect his ways."

"I did not ask Grandfather about the food." Yacov lowered his voice further still.

"Did you not know they follow Kashrut?" Moshe grinned broadly at the expression of relief that crossed Yacov's face. "And might I ask you, speaking of the law, Yacov. Is it not written somewhere that one must not steal that which belongs to another?"

Yacov gulped loudly and the color drained from his face as he struggled to pull on a pair of new wool socks. "Yes."

"There is word that a small boy like you and a very large dog have been seen about the streets . . ."

"This is a fine shirt I think . . ."

"It is certainly unlike the black coat of the pickpocket."

"And even without suspenders, this is a good way to keep one's pants from falling down."

"The thief, they say, wore suspenders."

"I am most grateful that these fine socks have no holes."

"They had no description of the lad's socks."

"They were most holey."

"Like you, eh, my holy Hassidim thief." Moshe mussed his hair. "It shall be our secret. But only remember to be thankful for each blessing even when it comes from the hand of a Gentile. Will you do that?" Moshe enjoyed the exquisite blackmail of the likeable little hypocrite. The boy nodded and pulled on his own ragged shoes.

"But may I not at least have a yarmulke?" he asked meekly.

"I thought perhaps a yarmulke might be required, even for

280

one who looks like he fits in the New City." Moshe pulled a beautiful embroidered blue silk skull cap from his pocket. Gently he placed it on the boy's head. "But a yarmulke does not a righteous man make," he said with mock sternness.

"Yes, sir, Reb Sachar."

From the other side of the curtain Ellie called impatiently, "What are you doing in there?"

"We are having, as you say in America, a 'man-to-man.' "

"Well, hurry up, Uncle Howard's probably already down in the car with Rachel."

Moshe straightened Yacov's yarmulke and put his arm around his shoulder. "Ready?"

Together they marched out and through the ward to a chorus of "Mazel Tov" and "Shalom." With each step, Moshe felt the boy's shoulders relax. When at last they emerged into the cold December afternoon, he was smiling and chatting about boys he had met and become friends with in the hospital. "We shall see one another again when we are all well and there is no more bombing in the streets." Ellie and Moshe exchanged glances. Moshe reached out quickly and rubbed Ellie's arm as if she had been stung and he could wipe away the pain.

"This is a happy day, Moshe," she said. "I'm fine. Okay?"

He nodded and pointed to the car where Howard sat talking with Rachel. His round face was animated and full of joyful expression. Through the windshield they watched as Rachel handed him the magazine and pointed happily to a page. Howard studied it for a moment, then burst into an off-key rendition of "Hark the Herald Angels Sing!" A slight breeze carried his rusty voice across the parking lot and Ellie was flooded with happy memories of carolers standing on busy street corners. She began to sing along:

"Peace on earth, and mercy mild,
 God and sinners reconciled!
 Joyful, all ye nations rise,
 Join the triumph of the skies;
 With angelic host proclaim. . . ."

"It's too high for me," she laughed. "That's always where I lose it."

Moshe cleared his throat and in a loud falsetto sang,

"Christ is born in Bethlehem!
Hark, the herald angels sing,
Glory to the newborn King."

From between them Yacov looked up and tapped his temple. "Meshuggener!" he exclaimed.

Howard spotted them and waved broadly. "Going my way?" he called.

"Just like Bing Crosby," Ellie laughed back.

"Moshe! Would you like a lift? As long as it is not to the Temple Mount."

"The Mufti's residence, please." Moshe poked his head in the window, feeling his heart catch in spite of himself at the sight of Rachel's blue eyes. "Hello to you, Rachel," he said, feeling awkward.

"You are looking well," she replied, looking away quickly. "Are you . . . well?"

"Yes . . . uh."

"Come on, Moshe, get in. We've got to get home." Ellie patted his back.

Moshe looked at his watch, then raised up and bumped his head. "Nearly four-thirty! I didn't realize it was so late." He put his hands on Ellie's shoulders and gave her a quick peck on the cheek. "I almost forgot. I have to go."

"I thought you were going to—"

"Thoughtless of me. A meeting. I have a meeting. Good-bye, darling. Howard. Yacov, it's good you are going home. And Rachel." He did not look in to see the bewildered expression in her face, but hurried off across the parking lot back to the Hebrew University.

"Well, I like that!" Ellie opened the car door.

"He is not going with us?" Yacov asked.

"I guess not, son," Howard smiled, then started the car.

Rachel stared out the window, certain that Moshe had not wanted to ride with them because she was in the car. She felt suddenly overcome with shame and barely looked up when Ellie introduced her to Yacov. Ellie and Howard made conversation with Yacov during the long drive home, but silence hung heavy from the backseat where Rachel gazed out the window at the rolls of wire that had made the city a prison.

26 Salvation Comes from the Sky

The British armored car wound slowly around Mount Zion and past the Tomb of David. Just ahead, the number two bus belched black smoke as it crept toward Zion Gate. The six members of the Highland Light Infantry leaned against the rough-hewn stone of the Wall and chatted quietly among themselves as they waited the arrival of the group they were to escort back through the crooked streets of the Arab Quarter and on to Mendelbaum Gate in the shadow of the synagogues.

"Here they come, mates." One soldier snuffed out his smoke and shouldered his rifle.

"The bus and that Jew-lover captain of ours."

"Watch your mouth, Tory. The captain ain't a bad sort."

"How much y' wanna bet there ain't but half of them Jews that came out this mornin'. They're cowards, y'know, these Yids."

"Five quid says twelve came out and twelve'll go back in, Tory."

"You're on, Williams. How about it? Any other takers? I say them Yids are scared runnin' on their holy day. No more'n half back through Mendelbaum. You'll see."

The brakes of the dilapidated blue and white armor-plated bus squeaked loudly as it pulled up in front of the waiting soldiers. The doors slapped open and the weary bus driver stared down at the smiling soldiers.

"Anybody gettin' off?" yelled one soldier.

Slowly an old woman disembarked, followed by the two Ashkenazi Yeshiva students and another young woman and her aged Orthodox mother.

One of the soldiers nudged a man next to him. "They've all gone to Beirut."

His smile began to fade as five more followed out the bus door. "That's still only ten."

Captain Thomas and Grandfather walked up behind the soldiers. "Ten what?" asked Luke.

"Ten passengers off the bus, sir." A soldier snapped to attention. "Me an' Tory 'ere got us a bet . . . I say twelve out, twelve in."

"Well, here is number eleven, then." Luke nodded toward the old rabbi.

"Any more in there?" shouted Tory.

One old man slowly descended the steps and looked around, blinking in the late afternoon light. "This is Zion Gate?" he asked feebly. "I meant to go to Katamon." He turned and disappeared into the interior of the bus.

"That's still only eleven."

A moment more passed, and Tory stood among the other soldiers with his palm outstretched as the little troop of Old City residents gathered beside the heavy steel-plated gates. Grandfather drew a deep breath and shook his head with a chuckle. "So," he said, "it looks like we are having more students for Yeshiva school." He jerked his head toward the bus door.

From the dim interior of the bus, eight more grim-faced, black-coated young men emerged one at a time. Cash was snatched from the palm of Tory, and a cheer went up among the other soldiers.

"Wait a minute! Wait a minute, mates!" Tory squawked. "These lads ain't part of the bargain. They didn't come out this mornin' and they ain't goin' back in, are they, Captain?"

Luke Thomas rocked back on his heels and eyed the young men as they stood with luggage in hand in a line along the side of the bus. "I don't see why they shouldn't be allowed to enter the quarter as long as they aren't bent on causing mischief." He frowned at a large rawboned Hassidim. "You going to cause trouble, lad?"

"No, sir," the man said in heavily accented English. "I am come only to study God's Word."

"There, you see?" The captain turned and walked away.

"Well, sir, y' ain't lettin' the Jews through without at least searchin' their luggage?" exclaimed Tory.

"Of course not. Open up, lads. Let's see what you've got in your grips."

One by one the newcomers opened their battered suitcases. Captain Thomas gently and nonchalantly nudged their clothes with the end of his sten gun, then, satisfied, ordered them to close up their valises. "Happy now, are you, Tory? Seems to me you lost the bet."

"How about the women? And that old guy there." He pointed at Grandfather.

"Come off it, Tory!" said another soldier. "Pay up."

"Shabbat will soon be over," said Grandfather. "We must be home."

Tory scowled and turned away, throwing his cigarette butt onto the cobblestones at his feet.

"Front and center!" Luke commanded. Then he turned once again to Grandfather. "If you would be so kind, Rabbi, to organize your people by fours."

A much larger band marched back through the Arab Quarter than had come out in the morning. And a much more prepared group as well. Three grenades were hidden in the bulky clothing of the elderly Orthodox woman, and rifle cartridges seasoned the sack of beans her daughter carried home for the Hanukkah meal. But the dearest Hanukkah gift to enter the Old City Jewish Quarter that afternoon was the disassembled sten gun strapped inside the trousers of the group's only rabbi.

"*Yakum purkan min shemaya*. Salvation comes from the sky." Michael Cohen patted the fuselage of the bright new Messerschmidt 109 and grinned broadly at David.

"Well, I shot enough of these German babies out of the sky. I sure never thought I'd be flying them." He turned a full circle, looking at the flock of German war surplus fighter planes clustered on the grass airfield of Budejovice in Czechoslovakia.

"So. What do you think?" asked Avriel, adjusting his wire-rimmed glasses.

"Well, they're real planes. Fighters." David shook his head.

"Unsteady and unstable." Michael drew a deep breath and exhaled loudly.

"Can you fly them?" Avriel frowned.

David and Michael looked at one another and said loudly, "Can we fly them?"

"Yes, yes. That is the question." Avriel peered at them suspiciously.

"We'll need a few hours in them, Avriel. You know they're not Mustangs."

"Or Spitfires."

"But it beats a Piper."

"I'll bet these'll even hang together without bailing wire."

"You think they've got real spark plugs, Michael?" David joked. "The only thing that's been keeping my engine running is an excess of fear. It radiates from me out to those antique spark plugs."

"All part of being a good pilot, David. You gotta have a plane that really challenges you."

"The word is *threaten*," David retorted.

Avriel grinned. "Am I to understand you fellows would like to have a go at these?"

Michael cocked his head thoughtfully. "We already had a go *at* them in the late war, Avriel. We'd like to have a go *in* them."

"Good. That's good. We can have twenty-five. In May."

"In May!" David exclaimed. "What are we supposed to do for the next four and a half months?"

"Pray." Michael said glumly. Then he frowned and chewed his lip. "So how are we going to get them from here to Tel Aviv? I mean the range on these things is . . ."

"We'll worry about that tomorrow." Avriel cut him short as he spotted the obese, obsequious little arms merchant waddling across the airfield.

"Well. Yes, yes, sirs, how do you like them?" asked the merchant.

"They're not Spitfires or Mustangs," Avriel grumbled. "Unsteady. Quite unstable, you know."

"Perhaps this is not to your liking." The merchant screwed up his face and stared mournfully at the planes.

"Our men would need training."

The merchant brightened again. "Ah, yes, there is a former Luftwaffe pilot . . ."

"A Nazi?"

The merchant spread his arms and shrugged broadly. "Who can say? Maybe he likes the Führer, maybe not. Did efery American who flies fote for Rosenfelt?"

"Roosevelt," David corrected.

"Whateffer," sniffed the agent, rubbing his shiny bald head. "So he flies for Germany. Maybe once you shoots at him and now he will teach you to fly a Messerschmidt."

The three Americans exchanged glances. Michael shrugged. "Why not?"

The agent smacked his stubby hands together gleefully. "Gute!" he exclaimed. "Twenty-fife?"

"If you will throw in one hundred thousand rounds of ammunition," Avriel bargained.

"No. No." The agent shook his head sadly. "Sefenty, perhaps."

"Ninety."

"Eighty."

"Eighty-five."

"Done!" The agent grabbed Avriel's hand and pumped wildly. "And as for that other matter."

"What other matter?" Avriel looked puzzled.

"The matter of arms shipment?" The agent pulled a sheet of paper from his pocket. "Yes. You see . . ." He ran his finger down a long list. "Ten thousand of rifle. Hmmm. Machine guns. Ammunition. Your other arms agent, the tall dark fellow, Kadar . . . he is worried about shipping. It is not to worry. We haf a little ship to carry. It is called the *Lino* and shall sail in only three weeks. Here is the schedule." He shoved the paper into Avriel's hand.

"Great." Avriel peered at the statement long and hard. Michael and David stared over his shoulder at the impressive list of weapons destined not for Jewish defense, but for the Mufti's arsenal. "Mind if I keep this?" He shoved it into his pocket without waiting for an answer. "Okay. Well, let's draw up the papers, shall we?" he patted David on the back. "You guys go on to the hotel. It shouldn't take me long."

Michael and David rode silently to Prague in the little green taxi. They were conscious of the tough-looking taxi driver glancing suspiciously into the rearview mirror at them. Occasionally David would smile and wink back, and the angry-looking eyes would quickly dart back to the bumpy dirt road.

When at last they entered the filthy postwar streets of Soviet-occupied Prague, Michael tapped the man on the shoulder and indicated that they wanted to be let out. They were still several blocks from the run-down Hotel Flora, but neither wanted to wait to discuss the list that had just fallen into their hands.

Michael counted out the fare to the driver as David attempted not to notice the glare of a ragged-looking young man in a tweed coat and wool sailor's cap. As they walked toward the hotel, it seemed to David that every eye was turned toward them.

"So," David said under his breath. "Looks like the Mufti's heard about war surplus too."

"Wonder how many planes the Arabs bought?"

"Wonder if the same Luftwaffe guy is going to teach their guys to fly?"

"Yeah. And where are they gonna get the pilots?"

"Probably the same place we're getting ours—war surplus Nazis and Americans, huh? Gonna do it all over again."

"How about that list of stuff? Machine guns. Rifles. Ammo."

"Enough to blow us off the face of the earth," David frowned.

Michael looked at him and smiled. "You know, David, it's good to hear you saying *us*."

"Blow *us* up. Shoot *us* down. Send *us* home in a box."

"It does have a certain ring to it, doesn't it?"

"I'll tell you, Michael, this is the craziest thing I've ever seen. *We* have an arms embargo against *us*—"

"There's that word again."

"So *we* can't do anything but buy this stuff and wait until the British pull out. After they're gone, then *we* can deliver it. In the meantime, the Mufti's shipping stuff like crazy to the other Arab nations and is getting it all delivered before the first Englishman leaves Palestine. *We* are definitely in a heap of trouble."

"Yeah," Michael sniffed, "I think maybe we oughtta see if there's not some way we can stop that Arab shipment. I don't know if . . ." his voice trailed off.

"You just cogitate on it a while, Scarecrow. You know, I figure if we're at this long enough, you just might get some brains."

"Maybe you'll find your heart."

"No problem."

"Yeah? You and Ellie back together?"

"I didn't say that."

"Well, what then?"

"I'm going to her place Christmas Eve."

"She asked you?"

"Her uncle."

Michael shook his head. "No problem, huh?"

"Maybe a slight deviation in plans."

"She loves that other guy? Moshe?"

"I don't know," David shrugged. "No. I don't think so."

"Come on, David. Why don't you just take her to some nice, quiet, out-of-the-way place and romance her a little bit?"

"Nope."

"Why not?"

"I tried it."

"Yeah? Didn't work?"

"Nope."

"You're in serious trouble, boy. Serious."

"There's still Christmas."

"What happens at Christmas?"

"I got her a new Leica."

––––––––

A strange, unexpected calm had settled over the city the last few days, though the warm turn in the weather had cooled the passions of hatred. For the first time since the commercial district riot, Jewish shops dared to stay open past noon. Today, two days before Christmas Eve and Hanukkah, the marketplaces would remain open until three o'clock, leaving plenty of time for merchants to lock their gates and scurry home before darkness and fear overtook the city once again.

Taxis had become scarce in the city. A few brave drivers had welded steel plates to their automobiles. They careened around corners and past barricades in defiance of the fact that taxi drivers had become a favorite target for Arab snipers perched on the Old City wall. Five died last month alone. Ellie preferred to walk the three blocks to King George Avenue with Rachel at her side and Shaul trailing along behind. The day was beautiful, and the walk gave Ellie a much needed opportunity to talk to Rachel.

Rachel had been strangely silent since Yacov had arrived, cooking and cleaning like a mute servant, then disappearing into her room.

"Talk to her," Uncle Howard had said, worried. "You know, that 'girl-talk' business." Then he had hurried off to the American school to meet with a member of the Beirut faculty about shipping remaining artifacts to safety.

"Now, aren't you glad you came?" Ellie asked, gazing up at the blue sky as a flock of pigeons fluttered to roost beneath the eves of a store on King George Avenue.

"Yes," Rachel answered, taking several more steps in silence. "He was quite unhappy, was he not?"

"Who?"

"The little boy. What is his name?"

"Yacov."

"Yes, Yacov. He wanted to come. I should have stayed at home and let him come instead."

A British armored car clanked by on patrol. Ellie raised her hand and smiled at the soldier perched on the turret. "He couldn't come," Ellie said. "You've got to help me find that dreidel thing his grandfather wanted him to have for Hanukkah. And by the way, kiddo . . ."

Rachel gave her a puzzled smile. "Yes? Kiddo?"

"How come you got so quiet all of a sudden when the boy came home with us?"

Rachel thought about Moshe in the parking lot of the hospital; the way he had seen her, then rushed away. She had not stopped thinking about it, but did not want to mention her feelings about it to the woman who loved him. Finally she answered—honestly, she thought. "I am not good with children," she replied flatly.

"What's that supposed to mean?"

Rachel frowned as she remembered the reaction of the children in the D.P. camps as she passed by. They had whispered words first uttered by their mothers. "They do not seem to like me," she shrugged.

"Why? Do you grow fangs during the full moon? You're a nice person. Yacov likes you. Or he would if you'd try."

"You do not know, Ellie. There are many who would say otherwise."

"Well, let me at 'em." Ellie thumped her on the back and smiled broadly, in hopes that Rachel would cheer up.

"But you see, there are things about me that a normal decent person would—"

"I have this philosophy," she interrupted. "You want to hear it?" Ellie continued without waiting for Rachel's reply. "*Nobody's* normal. Whatever *that* is. And hardly anyone is decent, not when you get right down to what goes on in our hearts. And anybody who would point a finger at somebody because of something that somebody else did to them . . ."

Rachel stopped in the middle of the sidewalk. "I am what is

called a *sotah* to my race." She looked at Ellie, the grief in her eyes stopping Ellie mid-sentence. "Do you know what this means?"

Ellie shook her head and frowned. "No," she answered, embarrassed at her glib attempt to cheer Rachel up.

"*Sotah*. It means faithless wife. Traitor. You know?"

"Because you survived and others didn't?" Ellie pleaded with her.

Rachel's deep blue eyes locked with Ellie's. Rachel pulled up the sleeve of her sweater, then clasped her hand over the tatoo. "I am called a *sotah* to my own people," Rachel repeated. "Mothers have forbidden their children to speak with me. They are right, I think." She held her forearm out to Ellie.

For the first time Ellie saw the mark Moshe had told her about, "*Nür für Offizere*." She stared at it, then glanced painfully into Rachel's eyes.

She is searching, looking from the depth of her soul, Ellie thought, *desperately, needing friendship.* Ellie took Rachel's outstretched hand and carefully, tenderly, pulled down the sleeve.

"The world is full of evil people, Rachel," she said softly, her heart aching for Rachel's burden. "But you're not one of them."

Unspoken gratitude passed from Rachel to Ellie, and she smiled when Ellie linked her arm in hers as they continued down the street.

David fired up the engine of the six-passenger Stinson aircraft, and prepared for takeoff from the dirt airstrip outside of Bari, Italy.

"Some surprise, eh, fellas?" asked Avriel.

"This thing feels like an ocean liner compared to those little dinghies you guys have had us buzzing around Palestine in," David remarked as they taxied out.

"Yeah!" Michael shouted over the roar of the engine as David revved the motor for takeoff. "There's enough booze back here to sink a battleship." He pointed to the cases marked Scotch and Seltzer Water. "You planning on setting up a nightclub in Jerusalem?"

"Don't be an idiot!" Avriel shouted back over his shoulder. "The Haganah has a military use for everything!"

27 Holiday Plans

Moshe shifted the bulky shopping bag into his left arm and bounded up the steps of the Moniger home. Two long loaves of bread protruded from the bag, and a heavy round of cheese filled the bottom. Moshe knocked loudly on the door, then looked over his shoulder, instinctively feeling the presence of hostile eyes observing his every movement. The bright voice of Yacov called from behind the new locks and bolts that Howard had installed on the door the week before. Shaul barked angrily beside the small boy.

"Who is there?"

"Moshe." He wiped his mouth with the back of his hand. "Has Shaul had breakfast, or am I to be first meal of the day?"

Bolts snapped and locks clicked open and Yacov threw the door wide open to Moshe. Shaul wagged hesitantly, then sniffed Moshe's leg as he crossed the threshold and shut the door behind him. Yacov then repeated the procedure in reverse, making certain that every lock was secure. "Good morning, Professor," Yacov smiled. "It is the professor, you see, Shaul."

Moshe held his hand out to Shaul palm down. "Just the harmless old professor," he cooed. "Good dog."

"He has become more fierce since I am hurt," Yacov apologized. "But he will not harm you unless you come between him and me."

Moshe blinked down at the dog, then took a step back from Yacov. "Good dog," he said again. He peered down the hall. "Is everyone up?"

"Oh, yes, for many hours. Rachel and I have done the shopping already this morning. There are quite long lines at the bakery now, but we have bought the bread."

"You took Shaul with you, of course?"

"Yes, I think he likes Rachel nearly as much as me, even though she is so very quiet and seems so sad that she rarely speaks even a word."

Moshe frowned with concern, remembering Rachel's beautiful smile as she had sat across from him at Fanny's the morning in Tel Aviv. He had hoped that being in Jerusalem would have helped her ease the heartache. "Maybe Shaul thinks she is very beautiful."

"Ah, yes," Yacov nodded. "He is a very smart dog, you see. Shall you like to see Miss Ellie and Rachel? They are in the kitchen, I think."

The faint aroma of coffee filtered down the hallway as Yacov led the way to the kitchen. Moshe followed behind Shaul at a distance, stopping in his tracks when the shaggy ferocious-looking animal turned around once and looked him over from head to foot. "Nice dog," Moshe repeated.

"Shaul!" Yacov reprimanded. "Come along." Then he said to Moshe over his shoulder. "Rachel is a good cook. Better than Grandfather and the public kitchen. And as you said, she cooks Kashrut. She is teaching Ellie to cook the same. But I think Ellie is not so good a cook."

Moshe bit his lip to keep from smiling as Yacov pushed the kitchen door open to reveal the two women washing and drying the dishes.

Ellie was still in her dark blue bathrobe; Rachel was dressed in a pair of powder blue trousers and matching sweater that he instantly recognized as Ellie's. "Good morning," he said cheerfully, setting the shopping bag on the table.

Ellie turned around with a look of shock on her face. "Good grief! Don't you call anymore? Who let you in, Moshe?"

"Shaul," he grinned. "And I've gotten a friendlier hello from the Arab High Command." He nodded at Rachel who had turned back to drying the dishes without a word. "Hello, Rachel."

"Hello," she said quietly.

"Look at me!" Ellie wailed.

"I have seen women in much worse shape than you."

"Egyptian mummies, right? Can you believe this man?" she asked Rachel, drying her hands on the towel and then rolling her eyes.

"Well, I hear Rachel has already been out to buy bread this morning," Moshe chided.

"This is so," Yacov agreed. Then he took Shaul by the collar and ducked out the door lest Ellie reprimand him for letting the professor in.

"How about a cup of coffee?" he asked, helping himself to

the dregs of the pot. "And a hello kiss?"

Ellie pecked him lightly on the cheek. "What's this?" she tapped the rim of the shopping bag.

"Bullets, guns, and grenades." Moshe sat down. "What does it look like?"

"Unique. Really unique. We toasted our grenades this morning and ate them."

"The perfect hiding place. Not even the British would think to look in your stomach. I'll mention it to the area commanders. So. Where's your uncle?"

Ellie put her hands on her hips. "I don't hear from you in a week except when you drop by the hospital and then run off to a meeting, and all you can say is 'Where's your uncle?' "

Rachel put away the last cup and, careful not to look at Moshe, started to leave the kitchen. "Excuse me," she said.

Moshe caught her by the hand. "Wait a minute, please," he said in Polish. "I have something to say that concerns you."

Rachel paused and looked at him briefly, then pulled her hand away. "Speak English, please. I am trying to learn English," she said haltingly.

"Please," Ellie added. "I took Polish for four years in high school, but the verb tenses always got to me."

Moshe smiled and shook his head. "I am sorry. I thought it would be easier."

Rachel stood before him, her eyes still downcast. "What is it?" she asked.

Moshe sipped his coffee and fixed his eyes on Ellie. "Is your uncle home?" he asked.

Ellie frowned and pulled her robe tighter around her. "Sounds serious."

"Important." He set his cup down and continued to look in her eyes.

"Give me a minute. I think he's in the shower. I'll get dressed." She slipped out the door, a sense of apprehension squeezing her stomach.

Rachel stood without moving as the kitchen door swung back and forth, then finally stopped. The silence grew uncomfortable for both her and Moshe. He pursed his lips and looked toward the window where the sun shone brightly in the courtyard beyond. "Would you like to sit down?" he asked.

"Could I make you another coffee?" Rachel asked, not waiting for his answer as she snatched the pot off the stove and hurried to the faucet to fill it.

"Thank you. Hmmm." He searched for words, careful not to let his eyes fall on her slim belted waist or his mind wander from the reason he had come here the morning before Hanukkah.

Rachel carefully measured fresh coffee into the pot. "It is a lovely morning, is it not?" she said finally, unable to bear the silence.

"Yes," he hesitated. "Rachel . . ." he began in a voice that sounded almost imploring.

She raised her eyes to his then for the first time. She frowned for an instant, unable to tear her gaze away. A rush of panic caused her to spin around and with shaking hands strike a match to light the stove burner. "The coffee is weak," she said in a rush. "At home when the war comes, we use the same grounds many times and finally there was no coffee at all."

"Rachel," he began again. "The other day when I saw you in front of the hospital, I just couldn't . . ."

She crossed to the window and looked out at the stone paving covered by dead leaves. "I understand," she said quietly. "I . . . I cause you to feel revolted."

"No!" Moshe jumped from the chair and stepped to her side, afraid to touch her but aching to put a hand on her shoulder. He looked down at her hands gripping the edge of the counter. "That wasn't it," he said, lapsing into Polish once again. "Not at all."

"I know that the Sabras have a name for us survivors. I heard it from the children on the kibbutz. *Sotah*. We are pitied, but somehow less than human. I have seen it in your eyes."

"You're wrong, Rachel," he said quietly. "I have never thought this of you. I don't know what I feel; now, after all you have been through, I must ask you to risk your life again."

"Risk?" she turned to him, a doubtful smile on her lips. "I have never risked my life, Moshe. I have only survived and in so doing I have lost my life. Ask what you will."

Moshe looked away from her, out toward the empty stone bench in the courtyard. "All right then," he said in English. He sat down at the table again, feeling a heaviness in his heart.

Ellie burst into the room with Howard in tow. She was dressed and seemed to glow in the rust-colored sweater and green and rust plaid skirt. Howard wore a black turtleneck shirt and heavy, drab green corduroy pants. Rachel self-consciously rummaged in the cupboard for extra cups.

"Moshe!" Howard extended his hand in genuine delight. "No, don't get up. Ellie tells me you have something exciting to talk to us about."

"Here, let me help." Ellie took the coffeepot from the stove and poured coffee into the cups. She pretended not to notice Rachel's trembling hands. "So what's this all about?" she asked, setting the full cup before Moshe, who did not look up at her. She had a sudden protective feeling toward Rachel and a desire to knock the cup onto his lap. *What*, she wondered, *happened in the few minutes while I was gone?*

"Tomorrow is Christmas Eve. And the beginning of Hanukkah," Moshe began as Ellie and Howard pulled up chairs opposite him. Rachel remained standing by the sink. "There is a British captain who has come forward to help. Tomorrow the English who guard Zion Gate will be a fraction of their usual force. This fellow has volunteered to stand duty. And he has volunteered to help us smuggle weapons into the Old City to the Haganah there. He has helped us before."

"What can we do?" Howard asked.

Moshe lifted a loaf of bread out of the bag and handed it to Howard. "We are baking bread for the hungry."

Howard gave a low whistle as he hefted the loaf. "Feels like something Ellie would bake," he grinned.

Ellie jabbed him with her elbow and took the bread from him. "Holy cow, Moshe!"

"I told you," Moshe smiled. "Bullets, grenades, and pistols." He rummaged for the round of cheese, lifting it with both hands. It was sealed with red wax. "The perfect Hanukkah gift, eh? Five hundred bullets in the cheddar."

"Sounds tasty." Howard hefted the cheese.

"It will be a gift for Rachel's grandfather," Moshe explained turning to face Rachel, who looked up in astonishment.

"My grandfather?"

"We have received special permission for you to enter the Old City. It is natural that you would bring gifts. But the gifts are to be delivered to the Warsaw compound. Rachel, there won't be time to . . ."

"I will not see him, then?" Rachel's eyes lost their brightness as quickly as it had come.

"Not tomorrow night. If this is successful, believe me, there will be more opportunities. In the meantime, write down his name; I'll see if someone at the agency can come up with an address for you."

"I see," she said, faltering. "Yes, I will do whatever I can to help." She scribbled her grandfather's name on a piece of shopping bag and folding it in half, handed it to Moshe. "Thank you."

"Good." He directed his gaze back to Ellie. "You're a journalist with a major publication. Your pass will be easy enough to get. The Old City on Christmas Eve, eh? Worth taking a photograph or two."

"What will I carry? Besides my camera and film I mean?"

"We've got that all worked out." He passed over her question. "Now, here's the clincher, Howard. And nothing can work without this."

"What is it?" Howard leaned forward in his chair.

"Without help, neither Ellie nor Rachel will have the vaguest idea of where they're going or where they've been."

"The Old City is not my domain, Moshe. You're the fellow who know the alleys and rooftop routes."

"Not you, Howard. We need to use the boy."

"Yacov?"

"He stands the best chance of getting through any Arabs that might stand between them and the Jewish Quarter."

"I can't allow it, Moshe. He's just a child. What if he was hurt? And his eyes are not . . ."

The kitchen door creaked open and Yacov stepped in. "I know the streets even blind, Professor. I have escaped from the angry British many times. Though I never stole from an Arab, for we are neighbors. But certainly if there was a problem, I am best to lead Miss Ellie and Rachel to the Warsaw."

"And can you lead them home again?" Moshe asked.

"I will come back. I will wish that I might light the Hanukkah candles, but I shall come back to this house." The boy stared hard at Howard with his one good eye, then adjusted his black patch. "I have to help you light the candles, yes?"

Howard nodded slowly. "You'll be back in time for supper."

"Yes," Yacov smiled jauntily, "if it is Rachel who cooks."

Rachel smiled shyly then, as Ellie sighed in exasperation. "You mean you like her stuff better than mine?"

Yacov shrugged. "Not I, but Shaul . . ."

Howard chuckled in spite of the seriousness of the moment. "And what about me, Moshe? How can I help?"

Moshe reached into the pocket of his shirt and pulled out a folded envelope. "This came last night to the university from Moddy Elaram in Bethlehem." He handed it to Howard.

"The Arab antique dealer?" Ellie asked, instantly recognizing the name of the merchant who had often visited the Moniger home. *His eyes are warm and brown like a Jersey cow*, Ellie thought, remembering the man. Usually he brought information or a small but authentic artifact for Moshe and Uncle Howard to look at.

"It was apparently mailed three weeks ago, we're lucky to have gotten it at all," Moshe said. "Go ahead, read it."

Howard studied the cramped writing on the envelope, then slipped the letter out and began to read. "Most Honorable Professor Sachar," he read aloud. "It is my hope that you have found great delightness in the watering jar you purchased yet a fortnight ago. I have, since all this trouble, grieved over the loss of my good Jewish friends and customers. Also it has come into my attention some very ancient writings brought to me by two Bedouin shepherds. Though I did not keep these scrolls"— Howard glanced up as Ellie gasped—"for their writing is obscure to me, I have agreed to act as agent. If perhaps you and the Professor Doctor Moniger shall like to see them, they have promised to come to Bethlehem on Christmas Eve to my shop at seven in the evening, for then will the Christians be traveling to worship and you will be less noticed. Truly, Your Servant, Moddy Elaram." Howard stared at the letter and gave a low whistle. Then he looked up at Moshe, who had an excited smile on his face. "It has to be the same men," he said finally.

"They threatened to go to the antique dealers in Bethlehem." Ellie took the letter from Howard and scanned it. "But that's an Arab stronghold."

"They were afraid to come back here, I suppose," Moshe said. "We must go, Howard. We must."

The heavy aroma of stale cigar smoke greeted David and Michael as they banged open the door to their room at the Atlantic Hotel in Jerusalem. It was early morning and Michael still looked as though he had not slept for a week, David noted, even though he had slept his way across Europe.

David pitched his canvas duffle bag onto a chair, then unzipped his leather flight jacket and threw himself across the bed, clutching a pillow for the first time since they had left Prague three days before. His legs hung off the opposite side of the bed, and as Michael passed, he gave them a little kick. "You better take off your boots, Tin Man," he warned. "You sleep like that, your knees are going to fall off."

David moaned and rolled over, sitting up and unlacing his boots. "You should know. You're the expert on weird sleeping positions. I can't figure out why your neck isn't permanently cocked off to one side, the way you squash your face up against the cockpit and lean on it for hours while I fly the plane." He pitched his left boot at Michael, who ducked into the bathroom.

"It's fear. Makes me sleepy every time you fly," he called. David stood and pitched the other boot into the bathroom, hitting Michael solidly on the rear end. Michael hooted and slammed the door. David pounded his fist on the thin wood. "You're not going to go to sleep in there, are you?"

The bolt slid shut. "Lay off, Meyer," Michael called. "Or you'll never sleep again, believe me."

"Says you." David lost the urge to razz his buddy, instead falling backward on the bed. For a few moments he studied his toes, poking out from hopelessly undarned socks. "If I hang these up on the mantle tonight," he said loudly, "Santa will have a terrible time filling them."

"What's that?" Michael stepped out of the bathroom.

"I said Santa won't be able to stuff my stocking." He wiggled his big toe.

Michael sniffed and wrinkled his nose. "He wouldn't want to."

"Now I know why he smokes a pipe. Aromatic tobacco," David said sleepily.

"I been meanin' to talk to you 'bout that, Tin Man." Michael opened his dresser drawer and pulled out a red-wrapped package. He pitched it to David, who caught it with his left hand and held it up as he stared at it.

"You want me to guess or open it now?"

"Open it now. Tonight's the big night, ain't it? You can't go over to Ellie's in holey socks."

"Don't tell me; it's a new wallet full of fifty dollar bills."

David laid the package across his forehead. "David sees all, knows all," he intoned. "A new 1947 Dodge . . . ah, no, no—I see it now . . ." He ripped off the wrapping. "A brand new pair of black and red argyle socks! Great!" he laughed, genuinely delighted. "Terrific!"

"Happy Hanukkah." Michael blushed. "It ain't much but if ever a guy needed somethin' . . ."

"Look in my top drawer," David instructed. "There's a little something for you. Under my tee shirts in the green paper."

"Aw, you shouldn't have." Michael pulled out the flimsy package.

"You better open it now, Scarecrow. I mean, I know you gotta live up to your name and all, but I swear I never saw a guy with patches on his boxer shorts before."

"Comes from flying by the seat of my pants." Michael smiled as he opened the package, revealing not one but three pair of undershorts decorated with red hearts. "Ah, you shouldn't have done it."

"Got 'em in Rome. The lady even embroidered your initials on 'em."

"Yeah?" Michael examined them closely. "Gee, Tin Man, thanks. You really do have a heart." He chuckled at his own pun and pointed to the hearts on the shorts.

"Well, anyway, Merry Christmas a little early, huh?"

"Thanks." Michael folded them neatly and tenderly put them in his top drawer. David clutched the socks and rolled over with a happy sigh as he thought about the gift he had wrapped and placed in his duffle bag. He hoped that Ellie would read the note he had written to her and know that he meant what he said that night in the plane above Jerusalem. *Tonight's the night*, he thought as he closed his eyes and drifted off to sleep.

28 Christmas Eve

The lobby of the *Palestine Post* newspaper was not unlike that of the little newspaper in Glendale, California, where Ellie had worked one summer. The floor was covered by a geometric pattern of small square tiles, a few missing or chipped. The long mahogany counter that separated the entry from the secretary had the mellow glow of age. A few awards hung on the walls next to framed copies of the paper that recounted momentous events in the existence of Palestine. Photographs of men like Theodore Hertzl, the man who made Zionism more than just a word, mingled with more recent photographs of David Ben-Gurion raising his hand in salute on Partition night. Three men and a woman worked busily behind cluttered desks, tapping away on time-worn typewriters.

As Ellie and Rachel walked in, only the woman glanced up. She continued her work as Ellie took a copy of the day's newspaper from the stack on the counter and began to skim the front page. The headlines were ordinary, reporting nothing more urgent than the lack of phone service between the Arab and Jewish sections of the city. *The world has reverted to worrying about mundane, irritating matters once again,* Ellie thought. There was one major difference between the *Palestine Post* and the *Glendale Herald*: the *Glendale Herald* was not in the middle of a war.

Ellie cleared her throat and slung her empty leather camera bag onto the counter with a thud.

The woman at the desk looked up. "May I help you?" she asked.

"I am Judith," Ellie replied, repeating the words as Moshe had instructed her the day before.

"Yes," the woman replied in a delighted voice. "You're early," she said, just as Moshe had predicted.

"My watch always runs a little fast," Ellie said in response to her words.

With that, the woman rose from her desk and opened the waist-high swinging door set in the counter. She stood aside as Ellie and Rachel passed through, then without another word

301

she led them to a door with a frosted glass window that led to a flight of steps to the basement. "Straight to the back. In the darkroom. He's expecting you." Then as Rachel and Ellie started down the stairs, the woman closed the door behind them.

The heavy slam and clank of the printing press greeted them as they entered the basement. Wheels churned, then reversed as the massive printing block slammed down in rhythm on the paper. A young man in a leather apron watched over the press, his face smeared with ink. He glanced up and smiled as he jerked his thumb back toward the door marked 'PHOTO LAB.'

Ellie knocked on the door, then, convinced that the noise of the press had overruled her knock, she simply turned the knob and walked into the cluttered, brick-lined lab. The sound of loud music greeted them. Ellie recognized the thundering cannon of the *1812 Overture* instantly as it roared from a large hand-cranked phonograph in the corner.

A bald-domed, thin little man sat on a three-legged stool at a counter. He was working intently on something. Behind them the thunder of the printing press slowed to a whine and a final bang, then it stopped. The *1812* boomed on.

"I'M JUDITH!" Ellie yelled over the music.

The little man raised his head as though he heard something; then he lowered it again and resumed work.

Ellie tried again. "I'M JUDITH!"

The man turned on the stool, his eyes lighting up as he saw the two women standing by the door. He stood and walked toward the phonograph. "YOU'RE EARLY!" he shouted in reply.

Ellie took a deep breath. "MY WATCH" she began as the man slid the needle off the record and silence fell. She lowered her voice. "My watch . . ."

"Yes, I know. It runs a little fast," he finished pleasantly. "So. Sit down, Miss Warne. And you are Miss Lubetkin, nu?" He pulled two more stools up to the counter, then disappeared into another room. Ellie and Rachel exchanged puzzled glances; Ellie's ears felt numb from the sound level of a few moments before. The man emerged carrying a large cardboard box which he set before them. Then he plopped down between them.

"Gets a little noisy in here, doesn't it?" Ellie asked.

"A necessary evil," he smiled. "If we should happen to get careless and blow ourselves up, you know, it would not be good to have the British investigate the noise, you see." He pulled a metal film can out of the bag and held it up. "An ordinary film can, eh?" He unscrewed the lid and showed Ellie the film inside the can. "Film, yes?" He dumped the can into her palm and tapped the bottom. "Primers. For blasting you see," he said triumphantly.

Ellie nodded as he carefully placed the primers back in the can. "Now I see why you chose the *1812 Overture*."

"Yes, you must be very careful. The bulbs—" He held up an ordinary-looking flash bulb, "I am afraid if you dropped it, the flash might ruin your picture." He smiled proudly. "Your camera is loaded as well."

Ellie swallowed hard. "Some kind of firecrackers you mix up here, Professor."

He carefully set the bulb down and slapped his hands on his knees with satisfaction. "For Independence Day," he said. "I will help you pack your bag. The English at the gates will not disturb you. If you are stopped by the Arab Militia patrols before you reach the quarter, do yourself a kindness and stand back if they insist on rummaging through your bag. No doubt what you carry will serve its purpose a bit prematurely if they are not gentle with the contents."

"This could blow me up?" Ellie asked gingerly.

He gave her an exasperated look. "Indeed, if you are not considerate."

Ellie sighed, then smiled with resignation. "It's dangerous."

"What did you expect—tea and cakes?"

"I don't know what I expected. But this is certainly much more than I had hoped for."

"Good. Good." He smiled and lifted her camera bag to the table. "Then I wish you Godspeed and good luck, my dear." He began packing the concealed explosive with a care that made Ellie's throat feel suddenly very dry.

Ellie held the camera bag carefully, though trying to appear natural, as they entered the bakery on the corner of King George Avenue and Julian Way. A crowd of women buying for the holidays shouted over the countertop at two harried clerks who bustled back and forth, shouting irritably into the back room to fill orders.

"This reminds me of Saks Fifth Avenue during a sale!" Ellie shouted to Rachel, as they took their place at the end of a long line. Twenty minutes later as they jostled their way to the front of the glass cases, a woman with her hair pulled severely back in a bun glared at Rachel.

"Well, hurry up, hurry up. There are others waiting!" she snapped as Rachel hesitated.

"My name is Judith," Rachel repeated the code name.

"You're early." the woman growled.

"My watch always runs a little fast."

"Well, I don't know if your order is ready." She turned and shouted back to the back room. "Order for Judith!"

A moment later a large shopping bag appeared at the window in the back. Two loaves of challah, the holy day bread, extended from the top. The woman grabbed it roughly, causing Ellie to wince as she wondered what the bread had been seasoned with. The woman slung it over the counter to Rachel who started to go. "Thank you!" Rachel yelled above the din.

"Wait a minute. You forgot to pay!" the woman demanded.

Rachel blanched. It had not occurred to her that she would have to pay for her bakery goods for the sake of appearance. "How much?" she fumbled in her pocket.

"Let me get it." Ellie stepped in quickly and counted out some change on top of the counter. Rachel, completely penniless, sighed with relief, watching as Ellie carefully shielded her camera bag from a heavyset woman who shoved in behind them.

Rachel cradled her shopping bag like a child as they inched their way back out of the stuffy little shop. "How about that Moshe?" Ellie said. "Making us pay." She shook her head indignantly. "I'm going to submit a voucher, and he can pay me back."

Their next stop was a small dress shop on King George, only three blocks away. A bell tinkled as they opened the door and a woman of about seventy stepped out from a back room. Her hair was gray and she wore a tailored burgundy suit of the latest fashion. "Dear me," she said in an elegant Austrian accent. "Custoomers. May I helf you?"

"My . . . name . . . is . . . Jud-ith," Ellie pronounced very carefully.

"You're early," the woman's accent dropped away instantly.

Rachel and Ellie exchanged amused glances. "Our watches always run fast," said Ellie.

The old woman placed a Gone To Tea sign in her window,

then locked the shop door. She led the girls down to the basement and there, for an hour and a half, she transformed them from slender and well-dressed young women, to dowdy and plump matrons with bullets and grenades appropriately concealed beneath layers of bulky clothing and padded brassieres.

"The main thing, my dahlings," the woman said as they waddled out the door, "is to make sure the men do not *want* to search you. I think we have accomplished this goal." She smiled and closed the shop door and pulled up the shade as they left.

Both Ellie and Rachel were breathing heavily when they finally reached home. Ellie wiped the sweat from her brow as they carefully laid their cargo down on the sofa in the front room. Uncle Howard peered in at their backs and stuttered loudly, "I b-b-beg your pardon!" The outrage in his voice was unmistakable.

They turned around and Ellie waved coyly, batting her eyes at her astonished uncle. "Yoooo-hoooo."

"Well for heaven's sake, girl!" He blustered. "What have they done to you?"

Ellie appraised the striped robes he held in his arms. "What are they doing with you?"

"I'm going as an Arab. I'll throw this on over my clothes once I get to Mamillah cemetery. Then I walk to the other side and enter Arab territory, and that is that."

"When are you leaving?" Ellie felt a wave of concern and hesitancy about the entire enterprise.

"Right now." Howard caught the panic in her eyes. He walked toward Ellie and Rachel. "But first I think we should commit this night and ourselves into the hands of God, children." He stretched his arms out and put his hands gently on their shoulders.

"Good idea," said Ellie, bowing her head. " 'Cause I don't know what I'm doing."

Howard tucked his chin and closed his eyes. Rachel, feeling awkward, did the same. Howard felt her stiffen as he prayed. "Dear Lord, we ask you to go with each one of us tonight. Keep us safe in your loving hands. Watch over our every thought and action, and guide us home again. We ask in the name of your Son who died for us. Amen."

"Amen," Ellie repeated, hugging Howard. "Be careful, you old teddy bear," she said.

Rachel looked away self-consciously. Howard kissed Ellie on the top of her head. "Be careful yourself," he said. "I feel like I've just hugged an armadillo. What have you got in there?"

"They said the idea is to make sure nobody wants to search us."

"It will be a rousing success, I assure you." He rubbed his ribs and winced. "Well, I'm off. I'll meet you back here before morning. If we're not back by daylight . . ."

"If you're not back before daylight, *what*. . . ?" Ellie looked at him with alarm.

"Send the cavalry." He chucked her chin, then hurried out the door to meet Moshe.

————

Gerhardt opened his second pack of cigarettes for the day and tossed the cellophane out the window of the slow-moving cargo truck as it crept up Bab El Wad. The haggard-looking English deserter behind the wheel glanced frantically at him.

"Blimey! You're not gonna smoke that thing in 'ere, are you?" He wiped beads of sweat from his brow as Gerhardt took the matches from his pocket. "There's enough explosives in this truck t' blow 'alf of Jerusalem t' kingdom come!"

Gerhardt narrowed his eyes and smiled as he leaned forward and struck the match on the dashboard only inches away from where the fuse protruded from a metal pipe. "Only the Jewish half."

The deserter swore and moved his hand to the door handle. "Do that again, mate, an' you'll find yourself another driver!"

Gerhardt threw his head back in laughter, then inhaled the harsh smoke. Two trucks, filled with explosives, driven by English deserters with a hatred of Jews almost as intense as his own—the plan was foolproof, he mused. It would be perhaps the greatest triumph of his career.

————

There was still more than an hour before the number two bus would leave for Zion Gate. Rachel fixed Yacov a quick lunch of cream cheese and strawberry jam on thin slices of bread.

"You are a good cook," Yacov said, attempting to make conversation. He gave his eye patch a tug, then took another bite.

"My mother used to make these little sandwiches for me," Rachel answered. "Out of wild blackberry jam. We had gathered the berries ourselves you see . . ." Her voice trailed off as she remembered picnics by a broad river and the sun sparkling through the green leaves above them.

"Very good." Yacov stuffed his mouth full.

"When you are done, please put your dishes in the sink," she said, afraid of the memories that so often crowded around her. She stood for a moment, her back against the counter, watching as Yacov happily finished lunch. How often she had seen that same expression on the faces of her brothers as they gulped their food and gathered their books and stood fidgeting as Mama had straightened their yamulkes and tugged on their jackets! Then they had slammed the door and run down the block to the synagogue for lessons.

Rachel swallowed hard and silently left the kitchen for the solitude of her own room. In less than an hour, she knew, she would be in the streets of the Old City. Perhaps she would walk by the very house where her grandfather lived. Perhaps she would pass him in the street, and he would never know her. *It is unfair of Moshe,* she thought, *that he has not allowed even five minutes for me to see him for the first time, to touch his face and know that I am not alone in this world.* But then, Moshe must have known that there could never be enough time in the world for her to say all the things she wanted to say to the old man. Five minutes, one hour, one day, could never be enough.

Ellie tapped on the door, then poked her head in. "I'm taking my 35 millimeter camera along, just in case . . ." she began, stopping as she saw the emotion in Rachel's eyes. "What's up?" she asked, sitting on the bed next to her. "Are you afraid?"

Rachel shook her head. "Oh, no!" she exclaimed.

"You worried about something?" Ellie coaxed, not one to give up, even though she wondered if she should mind her own business.

"I am . . ." Rachel controlled the quaver in her voice, "homesick," she finished.

Ellie gave her a quick hug. "So close, huh? You know we've got to get out of there before dark, and the captain doesn't even come on duty at the gate until four o'clock. That gives us an hour, Rachel. Maybe a little more. Are you telling me you think we could deliver this stuff, *and* track your grandfather down?

And that would be enough time for you two to get reacquainted?"

"You are right, of course." Rachel's voice sounded calm again. "To see him and not to stay would be torture."

"The only people going in to stay are men. And Moshe is having a difficult time just getting enough food to them. I am sorry, though."

"It is silly and selfish of me. I must wait, if it means I am helping what Moshe is doing. But they say my grandfather does not even know I am alive. No message can reach him. If there were only some way once we are in the Old City..."

Ellie frowned and bit her lip thoughtfully. "Well, it's possible we could leave a note for him someplace. Have you ever talked to Yacov about it?"

"No. What purpose...?"

"The boy's from the Old City. There can't be that many old rabbis living there. Maybe *he* knows him. Or at least knows somebody who knows him. I keep telling you Rachel; *Talk to him!* He even speaks Polish!" Ellie's enthusiasm had more than a touch of irritation to it, and Rachel felt ashamed of her reluctance to talk to the boy. "He's been here three days. For heaven's sake, come on, Rachel! You sit around here feeling sorry for yourself, and in three days you've never even asked the one person who might be able to give you some answers."

Rachel looked away, tears welling up. "Are you angry with me?" she asked, afraid she had lost her only friend.

"Angry?" Ellie said loudly. "Are you kidding? I just think we're both a little dense not to think of it before this." She rolled her eyes in frustration as a tear trickled down Rachel's cheek. Rachel smiled with relief.

"I thought you were angry."

"No. Just noisy. It's the Irish in me." She patted Rachel's hand. "So. Now that I've had my say, what do you suggest we do?"

"Talk to the boy?"

"Right. To Yacov."

"To Yacov." Rachel stood and brushed her tears away, then she left Ellie sitting on the bed and returned to the kitchen.

Yacov was licking jam from each finger with the contentment of a cat who just finished supper. "Is it time to go?" he asked, eager for the adventure.

"No," Rachel quietly replied, filling the teakettle, although she did not especially want tea. "Little boy—" she began tentatively.

"I am not so very little, you know. I am ten," he said defiantly.

"*Yacov*," she began again. "You know I have a grandfather in the Old City, where you are from also, I am told—"

"No, I did not know this." He folded his hands on the table and looked at her with new interest.

"No, I suppose you would not know." She put the kettle on and lit the stove, afraid to ask him. *What if he cannot help?* she thought. "Yes. This is so. And I have been away for a very long time."

"You were in a camp?" Yacov asked.

"Yes."

"I thought as much. Except that your hair is very long and beautiful. I thought they shaved the heads of women in the camps."

A rush of panic overwhelmed Rachel. She turned dizzily and started for the door. Ellie walked in at that instant and, taking her hands, stopped her.

Rachel's head bowed with shame. Ellie lifted her chin and looked squarely in her eyes. "You have to live, and you might as well start now," she said softly. "Sit down."

"Did I say something bad?" Yacov asked.

"No, Yacov," Ellie replied, as Rachel sat at the table across from him. "You are right that Rachel has beautiful hair. But that's not what we're really talking about." She sat down beside him. "You see, Rachel's grandfather doesn't know that she is alive. He just doesn't know, you see?"

"But why?" Yacov asked in astonishment.

"Because Rachel has been gone a long time. We thought that if we could get a note to him somehow."

"Does your grandfather have any other family?" Yacov asked.

"No." Rachel looked up at him. "I am the last."

"Then surely it is important that he hear this news soon." He stuck his lower lip out. "To live alone can break one's heart. So says Grandfather."

"He's right," Ellie agreed, touching Rachel's hand reassuringly.

"Rabbis know these things," Yacov said proudly.

Rachel brightened. "My grandfather is also a rabbi."

309

"Then surely they shall know one another!" Yacov's voice quickened with excitement. "What is his name, please?" he asked.

"Rabbi Lebowitz," she replied.

Ellie gasped, and Yacov frowned. "Shlomo Lebowitz?" he asked cautiously.

"You know him?" Rachel reached across the table and joyfully took his hand; then she pulled it back when she saw the look of utter disbelief and horror on his face. "Is he . . . dead?" she asked.

"No." Yacov answered, feeling as though he were choking. He leaned closer and studied her face, trying to remember the photograph Grandfather had shown him so long ago. This could not be the face of his sister; it simply could not be! "Rabbi Shlomo Lebowitz is *my* grandfather!"

"Cousins?" Ellie stammered, looking from one to the other. She gazed at the softly rounded chins, each with a small cleft; and the vivid, incredible blue eyes.

Rachel's face was pale; her eyes bright with emotion. She reached her hand gently toward Yacov's face. "I had no cousins," she whispered.

"Nor I," Yacov answered, believing at last the clear gaze of the sister he had never known except in the dried, cracked reflection of a yellowing photograph.

"You are Yani?" Rachel asked, caressing his face with trembling hands. "Yani Lubetkin?"

"Yani. Yes, I am Yani. Though Grandfather has not called me that for many years." His words came in a rush. "And I had forgotten that my older sister had a name. I had forgotten your name." He began to cry, his slender shoulders shaking with silent sobs.

Rachel went to him then, and wrapped her arms around him, cradling his head in her arms. "Baby Yani, don't cry. Oh, Yani! I am your sister who was lost. I am Rachel."

310

29 Hanukkah Gifts

Moshe adjusted the headband of his keffiyah. He felt almost too warm beneath the heavy black and brown striped wool robes he wore, but he knew that once night fell he would be grateful for their warmth. The little donkey he held at the end of a lead rope nudged him gently with her nose. Moshe scratched her behind the ears and peered impatiently up the Bethlehem road for Howard, who was supposed to meet him within the hour. Moshe had left his watch back in his apartment, fearful that it might give away the fact that he was not a Bedouin nomad. Now he wished that he knew the exact time of day. He searched the sky above the power station that bordered the railroad tracks and the road that led deep into Arab-held territory. The afternoon was beautiful and cloudless. *Full of hope*, thought Moshe, watching as the few remaining Christian pilgrims passed him on their way to worship in Bethlehem.

Usually, Moshe knew, this road was jammed with families traveling to the ancient site of Christ's birth on this night. The crowds had dwindled to a devout few this year. The Bedouin shepherds he and Howard were to meet tonight had been right about one thing, however—no one seemed to notice him or the little donkey. Today they could travel to the shop of Moddy Elaram without an armored car and a brigade of Haganah soldiers to accompany them, but this would doubtless be their last journey for many months. He shielded his eyes against the bright afternoon sun and searched the faces for the familiar sight of Howard's jovial smile beneath an Arab keffiyah. *I should have waited by the deserted windmill of Montefiore for Howard*, Moshe worried. At least that was the fringe of Jewish territory. He had been warned that Arab snipers had been at work in the area, but dressed as they were, they would have more worry about being shot by the Haganah. Only a quarter of a mile away from Montefiore, down Julian Way and past the rail station, Moshe was already deep in hostile territory. He hoped that nothing had happened to delay Howard or keep him from coming. They had several miles to cover on foot before they would finally enter the protection of Elaram's little shop.

Moshe was startled by the sound of a deep voice behind him, "Salaam, Professor Sachar."

Moshe spun around and found himself face-to-face with Howard, dressed in the garb of a poor shepherd; he even smelled as if he had been living among the sheep for a while. He was grinning from ear to ear at the expression on Moshe's face. "Where did you come from?" Moshe asked in fluent Arabic.

Howard answered without a trace of accent, "I walked right past you just a moment ago. You didn't recognize me?"

"No, but I must have smelled you," he smiled.

"Who will doubt that I have been tending sheep?" He clapped Moshe on the back and took the lead rope from him, clicking his tongue in Arab fashion at the little donkey. "And if we were to look truly native, Moshe, both of us should climb onto the back of this poor little beast and goad her all the way to Bethlehem."

"When our feet tire, perhaps," Moshe replied, following after Howard.

A small boy rode high atop his father's shoulders, gripping his tiny hands across the lean young man's forehead. An infant in the arms of her mother wailed loudly in protest of the dust of the road. Her cries were answered by a soft gentle voice singing a song that had been sung through the centuries by mothers carrying their little ones along this road.

"But thou, Bethlehem Ephrathah, though thou be little among the thousands of Judah, yet out of thee shall he come forth unto me that is to be ruler in Israel; whose goings forth have been from old, from everlasting. . . ."

The melody spread from one group to another until at last the words echoed from the barren hillsides that lined the ancient road.

"I think," Howard said when the song had ended, "that Mary must have sung those words as she traveled to Bethlehem to have her baby."

Moshe smiled and said, "I do not doubt it, Howard. There is no Jewish mother who does not teach those words to her children. The prophet Micah, is it not?"

Howard nodded, feeling the continuity of those who had traveled this very road two thousand years before. "Moshe, my

312

dear friend," he said at last. "You know all the messianic prophecies. We have spoken of them many times together. As an archaeologist you know how the prophecies were perceived by
the Jews of the first century."

Moshe nodded. "Or course."

"And yet you have never told me why you do not believe in
the One who fulfilled those prophecies."

Moshe squinted, gazing straight ahead through the sea of
people and the dust that rose in a steady cloud above them. "I
have never said I do not believe in Jesus." He turned his dark
eyes toward Howard and for an instant their souls locked in understanding. "Although the rabbis do not believe that He was
the Messiah, only the ignorant deny that He was a great prophet
and great among the rabbis."

"Then tell me what it is about Him that you deny," Howard
pleaded in an earnest desire to understand.

"I deny those who since the early centuries have denied His
Jewishness. Jews have known little of Jesus and have wished to
know less."

"But why?"

Moshe looked at Howard in disbelief. "You are an intelligent
man, Howard. Surely you know that the name of Jesus is to a
Jew the scourge of God, the fiend in whose name children have
been torn in two while their Jewish parents were roasted alive
in every city of Spain! When the Crusaders burned Jewish villages, plundered Jewish homes and hung Jewish men from the
rafters while they raped their women, it was all done in the
name of the Prince of Peace, was it not?"

"Surely you cannot equate these things with Him, Moshe?"

"Not I, Howard. But in the Middle Ages in the Jewish ghettos,
after the thumb-screws and the rack had pulled conversions
from a number of Jews, a collection of legends called the Toldos Yeshu grew up about Jesus, slandering His name and per-
verting His messages. A natural consequence, I think, after the
unspeakable things that were done in His name to the very race
from which He sprang . . ." Moshe frowned and pursed his lips.
"The spirit of Toldos Yeshu still exists. For many, the name 'Christian' is a label to fear."

"The Inquisition was so long ago. A hideous crime. Terrible."

"For my people the Inquisition has never ended." He lowered his voice. "In Europe we have not even finished counting

313

the dead. And do not ignorant men who call themselves Christians still herd the survivors into camps and blow our boats from the water? I have heard it said that the Christ-killers deserve no less."

"You are looking at men, not Jesus."

"I know that, Howard. I am well acquainted with the teachings of the gentle master." He smiled sadly as they walked along. "I tell you these things only so you will understand."

"It is not every Christian who denies the people of God."

"The names of those who risked their lives to save Jews from the Nazi death camps are engraved on my heart. I am not bitter against every man who calls himself by the name Christian— only very careful, my friend."

Howard sighed. "I remember a quote by Martin Luther. My father used to repeat it often," he paused. "Now, let me get it right." He rubbed his chin thoughtfully and spoke the words in English, " '*Our fools, the popes, sophists, and monks, have hitherto conducted themselves towards the Jews in such a manner that he who was a good Christian would have preferred to be a Jew. And if I had been a Jew and had seen such blockheads and louts ruling and teaching Christianity, I would have become a swine rather than a Christian, because they have treated Jews like dogs rather than like human beings.*' "

Stunned, Moshe asked, "He said *that*? Must have changed his mind later in life," he added cryptically. "He said some really awful things about the Jews.—Anyway, well said, Rabbi, well spoken. Do you know what the church required for a Jew to become a Christian?"

Howard shook his head. "No."

"He had to eat pork; not serious, I suppose, but it constituted a denial of the kosher diet as prescribed in Deuteronomy. Now I ask you, can't a man be a Christian and follow Kashrut as well?"

"I see no hindrance," Howard answered in mock seriousness.

"Ah, well, that was the least of the requirements. A Jew had to deny the Holy Books, deny all Jewish holy days and festivals. What, I ask you, did they think Jesus celebrated during Passover in Jerusalem? The Gospels are full of festivals sanctioned by the Lord. And yet even now, Christians have only a vague glimmer of what significance those times had in His life and teaching.

314

They have made Jesus a Gentile."

Howard's eyes twinkled with delight at Moshe's explanation. He had not heard him talk so much on the subject in their entire eight years of association. "But He is still not a Gentile, is he, Moshe? No matter what small and wicked men have tried to make of Him."

"No. He is a Jew." He held his chin up. "But I believe He came to all men who would seek Him. As I read the messianic prophecy of Isaiah 53, the Messiah came to heal our sins by His wounds as the final sacrifice. He did not come for only one nation."

"And yet if there had been only one man on earth who needed Him to come and to die, He would have done so. God's love is so great."

"As a Jew I know the laws, and have done my best to live them from my heart. In the old days, before the temple was destroyed, a man sacrificed a lamb to pay a penalty for his sins. After the temple was destroyed, we still had the laws; still sinned, but there was no more sacrifice. It is only recently, since we found the scroll, that I began to understand the meaning of Isaiah 53. I will never call myself by the word Christian, but I understand why the Messiah came into this world, and I believe I have found a truth that is as old as the Jewish people. He does not want our sacrifices, He wants our hearts. The ultimate sacrifice was one He made for us. Jesus did not destroy Jewish law, He fulfilled it." He paused and looked at Howard. "Does this make sense?"

"Perfectly. But why won't you call yourself by the name of Christian if you believe this?"

"Did I not tell you the final requirement for a Jew to convert? He had to deny his people and never again speak to his family. He had to turn his back on everything he held dear."

"No one requires any such thing now, Moshe," Howard frowned.

"Well, that was one law that those who remained in the faith of their fathers approved of. Now, if a man becomes a Christian, the Orthodox no longer consider him a Jew. He is cut off and considered dead."

"But, Moshe—"

"I am a Jew, Howard. As do many Jews, I believe in the coming of the Messiah. I just happen to believe that He has been here once already."

"An interesting way of looking at it," Howard smiled. "You cannot call yourself by the name that has for so many centuries murdered your people."

"But truly, Howard, I will tell you that I believe that Jesus lives in the hearts of those who really know Him. It was through your friendship that I first saw His gentleness. For this I am grateful."

Emotion flooded Howard's face and he looked at Moshe and smiled. "I only wish I had been born a Jew," he said.

"When you found our Messiah, is it not written that you were grafted into the family?" Moshe clapped him on the back. "I never think of you as a Gentile, Howard. You never have pushed me or tried to convert me to the angry Gentile religion called the church. You have only walked by my side."

"How can I begin to say what I have learned from you?" Howard said.

"Really?" Moshe beamed.

"Of course."

"Well, then, I will teach you one more thing; thank God you weren't born a Jew! Chances are you would be dead right now!" Both men laughed, although the truth of Moshe's statement was a harsh reality that neither could deny.

———

The number two bus alternately whined and growled up the slopes of Mount Zion toward Zion Gate. *We probably could have walked faster than this bus is moving*, thought Ellie. But nobody walked to Zion Gate anymore. The slope of the hillside and open exposure to Arab snipers perched on the Old City wall above made her shudder, even inside the protective armor plating of the bus.

Afternoon sunlight streamed in through the slits that served as windows. A few of the more adventurous travelers leaned forward in their seats and marked their progress. Ellie sat across the aisle and one row back from Yacov and Rachel, who chatted shyly together in Polish. Even inside the gloomy interior of the bus, this seemed to Ellie to be the brightest spot in the world. She watched them, then looked away until a moment later she found her eyes irresistibly drawn to them once again. For her they were living proof that God was paying attention. As

Uncle Howard had said, even an unhappy situation had been turned to good. And theirs was not a rare or isolated instance. Moshe had spent hours telling her about similar miracles. *But*, Ellie thought, as Rachel threw her head back in laughter at Yacov, *this is my miracle, too. I have watched it happen*. Somehow that brought the reality of it home to her. She was no longer afraid of the uncertain future that loomed ahead. God knew the end of the story. He, after all, had written the Book.

As the bus rolled to an uncertain stop and the doors clanged open, Ellie stood and retrieved her camera bag from beneath her seat. Rachel carried a canvas shopping bag filled with the bread and the round of cheese Moshe had brought her. Shaul and Yacov leaped from the top step of the bus in the joy of the prospect of once again walking the streets of their home. Conscious of their fragile cargo, Rachel and Ellie stepped down with more caution.

A group of six soldiers waited by the great iron doors of the gate which were bolted shut. One young man glanced her way, then nudged his companion and quietly remarked about her bulky form. The two of them snickered and shrugged, then returned to their previous conversation. The woman in the dress shop had been accurate in her appraisal of where their safety lay. These men were less than anxious to search a woman who appeared to be at least forty pounds overweight. Rachel looked at Ellie and raised her eyebrows, then winked. It was a new experience for both of them.

No other passengers got off the bus. As its doors slapped shut and its complaining engine rumbled back down the hill, one of the soldiers approached Ellie.

"Jus' what d'ya think you're doin' 'ere, miss?" he asked.

"I'm a journalist. *Life* magazine. I have special permission to enter the Jewish Quarter for pictures this afternoon."

"This ain't no school dance, y'know," he frowned and stared hard at her. "We ain't 'eard nuthin' about it, miss, and y' ain't going in until we 'ear otherwise."

"Who's in charge here?" Ellie demanded.

"I am. Sergeant Albert Tory," said the belligerent soldier.

"Leastways, until the captain gets 'ere, ma'am," volunteered another soldier as he glanced at his watch. "You're a bit early yet. 'e ought to be 'ere in another few minutes."

Tory wheeled on him. "Well, I say nobody goes in. An' if tha'

317

Jew-lovin' Captain Thomas says otherwise, at least these'll 'ave a proper searchin' first," he growled. He turned his angry gaze on Rachel who stood with her arm protectively around Yacov's shoulder. "All right, we'll start with the kid. Against the wall!" He grabbed Yacov by the arm and was instantly answered by Shaul, who leaped to his feet and lunged for the startled Tory, his teeth bared in the angry snarl. Tory fell back in fear, snatching his revolver from its holster.

"No!" Yacov screamed and threw himself between Shaul and the gun. "Don't shoot him!"

Shaul continued to growl at Tory, who cursed as he tried to aim past the boy.

"Leave them alone!" Ellie shouted, raising her camera. "Unless you want to be known around the world as a man who shoots children and dogs."

Fearfully, Tory looked from her camera to the dog and back to Ellie again. "Put that thing away!" he bellowed.

Ellie focused the lens. "Not until you put your weapon away."

"You saw the dog," Tory looked at his startled men. " 'e tried to attack me, right, lads?" A few nodded. "There. Y' see? I'll 'ave y' arrested if you try to interfere with this one, miss. And you'll lose that precious camera of yours all the same."

Rachel knelt beside Yacov and put her hand on Shaul's head. "You will have to shoot me as well," she said calmly.

"Arrest the girl with the camera." Tory waved the pistol toward Ellie.

Two soldiers hesitantly stepped forward. Again, as they moved toward Ellie, Shaul lunged and snarled fiercely. They jumped back with the other men. "Sorry, Sarge—she's all yours."

"Get 'er, I say!" he ordered. "I'll take care of the dog."

The roar of an armored car caused them to all glance away.

"Captain'll settle it, Tory," said one of the men, as the car screeched to a stop in front of the gate.

"That's fair enough," said Ellie, snapping the shutter of her camera at the horrified face of Tory.

Captain Luke Thomas opened the door of the car and climbed out, taking in the scene in one glance. He instantly recognized Ellie, and nodded curtly. Then he scowled at Tory, whose cap had fallen to the pavement. "Got yourself a burglar, Sergeant Tory?"

Luke raised his chin and peered down his nose at the disheveled Tory.

"Watch the dog, Cap'n. 'e's a mean brute. Tried t' take m' leg off." Tory wiped his brow.

"Is that so, lad?" He looked at Yacov, a twinkle in his eye.

Yacov slowly shook his head. "No, sir."

"Put the gun away, Sergeant," he said, approaching the dog.

"But, Cap'n!" Tory protested.

"Holster it! That's an order!" Luke snapped.

Reluctantly, his eyes never leaving Shaul, Tory obeyed. Luke walked slowly to Shaul and extended his hand. Shaul sniffed suspiciously. "There's a good dog," Luke said soothingly.

Shaul nosed his hand, then wagged his tailless hind end. "He will not harm you," Yacov said, eyeing the surly sergeant. "If you do not harm me."

Luke scratched Shaul behind the ears. "Good fellow," he said crisply. Then he turned to Tory. "Your duty is at an end, I believe. You are free to celebrate Christmas."

"But, Cap'n!" Tory protested.

"Unless you wish to walk back to barracks, I suggest that you consider target practice on someone else's dog."

Tory scowled and sulkily returned Luke's salute. Then he retrieved his cap and climbed into the armored car with three other members of the guard. With one last angry glare, he slammed the door.

Ellie sighed deeply as Luke turned toward her. "Miss Warne, is it? Yes, I remember. Sorry about all this. At times the lads are a bit trigger-happy. You're here to photograph the Old City, I believe?" Without waiting for her answer, he turned to Rachel. "And you are . . ."

"I am Judith," said Rachel, using the code name.

"You're early," replied the captain. "I have a pass here. Going in for the holy days. Well, we'll have to search your packages, I'm afraid," he said. Then without ceremony he turned toward one of his men. "Andrews. See to it." He turned his back and sauntered toward the gate as a young rosy-cheeked soldier quickly glanced through the bag of bread and cheese.

"All right, sir," said the young man.

"Good, good," said Luke. "You don't look the type to be smuggling weapons into the Old City, now do you? Enjoy your holiday." He turned his kindly gaze on Ellie. "*Life* magazine or not, you'll have to be out before dark. We cannot guarantee your safety if you're wandering about the Old City after dark."

Ellie nodded. "Thank you. You've been most kind."

"Open the gates, lads," he instructed.

The great iron hinges groaned as the soldiers opened the gate. Ellie remembered watching *The Wizard of Oz* with David. He had made a face and laughed as the gates of Oz swung wide and Dorothy had entered with Toto and her friends. She looked back at Rachel and Yacov and Shaul and grinned in spite of herself. Rachel winked as if to say, "That wasn't so hard."

The hundred-yard stretch into the Jewish Quarter was deserted. Two soldiers scanned the rooftops as they escorted them to Mendelbaum Gate, but the narrow corridor reminded Ellie of a ghost town. Windows and doors were covered over by planks and sheets of wood. This street, which had once echoed with the happy shouts of playing children, now stood desolate. "Mufti's gang chased the Christians out," volunteered a soldier. "Now they 'ave the run of the place after dark. Prowlin' on the rooftops, takin' pot shots at anything tha' moves over in the Jewish sector. Mind you're 'ere before sundown, like the captain says. We ain't comin' in after dark."

The soldiers turned and quickly hurried back toward the gate as Ellie and Rachel and Yacov approached a barricade of sandbags and barbed-wire manned by black-coated Yeshiva students.

"Halt!" demanded one boy of about sixteen, brandishing a pitchfork.

Yacov recognized him and greeted happily, "Israel Ditkowitz! It is I, Yacov!"

"What's the password?" barked the young man.

"I am Judith," Rachel answered.

The young man grunted, "Well, then, come along." He raised his pitchfork and allowed them to pass, somewhat grudgingly.

"You make a fine soldier, Israel," Yacov called as they rounded a corner.

Ellie snapped the shutter of her camera, amazed at the changes inside the Old City. A group of men huddled together on a rooftop position just below where a member of the Suffolk Regiment stood watch over them and the Arab sector. They had no weapons that Ellie could see. They simply made their pres-

320

ence known. They were willing to defend, even if they were not yet ready.

"How far is it to the Warsaw Compound?" Ellie asked Yacov.

"Quite far. And now you must hurry or we will not finish before dark. There is yet another stop I must make with my sister," he said in a determined tone of voice.

"Wait a minute!" exclaimed Ellie as Yacov bounded up the Street of the Stairs two steps at a time. "You don't have time for that."

"If we hurry," Rachel replied, following doggedly after Yacov. "It is different now, Ellie. Now that we have found one another, we must see him. It is Hanukkah. God has given us a gift."

Ellie frowned, understanding their desire, but uncertain of how she could dissuade them. "We won't make it out."

"Not if we dally and take photographs," Yacov leveled his gaze on her.

"But Moshe said—" she began, then stopped. Yacov and Rachel were determined. There would be no convincing them otherwise.

The walls of the Warsaw building loomed ahead of them. Yacov broke into a stiff jog, which Ellie and Rachel were unable to keep pace with. Their hidden cargo was heavy, and Ellie found herself panting after the first few feet.

Yacov turned and called after them, then ran head-on into the towering figure of Rabbi Akiva.

Yacov stumbled, then looked up into the glaring, angry face. "Pardon, Rabbi Akiva." He lowered his eyes quickly and stood respectfully before the broad black-coated belly.

"You!" snapped Akiva. "Yacov, is it not?"

"Happy Hanukkah, Rabbi Akiva." Yacov looked up hopefully and smiled.

"The gates are locked. No one enters and no one leaves unless they desire to evacuate. So how have you come to be here? You have transgressed our bargain." He looked up at Ellie and Rachel as they lumbered up the steps. "And who are these strangers? They are not dressed in the modest fashion of the Hassidic women. Have you led them here, Yacov? And for what purpose have you done so?" He turned his head and suspiciously appraised them.

"This is my sister, Rachel," Yacov answered. "We have come to find my grandfather. Have you seen him about?"

321

"You have no sister!" Akiva snapped. "Your sister died these many years ago. Who is this woman?"

Ellie interrupted his growing indignation. "I am Ellie Warne. I am a magazine photographer." She extended her hand. "I have received permission to photograph the situation in the Old City."

"Situation?" he said coldly. "There is no situation, save the peril these Haganah intruders put us in." He fixed his angry eyes on Rachel, who looked down at the cobblestones at her feet. "If they would leave the business to those of us who know how to get along . . ." He spurned Ellie's hand, then, with his lip curled in bitter fury, he pushed past them.

Yacov stood dumbfounded for a moment, watching the large, swaying back of Akiva as he stomped down the steps and turned a corner. "Come," he said softly. "We must hurry."

"But who is he?" Ellie asked.

"He is . . . maybe was . . . mayor of the Old City. He does not believe in Zionism. I do not know what Grandfather shall say when I tell him of how angry Rabbi Akiva is that we have come past the blockade." He turned and hurried up the steps and into the shadow of the Warsaw. High atop its pinnacle, Ellie saw another small group of men, staring intently to the north, where Arab muzzien stood in minarets and called the faithful to prayer. The songs they sang drifted over the Jewish Quarter and mingled as a backdrop to conversations of the Orthodox who talked in hushed tones as they stood in small groups around the compound. Eyes wandered curiously to Ellie and Rachel as they lugged their burdens across the courtyard and down a narrow flight of stairs to a basement classroom.

Yacov pushed the door open. "It is here that I study the—" His happy words were interrupted by his astonished gasp as he saw the tables covered with sacks of beans. Young and old women sat in long rows, busily sorting bullets from the beans. They looked up at Yacov, several smiling and calling out in recognition.

An old woman—ancient, Ellie thought—slid off her stool and shuffled over toward where they stood. Rachel closed the door behind them and smiled as she watched the assembly line munitions factory. "Shalom, Yacov!" the old woman said in a cracked voice. "We have missed you at the kitchens."

"Shalom, Mrs. Cohen," he said. "Shaul and I have been gone. But we are back," he said proudly. "And we have brought gifts for Hanukkah!" He pointed happily at Rachel and Ellie who both felt somewhat self-conscious beneath their bulky, ammunition-laden clothing.

"You're a good boy, Yacov." She patted his cheek with approval. Then she fixed her kindly gaze on Rachel and Ellie. "You must be Judith, eh? You have brought us maybe another sten gun?"

30   Reunion

The bright blue of the afternoon sky had begun to soften with muted pastels as the sun dipped lower in the sky. Ellie looked anxiously upward past the domed rooftops as darkness threatened the little band. Relieved of their burden, Rachel and Ellie now kept pace with Yacov's rapid footsteps as he hurried toward number 8 Chaim Street, and home.

Rachel's face was tight with emotion. After so many years and so many dreams, she was finally in the streets where her dear mother had grown to womanhood and married. Her heart absorbed every silhouette; her feet memorized the cobblestones, and every footfall seemed to echo, "You are not alone. You are not alone." Here—ironically, once again in the midst of siege and war—she finally felt safe. She reached her fingertips out and brushed the rough stone of the buildings. Had her father not always ended Passover with the words, "Next Year in Jerusalem"? And had they not prayed each night for the peace of the beloved city and proudly remembered that their grandfather lived out his life among these sacred sites? *I am here, Papa*, her heart whispered, as she remembered the emotion with which he had spoken of the Holy City. *I am here.*

Yacov rounded a corner to the narrow alleyway of Chaim Street. "This is my home!" he shouted joyfully. Shaul spun in a delighted circle, then ran to the steps that led down to their little basement apartment. He paused and looked at Yacov with solemn eyes to make sure that he was really coming, then skipped down the steps and barked twice to be let in. Yacov ran faster, leaving Ellie and Rachel jogging behind. "Come on!" he cried. "Hurry up!" Then, impatiently waiting as they caught him at the top of the stairs, he took Rachel's hand. "This is your home, sister," he said, gently leading her down to the door.

Ellie hung back, feeling like an intruder. The sun was setting. She remained at the stair-railing as Yacov knocked softly, then turned the door handle.

"Grandfather?" he called, pushing the door open. There was no answer.

"Please, God," Ellie prayed. "Let them find him."

Yacov and Rachel entered the apartment, then emerged a moment later. "He is not home," said Rachel, her voice thick with the pain of disappointment. Her head was bowed as they climbed the steps to where Ellie waited.

"I'm so sorry." Ellie searched for words of comfort, but found that her only thoughts were of the approaching darkness. "Maybe if we wait a few minutes, he'll come back. We can wait another minute."

"He is gone." Yacov's voice was puzzled. His eyes scanned the street. "Gone."

Ellie rubbed her hand over her face in frustration. "Where, Yacov? Where is he?"

"Perhaps at Nissan Bek Synagogue. At afternoon Hanukkah service. Although always before we have gone in the evening."

"Where is it?"

"Back by the Warsaw buildings."

"That far? Why didn't we check there before we came here?"

"Can we make it?" Rachel asked, the light coming back to her eyes.

"I think not," Yacov said.

"But can we *maybe*?" Ellie asked.

"Perhaps," Yacov answered. "But we must hurry. I know a shortcut. I know how good Ellie climbs on rooftops. But can you do the same, my sister?"

Ellie grabbed him by the arm. "So go. Hurry up. I'm a fool, but I love happy endings. Hurry, will you?"

Yacov bent down and spoke the words "Nissan Bek" to Shaul, who tucked his hind-end beneath him and ran quickly back the way they had come. Yacov took Rachel by the hand and pulled her to a ladder nearly hidden between two buildings; then he climbed up and motioned for the two girls to follow. Ellie tucked her skirt up and climbed quickly up to the flat roof. Rachel followed more hesitantly. Once there, Ellie saw that perhaps they had made a mistake. A large orange sun was flattening against the horizon, and soon it would be too late. *We may as well try*, she thought, following Yacov from rooftop to rooftop toward the massive dome of Nissan Bek.

No longer did Rachel think of the setting sun. As they neared the great Nissan Bek, her heart raced with hope. Yacov climbed deftly down a ladder still a block away from the entrance to the synagogue. The sound of Jewish hymns filled the air with a haunting dissonance as the Muslim muzzien called an end to the day and the setting of the sun. Ellie helped Rachel down, then followed her to the street. Shadows were collecting now as they ran up the worn stone steps of the ancient temple.

"You must go to the women's gallery. I will go among the men and search for him," Yacov instructed after they entered the outer court, frescoed with paintings of Moses standing on the Mount with the tablets of God's law held high in his arms. The voice of the cantor echoed from the vaulted ceilings as Ellie and Rachel covered their heads with their scarves and climbed the stairs to the women's gallery.

Women, young girls, and small children stood against the lattice work that separated them from their husbands and fathers worshiping below them. Rachel inched her way up to the lattice panels with Ellie at her side and peered down at the men, reading as they swayed in their prayer shawls.

"There's Yacov," Ellie whispered, spotting the little boy weaving through the large crowd of men, peering up into every face. Rachel did not hear her. Her own heart was pounding too loudly.

"I love Him, for the Eternal hearkeneth unto my voice in supplication." Voices were raised as one as they read Psalm 16 in the hymn of the Hallel. "For He hath inclined His ear unto me; therefore, while I live, I will call to Him . . ."

Rachel leaned against the screen, her eyes following the little boy as he anxiously searched the faces raised in song beneath the blue and white talliths. Ellie put her hand on Rachel's shoulder. *Please, God*, she prayed for them. Rachel's eyes were full of hope and fear, her hands clutching the lattice like bars. Ellie eagerly scanned the crowd, hoping for a glimpse of the kindly old man.

"Oh, Eternal!" rose the cry, "deliver my soul! Gracious is the Eternal, and just, and our God is compassionate."

Ellie watched, scarcely breathing as Yacov's face lit up with delight. Rachel gasped and pressed forward as Yacov tugged on the fringes of Grandfather's prayer shawl. The old rabbi's back was to them, but he knelt and brushed the excited tears from Yacov's cheek as the boy talked animatedly to Grandfather in the midst of the chanting of the Hallel. The old man embraced the boy, wrapping his prayer shawl around him, enfolding him with his joy. Yacov pushed away and began to explain about Rachel.

"For thou hast liberated my soul from death, mine eye from weeping . . ."

Rachel's eyes were riveted to the back of Grandfather's head. "I am here, Grandfather," she whispered, tears streaming down her cheeks. "Grandfather!" she cried aloud, causing a stir among the men.

The old man turned around then, his eyes searching the lattice that concealed the faces of the women from view. Yacov pointed as Rachel reached through the gap in the screen. Grandfather's face was etched with feeling as he raised his ancient gnarled hands toward hers and walked through the swaying crowd of men until he stood beneath her outstretched hand. "Rachel!" he called. "You have come home." Tears streaked his face and dropped like dew to his beard.

It seemed as though their hands had touched over the gulf and for a moment their eyes, old and young, caressed. Rachel's voice was choked by emotion as she cried out, "I am here!"

"Dear in the sight of the Eternal is the death of his pious ones," read the congregation as eyes darted to Grandfather, then back to the prayer book.

"Rachel!" He cried again, reaching out for her as he clutched his chest with pain and dropped to his knees.

A murmur rose from the congregation as Rachel screamed and ran from the gallery and into the main floor below. Yacov sat on the floor, cradling the old rabbi's head. Rachel ran to his side and knelt beside him, taking his hand and holding it to her cheek. "Grandfather," she said again and again.

A cluster of men formed a circle around them and Ellie elbowed her way through, then stopped as the old rabbi looked into Rachel's eyes. "Is it really you?" he asked weakly.

"Yes. Yes. It is Rachel," she wept, kissing his fingers.

"I should have known," he tried to smile. "You have the eyes of your mother."

"Shhh. Don't talk. Not now. We will have time to talk," Rachel touched his cheek.

"Perhaps not so much time. But you have Yacov and he—" His breath came in short gasps.

A large man crowded past Ellie. "Please," he said, and the crowd parted for him. He knelt beside Grandfather and quickly loosened his collar. He put his ear to the old man's chest and silence fell as he listened to the weak heartbeat. He looked up at the younger faces in the group. "Help me move him," he ordered, as Rachel and Yacov moved back and embraced one another.

Gently, four men lifted Grandfather from the floor and carried him to the back of the auditorium and into a small anteroom. Then, as Rachel and Yacov followed after, they shut the door behind them.

———

The stars shone like diamonds against black velvet over the little town of Bethlehem. Campfires of pilgrims dotted the hillsides around the city and, Moshe thought, nothing much had changed in the two thousand years that had passed since the birth of Jesus in a cave above the little town. As shepherds had first come to find the infant Messiah, King of Israel, Moshe and Howard now came seeking a treasure.

It was nearly six o'clock when they passed into the narrow, cobbled souks of Bethlehem. Vendors hawked their wares to hungry travelers, offering the warmth of fires to any who would stop to purchase a meal of skewered lamb chunks and onions. The aroma drifted deliciously into every corner and alleyway, tugging at the appetites of Moshe and Howard.

"What is the time?" Moshe asked a grizzled vendor, who held two sticks of roasted meat out to him.

"Listen to the bells," the man replied. "Soon it will be six. But an hour before the masses begin. Will you buy?"

Moshe flipped him a coin and took the meal from him, handing one of the sticks to Howard, who savored the heavy garlic flavoring. Moments later the church bells began to chime from every corner of the city.

"We have an hour," Howard remarked, handing the donkey's rope to Moshe and purchasing two ears of roasted corn from yet another merchant. He handed an ear to Moshe, then proceeded to clean three rows of kernels in one bite. Despite the sparse crowds on the road that afternoon, the streets now teemed with people crowding to buy food and candles for the evening's candlelight procession that would begin in an hour. "Now I understood what was meant by 'no room in the inn,'" he said, finishing off his corn and handing the still-warm cob to the donkey.

"Let's just hope we find what we're looking for, eh?" Moshe said.

"This is certainly not the Christmas dinner I had planned for us." Howard looked around him, choosing from the myriad of food sellers. Then he blanched and struck his forehead with the palm of his hand. "Oh, no!" he muttered.

"What is it?" Moshe asked with alarm.

"That young fellow, David. I asked him to dinner. I thought maybe he and Rachel—"

"Yes?"

"Well, I forgot to tell him we wouldn't be there, that's all. I simply forgot about it with all the excitement."

"Maybe Ellie will call him." Moshe purchased two more skewers of meat.

"She didn't know he was coming," he shrugged.

Moshe eyed him disapprovingly. "I did not know you were so devious."

"I was . . . I thought she would say no. Young David seems like the sort who could cheer up a girl like Rachel."

"Where I come from you would be called a matchmaker. Though I do not know if I approve of the match." Moshe frowned and wiped his mouth on the fringe of his keffiyeh in Arab fashion.

"Do I detect a note of jealousy? I thought that you and Ellie—"

"I am not jealous. It is simply that Rachel is . . . she is wounded, you see, and I think quite fragile. I do not approve of this David person. After all, it was he who wounded Ellie."

Howard arched his eyebrows, "Oh?" He glanced away self-consciously. "Funny how you can live in the same house with someone and never know what's going on. I never have been very perceptive when it came to women."

"Nor have I, my friend."

"Well, you seem to have a fix on the two women of my house."

"They are both innocents," Moshe smiled. "Each in a different way. Until now, Ellie has had the innocence of one who has never seen the pain of others suffering. And Rachel, dear Rachel, has suffered without understanding, like a small child lost in the marketplace. Now Ellie's eyes are beginning to open, and in the end it may be she who takes the lost child by the hand and leads her home."

"This doesn't have the sound of a man who doesn't understand women."

"I only know this because once I lived in blindness, and once in hopeless confusion at the horror around me. The very thing I have come to love about Ellie is her ability to act in the face of terror. Rachel has not learned this yet, and she is still a victim waiting for the next blow to be struck against her. It is only when our eyes are opened and we rise up in indignation against those things that are wrong and evil that we become what God would have us be, is that not so?"

"I see what you mean," Howard answered, munching thoughtfully on a chunk of lamb.

"Ellie knows this instinctively, I think."

"She's fairly tough, all right."

"Not tough. Unafraid. Even when she is afraid, she looks for the answer that will give her victory over her fear. Rachel is simply afraid. Without hope in her soul, she lives among those whose hearts have died. I grieve for her. There is so much beauty in her heart. She has forgotten, and I only wish I could . . ." his voice trailed off.

"I didn't know you felt this way. And I am ashamed to admit I didn't think that far."

"Earlier today you quoted Martin Luther to me." Moshe warmed his hands at the fire. "And now I wish to share with you a poem by Bialik."

Howard squatted and put his hands out toward the flame. "Please," he said quietly.

Moshe knelt beside him, the orange glow of the fire illuminating his face. The anguish of concern about his eyes was highlighted by the fierce, flickering shadows. He began:

"All, all of you do I remember yet,
  In all my wanderings you go with me—
  Your likeness graven on my heart forever.
  And I remember, too, how strong, how sturdy
  The seed must be that withers in those fields.
  How rich would be the blessing if one beam
  Of living sunlight could break through to you.
  How great the harvest to be reaped in joy,
  If once the wind of life should pass through you,
  And blow clear through to the Yeshivah doors."

Moshe lowered his voice. He faltered for a moment, then
began again:

"All, all of you do I remember yet—
  The hungry childhood and the bitter manhood,
  And my heart weeps for my unhappy people. . . .
  How burned, how blasted must our portion be,
  If seed like this is withered in its soil."

31 The Trap

A warm breeze greeted David as he pushed through the revolving door of the Atlantic Hotel and onto Ben Yehuda Street.
For the first time in weeks, the shops and cafes of Ben Yehuda
were brightly lit and crowded with men and women picking up
last-minute gifts for the holidays. The last week and a half had
been quiet in Jerusalem, David reasoned, lulling everyone into
a sense of safety and well-being despite the news from Cairo
about the Arab meeting. Christians and Jews alike welcomed
this night, and the stone walls of Jerusalem echoed with happy
laughter once again.

David tucked Ellie's present under his arm and stood for a
moment looking at the ruler-edge crease in his slacks. Even his
tie was pressed, and his shoes glistened with the reflected lights
from the blinking neon of the Atara Cafe across the street. The
Atara was the hangout for the volunteer forces of the Haganah,

as well as a number of newsmen who were on their own. Through the windows David could see groups of young men in animated conversation at tiny tables crowded with large mugs of beer. "Sorry, fellas," he murmured happily, "this is one party you're going to have without ol' David."

Under his leather flight jacket he carried a small balsa wood model of a Mustang fighter plane for Yacov and two rolls of Italian salami for Shaul. He had purchased twenty pounds of salami in Rome, stuffing every available corner of his duffle bag with the spicy cargo. Only moments before, he had untied the bag to find that everything inside smelled like a deli. He sniffed the thin, six-inch-square package he carried on top of the camera box. Only a vague aroma drifted from the paper and David hoped that the beautiful silk scarf he had purchased in Rome for Rachel had not absorbed any of the smell.

It was only a few blocks to the bus stop, but David had borrowed Michael's beat-up car for the occasion. He dumped the gifts onto the front seat of the car and climbed in. Glancing at his watch, he felt a wave of impatience. It was still only six-thirty; he was a half an hour early. He sat for a moment watching through the windshield as two lovers strolled happily down the street, stopping in the shadows to kiss. An ache started in his stomach and spread to his arms as he remembered Ellie looking up into his face and leaning against him as they strolled along the boardwalk in Santa Monica last Christmas Eve. *Had it been only a year?* he wondered in amazement. Then he thought how fresh the feelings were inside his heart. Every emotion, every stirring seemed like only yesterday. He sighed deeply and started the car. "So," he said, "you'll be a little early. You can help her mash the potatoes."

David took the long route to the Moniger home, avoiding the barbed-wire roadblocks along the dark and bleak military areas. He passed through a Haganah checkpoint and was instantly recognized by a man he had seen in the office of the Old Man.

"Let him through," came the order. "He is okay." David waved, then rolled down the window to shout at the grim collection of men at the outpost just in front of the Jewish Agency.

"Merry Christmas," he called.

The men smiled and waved in return. Then, on impulse, David tossed a salami into the hands of their leader. For a moment the man seemed startled, then he smiled and looked down at David. "Be careful who you throw salami at. Someone might think it is a grenade you toss and ... kablooey!" He pointed his index finger at David. "But thank you! Merry Christmas to you as well!"

Lights glimmered through closed shutters of the Rehavia homes. A few houses stood dark and desolate, abandoned by their owners for safer places in the world, but for the most part, the Jews had held firm to Ben-Gurion's pleas that not one inch of the city be given up without a fight.

The Jewish outposts and kibbutzim that David and Michael had flown over today also bustled with activity. Even from their high vantage point, David had seen men and women at work digging jagged trenches on the perimeters of their tiny settlements. Most of the Jewish land had been purchased nearly a century before by Jews in Europe who had foreseen this moment in history. Now the land that had been desolate and barren had begun to bloom with the hope of a new nation. At this point, David knew, it was only hope that sustained these people. They had very little else to combat the constant threats and ever-increasing incidents of terrorism.

Some Jews had turned to counter-terrorism, and David thought, *If anything will destroy the United Nations' resolve to support Partition and a Jewish homeland, it will be atrocities committed by Jews.* The world's conscience was raw with the sight of the Nazi death camps. Militancy among the Zionists only served to dull the edge of the world's guilt. He hated to admit it, but Moshe had been right about Ellie's photographs; they showed the truth of the situation to a world that sought any excuse to forget that the chosen people struggled not for land or territory, but for survival.

He rounded the corner of Ellie's street, and patted the red tissue-wrapped box that held her new camera. He had been wrong about her staying; he knew that now. He only hoped that the Leica would convey the message that he believed in what she was doing. Not a day passed but one of the Haganah men mentioned a letter from a relative in the States who had seen one of her pictures. Every image struck deeply back home, and momentum for private assistance seemed to be growing. As the official United States policy teetered precariously between support of Partition and the threat of repeal, men and women gathered at banquets across the U.S. to hear Golda Meir speak of the Yishuv's urgent needs. Money was flooding in daily. David thought about the Messerschmidts and smiled grimly. He only wished there had been money enough to buy a flock of Mustangs. They were neat and stable, and there wasn't an ME 109 that stood a chance against him in the cockpit of his own little fighter.

He pulled up in front of the Moniger home and set the brake. He stared up at the house for a long moment, puzzled at the darkened windows. The structure seemed deserted. "Maybe they're at the back of the house," David murmured as he stepped out of the car onto the sidewalk. He stood and scratched his chin, then retrieved the packages from the seat and strode up the front steps. He knocked sharply on the door and waited, looking at his watch. *I'm a little early, yes, but certainly they should be here,* he thought. He knocked again, harder; when no one answered, he climbed back into the car to wait.

The kerosene chandeliers of Nissan Bek Synagogue smoked and flickered above Ellie's head. The great auditorium was nearly deserted now. A rabbi talked in hushed tones to two young defenders. A third man lay on a scaffolding suspended from the roof of the dome far above the floor of the great hall. Ellie glanced up as he coughed. From her angle far below, she could see him gazing intently through the window to the north, scanning the darkness of the Muslim Quarter just on the other side of the thick walls of the building. A young woman in a long black dress, her hair covered by a scarf, hurried in and placed a small basket into the larger basket that hung from the scaffolding.

"Happy Hanukkah, Shimon," she said, smiling up toward him. Her voice echoed throughout the building.

"Thank you, Tikvah," he said back in a low voice. "And could you fetch me another blanket as well? It is cold up here."

The woman waved, then hurried out, casting a curious look in Ellie's direction. Ellie watched as the man on the scaffolding hauled the basket up and carefully unwrapped his lonely supper. Ellie thought about all the flagpole sitters and wire-walkers who had covered the front pages of the newspapers of her childhood. The folks back home had cheered them on, even though their only purpose had been to achieve some senseless record. Now, here was a man perched on a few boards high above her head in the dead of winter in Jerusalem. Surely he deserved some title: *World's Loneliest Outpost*, or *Guard Duty Closest to Heaven.* Ellie tapped her black camera case with her thumb. *What a front-page picture this man would make!* she thought. But she was out of film. The man coughed again, and Ellie looked up as he sipped hot coffee and hungrily devoured a slice of bread. *Every Jew in Palestine is a flagpole sitter in a way*, she mused. And down on the ground, the United Nations and the peoples it represented, watched with detached interest to see whether the Jews would finally and irrevocably lose their balance and fall into the angry hands of the Arabs. She wondered about her photographs, popping up between ads for soap and cigarettes. Perhaps people back home looked at them, shook their heads and muttered words like "crazy"; then they turned the pages and forgot about it. "I guess you must be here on the flagpole, huh, God?" she said quietly. The guard heard her and glanced over the edge of his perch. Ellie grinned and waved. He waved and then returned to his meager supper.

Moments later the door to the little room opened and Rachel and Yacov came out, followed by the large man who had first attended Grandfather. Ellie stood and walked to meet them, embracing Rachel, who laid her head against her shoulder like a child.

"How is he?" Ellie asked.

The big man shook his head. "I was a medic in the war, nothing more. I cannot do anything for him here. He needs medical attention. At Hadassah."

"It is his heart. The kind doctor says for many months . . ."

"He never told me." Yacov clouded up and looked quickly away.

"I cannot . . ." Rachel began. "We cannot leave him now."

"I didn't think you would. It's okay. I'll explain to Moshe."

"Moshe." Rachel repeated his name with a tenderness that caused Ellie to frown briefly.

"He'll understand, Rachel."

"He will think I have . . ."

"He won't think you've run out on him. He's an understanding man. You'll see him again, and it'll be all right." Ellie put her hand on Rachel's arm and said gently, "You love him, don't you?"

Rachel glanced down and stared at the marble floor. "Ellie, I would never presume to . . . I care so much for you, too. For you both."

"I'm a real dope sometimes, you know, Rachel? If there's one thing more obvious than two people staring at each other, it's two people trying *not* to."

"But Ellie . . . Moshe doesn't—"

"Never mind. I think Moshe is trying *not* to. There's a big difference." She smiled, certain that she was seeing the truth. She looked at the big man. "How can I help with Rachel's grandfather?" she abruptly changed the subject.

"Unless you have an ambulance to take him to Hadassah, I cannot think," he said grimly. "No ambulance will come here."

"I see." She lifted Yacov's chin. "I know you're staying, but you've got to help me get out of here, son."

"Shaul will take you home. And when you are done with him, send him back."

"I'm probably safer with him than the whole Suffolk Regiment," Ellie said under her breath. She turned to the big man.

"Where are you taking Rabbi Lebowitz?" she asked.

"We shall not move him. At least for tonight."

"He'll be here until morning at least? Good. That's good," she said. She touched Rachel's cheek. "I'll see you again."

Rachel's chin quivered and she bit her lip. "Oh, my dear friend!" she cried. "Please be careful."

"Okay, Yacov." She headed toward the door. "Where's Shaul?"

Thousands of candles flickered in the dark street, illuminating young and old faces—faces filled with hope, yet despair. Flames danced in the breath of mouths that sang an ancient hymn, celebrating the birth of the one called Immanuel, God with Us.

Their donkey in tow, Moshe and Howard inched their way against the tide of the crowd moving slowly up the main thoroughfare of Bethlehem toward the church that some said marked the manger where Christ was born. Both Moshe and Howard had been to the shop of Elaram a hundred times, but

335

always before the streets had hummed only with the sleepy sound of flies buzzing in the marketplace against the backdrop of tourists haggling over the cost of a carved olivewood creche. And like the tourists, always before, these archaeologists had haggled over the price of an ancient coin or Bronze-Age tool. Elaram drove a hard bargain, Moshe knew. He carried crisp new British pounds beneath his robes, tucked safely in his pocket beneath the heavy Smith and Wesson .38 in the holster at his waist.

At last they reached the corner that marked the street of Elaram. Instantly they fell off into the deserted alleyway and turned yet another bend that led up a small incline. The voices of the pilgrims followed them, echoing softly like a choir in a cathedral. The donkey stumbled on a step in the street.

"Let's tie her up here," Howard suggested. "No one will steal her."

Moshe smiled at him doubtfully. "How do you think I came by her?"

Howard clicked his tongue disapprovingly. "Well, then, maybe her owner will steal her back." He looped the rope around an iron bar on the window of a deserted-looking house.

Moshe patted her on the rump, then followed Howard up the steep stairway that led to the tiny shop of Moddy Elaram. Howard was panting when at last Moshe rang the shop bell that hung beside the rough-hewn wooden door. Only a faint light shone from the windows. Moshe lifted the latch and gingerly pushed the door open, ringing yet another bell that hung above the door.

"Moddy?" he called, glancing around the musty shop. A gaslight hissed from the wall above a short counter covered with what, to the unpracticed eye, appeared to be debris from a potter's trash pile. Broken bits of clay pots were mingled with small unbroken bowls and half an ancient clay household god. "Some things never change." Moshe stepped in, eyeing the jumbles of pots stacked against the walls.

"Trash and treasures," Howard said, following him.

"Moddy?" Moshe called again.

"I don't think we're early."

Dark green tapestry curtains covered the doorway into the back of the shop. Suddenly they parted and a young man, dressed in an ill-fitting suit with frayed cuffs and collar, stepped from behind the curtain.

"You wish to see my uncle?" he asked, eyeing them warily.

Moshe and Howard exchanged glances. "He asked us to meet him here." Moshe fumbled in his pocket and pulled out the letter which he handed to the grim-faced lean young man. Moshe watched him as he read the letter. His black eyes seemed almost lifeless. He had several days growth of beard around a mouth that seemed pinched and hostile, drawn down at the corners as if stitched by some thread of bitterness. His tousled hair fell in greasy curls across his forehead. He finished reading the letter and looked up at Moshe without expression. "My uncle is in hospital at Jerusalem, unfortunately. But I look after his affairs."

"What is it? How long has he been ill?"

"His heart, alas." His voice had no emotion. "Just a week ago. We have hope for his recovery. But now I must look after his affairs."

"As you can see, he asked us to meet him here along with the Bedouin shepherds. In regard to the scrolls."

"Ah, yes. You are expected. My uncle tells me you are coming and when you are coming and what you shall wish to see."

"When are the shepherds to arrive?" asked Howard.

"Alas, no. They shall not come."

"But what about—" Moshe protested.

"They have come and gone again, leaving this matter in my hands. If you will have patience, Doctor Professor Sachar . . ." He raised his index finger and shook it at Moshe. Then he gave a half smile. "There is time. There is time." He turned toward the curtains and disappeared behind them once again.

Howard leaned close to Moshe's ear. "If it took the first letter three weeks to reach us, there just wasn't time enough for him to get word to us," he whispered.

"I just hope all of this is not for nothing." Moshe frowned with irritation.

The young man slipped from behind the curtain and stood quietly watching until they noticed that he had once again entered the room. When their eyes met his it was as if he clicked to life. "Be seated, gentlemen. Be seated." His smile seemed more genuine, putting Moshe at ease.

Moshe looked for a chair, noticing that every available space had been taken by piles of old newspapers and artifacts. Howard eyed a rickety-looking stool shrouded beneath a jumble of dusty prayer rugs. His feet ached from the long day of walking, so he simply shrugged and moved the pile onto another pile. Then he scooted the stool up to the counter and plopped down with a sigh.

"Ah, my uncle," the young man sighed. "His little shop is far from neat, is it not? Perhaps one day if it is mine—" he left the sentence unfinished and directed his black gaze toward Moshe. "Sit. You see this gentleman here, he moves things from the chair. It does not matter."

"No, thank you." Moshe leaned against the counter. "I will stand."

"As you will have it."

Moshe looked at the heavy leather pouch the young man held tightly in his hands. "You know our names, but I don't believe you mentioned yours?"

"A thousand pardons, Professor Doctor," he bowed slightly. "I am Ral Irman. Forgive my rudeness; you see, one cannot be too careful. I was told of what you look like and was not expecting one dressed as you. Also, I was expecting only one—" he nodded toward Howard—"not two such distinguished persons such as Professor Moniger."

Moshe frowned and waved his hand toward the leather pouch. "We have come a long way and have a long way yet to go. What is it Moddy wanted us to see?"

Ral Irman arched his eyebrows and pursed his lips. "Ah, yes." He laid the pouch on the countertop, then swept back the broken pottery with his arm. "The scrolls," he said.

Howard leaned forward, his eyes intent on the cracked leather of the pouch. Moshe fought the urge to tear the thing from the spider-like hands of Moddy's nephew. "Yes," Moshe said quietly, "the scrolls."

The mouth of Ral Irman turned slightly upward as though he enjoyed the tension he had engendered in the two men. Slowly he untied the pouch, his eyes never leaving Moshe. His hand seemed to crawl into the opening and his eyes widened as he grasped something and pulled it out.

Moshe's heart fell. There before him was a shriveled brown roll about the size and shape of a newspaper. It had the appearance of tree bark, and time had welded its folds together.

338

Ral Irman's smile faded. "You are not pleased, Professor Doctor?"

Moshe and Howard leaned over the scroll, examining it in the dim light. Tar and small bits of fabric clung to it.

"It's never been opened," Howard said.

"And it will not be without special equipment," Moshe returned.

"We have others." Ral Irman upended the pouch, dumping its contents carelessly onto the counter. Five more crumbling scrolls tumbled out as Moshe snapped at the young man in irritation.

"You idiot! Didn't your uncle tell you these are fragile!"

"A thousand pardons, then," he pouted, stepping back near the shaky shelf of clay jars behind him.

Howard and Moshe pored over the pile of six ancient cylinders, reverently and carefully placing them in a row. One appeared to be made of papyrus, and another, sealed tight, was definitely copper. "We don't dare attempt to examine them in these conditions," Howard said. Then he looked up at the brooding face of Ral Irman. "Where is the other scroll?" he asked, certain that Ellie's Isaiah scroll was not among the row of fragile items before him.

"The other?" Ral Irman glanced at him doubtfully. "I have been instructed first by my uncle to settle a price on these six before you."

"And what is his price?"

"A thousand pounds. Cash. Tonight."

Moshe peered at the young man. "A thousand, you say?"

"For the six. Together."

"And what of the seventh? We want to see it before we settle any price on these six," Moshe insisted.

Without a word, Ral Irman slipped behind the curtain again. After what seemed like several minutes, he returned carrying another cylinder, this time carefully wrapped in a soft cotton fabric. Moshe felt his heart pounding wildly in his throat. *The scroll of Isaiah,* he thought, *perfect and unchanged after two thousand years. The Word of God as it existed in the day of Christ!* Its prophecies concerning the return of Israel and the coming of the Messiah had remained unchanged over two thousand years of the Diaspora.

"Let me see it," Moshe demanded, unable to conceal the emotion in his voice.

"I am instructed to see your money first," Ral Irman taunted, holding the precious cargo tighter to him.

"For goodness' sakes, Moshe," Howard pleaded, "pay him for the other six." He began to carefully replace them in the pouch, making room for the scroll on the countertop as Moshe dug into his pocket and pulled out a wallet containing more than enough to pay for the six. He counted out ten 100-pound notes, watching as Ral Irman's eyes suddenly danced to life.

"All right," Moshe said. "One thousand pounds. Now let us see the seventh scroll."

Ral Irman grabbed the bills from the counter and dropped the final scroll before them. His eyes gleamed with greed, but Moshe and Howard did not notice. Carefully, gently, they unwrapped the covering of the scroll. Howard drew a deep, astonished breath, feeling tears come to his eyes as he gazed at the warm, rich texture of the scroll. The edges were crumbling, but unlike the others, it unrolled easily with a mere touch of Moshe's index finger, its perfect, precise lettering revealing the ninth chapter of the book of Isaiah. Moshe cleared his throat and read the words, caressing them with his eyes, lifting them high with his voice.

"For unto us a child is born, unto us a son is given: and the government shall be upon his shoulders: and his name shall be called Wonderful, Counsellor, The Mighty God, The everlasting Father, The Prince of Peace.

"Of the increase of His government and peace there will be no end . . ."

When he had finished, Moshe looked at Howard and smiled. "We have found it together, my friend." Howard nodded, emotion cutting off his ability to speak. Moshe felt startled at the greasy voice of Ral Irman.

"You learned doctors are pleased with our little gem? We do not doubt, seeing you read it, that it is indeed genuine and valuable perhaps?"

"How much have you been instructed to ask for this scroll?" Moshe resumed his businesslike posture.

"This scroll is not for sale," Ral Irman smiled cruelly.

Moshe lifted his chin, feeling a rush of anger at this sleazy little insect. "Why not?" he demanded brusquely.

"Because," the voice became arrogant, "it belongs to another."

"Who?" Moshe's voice became louder and he stepped menacingly toward Ral Irman, whose smile faded instantly.

From behind him, the curtain rustled, then parted. Moshe's eyes fell first on the gleaming blue barrel of a revolver extended by a black-gloved hand over the shoulder of Ral Irman. Framed by the curtain, a cruel face smiled a gap-toothed smile. "It belongs to Haj Amin, the Grand Mufti of Jerusalem," said the sinister voice of Hassan.

Moshe stepped backward as though he had been struck. Howard sat frozen in the realization that this had all been set up as a trap.

"Hassan!" Moshe said, spitting out the hated name like poison.

"And so we meet again, brother of my friend." Hassan shoved Ral Irman to the side, leaving him to scramble into a stack of books.

"You are no man's friend, Hassan," Moshe returned.

"Perhaps not. But it is not wise to hurl insults at the one who holds the gun."

"What have you done with Moddy?" Moshe demanded.

Hassan's eyes narrowed in cruel amusement. "Did you not hear? His heart." He jerked his head toward the back room. "Messy business, these weak hearts." Hassan stepped forward as Ram Kadar parted the curtains behind him and entered the room.

"I have not had the pleasure," Kadar sneered toward Moshe.

"This is the brother of your dead wife's lover, Kadar."

Kadar shot him an angry glance, silencing Hassan momentarily. "You are the Zionist, Moshe Sachar, are you not?" His hand rose, also revealing a revolver.

Moshe glanced at the gun. "And what have you done with the Bedouins?" he asked. "Are they dead, too?"

"Oh, no," Hassan said. "They were most happy to assist us in our little party tonight. Most happy to leave the scrolls and scurry back to their tents. But you shall not worry. These scrolls will find their way into the hand of a Jew. The chief rabbi of the Old City has purchased them."

"And what was the price?"

Hassan smiled, delaying the agony of Moshe's question as long as possible. "Information, my dear Moshe. And the blood of your pitiful little band of Haganah soldiers behind the walls of the Old City."

Moshe glanced quickly at Howard; the realization that Akiva had sold out was clear on his face. "I see. Men for the scrolls. So the Mufti has a trained ape inside the Jewish Quarter as well as out."

Hassan lunged forward, angrily slamming the barrel of his gun across Moshe's cheek. Moshe fell hard against the wall, barely missing Moddy's clay water pots that stood stacked precariously all the way to the ceiling. Howard jumped to his feet and rushed toward a dazed Moshe, then was stopped abruptly by the thrust of Kadar's pistol barrel in his middle.

"And who are you, little man?" Kadar asked contemptuously. Howard did not answer, instead meeting his gaze defiantly. "It does not matter," Kadar growled. "You are just as dead without a name."

Ral Irman snickered as Moshe moaned and tried to sit up. Kadar twisted Howard's arm hard behind his back, then shoved him down beside Moshe. "Get on your knees. Kneel, I say. Next to this vermin Jew."

Howard knelt beside Moshe, glancing around the room. *My last sight will be ancient clay pots and artifacts in such disarray as to scare the life out of any archaeologist,* he thought with grim amusement. *A fitting end for one in my profession.* He heard Hassan cock his gun and looked into the mouth of the barrel, strangely at peace.

"Wait!" shouted Ral Irman, rushing forward. "Do not shoot them yet. Their pockets are filled with hundred-pound notes, and you will make them bloody!" he whined. "You promised me their money for my part. You promised!"

"You!" Hassan snapped at Howard. "Empty your pockets. Slowly." Howard emptied his pockets, reaching beneath his robes and pulling out his wallet which he tossed on the floor.

"Now his." Hassan pointed the gun at Moshe who shook his head, attempting to clear his mind as Howard reached toward him.

Howard caught his eyes and held them. They were full of message; full of meaning. Howard frowned and lifted Moshe's robe. Moshe glanced toward the stacks of pots, then quickly closed his eyes again. Howard reached for Moshe's wallet, feeling a cold rush of adrenaline as his hand brushed the hard steel of the .38.

"No tricks. You are a dead man anyway," Kadar warned. "Bring your hand out slowly." Howard felt the presence of the two guns trained on him. He could never outshoot them both. His hand tightened around the pistol grip. He glanced quickly at the jars, suddenly knowing what he must do. "I have it here," he said. Then, he pointed the revolver through the cloth of Moshe's robe and squeezed the trigger. The bullet exploded through the cloth and into the bottom row of jars, sending shards of clay into every corner of the shop. The wall of teetering jars crashed down upon the startled heads of Hassan and Kadar and Ral Irman. Hassan shrieked and fired his gun as the avalanche of pottery caused a chain reaction of jars falling from the walls behind them. Moshe cried out and gripped his upper arm as Hassan's bullet slammed into him, splintering the bone and passing through the other side. Howard jerked him to his feet and, supporting him, half dragged him over the pieces of jars that littered the floor. He grabbed the leather pouch and the scroll of Isaiah as he hurried through the curtains and into the back room where a stairway led down to the street. There on the floor was Moddy, soaked in his own blood, his gentle brown eyes gazing in sightless horror. It would be only seconds, Howard knew, before the murderers would recover and pursue them.

"Come on, Moshe!" he cried. "Get your feet under you, boy! I can't carry you!" Howard threw the back door wide and dragged him out.

In monumental effort, Moshe rose and leaned on Howard, willing his legs to move in spite of the wound he suffered. The fresh cold air helped bring him to his senses, and Howard guided him quickly down the steep stairway and onto the street below. He glanced up as Hassan, framed in the doorway, aimed and shot at them. The bullet ricocheted off the cobblestones only inches from his feet. Howard raised Moshe's gun and without bother to aim, he shot back, causing Hassan to dive back into the shop for cover.

"Come on, Moshe! We've bought some time at least!"

32   Sanctuary

Ellie clutched the frayed rope around Shaul's neck tightly. He pulled her through the dark streets like a hound on a hunt. Often the dog's path took Ellie beneath low overhangs and around pails of overflowing garbage in tiny alleys, but Ellie had to give him credit; he seemed to be going *somewhere*.

"Are you sure this is out, dog?" she muttered breathlessly, uncertain that she should have trusted her safety to a shaggy four-legged beast.

"Shaul will take you home," Yacov had guaranteed. "But you must not let go of the rope or he will be home and you will be where you wish you were not." Then the boy had whispered some magic words to Shaul, and off they had gone.

Right now, as they squeezed through an alley, upsetting stinking garbage cans that rolled and clattered after them, she was tempted to let go and follow her own nose to cleaner air. But she hung on, scrambling up the steps in the final ascent to Mendelbaum Gate. Up ahead the small group of Hassidic guards lounged indolently on the sandbags.

"Shalom!" Ellie called as Shaul dragged her toward their outpost.

"Halt!" cried the same young man whom Yacov had greeted by name. The men jumped to attention and blocked their path. "You cannot go from here. You must go back," he instructed.

Shaul growled and the hair on his ruff bristled as he and Ellie stood before the men. "Easy." Ellie stroked his head. "I have to get to the New City," she explained as Shaul growled once again and the four men stepped back a pace.

They spoke rapidly to one another in a language Ellie did not recognize, then directed their attention once again to her. "Rebbe Akiva and a small group of rabbis have gone to pray at the Wailing Wall this night, as they have always done on Hanukkah. They have not returned, and we fear for their safety. Surely the Arabs have taken them, and you, a woman, may not safely pass into the streets beyond this point," a man explained.

344

"Have you sent word to the British soldiers at Zion Gate?" she asked.

The oldest guard laughed bitterly. "And what shall they do? Arrest us for standing guard, that is all."

"I've got to get out to the New City!" Ellie insisted, staring past them into the dark corridors of the sector beyond.

"Madame," said another in a thick French accent. "You do not understand . . ."

"I understand perfectly. A man's life is at stake; you may be too proud to ask for help, but I am not."

The sound of shuffling feet beyond the barricade stopped her mid-sentence. The guards whirled around and took their positions behind the barricade.

"Halt!" cried one in a shaky voice. "Who goes there!"

From the dark street beyond, vague shadows moved toward them. Ellie pushed Shaul's rump into a sitting position and sat down on the cobblestones beside him.

"Who goes there!" a guard demanded once again.

The older man had drawn a revolver from between two sandbags, and the barrel gleamed in the starlight.

"Rabbi Akiva," came the solemn reply.

A cheer went up among the little band, and they scrambled to remove the barrier and open the passage for the stout bear of a rabbi and his group of four others.

"Welcome, Rabbi!" they cried. "We feared for your safety when you did not return."

"When will you learn?" Akiva answered harshly. "This barrier is unnecessary. Our friends mean us no harm. The Haganah and the Zionist are the enemy of our peace in the Old City."

"Were you not stopped by the Arabs?"

"Though the other rabbis refuse to join us, we are living proof that there is yet goodwill. There is no need for all of this—" he gestured toward the barricade angrily. His hands fell to his side as he saw Ellie still sitting near the edge of the barricade. "And what is this?" he sneered. "Have you taken all your photographs?" He eyed her clothing carefully, noting that she seemed much thinner than during their first meeting of the day. "You! You are a journalist, you say! Well, take a photograph of this, for we are the only sane men left in Jewish Palestine!" He drew himself up to his full height, and glowered down at her.

"Rabbi Lebowitz is very ill. He needs an ambulance," Ellie

explained softly. "Do you think there is a way—"

"Rabbi Lebowitz!" he spat the name. "A traitor. God's punishment is just." His eyes narrowed and he smiled at Ellie. "But go, child. You see, we have walked the streets of the Arab Quarter and no harm has come to us. Go, if you must."

Ellie stared up at him, drawing a breath as if to speak; then she looked at the guards who stood shamefaced against the barricade.

"Come on, Shaul," she said to the dog. She passed out of the safety of the compound and into the no-man's-land of the street beyond.

The sound of Shaul's feet scrabbling over the stones mingled with her heavy breathing; there was no other sound along the empty corridor. Darkness pressed heavily against her mind and she imagined a face in every shadow, a hand reaching out from every alleyway. Her hands grew clammy, and a cold knot formed in the pit of her stomach. She suddenly wished she had taken the time to find a bathroom before she left the safety of the Old City. "You're scared, Ellie old girl," she said to herself. "Still watching, God?"

Suddenly, as they turned a corner, Shaul stopped in his tracks, sending Ellie tumbling over the top of him onto the pavement. She cried out and groped for the end of the rope. Shaul growled, then backed a step; Ellie caught her breath and shivered in her sweat-soaked blouse. "What is it?" she whispered to the dog. She breathed unevenly, caught in a net of fear. She grabbed the rope and pulled the dog tightly to where she sat, wrapping her arms around his neck. She whirled around as the sound of footsteps closed in behind her, then, twenty feet from her in the other direction, a shadowy figure stepped from between two deserted buildings. Three more men followed behind him, their robes billowing, ghostlike, flapping in the wind. Ellie cried out and struggled to scramble to her feet. She searched for a way of escape, but both routes were cut off. She backed up until she slammed against a wall, dropping Shaul's rope. The big dog barked, then snarled and charged away from her, passing through the legs of the startled Arabs as they closed the circle around Ellie. "Shaul!" she cried. "Come back!"

One of the Arabs laughed a short, brutal laugh. "We have been searching for you, Haganah woman," he said. "Your dog will not save you."

"No, you see, you've made a mistake." Ellie held her camera out. "I'm a news photographer, you see." She said in a panicked rush.

"So this is the picture-taker," a voice whined from beneath the checkered keffiyah on her right. She could not see their faces, only dark shadows framed by the light head coverings. There were eight men pushing nearer to her.

"Yes. For *Life* magazine."

"Ah, a woman journalist." The voice sounded with a crisp British accent.

"You are the one we have been looking for." Others nodded and an argument broke out as one of the men reached out and laughed as he brushed her neck with his fingertips. "Where are the others, Haganah woman?" a voice demanded.

"I don't know what you are talking about." Ellie tried to sound calm and defiant. "I am an American citizen, and I demand that you—"

A white-clad figure grasped her at the throat and pushed his body hard against hers. "You demand nothing, woman!" he snarled, his hot breath filling her nostrils.

"Let me go!" She struggled against him.

"We shall let you go, before Haj Amin. But first we shall have our way with you, Haganah woman!" His hand wandered over her body and she felt as though she would be sick.

"Please," she choked.

"Break the door down!" the man shouted. A rattle of gunfire sounded as the lock was blown from the door of a deserted house. Ellie screamed as two men dragged her toward the darkness of the doorway. Hands reached out, touching her, and she kicked out against them.

"Let me go!" she cried.

Someone lit a lamp which flickered dimly on a rough wooden table. They tore at her clothes and slammed her roughly onto the floor; then the jeering, shouting men swarmed around her.

"God! Help me!" she screamed as the leering face of a bearded Arab came close to hers.

Suddenly the burst of sten gun fire exploded from the doorway. Bullets crashed into the ceiling above them, sending plaster cascading down on Ellie and the men. The Arabs leaped up and whirled around. The laughing stopped, and instantly silence fell. Ellie closed her eyes as sobs wracked her body. Then she heard the low growl of Shaul. From the door came the heavy accented voice of Captain Luke Thomas.

"Having a bit of fun, here, are you, lads?" he asked.

Ellie opened her eyes as the Arabs backed away from her, their eyes riveted on Luke's sten gun.

"She is Haganah!" shouted a young Arab man. "She smuggles weapons into the Jews. We are told this. Arrest her!"

"You ignorant scum," said the captain angrily. "I ought to blow your heads off and leave you for the buzzards. Hanging is too good for you." Four more English soldiers filed in past him. "Handcuff them. Tightly," he demanded. "Get against the wall!" he shouted.

Shaul padded quickly to Ellie's side and licked her tears, nosing her on the cheek. She wrapped her arms around him, still too shaky to stand. "You," she sobbed. "Good dog."

The tall, lean captain bent low over where she lay. "Are you all right, Miss Warne?" he asked gently.

Ellie wiped her face with the back of her hand. "I think so. Just scared." She tried to smile.

He handed her a handkerchief and she blew her nose. "So was I, a bit." He took off his coat and wrapped it around her shoulders, covering her torn clothing. Then he helped her to stand and led her back out to the darkness of the street. "Keep your guns to their heads," he instructed his men. "And if they give you any trouble, leave their brains for the Mufti to clean up."

"How did you find me?" Ellie asked, leaning against the building.

"We have been watching for you. When the animal came out barking like a mad dog, I figured something was up. You are not more than fifty yards from the gate. We heard the gunfire, then saw the light."

Ellie nodded. "Thank you."

"Where are the others, miss?"

"Yacov's grandfather became very ill. They stayed behind."

"Rabbi Lebowitz?" Concern etched his voice.

"Yes. Heart attack, I guess. I came out to get an ambulance."

"Dear God," he clicked his tongue. "He is a grand old man; that was very brave of you."

"There has to be something we can do." She felt as though

348

she might cry again; and again, the captain pulled his hand-kerchief from his pocket.

"Come on." He put his arm around her shoulders and led her toward Zion Gate. "We must get you home. I'll see what can be done about the rabbi."

"Wait a minute," Ellie hesitated. "My camera is around here someplace."

She and Luke scanned the cobblestones, finally retrieving the smashed camera. Luke handed it to her, its film dangling from the cracked case.

"It seems a bit the worse for wear," he said.

"This is the second camera I've lost. You know, pretty soon these guys are going to make me mad."

———————

It had begun to get cold again. Steam from David's breath clouded the edges of the car windows. For what seemed like the hundredth time, David pulled up his sleeve and looked at his watch. It was nearly nine o'clock. He smiled ruefully, feeling foolish for having waited like a lovesick adolescent for two and a half hours. They weren't coming. They had made other plans. Maybe somebody had left a note for him at the desk of the ho-tel. He hadn't checked, after all.

He gathered the packages together and stepped out into the chilled night air. Tucking the packages into his coat, he climbed over the stone fence and into the narrow stone-paved side yard that led to the back of the house. He laid the packages on the back doorstep and then made his way to the front of the house. Unzipping a pocket in his flight jacket, David pulled out a small notebook and pencil. "Els," he scrawled. "Sorry I missed you. Packages are around back. Merry Christmas. David." He slipped the note between the door and the doorjamb and then, feeling the weight of lonely disappointment, climbed back into the car. David sat for five minutes longer, hoping to see the lights of Howard's Plymouth. He imagined them arriving and Ellie throw-ing her arms around him in delight that he had waited. "We had a flat. We ran out of gas. We got caught in a traffic jam," she would explain apologetically. Then they would all go to the King David and have dinner after all. It was Christmas Eve, and his excitement had been shot down in flames. He glanced at his watch again, then started the car with a roar and squealed away, leaving a strip of rubber on the pavement in front of the house. Slamming his hand on the steering wheel, David headed back to the Atlantic Hotel, certain that this was all his fault. Certainly there had been a note or a phone call. He would check at the desk; then find Ellie. Better late than never.

The car screeched to a halt in front of the Atlantic. David bounded from the car and through the revolving door into the nearly deserted lobby. He strode to the desk and rang the bell impatiently.

"Yes, sir?" asked a sullen desk clerk.

"David Meyer. Any messages for me?"

The clerk eyed him for a moment. "Room number?"

"349."

The clerk shuffled to the mail rack, scanning the numbers on the boxes myopically. David had already seen that the box to his room was empty.

"No messages."

"Maybe a phone call?"

The clerk shrugged. "Not that I know of."

"Well, check!" David snapped.

The clerk stuck out his lower lip and grudgingly shuffled through a slim stack of scribbled phone messages. He slapped them down on the desk and smiled patronizingly. "No messages," he said with satisfaction.

David pursed his lips and frowned. Then he looked back at the man. "Okay. Thanks anyway." He turned away, feeling more alone than he had ever felt. Stepping out onto the crowded street once again, he stared through the window of the Atara Cafe. *By now the guys will be good and drunk*, he thought. *And every one of them will ask about my hot date with Ellie.* He looked down at the sidewalk, trying to muster the bravado he would need to fend off their questions. His rumbling stomach reminded him that he had not eaten since a light breakfast in Tel Aviv that morning. He rubbed his hand through his hair with a sigh, then climbed back into the car, unable to face his friends at the Atara. *If Michael is right and the one thing I have going for me is my ego,* David thought, *my ego just crashed and burned.* Ellie had simply not wanted to see him, he reasoned. When her uncle had told her he was coming, she had demanded that they move the celebration somewhere else.

He drove toward the massive citadel of the King David Hotel, determined at least to have a good meal; half-hoping that Ellie would be there so that he could saunter coolly by her table and tell her how sorry he was that he had forgotten the invitation. The red-coated valet opened the car door as he pulled up in front of the main building. David dropped the keys into his hand.

"Are they still serving dinner in there?" David asked.

"Until ten o'clock, sir."

"Thanks." David tipped him without looking at the denomination of the bill.

"Thank you, sir!" exclaimed the astonished valet. "And a very Merry Christmas to you!"

Blood from Moshe's wound marked an easy trail down the cobbled alleyways of Bethlehem. Howard glanced back, watching as a swinging lantern dipped low to the cobblestones. Hassan and Kadar were moving slowly; he and Moshe had some advantage in that.

Moshe's steps faltered and he leaned heavily against Howard. "Go without me," Moshe breathed. "Leave me the gun and go."

"You're bleeding heavily, my friend." Howard propped him against the wall of a building and pulled the headband from his keffiyah. Moshe stifled a cry as Howard bound the wound tightly. "Just a little further, Moshe. We'll see if the little mule is still there." Then he whispered, "Please, God."

Moshe wrapped his good arm around Howard's shoulders and they started out again, staggering down the alley like two drunken buddies out for the night. Blood still dripped from Moshe's fingertips; his arm hung uselessly at his side. He stumbled again, nearly unconscious from loss of blood.

"We're going to make it, Moshe," Howard prompted. "Come on, boy."

Moshe smiled at him in drunken amazement. "Didn't know you had it in you."

"I haven't always been fifty years old, you know. This isn't half as bad as Verdun in the first war. There it was all hand-to-hand." He tried to keep a steady stream of quiet conversation going, asking questions of Moshe in hopes that he could retain consciousness.

351

At last they rounded a corner and bumped directly into the rump of the little donkey. "Thank God," Howard sighed, lifting Moshe onto her back and quickly untying her rope. Behind them, Howard heard the voice of Hassan as he discovered the trail of Moshe's blood that led down the alley. "Hold on!" Howard cried to Moshe, clicking the little beast into a trot down the slippery incline that led to the main thoroughfare of the city.

The bells now tolled through silent and empty streets. A few pilgrims slept around fires in the souks, but none looked up as Howard jogged past them, the donkey's hooves clip-clopping against the stones. He looked back over his shoulder just in time to see the figures of Hassan and Kadar run to the center of the street and look both directions. Quickly, Howard guided the donkey into the shadows and briefly closed his eyes in weariness. Moshe leaned forward, lying down on the donkey's neck. Hassan motioned to Kadar, who ran in the direction opposite them while Hassan strode purposefully toward them. Hassan paused briefly at every fire and in every shadow to search the faces of those who slept peacefully. With a sweaty palm, Howard gripped the handle of the revolver. He looked up at the edifice in whose shadow he stood. Tall spires rose into the night skies. Hugging the rough stone of the church building, he softly urged the donkey to follow him. "Moshe," he whispered, "are you still with me, boy?"

"Uh," Moshe groaned.

Suddenly, Howard bumped into a man, an ancient Arab, smiling toothlessly from beneath his checkered keffiyah. He lifted his chin and stared at Howard; then he looked past them at the rapidly approaching figure of Hassan.

"Come," he demanded. "You are under my protection." He turned on his heel and scuffed slowly ahead of Howard and Moshe, rounding the corner to the back of the church. "Come," he said to Howard again, who was simply too startled to resist. The old man led the way to a small alcove in the side of the building and, with a click, turned the latch. "Enter." He stood aside.

"The donkey—" Howard protested.

"I will hold her. Go." Howard pulled Moshe from the donkey's back as the sound of Hassan's running footsteps neared the corner of the building. He dragged the now-unconscious Moshe through the small, nearly hidden door, and the old man pulled it shut behind him. The room they had entered was pitch black, and the smell was dank and musty. Howard squatted on the floor, cradling Moshe in his lap. He listened as the sound of Hassan's footsteps approached nearer and nearer, echoing in the sleeping streets. He could scarcely breathe, and as Moshe moaned, Howard covered his friend's mouth with his hand. The footsteps stopped at the door, and the latch rattled violently as Hassan tried to force the lock. He cursed loudly in Arabic, then ran on down the street, the sound of his footsteps diminishing in the distance.

Exhausted, Howard closed his eyes, feeling weariness overtake him. His head nodded low, his chin touching his chest as he fell almost instantly asleep.

———

Ellie climbed stiffly from Luke's armored car. He waited for Shaul to jump out behind her, then smiled grimly and shut the door.

"I think, miss, perhaps it would be wise if I checked the house for you, since your uncle is away and you are alone."

"Really, I'm okay. I wish you would let me go with you to Hadassah to get the ambulance."

"I should think you have seen enough front-line action for tonight." He took her key and climbed the steps two at a time. Then he pulled David's note from the door and handed it to her as she huddled against the stair railing.

Ellie scanned the note and smiled. "David. Dear David," she said softly.

"Important, miss?" asked Luke, throwing the door wide and stepping aside for her.

"Yes," she answered. "I had forgotten that it was Christmas."

"And so it is. And may God bless you." He tipped his hat.

Shaul ran into the house ahead of her and she followed. "He already has," she returned. "Merry Christmas, Captain."

"The same to you." He climbed into the armored car and roared off toward Mount Scopus and Hadassah.

Ellie shut the door, careful to bolt all the locks. Then she switched on every light she passed on her way toward the back porch. She had had enough of shadows for one night. Shaul plopped down in the kitchen in front of the stove and gazed up at her with forlorn eyes as she put the kettle on, then unbolted the back door and gathered in the gifts that David had left, then bolted the door again. She put them on the table, smiling as she wondered how he had spent his night. In spite of her weariness she found herself remembering Christmas Eve the year before, walking along the boardwalk with waves crashing against the shore.

Pulling up a chair, she sat in front of the packages and, chin in hand, read the labels, laughing out loud when she read the one to Shaul. The dog raised his head in response to his name. She pitched the roll of salami to him; he caught it in his mouth with very little effort and chewed away at it as Ellie tore the white envelope from her package and read the note that David had written to her.

Merry Christmas, my darling Els,
As I write this my feet are firmly on the ground. I can only say that over the last few weeks, I have come to see how very right you were about my life. I have lived only for myself; only loved for my own benefit, never seeing who you really are. Maybe these words come too late and you have closed the door to me. I hope not. We have shared so much and I have found a new love for you as I have come to understand and respect the woman you have become. I am also finding a purpose in my life, although I still have a long way to go. Regardless of what the future holds, I am certain of one thing: I will always love you. David.

Ellie read the letter again and again until her eyes blurred with exhaustion. Gently she laid his letter on the table before her. She was still so very angry at him, yet she knew she loved him. For the first time she bowed her head and prayed for him and for herself, that an answer would be clear in her heart. She had been torn for so long between him and Moshe. Now, she knew that perhaps Moshe was falling in love with someone else in spite of himself, and she did not want to make any decisions based on the fact that she might have to be alone.

She carefully unwrapped the big box in front of her, trying not to tear the paper. She lifted the lid of the box and pulled the wadded newspaper out from around the present. She gasped as the glistening black body of a new Leica was revealed before her. Gently she lifted it from the box and cradled it on her lap. A note dangled from the lens: "For the woman who etched the face of God's Chosen on the hearts of the world. I am proud of you. David."

"Merry Christmas, David," she sighed. "Thank you." Then she turned off the stove and switched off the light, too tired for tea after all.

33   The Tomb

Howard opened his eyes as the door popped open and slowly swung on its creaking hinges. He scrambled for the revolver, feeling beads of perspiration form on his forehead as he waited for the face of Hassan to peer in the door. It was still dark outside, but he could make out the soft gray shadow of the donkey outside the door. After a moment he laid Moshe on the stone floor and stood to peer out the door. The street was deserted. Even the old man had gone, leaving the little donkey loose on the end of her rope.

Howard had no way of knowing how long he had slept, but he felt refreshed. He touched his wrist for the watch that he had left at home, wishing he had an idea of what time it was.

He returned to where Moshe lay and felt the pulse in his neck. His heart was still strong. "Moshe," he called. "Moshe," he said again.

"Where am I?" Moshe moaned softly.

"In church, boy. Help me. Get up. We've got to get these scrolls back to Jerusalem. We've got to warn your men about the Rabbi Akiva. And we've got to get you to a safe hospital."

Moshe struggled to sit up, wincing with pain. His arm throbbed in agony as he leaned on Howard, and together they left their hiding place. Howard boosted Moshe up, then clucked the donkey into motion, sighing as they passed from the confines of the town and back along the road that he hoped would take them to Jerusalem—or at the very least, into the refuge of Mar Elyas Monastery—before daylight.

Dressed in the uniform of a British officer, Gerhardt looked strangely out of place as he knelt in prayer beside Haj Amin in his private mosque on the grounds of the Dome of the Rock. Haj Amin lifted his face from the darkness of the eastern sky and turned to Gerhardt.

"We have no doubts about the success of your mission," he said serenely.

"I am most honored that you would rise up so early to pray in my behalf." Gerhardt washed his hands in the bowl set before him.

"It is never too early to beseech Allah, the ever-merciful Lord of the Universe, on behalf of our people here in Palestine." Haj Amin flicked the water from his fingers, then dried them on a towel extended by his servant. He rose slowly as Gerhardt waited respectfully, then stood.

"And what is the word from Hassan and Kadar?" Gerhardt asked.

The Mufti waved his hand, dismissing his servant. He smiled reluctantly. "Alas, I fear Hassan is somewhat of a bungler. Our quarry escaped. Mortally wounded, so says Hassan. He has members of the Jihad Moqhades fanning the countryside at this very moment. They will be found," he said assuringly. He put his slender hand on Gerhardt's back. "Ah, but *you* are our general, are you not? And what you do this morning shall shake the foundations of the world."

"Let us hope that the Jews will see their folly and give up."

They walked toward the luxurious residence of Haj Amin. "And if they do not, it will make little difference. What was that little song the Führer used to sing? 'Crush the skulls of the Jewish pack and the future, it is ours and won.' Eh?"

Stars still glistened brightly in the sky and Gerhardt looked upward. "Those were good times," he sighed.

"And these will be better, you shall see. Are you sure you have not time for coffee?"

"I am indeed honored. But the trucks are waiting. Soon it will be daylight."

Haj Amin nodded with understanding. "This is only the beginning for us, Gerhardt. Do well and there is no end to the heights you may scale."

———

Moshe leaned heavily on Howard as the little donkey plodded past the tomb of Rachel. They had gone nearly a mile, and the towers of Mar Elyas Monastery loomed beyond a sharp bend in the road. Small lights seemed to dance across the hillsides surrounding them, and a large bonfire blocked the road a quarter mile ahead as they rounded the outcropping of limestone cliffs just before the monastery.

"Hassan didn't waste any time," Howard said aloud.

Moshe raised his head and glanced to the east. "Soon it will be dawn, and we are finished."

The first light of day outlined the jagged black hills with a thin line. Hassan had obviously set his trap very well. He had gone ahead to the Arab stronghold of Talpiyoth where young Jihad Moqhades had flocked joyfully to the first call of Haj Amin. They were strong and tough and knew every inch of this territory. "You've got the advantage of age," Howard muttered to himself. "You old fool, after twenty-eight years of rooting around for old pots, you think they know this place better than you?"

"What are you saying?" Moshe asked weakly.

"Nothing," he answered. "Lean on me." They followed the road for a few more yards, Howard frowning grimly at the lights ahead. He turned and looked behind them. A pair of headlights swept toward them. "We've got to get off the main highway, Moshe. Can you stand the jolting?"

"Yes," Moshe said, wincing as Howard led the donkey down an incline and into a ditch.

Howard laid the scrolls on the ground and quickly helped Moshe slide from the donkey. "Get down, close to the bank," Howard instructed. Then he turned the head of the animal away from the on-coming car so that her eyes would not reflect the headlights. He lay down flat behind her and waited, hardly daring to breathe as the engine shifted into second gear to begin the long pull up the road to the waiting group of Jihad Moqhades. For a moment the lights shown on the bank behind them, and Howard closed his eyes and prayed as shadows danced around him. Then the red glow of the taillights diminished in a swirling cloud of dust, the engine whining up the slope.

Howard stood and looped the lead rope around the branch of a shrub. He knelt beside Moshe. "Are you still with me, boy?" he asked.

"I can go no farther," Moshe replied haltingly.

"Of course you can." Howard rubbed his hand over his mouth and swallowed the fear that pushed against his own throat. "You just feel like you can't." He looked around wildly, noticing the glimmer of three more torches bobbing toward them. One extended far over the edge of the bank, illuminating the rocks and brush just one hundred yards from where they lay. His mouth went dry as he heard the cry:

"Yehudah! Yehud!"

Moshe lay with his head against the dirt bank. His face was as white as the stones in the darkness. "Please go, Howard. Take the scrolls."

Howard wrapped Moshe's arm around his shoulder, then pulled him to his feet. "Did I ever tell you about the time in the Argonne?" he panted. "The Germans were lobbing gas into the trenches, and even the rats were running." He bent down and slung the scrolls over his other shoulder. "Lost my gas mask. Thought I was a goner," he whispered, more to himself than Moshe. "Thought I'd never be that scared again." He propped Moshe against the donkey, then pushed him across her back. Moshe cried out once and then was silent. Howard felt him go limp, thankful that he was at least no longer conscious of the pain. The torches seemed to respond to the sound, bobbing more rapidly toward them.

"Yehudah!"

Howard scrambled over a pile of rubble and headed due east where the crack of daylight was growing ever wider. The sure-footed little beast followed him through the shrubs and up over a small hillside. Howard glanced around him. In five more minutes they would be an easy target. He looked to the north to where the monastery loomed, then back toward Bethlehem. Then he slapped his forehead at his own stupidity. He stood not more than twenty-five yards from the very archaeological dig he had worked at only three months before. Quickly he slid Moshe over his own shoulder, astonished at how light he felt. He removed the halter from the donkey and whipped her into a frenzied gallop toward the approaching men. He turned and scrambled as quickly as he could, trying not to stumble over rocks and bushes as he made his way to a rock wall fifteen feet high.

"Somewhere along here—" He picked his way along the wall, touching its rough surface for support. He searched the bottom edge of the wall for a small opening, two feet square, that led to a first-century tomb chamber beneath the ground. At the time, members of the crew, including Moshe, had suggested they leave it at least partially concealed beneath the shrubs so that artifact seekers and robbers would not plunder its contents. Howard stumbled onto a large pile of rocks and rubble. He had gone the wrong direction. Twenty yards, maybe more.

He glanced anxiously toward the torches, now directly across from him, gathered in a circle in the road. He turned and scrambled back to the north along the wall, clutching Moshe and the scrolls as he counted his footsteps back from the rubble heap. "Fifteen, sixteen." He glanced anxiously toward the sun, praying that he would find their refuge before daylight slammed into the darkness and left them as exposed targets lined up against the wall for the firing squad. "Twenty-four, twenty-five, twenty-six. You've missed it." He turned and slowly retraced the last six steps, finally falling to his knees and laying Moshe down, feeling beneath the brush for the opening. "*God, God. Where is it, God?* He reached out and suddenly put his hand into a hole only inches from where he had walked. He dropped the scrolls into it with a thud, then dragged Moshe feet first until his legs dangled in the hole from the knees down.

"I'm going down first," he whispered. "Then I'll pull you in." Moshe moaned in response. Howard scrambled over his body, then dropped into the antechamber of the tomb as the first shaft of light split the night like an explosion. He grabbed Moshe and pulled with all his might as daylight raced across the land and suddenly beamed into the shaft where they tumbled to the soft earth.

David rubbed his aching head and stared up at the fogged windows of the car. The first light of morning filtered in, accompanied by the steady roar of heavy trucks. "Where am I?" he said aloud, sitting up and feeling the clout of last night's Scotch. Rubbing a small round peephole on the window, David peered out as an armored car moaned past, followed by two huge British army cargo trucks. David tried to start the car, but it responded with a solitary click every time he turned the key. He had left the lights on last night. The battery was dead. He wiped the windshield with his sleeve, laughing at himself as he recognized the familiar shops of Ben Yehuda and the still blinking neon sign of the Atlantic Hotel three blocks away. The army trucks slowed to a halt in front of the hotel; gears shifting lower and engines sputtering to a stop. David frowned and squinted. "What are they doing?" he said aloud.

Suddenly the door of the trucks flew open and four men scrambled out and ran toward the armored car. "What the . . . ?" They clambered into the car which roared and sped away from the trucks. David reached for the door handle, then froze in fear with the certainty of what was about to happen. "They're going to blow us up!" he shouted, throwing his door wide and jumping onto the pavement. "It's a bomb! A bomb!" he cried into the quiet morning air. An instant later a flash of white light ripped through the street as the trucks exploded. Two tons of dynamite sent a thousand white-hot shards of steel through the walls of buildings, collapsing them like firecrackers bursting inside a house of cards. David only saw the light; he did not hear the blast that tore the souls from Ben Yehuda Street and the Atlantic Hotel on Christmas morning.

———

Howard lit a candle from a stash of supplies that had been left behind during excavation. He rummaged through the knapsack, finding a Coke and a rotten orange. He threw the orange to the ground and it rolled down the shaft and dropped into the main room of the tomb.

"What is it?" breathed Moshe.

"The last of Tommy's lunch." He took out a paper-wrapped piece of cheese and unwrapped it. "Not in bad shape."

"I'm thirsty," Moshe said with difficulty.

"I've got just the thing." He helped Moshe scoot down the shaft and through a small opening into the dusty gloom of a chamber ten feet square by four feet high with an oblong pit sunk in the center of the floor to give standing room. The museum had long since removed the bones of the first-century Christians who had been buried here. Now all that remained were six loculus crypts in which bodies had been sealed until the flesh decomposed. The candle flickered eerily inside the chamber. Howard held it until wax dripped on the stone and then he set the candle in it. He settled Moshe against a wall and went back to the shaft to recover the scrolls.

He looked up at the bright sunlight streaming in through the opening. "God help us," he whispered; then he gathered the treasures and slid back toward the tomb chamber.

He stopped short as he saw again the ashen face of Moshe and heard his shallow breathing. He shook his head with concern, then climbed into the room.

"All the comforts of home," he said, cheerfully depositing the scrolls next to Moshe. He pulled the Coke from the knapsack and popped the top from it on the ledge of the tomb. His own throat burned with thirst, but he held the bottle to Moshe's lips and helped him sip. "Go easy," he warned. "Just a little bit at a time."

Moshe sighed gratefully and stared at the candle. "Thank you." Howard crammed the lid back on the bottle and leaned it against the wall.

"What about you?"

"Not thirsty. You know how I am about warm Coke, eh?"

Moshe did not argue; instead, he looked at Howard. "You are a good friend. You could have gone ahead. The countryside is covered by now with the Jihad Moqhades. What if they find us, Howard?"

"Then they find us," he shrugged. "What is this? We could take a few of them with us, you know."

"Five bullets." Moshe closed his eyes. "Three for them and two for us."

"Shut up, Moshe, or I won't give you any more to drink. A little too much Coke, huh?"

Moshe smiled and closed his eyes. "If I don't make it, Howard—"

"You'll make it," Howard said, questioning his own words.

"If I don't, there is so much I would have wanted to say. To Ellie—" He paused. "To Rachel. But you, Howard, you know you have been to me the brother I lost."

"We're both going to make it, Moshe. So just go to sleep. Shut up and go to sleep."

"I think if I sleep I shall never again awake in this life." His voice sounded very much like a small boy's as he drifted off to sleep.

Howard glanced around the chamber as Moshe's breathing became more deep and even. "If I descend into the tomb, lo,

God is there," he said quietly. Then he picked up the scrolls and carried them to a loculus that was blocked by a flat stone slab. He moved the slab to the side and wiggled into the hole, knowing that near the back was a depression in which he could safely hide the scrolls. If he and Moshe were to die together in this tomb, he thought, at least the scrolls would be safe from the hands of the Mufti. And one day, when at last peace came to Palestine and the American school again opened its doors, he was certain that another archaeologist would return to the dig and find them. He placed the slab back over the opening and sat for a long time staring at it. He thought perhaps he knew what had been in the heart of the men who had hidden the scrolls in the caves nearly two thousand years before. "You were there then, too, Lord," he said, facing death without fear. "But if you could arrange it, I would like to stay around a while longer."

————

The men of Hassan cheered lustily as the great pillar of smoke rose high above Jerusalem in the distance. They stopped their search and gathered near the roadblock by the monastery.

"The war for Jerusalem has begun!" shouted the leader of the men from Talpiyoth.

"Enough of this search for two small men and worthless baggage," came the cry of another. "We are needed in the city, as you can see!" A rumble of dissatisfaction swept through the group as all the eyes of the Jihad Moqhades turned toward the Holy City.

Hassan leapt to the top of the barricade and raised his pistol, firing a round angrily into the air. "It is the wish of the Mufti that these thieves be found!" he cried. "Their heads are worth more than the loot of Jerusalem."

"It is for your glory that you say this!" shouted the leader. "It was through *your* bumbling that they escaped. It is *your* head which is in peril with the Mufti."

The gathered troops echoed approval at their leader's words. Raised fists and weapons reinforced their dissatisfaction with Hassan.

"We are going to the Mosque. To Jerusalem," the leader cried.

"JIHAD! JIHAD! JIHAD!" came the frenzied call of the men.

"Leave me ten men!" Hassan shouted at their leader. "Ten can do the work of a hundred in daylight."

The leader rubbed his hand over his grizzled face. "Perhaps."

"There is great reward if the men are found. My word of honor," Hassan said.

"Ten. Only ten? Perhaps." He pointed his finger at a disgruntled collection of men who stood to the side. "You. You will stay and aid our brother Hassan in this search. He has promised great reward from the hand of Haj Amin if they are found."

With a great cheer, the hundred Jihad Moqhades swarmed past the barricade and up the road toward Jerusalem.

34   The Cavalry

The windows above Ellie's bed rattled insistently. Shaul sprang to his feet beside her and whined. Still wrapped in a towel, having fallen into bed after her shower the night before, Ellie opened her eyes and focused on David's present. It sat on her dresser beside Miriam's red-wrapped package. She reached out and languidly scratched Shaul behind the ears. "Merry Christmas, mutt," she croaked sleepily. Then she sniffed and sat up suddenly as she remembered Moshe and Uncle Howard. She had not heard them come in last night; surely the dog would have had something to say about it if they had come home.

Jumping from bed, she hurried to find her robe. Then quickly brushing out her tangled hair, she rushed down the hall.

"Uncle Howard!" she called loudly, throwing his door open to reveal a perfectly made bed and an alarm clock that read 5:45.

If I'm not home before dawn, he had said, *send the cavalry.*

Ellie threw down the brush and ran back to her room. Rummaging through her drawers for clean underwear, she tried to think of whom she could call. Captain Thomas? Surely he was off-duty by now and she did not know where to find him. Her hand brushed the camera. "David!" she cried with relief as she hurriedly pulled on her clothes. She buttoned her jacket and, as an afterthought, snatched up Miriam's gift and slipped it into her pocket. *I'll open it over breakfast*, she thought. "Come on, Shaul," she said, grabbing the camera and loading it. She would take her first photographs of David climbing groggily out of bed.

The dog followed her out onto the front steps, bumping into her legs as she looked across the rooftops of the city in the soft morning light. A huge funnel of smoke rose up from the downtown section of Jerusalem. "Dear God!" she cried, running to the Plymouth and jumping in. Had that been what had rattled her windows? The sight of the smoke sickened her with fear for David. She had seen the aftermath of a bomb before. "Please, God," she cried as the car careened nearer to the sight, following ambulances and screaming police cars to the scene.

An ashen-faced officer waved his arms and flagged her down a full six blocks from the center of the blast. She rolled down her window and shouted to him.

"What happened?"

"The Arabs bombed Ben Yehuda Street."

Ellie felt the world spin around her. She laid her head down on the steering wheel of the car and fought for control. Horns and sirens blared behind her.

"Move your car, miss! We have to get through," shouted the officer.

Her breath coming in short shallow gasps, Ellie managed to slip the car into gear and drift to the side of the street. She laid her head back on the seat then, unable to make her legs move or her hand slide to the door handle. Shaul whined and nudged her gently. Cries of the officers filtered in through the windows as rescue vehicles rushed by. "Ben Yehuda Street. Atlantic Hotel. The whole place is leveled . . ."

A wave of nausea overcame her and she opened the window of the car and gasped for air. Then, feeling her breath come easier, she grabbed her camera, a certain pass into the scene, and pulled herself from the car. Shaul followed on her heels as she staggered up the sidewalk against the flow of neighborhood survivors who clutched each other and wept as they fled the carnage.

"Nothing is left!" screamed a woman hysterically. "No one— they are dead! All dead!"

Most were still dressed in their nightclothes, and in the frosty morning air children cried out from the cold. Three blocks from

Ben Yehuda an officer stopped her.

"Can't go in there, miss," he said

She held up her camera. "Press." She heard her voice echo hollowly. "*Life* magazine."

He allowed her to pass, restraining a weeping mother who cried that she had lost her child in the wreckage. Ellie raised her camera and snapped the shutter. Glass from the windows of shops and apartments crunched beneath her feet. Worried about the dog, she moved to the center of the street, more crowded with hysterical women and men than the sidewalk. Everywhere, there was blood: on the starched white nightgown of a little girl who wailed as a rescuer carried her from the bomb site; on the face of a man limping in anguish toward the makeshift medical post. A woman darted frantically through the crowd. "My husband!" she cried. "You have to help me find my husband!"

Nothing in her life had ever prepared Ellie for the devastation she witnessed as she stepped onto what had been the Street of the Jews.

Nothing but rubble was left of the Atlantic Hotel. The buildings that remained standing were marred by great gouges; whole walls had been blasted away, revealing the wreckage of bedrooms and the bodies of victims. Here and there a rescue worker scrambled over the wreckage or dug toward a feeble cry for help. Smoke rose from the ruins. The body of an old man lay against a fire hydrant. Firemen quickly shoved it to the side as they connected their hose. There was no time to worry about the dead; rescuers had to attend to those living who faced being burned alive beneath the wreckage as fires from the gas mains began to spring up. Wrought-iron railings dangled from what had once been balconies. Torn clothing littered the streets. Two young men hurried by carrying a maimed man who had been pulled from beneath the concrete only moments before. His moans punctuated the heavy silence of the street.

Ellie's hands dropped to her sides, and the Leica jerked and dangled from the strap around her neck. The remains of Michael Cohen's car—a huge piece of metal had crushed its roof.

"David!" she cried, her heart breaking in anguish as she surveyed the scene. "David!" she shouted, stumbling slowly toward where the Atlantic had stood.

Four volunteer firemen rushed past her. A shout of joy echoed in the street as rescue workers found another survivor. "Over here!" They shouted from across the street.

Sobs choked Ellie as she tried to control her grief. "David," she said softly. Shaul jumped up on her and wagged his rump. He spun around and barked.

"Els?" questioned a soft voice behind her. "Els? Is that you?"

She turned toward the husky voice to see David, standing in the street in his stocking feet, his clothes torn, but his necktie still in place around his neck. A deep cut above his eye bled heavily, and he seemed dazed. "David!" she cried, throwing her arms around him. "Oh, darling, you're alive."

"Help me," he pleaded. "The guys are in there. They were in there when the trucks exploded." He gazed at the demolished car. "I almost stayed in the car." He covered his face with his hands. "The guys are in there," he said again.

"Come on." Ellie took his arm as he began to walk toward the ruins of the hotel. "You have to get out of here, David. There's nothing we can do."

David ignored her and picked his way toward the hotel, searching frantically for a place to begin digging. "I gotta find Michael," he said simply. Then he bent down and began tossing chunks of the building to the side.

"David, please," Ellie begged.

Shaul ran to the top of the mountain of rubble and barked frantically. Ellie glanced up and said to David, "Maybe he can help. Maybe he knows something."

David dropped a large piece of wood and scrambled up to where Shaul perched. "What is it, fella?" he asked, kneeling beside the dog. Shaul continued to bark and David followed his gaze down the opposite side of the remainder of the building. As Ellie climbed up after him, David stood slowly and gave a strangled cry, then disappeared as he slid down out of Ellie's view.

"David?" Ellie called as she reached the dome of the rubble. Down below her, in tearful reunion, David embraced Michael Cohen as two other unshaven men happily stood by.

"We thought you was dead," said Bobby Milken.

"I thought we were all goners." David brushed the tears from his face. "Man, am I glad to see you!"

"We got drunk and spent the night down in some dive on Julian. Lost all my money in a crap shoot," said Michael.

"Yeah," said David, embracing his friend once again. He wept openly, unashamedly. "I'm glad to see you bums."

Ellie half-climbed, half-slid down to where the men clustered. Relief filled her heart as she snapped a photograph of their happy assembly.

"Merry Christmas, Els!" David cried. Then as Ellie spoke, his smile faded.

"David, I need help. This is awful. But Moshe and Uncle Howard were supposed to be back before morning. I'm worried, David. Please, can you help me?"

He drew a deep breath and got control of himself. "Sure," he said in a husky voice. "Yeah. Where are they?"

"On the road between Bethlehem and Jerusalem someplace. That's all I know. I need someone to drive down with me to help me find them. David, I'm so worried."

Michael and the others turned aside to help with the rescue efforts as David took her by the arm. "You'll never find them in a car. If they're in trouble, the last thing they'd want is to have you out there in the middle of it. I'll fly down and have a look. If they're along the road, I can land and get them home."

"I'm going too, David. Okay? I'm going."

"No, you're not. It could be dangerous."

He rolled his eyes at the look on her face. "What do you think I'm doing here?"

"All right. All right. Where's your car?"

He followed her back through the wreckage, walking carefully around broken glass in his argyle socks. Shaul kept his nose right at Ellie's heel as they snaked through the crush of humanity misery that waited for vehicles to carry them to Hadassah.

Far above the destruction of Ben Yehuda Street, Ellie focused her camera on the gray plume that rose from the carnage below, then snapped the shutter.

Slowly David banked the plane and shook his head in grim silence as they set course for Bethlehem. "Looks like a B-29 dropped a full load down there," he remarked. "I thought I saw enough of this in Europe to last a lifetime. Never expected to be right back in the thick of it."

"Why are you still here, David?" Ellie put her hand on his arm.

"Because it's the right thing to do. And looks like there's nobody else gonna do it."

She pulled a clean handkerchief from her pocket and dabbed the cut on his forehead. "I came to the same conclusion a few weeks ago," she said.

"You know something else?" He took her hand and held it.

"What?"

"You're still in love with me."

She drew her hand away. "You arrogant lout. Why don't you let *me* say that?"

"Okay. Why don't you say it?" he grinned, looking ridiculous in his torn, collarless shirt with his tie around his neck. "I saw your face when you thought I was dead. Why don't you stop playing games and we can get down to the business of being in love. That takes a little work and effort, you know."

"In the first place, I don't care what you thought you saw on my face. Yes, I was sorry you were dead. I thought you were dead. Anybody would be sorry. In the second place—"

"You better tell the truth, Els—God's gettin' this on record, y'know. Go ahead and tell me you're not in love with me." He raised his eyebrows expectantly. "Go ahead."

Ellie sniffed and reached back to scratch Shaul behind the ears. "I can't," she said sulkily. "Because I'm not sure."

David shrugged. "God's gonna get you," he teased.

"You are the most egotistical, arrogant—"

"Truthful, honest, loyal. A real boy scout. I even do a good turn every day." He pushed the Stinson into a steep dive and buzzed over the top of Allenby Barracks and the train station, leveling a mere fifty feet above the road to Bethlehem. "Keep your eyes peeled," he instructed. "Every face on the highway is gonna be looking up here cussin' this plane before I'm through. If they're down there, you'll see 'em."

Ellie turned her attention to the travelers below, laughing at the Arab camel drovers who shook their fists in fury as their camels bucked and bellowed beneath the shadow of the plane.

"Trouble up ahead!" David shouted, pulling the plane up as they roared over the heads of a large group of Jihad Moqhades.

Ellie instinctively ducked back as rifles raised to shoulders and barrels flashed in their direction. "Who are they?" she cried.

"Arab irregulars," said David grimly. "Your uncle might be in more trouble than I thought."

He banked the plane and made one more pass over their heads, this time high and hopefully out of range. "They all have guns. Every one of them," said Ellie. "Do you think they could have found Uncle Howard and Moshe?"

He looked at her and shook his head. "We'll know soon enough. These fellas never stop to bury their victims."

A look of horror and fear crossed Ellie's face. "You think they're dead, then?" she asked.

"Tie up the dog back there," David instructed her. "We might have to do some fancy flying and the last thing we need is the mutt flopping around."

Ellie shook herself back to reality and climbed back to secure Shaul's frayed rope to a handle on the side of the plane. "What's all this stuff?" she yelled over the roar of the engine as she spotted the crates of seltzer water and Scotch.

"Bombs," said David. "Get up here. I think I've spotted something."

He brought the plane low over the barricade on the highway just before the monastery. "Over there," said Ellie. "That's my uncle's dig. I spent the first three months in Palestine rooting around in an old tomb down there."

"Well, something's up!" cried David. "Look at those guys!"

Ellie peered out the window as a small group of men scoured the area around the dig.

"Either somebody's lost their car keys, or I'd say Moshe and Howard are hiding out down there someplace." He banked the plane back toward Jerusalem as a volley of rifle fire filled the sky around them. "So much for the car-key theory," he said.

"What can we do? How can we land the plane with those men down there at the dig?"

"I don't know," he frowned. "We're going down again. See if you can count them."

Ellie pressed her face against the windowpane and gazed down at the barren rocky countryside below. She counted softly to herself as rifles raised and took aim on the Stinson. "Ten. Maybe more," she said. "I can only see ten. They haven't found the tomb yet."

"The tomb?"

"The tomb. I just told you about the tomb. It's the only place they could be if they're down there, David. There's no other place they could be."

"They aren't dead yet, anyway."

"How do you know?" she asked hopefully.

David looked at her in exasperation and tapped his temple. "That's what I like about you, Els; you got a lot upstairs." He pushed the plane into a gentle dive once again. "Look at those guys down there. If they had killed your uncle, do you think they'd be wandering around looking for their bodies? They'd know right where to find them."

Another volley of gunfire greeted the plane as they passed overhead. David pulled up and circled over Bethlehem, then returned to the dig site. Ellie clambered over the back of her seat to the crates.

"We've got to do something," she said. "Something."

She pried the lid from the top of a crate of seltzer bottles.

"What are you up to?" David called back, continuing to circle.

"You said these were bombs." Her voice was filled with angry frustration as she wrenched a bottle from the crate.

"So, what is it?"

She pushed down the button on top of the bottle sending a bubbling stream of seltzer toward David. "Seltzer water!" she cried in disgust.

"Knock it off," David snapped, wiping the back of his head. "Don't you have any imagination, girl? This is a war of imagination. That's a bomb you're holding. Let's have a little respect."

"Stop babbling, David!" she shouted. "Moshe and Uncle Howard are going to be killed and all we have is a couple crates of fizzy water and you're—"

"Shut up and listen, will you!" he demanded. "Remember I told you about my buddy who used to tend bar during the war at the Top of the Mark in San Francisco?"

"Yes. So what?"

"He used to save the nearly empty seltzer bottles. Remember I told you?"

"Yes."

"Remember what we used to do with them?" He turned and

370

grinned broadly as Ellie's face flooded with the delight of understanding.

"You used to shake them up and toss them off the roof of the hotel during blackouts!" she cried.

"And they screamed like bombs all the way down and blew up when they hit bottom. Scared the bejeebers out of the whole city. Thought the Japs were attacking for sure!"

"Oh, David! You think it'll work?" She shook the bottle and began to pry open the cockpit window.

"What would you do if you heard a bomb screaming down out of the sky?"

"I'd run!" She braced the window open and began to pull the bottles from their crates.

"Exactly. It just about got me arrested in Frisco. Harold got fired. Let's see what kind of damage we can do to those blanket heads down there." He whooped and banked the plane toward where four Arabs stood atop a high stone wall. They were only a few feet from the entrance to the tomb, Ellie knew. "Shake those babies up real good now," David instructed. "Ready?"

"Any time." Ellie sat up on her knees at the window, two bottles in hand. "Say when."

"We're gonna give it plenty of altitude so they can whistle a long time before they hit." David brought the nose of the plane up to an altitude of five hundred feet as they passed over the Arabs. "Okay, Els. When I count three. One . . ."

Ellie continued to shake the bottles until their contents began to push at the nozzle. "Right."

"Two . . ."

The Arabs raised their rifles to their shoulders and the popping of gunfire filled the air.

"Three! Let 'em go!"

Ellie threw first one bottle from the plane then paused a second before throwing the next. The scream of escaping seltzer water drowned the popping bullets and the shouts of the Arabs who looked up in terror at the sound of falling bombs. They threw down their weapons and jumped from the wall, scrambling for cover as the bottles hit and exploded into fragments of glass and tall geysers.

David and Ellie whooped with delight.

"It's working!" cried Ellie, throwing her arms around David's neck. "You're wonderful!"

"I keep trying to tell you that!" he laughed. "Hold on. We're going to make another pass." David pushed the plane into a steep dive, nearly brushing the heads of the now defenseless Jihad Moqhades. They cowered low behind a cluster of rocks and Ellie could see their fearful faces as they looked at the belly of the plane.

"We've got to get them out of there, David. We can't land if they're still hanging around."

"Time for another run, bombardier." He pulled the plane up into a steep climb and circled to where five other Arabs lay spread-eagled against the earth. "Shake 'em up good now."

Ellie had already taken four bottles from the crate and was hard at work agitating the contents. "Ready when you are."

"Just don't shake 'em so much they blow up in here, okay?" He glanced over his shoulder.

Down below them, the Arabs were scrambling for their rifles, searching for a safe place to hide from the menacing little plane. Ellie gasped in horror as an Arab crouched dangerously close to where the entrance of the tomb was hidden. "David!" she shouted. "They'll find it! Hurry."

"One . . . Two . . . Three. Let 'em fly!"

Frantically Ellie dropped first one, then two and three bottles from the window. The whine filled the air.

"Now the other one!" David shouted.

Beneath them, the terror-stricken warriors ran from the site of the tomb entrance, which seemed to be the target area for the howling death that rained down on them. Like ants on a ruined anthill, they ran from the sound, they ran from the explosion, they ran from one another, each taking a separate route back to Talpiyoth.

David dipped the wings of the plane as he buzzed their heads dangerously close once again. Ellie laughed with delight as they screeched and ran from the oncoming plane. David climbed and circled one last time, convinced that, at least for now, they had seen the last of the Arab band.

———

Howard raised his eyes to the roof of the tomb as the roar of the aircraft engine and the sound of explosions penetrated the earth above them.

"What is it?" Moshe asked weakly.

"The cavalry, I hope," said Howard, turning his eyes with concern to the blood-soaked bandage on Moshe's arm.

Again and again the plane passed directly above them and was answered by the popping of Arab guns. Howard closed his eyes and prayed for whoever was in the plane—and for himself and Moshe as well.

Finally the sound of gunfire ceased, but the roar of the plane engine crisscrossed the sky above them. "They are searching for us," said Moshe flatly.

"I've got to go up." Howard scrambled toward the opening. "Got to let them know we're here."

"Howard!" Moshe called after him. Howard paused at the entrance to the shaft and turned, looking into the eyes of his friend.

"We're either going to make it together or not at all." He grinned at Moshe, then climbed up the shaft toward the sunlight. Cautiously he stuck his head out. The shadow of the Stinson touched him, and he pulled himself out of the hole and pulled off his filthy Bedouin robe. He stood beneath the rock wall and waved his robe as the bright silver bird banked and turned toward him.

Ellie looked down from the airplane, her heart filling with joy as she spotted the portly figure frantically waving below. "It's Uncle Howard! He's alive!" she wept.

David passed directly over his head and dipped his wings in salute before he turned and lined up with the ribbon of highway that would serve as his landing strip.

Howard threw the plane a kiss, then scrambled back down the shaft to where Moshe waited. "They're landing!" he shouted. "Moshe! Come on, boy!" He slid into the tomb and crawled quickly to Moshe's side.

Moshe smiled wearily at him. "Your cavalry, eh?"

"We've got to go. Hassan's men can't be far." He slipped his arm around Moshe and helped him toward the opening of the shaft, boosting him up from behind. Carefully he lifted him toward the sunlight. Moshe groaned once as his arm bumped the rocks at the entrance to the tomb; then he lay beneath the shrub as Howard clambered out over him.

The plane taxied to a stop a mere fifty yards from where Howard helped Moshe to his feet. David smiled and waved broadly as he hopped from the plane and Ellie followed. They ran across the rough terrain toward the weary fugitives.

"It's about time!" shouted Howard, supporting Moshe as they stumbled toward the plane.

"Uncle Howard!" cried Ellie, triumphantly wrapping her arms around him.

"Moshe is wounded. He has lost a lot of blood. Left a trail for the Arabs to follow. I thought we were goners," he said, gushing happily as David took Moshe from him and helped him to the plane.

"But you're all right! Thank God you're alive. Oh, thank God!" Ellie cried, as Howard picked up an Arab gun and put in into the cockpit, then helped Moshe into the plane.

Howard blanched and whirled around to face the rock wall. "Dear God!" he exclaimed. "I've forgotten the scrolls!" He ran back across the field as David called angrily after him.

"Where's he going? He'll get us all killed!"

"Uncle Howard!" Ellie screamed and ran after him.

Howard leaped into the shaft and slid down into the tomb. He shoved away the stone that leaned against the loculus and crawled into the narrow chamber. He reached out and grasped the leather pouch and the fabric-wrapped scroll of Isaiah. With infinite care he lifted them from the depression and wriggled back out to the shaft and the open air. He gently laid the scrolls on the lip of the opening, then pulled himself out of the hole and onto the dirt. "I got them!" he called joyfully. Then he gasped as a foot stepped firmly on his arm and the barrel of a machine gun rammed beneath his chin and lifted his face into the sunlight. The smiling face of Hassan gazed down on him.

"Thank you so much, my friend, for returning what is mine." Ellie and David stood a few yards away. Howard turned his eyes on them and then on the scrolls. "I'm sorry," he said softly.

Ellie and David did not reply. Ellie's face was chalky white and David glared at Hassan angrily.

"You will get up," instructed Hassan. "Slowly, please. And pick up the scrolls, if you will."

Howard carefully obeyed, not willing to defy the gun at his head. His eyes met Ellie's and seemed to speak to her. She nodded slightly.

"Now you will all please walk to the plane," Hassan's voice had the patronizing tone of a man who had finally and decisively won. "My companions were cowards. Cowards. But I remained behind," he cooed. "As my father said many times, where the vulture circles, there is the body, yes?" He seemed amused by his monologue.

"Which rock did you hide under?" snarled David as they reached the wing-tip of the plane.

Hassan bellowed with rage and slammed the gun barrel down hard on David's shoulder, breaking his collarbone and sending him to his knees. "Insolent!" he shouted. "Insolent Jew! But it is I, Ibrahim El Hassan, who is the victor now." His breathing was labored with fury. Then he looked toward Ellie and Howard and the sten gun that lay on the seat of the open cockpit. "Young woman," he said smoothly, "if you would be so kind? Carefully remove the weapon and drop it to the ground. One false move and you are instantly dead."

Ellie sidled to the door and holding one hand above her head, she took the gun from the cockpit and lowered it to the ground. Hassan sniffed and walked to the door, peering in at Moshe who lay across two backseats, nearly unconscious. "We meet again, Moshe," he sneered. "Perhaps for the last time?"

"Hell is not deep enough for you to hide, Hassan," Moshe coughed, as Shaul snarled from the rear of the cabin.

Hassan quickly stepped back, then eyeing the leashed dog, he smiled. "Then perhaps we shall meet in hell, eh, my friend?" he cocked the gun and raised it toward Moshe's head, meeting his eyes with cold hatred. Then he lowered the gun barrel. "No. You shall die last. As I have died, slowly died inside. You shall see those you love fall around you and writhe in agony." He turned his gaze toward Howard. "On your knees, fat man!" he screamed, knocking Howard to the ground.

"No!" cried Ellie. "Please don't!"

"You are next, woman!" Hassan's voice rose and cracked with hatred. He shoved her roughly to her knees beside Howard and raised the barrel of the gun. Shaul lunged against the rope, and it snapped just below the knot. He jumped from the cockpit and hit Hassan just as he pulled the trigger of the gun. The shot went wild, as fangs bared, Shaul slammed Hassan against the ground.

"Help me!" cried Hassan. Howard grabbed the gun and jumped to his feet. Ellie turned her head away as Shaul tore at the throat of the man who had attacked her so many weeks before. Hassan's shrieks faded to a gurgle, and Shaul stood proudly over the body.

"Get in," Howard said in a barely audible voice. "Don't look at him. Just get in."

Ellie ducked beneath the plane and climbed in from the opposite side. Howard helped David to his feet. "Can you still fly this thing?" he asked.

David staggered against him. "Flew all the way to England once with a busted leg," he gasped, as Howard helped him into the cockpit and tossed the scrolls in after.

"Get us out of here," said Howard, his eyes on four Jihad Moqhades lined up atop the rock wall. He jumped in as the engine coughed to a roar and the plane began to roll up the highway.

"Shaul!" Ellie shouted to the dog. "Come on, boy!"

The Arabs raised their rifles and bullets popped all around where the dog still stood over his victim. He spun instantly and ran after the plane. Howard held the door wide as Shaul ran alongside. "Come on boy! You can make it!" he called.

With a mighty leap, Shaul cleared the ground, landing squarely on Howard's lap.

The wheels of the plane cleared the top of Mar Elyas Monastery, and they slowly spiraled upward out of range of the bullets of the Jihad Moqhades.

Epilogue

In a quiet hallway at Hadassah Hospital, Ellie sipped coffee as she awaited word on Moshe's surgery. Howard had already taken Rachel and Yacov back home from the bedside of their grandfather to a much-needed rest, and David slept in a room on the floor below.

Ellie reached into her coat pocket in hopes of finding a handkerchief. Instead, her fingers closed around the small package that Miriam had given her. She pulled it out and placed it on her leg. Then she glanced at her watch. It was eight o'clock in the evening. Ellie closed her eyes and imagined her mother and father and brothers gathered beneath the Christmas tree opening their gifts. "It's morning back home," she said quietly. "Christmas morning, Miriam, and I'm thinking of you." She carefully unwrapped the package, smiling softly as the intricately carved, olive wood cover of a small Bible emerged from the red paper. She traced her name, carved beneath a cross covered with tiny rosebuds. The old woman had had it made especially for her. She opened the cover and recognized Miriam's cramped handwriting.

"Little Ellie: And so you are home this Christmas in peace and safety among those you love. On this day as you remember us, I wish to pass along a gift I received so very long ago. It is a promise that has never dimmed and never changed. You will find it in the book of Romans, chapter the eighth, the verses thirty-five through thirty-nine. I was young once and wondered as you do. Now I am old and I doubt no longer. And so I give this gift to you. With much love for you in this old heart, I wish you Merry Christmas. Miriam."

Ellie smiled tenderly and touched Miriam's name with her index finger. She wondered now what her life would have been if she had gone home to the safety of California. If Uncle Howard had sent a short note explaining Miriam's death; if she had not stood on the deck of the *Ave Maria* and wept as she ran aground; if she had not seen Rachel touch the face of Yacov and call him brother—would she ever have known that God's love was bigger than heartache?

Ellie laughed aloud at the foolishness of her thought. Once she had doubted that God could ever stay in a place like Jerusalem; now she wondered if she ever would have found Him in Los Angeles. "But you're even in L.A., aren't you?" she whispered with a smile. "Merry Christmas," she said as she opened her little gift and read the promise.

*If you would like to contact the authors,
you may write to them at the following address:*

Bodie and Brock Thoene
P.O. Box 542
Glenbrook, NV 89413